THE ROMANCE OF THE ROSE

The Poet dreams a dream; imagines that he rises, washes, and dresses; wanders by a stream, basting his sleeves; and enters a garden surrounded by a wall decorated with personifications. *Morgan 324, f. 1r.*

THE ROMANCE OF THE ROSE

By

GUILLAUME de LORRIS

and

JEAN de MEUN

Translated into English verse by
HARRY W. ROBBINS

Edited, and with an Introduction, by
CHARLES W. DUNN

A Dutton  *Paperback*

New York
E. P. DUTTON

English Translation
Copyright, ©, 1962, by FLORENCE L. ROBBINS
Introduction by CHARLES W. DUNN
Copyright, ©, 1962, by E. P. Dutton & Co., Inc.
All rights reserved. Printed in the U.S.A.

Published simultaneously in Canada by
Clarke, Irwin & Co., Ltd., of Toronto.

A C K N O W L E D G M E N T

Grateful acknowledgment is made to the
Trustees of The Pierpont Morgan Library for
permission to reproduce in this book illustrations from three manuscripts of *The Romance of the Rose* in the Library's collection.

Library of Congress Catalog Card Number: 62-8218

SBN 0-525-47090-5

CONTENTS

(The numbers within brackets are the line numbers of the original text in Old French; the lines of the English translation are numbered in the text)

ILLUSTRATIONS

INTRODUCTION

The Romance of the Rose is one of the great monuments of medieval literature. Guillaume de Lorris began the poem around 1237 but left it incomplete at line 4058. An anonymous poet provided a seventy-eight-line conclusion, which proved to be of only temporary value, for Jean de Meun around 1277 wrote a vast new amplification which reached its ending at line 21,780.

Thus *The Romance* stands today like some great French cathedral, conceived by its first architect in early Gothic, temporarily enclosed by a modest apprentice, and then extended on a grandiose plan and executed in an advanced and ornate style.

Like a Gothic cathedral, it includes both the grotesque and the sublime, the profane and the sacred. The uninitiated can enjoy its individual details; the sophisticated can appreciate its complex architectonics. For despite its varied workmanship, the whole is controlled by the Gothic instinct for the order which underlies diversity.

1. GUILLAUME DE LORRIS

GUILLAUME DE LORRIS, the initiator of *The Romance*, took his name from the small village of Lorris on the Loire River above Orléans in the north of France. Nothing is known about his origin or career except by inference from the text of *The Romance*. He may have been born around 1212 and died about 1237. He was both literate in style and courtly in manner. Well read in the

Latin classics, he particularly enjoyed Ovid, understood the devices of medieval allegory, and appreciated the subtleties of courtly love and of romance.

Guillaume describes his love affair in a dream-vision, which he narrates in the allegorical manner favored by medieval tradition. Long before the thirteenth century, the Church fathers had developed the theory that everything in the Bible could be interpreted allegorically; by exegesis, the bare narrative could be shown to have a concealed spiritual meaning. The allegorical method gradually became extended from mere biblical commentary and was widely applied in a number of entirely different ways. Prudentius, for instance, wrote (in the fourth century) a moral poem, the *Psychomachia* (*The War of the Soul*), which represented the struggle waged between the virtues and the vices for possession of the human soul. Fulgentius (in the sixth century) applied the exegetical method to the discovery of spiritual truth in the pagan classics. "In the nut," he wrote, "there are two parts, the shell and the kernel; so in the songs of the poets there are two, the literal sense and the mystic." The allegorical mode thus came to dominate the arts just as it had dominated religious writing. For the age of Guillaume de Lorris, to quote Emile Mâle the art-historian, "the whole world was a symbol."

Allegory, though omnipresent, varied in degree. At the end of the thirteenth century, Dante constructed his own epic, the *Divine Comedy*, to be read at four levels, literally, morally, mystically, and anagogically. From Prudentius' simple personifications of the forces affecting the human soul, Dante moved on to the use of a complex typology by which legendary and historical personages represented various aspects of the Divine Plan.

Guillaume de Lorris is, however, no Dante. He has an uncomplicated story to tell and follows Prudentius' clear-cut example. Human action is represented by personifications of the various forces that affect behavior. A Lover wishes to win his Lady (the Rose); her responsiveness (Fair Welcome) encourages him; her sense of modesty (Shame) fends him off; the dominance she exercises upon him (Danger—a French form of the Latin word *dominarium* meaning "domination") blocks his advance. Modern readers, accustomed to similar Freudian abstractions, can hardly fail to translate Guillaume's transparent terms.

The attendant conventions of the love affair are less self-evident than the action. The lovers seem to be engaged in a kind of ceremonial ballet. The movements were all perfectly familiar, however, to Guillaume's readers. By the end of the twelfth century, Chrétien de Troyes' well-known romances, Marie de France's lays, and Andreas the Chaplain's treatise on *The Art of Courtly Love* had established the standard pattern for French literature.

The love which these writers celebrated so gracefully was not Christian love but erotic passion. Their code was loosely defined and may represent no more than an unreal and impracticable literary convention. Courtly love was always secretive, for its object was extramarital. It was an irresistible force, seizing bachelor or married knight, maiden, wife, or widow. If, as is true in some romances, the lovers do eventually marry, their marriage is a comparative irrelevancy. Andreas the Chaplain, indeed, flatly states that love cannot exist between two people married to one another.

Love, according to Andreas, is an "inborn suffering." Hence the long tradition of the lamenting lover—Chrétien's Lancelot, Chaucer's Troilus, and even Shakespeare's Romeo. Hence the plaintive arguments, which, in bare summary, generally run the same course: "May I?" "You mustn't." "I'll die!" "That would be sad. But I'm a maiden." "I'm a worthy courtier. I can prove it." "Oh, well."

Yet the courtly lover is not the cynical seducer as portrayed by Ovid in his *Art of Love*. He may be inspired by what the French called "refined love," an ideal rooted in the feudal concepts of duty, service, and reward.

Guillaume de Lorris, who knew well the discourses of courtly love, provides his audience with a fresh approach to this familiar matter. By his use of allegory he supplies a refinement sometimes lacking in explicit narrative. He subordinates action to tableau or pageant, panorama or procession. He translates his experiences as a lover into the world of dreams. But, even though the motivation is allegoric and the events dreamlike, *The Romance* has an immediacy that more realistic narratives fail to achieve. In the dream, the Lover is not only the Poet but also Everyman, or, at least, Every Courtier. The Rose is not only the Poet's Beloved; she is also Every Lover's ideal Lady.

Guillaume is a master of allegory. His setting has a warmth and color and fragrance that relieve *The Romance* of the frigidity of abstraction. His personifications, such as the grumpy boor, Danger, become very lively indeed when awakened into action. Many of the details of the action and setting, as scholars have shown, are drawn from the long tradition of love poetry; but Guillaume always borrows intelligently and creatively, as a skilled medieval craftsman knows how, in order to construct and adorn his own original masterpiece.

2.   THE ANONYMOUS CONCLUSION

NOTHING is known about the origin of the seventy-eight-line conclusion (inserted here at the end of Chapter 19) apart from the fact that it appears in several manuscripts of *The Romance*. Presumably, Guillaume de Lorris died before he could complete his great work. The devotee who provided this ending posesssed sufficient knowledge of poetry to compose lines that rhyme and scan, but his imagination was severely limited, and he supplied only the barest and most obvious dramatization of the Lover's winning of his Rose. His chief service lay in his rounding out of Guillaume's fragment so that it could be appreciated as an aesthetic whole.

3.   JEAN DE MEUN

JEAN DE MEUN, the author of the vast amplification, apparently came from the village of Meung on the Loire below Orléans, not far from the birthplace of Guillaume de Lorris. Apart from this geographical coincidence, the two poets have little in common. Guillaume was the conservative celebrant of courtly love. Jean de Meun, who was probably born shortly after Guillaume died (*ca.* 1237), speaks for a later generation and reflects a new poetic sentiment, which might be called anti-courtliness. Though his theme is nominally the same as Guillaume's, he is a devotee, not of courtly, but of scholastic love.

The source of Jean's point of view is readily explained. He was a product of the University of Paris, a student of the seven liberal arts—the *trivium* (grammar, rhetoric, and dialectic) and the *quadrivium* (arithmetic, geometry, astronomy, and music). A universal scholar, he was interested in law and medicine and well versed in the advanced studies of philosophy and theology. That he did not lead a celibate or cloistered life seems evident from many details in *The Romance*, and particularly from the poet's encomium of his own virility (Chap. 99, lines 25 ff.). Also, his tone suggests that he would not willingly submit in courtly obedience to any lady.

Jean de Meun the scholar, it should be noticed, was also a professional writer and popularizer, interested in gaining rewards from the patrons to whom he presented manuscript copies of his works. As might be expected of the author of *The Romance's* continuation, his interests as a writer ranged widely. He translated the *Military Art* of Vegetius, a fourth-century Latin writer from whom medieval strategists learned how to besiege a castle, and from whom Jean himself perhaps drew inspiration for the allegorical siege of the Rose. He translated Boethius' sixth-century *Consolation of Philosophy*, that famous debate which demonstrates that Fortune is subject to Providence—a topic to which Jean frequently alludes.

He also translated the *Life and Letters of Peter Abélard and Héloïse*, whose love affair he obviously followed with a warm sympathy; for Abélard (1079–1142), the scholastic philosopher, theologian, and lover, although a much more profound thinker than Jean, foreshadows the translator. Jean translated the *Spiritual Friendship* written (*ca.* 1160) by the great English Cistercian, Ailred, Abbot of Rievaulx, whose essay presents a Christian counterpart to one of Jean's favorite classical works, Cicero's *Friendship*. He translated the *Topography of Ireland* (under the title *The Wonders of Ireland*), written (*ca.* 1188) by Giraldus the Welshman.

Several other works were attributed to him in the Middle Ages, two of which are almost certainly his. One is a poem entitled *The Testament of Jean de Meun,* in which the author renounces the follies of his youth; the other, a poem entitled *The Codicil of Master Jean de Meun,* which satirizes the Mendicants just as they are satirized in *The Romance.*

Jean's distinction as a writer seems to have won important contacts for him. He dedicated-his Vegetius (in 1284) to Jean de Brienne, the Count of Eu, and his Boethius, to King Philip IV (the Fair), who reigned 1285–1315. In *The Romance* he pays particular compliment to the King's great-uncle, Charles of Anjou, the King of Sicily (reigned 1266–1285), and to Count Robert II of Artois, the patron of poets. The author of the *Testament* speaks truly when he says:

> God has granted me honor in the highest and great substance;
> God has granted me to serve the greatest people of France.

In his later years up to the time of his death in 1305, he lived in a comfortable residence in the Faubourg St. Jacques, near the meeting-places of his spiritual home, the University. Here he could listen to, and engage in, endless disputations, for the accepted method of reaching scholastic results was to match thesis with antithesis and draw conclusions in public debate.

His exact relation to the University remains unknown. Later documents always refer to him as Master Jean de Meun, from which title we may conclude that he was at least a Master of Arts; and he may, in fact, have been a teaching Master. The conventional portrait of him which appears in the manuscripts of *The Romance* shows him wearing the biretta appropriate to that rank. (See p. 213.) But whatever his status, he lived in the midst of an intellectual ferment which is reflected in his writing.

Jean's personifications in *The Romance* all speak like academics. Each defends his role in life. Each interprets, quotes authorities, disputes, refutes, defines, and rationalizes. The process of oral questioning on "whatever you wish," known as the *quodlibet*, to which Masters submitted, lives in *The Romance*. The entire work portrays an intellectual chain reaction among scholarly specialists occasioned by the Lover's dogged determination to persevere in his pursuit of love. Reason proves (Chap. 21) that love is vain and unprofitable, but the Lover persists in his unreason, and so *The Romance* continues through a delightful series of arguments, half serious, half comic in tone.

Because of the wide range of the discussions in Jean's *Romance*, some literary historians have persisted in describing the work as an encyclopedia. This title is entirely misleading. When some of the speakers seem to say more than is necessary, the modern reader may feel that the wealth of their discourse is indeed encyclopedic. But Jean is himself a poet, not an encyclopedist, and his theme is always love. The source of confusion lies in the fact that he follows the precepts of medieval rhetoric and the methods of thirteenth-century scholasticism.

The essence of poetry, according to the accepted authorities such as Matthew of Vendôme and Geoffrey of Vinsauf, lies in amplification. The poet's task is to expand and adorn and illustrate his subject. Jean is merely following their advice when he introduces parallels such as the extensive account of Pygmalion (Chap. 97). Even his apology for having interrupted his narrative at this point is a part of the recommended rhetorical practice. He is not writing an encyclopedia article on Pygmalion; he is drawing a highly appropriate and moving poetic parallel between the ravishing beauty of the sculptor's statue and the irresistible charm of the Lover's Rose.

As a rhetorician, moreover, Jean never loses the thread of an argument. The debaters sometimes prolong their debate to such extraordinary length that the casual reader (or critic) may forget the main point, but the author himself has not forgotten it. Thus Reason, for instance, calmly holds her ground when the Lover accuses her of indelicacy. She has referred to Jove's cullions (Chap. 26, line 228); the Lover is shocked (Chap. 27, l. 76); she promises to justify herself later (Chap. 27, l. 82); proceeds with her main argument; and then disposes of his minor quibble (Chap. 33, l. 21). Everywhere this same deliberate progression is maintained.

A larger question remains unanswered, however, by the examination of rhetorical details. Did Jean de Meun attain, or even wish to attain, any over-all unity in the development of his theme? In continuing Guillaume de Lorris' poem, Jean chose to follow a difficult and typically scholastic method; and, once again, an appreciation of his intentions vindicates the poet. In portraying the Lover's career, Guillaume de Lorris was able to follow the customary and well-established conventions of courtly love. But the age of Jean de Meun was animated by the Aristotelian dictum, *Sapientis est ordinare*. As a man of learning he instinctively ordered his theme and related love to the whole scheme of things.

The simple method of the old allegories such as Prudentius' *War of the Soul* no longer sufficed. Jean realized that truth has many parts, each one complex. Hence the rich conflict of opinion between Jean's personifications. Reason reveals love's folly, Genius argues its necessity, the Duenna describes the sordidness of its stratagems, Forced Abstinence suggests the unhealthiness of its renunciation, and so on, until every aspect of love has been ordered within the totality.

The order which Jean achieves is not the clear, self-contained order of Milton's *Paradise Lost*. It is the order of the thirteenth century. Jean is at times ambiguous and paradoxical. Yet he shares the intellectual excitement of the age which undertook to reconcile faith with reason, authority with experience, and the philosophy of Plato and Aristotle with the theology of the Church. He, perhaps, accepts the Averrhoistic theory of double-truth, by which a proposition can be true philosophically though false theologically, or false philosophically though true theologically. However, he boldly embraces the same important questions with which Aquinas had wrestled, concerning the nature of God, of man, of the universe, of providence and fate, of free will, and of the real and the ideal.

The guiding principles of Jean's order of love, which become clear when once their source is recognized, are centered upon the relationship between the Lover and Genius and God. According to the scheme envisaged in the *Universe of the World* (*ca.* 1145–53) by Bernard Silvester of Tours, the Divine Mind created all things in a hierarchical system, within which the generative principle (Genius) serves to conquer Death and avert the return of Chaos. Alan de Lille (d. 1202) gave Bernard Silvester's idea a dramatic development in his *Complaint of Nature*. Perhaps because he was an opponent of the heretical Cathars, who held that intercourse was evil, Alan represented Nature as complaining that Man alone of all her creatures had turned the principle of love awry. On behalf of Nature, Alan's Genius pronounces an anathema upon all those who may be guilty of this dereliction. Naturally enough, then, in *The Romance* we find Genius delivering advice to Love's followers, which in any other context might seem startling:

> Be active in your functions natural. . . .
> Plow, barons, plow—your lineage repair;
> For if you do not, there'll be nothing left
> To build upon.
>
> (Chap. 91, ll. 151 ff.)

Jean's Genius is not endorsing hedonism. The author is not echoing the ancient cry of Catullus:

> Let us, my Lesbia, live and love. . . .
> The suns can set and rise again;
> When once our brief light has set,
> We must sleep one endless night.

On the contrary, Jean relates human love to the Divine scheme, just as Bernard Silvester did. After mortals have fulfilled Nature's purpose, Genius tells us, they may be privileged to pass to the Good Shepherd's Paradise. It is an abode of everlasting and incorruptible joy.

Genius adumbrates its quality by two indirect but effective comparisons. Jupiter, he remarks, established a Golden Age dedicated to the proposition that "delight's the best thing that can be

—the sovereign good in life, which all should seek." (Chap. 93, ll. 50–51) But Jupiter was a bad administrator, and his Golden Age declined to an Age of Iron. The Shepherd, on the other hand, perpetually guards his charges against any harm.

The delights of the Shepherd's Park, moreover, are real, while those of the Lover's Garden are evanescent. In Guillaume de Lorris' part of *The Romance*, the Lover had witnessed the apparent delight and happiness of the dancers in the Garden, but Genius assesses their true worth:

> These things are fables—vain imaginings—
> No stable facts, but fictions that will fade.
> Dances will reach their end, and dancers fail.
> (Chap. 94, ll. 52–54)

Jean de Meun is not attempting here to atone for the outspoken sexuality of his writing. He does not pretend to be a theologian or a philosopher. He is a scholastic poet, not a poetic scholastic, and draws his ideas eclectically from the vast range of his reading in order to weave them into his own representation of reality. Like his contemporaries, he strives to see life whole; and, as a consequence, his *Romance* is itself a whole.

Jean does even more, however, than transform Guillaume's simple allegory of courtly love into a panorama of scholastic love. He extends the role of the personifications so that, while still functioning within the allegory of love, they also become the spokesmen of a contemporary social satire directed especially against the Mendicant Orders and women.

To appreciate Jean de Meun's violent opposition to the Mendicants, certain distinctions must be understood. The secular clergy, with whom Jean sympathizes, ordinarily served the church as parish priests and had provided the main source of teachers in the University. Monks, such as the ancient Benedictines (Black Monks) and the recently formed Cistercians (White Monks), lived a contemplative life in the seclusion of monasteries. The Mendicants, in contrast, were dedicated to the active life. They belonged to orders, the most important of which were the Franciscan Order of Friars Minor and the Dominican Order of Preaching Friars (known in Paris as Jacobins). They were under vow to own no property and begged for their subsistence. Although most of them served as wandering preachers, some entered the University and soon rose to important heights as rivals of the secular clergy. Within their orders in the thirteenth century they numbered many distinguished and admirable men, including Roger Bacon, the Franciscan, and Thomas Aquinas, the Dominican.

Jean alludes indignantly to two early incidents associated with the growth of their power. In Paris, in 1254, Friar Gerard (a Franciscan) began to circulate an interpretation of Joachim of Fiore's prophecies entitled *Introduction to the Everlasting Gospel*. This fanatical work, which seemed to elevate St. Francis above Christ, and the Mendicants above the Pope and secular clergy, was condemned in 1255 with quiet tact by the Bishop of Paris. But a secular master, William of St. Amour, had retaliated with an unmeasured attack upon the Mendicants, whom he described as the forerunners of Antichrist. His behavior instigated a *cause célèbre*. He was tried before the Pope, was condemned to exile, and never lectured again. As a secular partisan, Jean revives the old quarrel when (in Chap. 55) he attacks the *Everlasting Gospel* and bewails the fate of Master William, who had died in obscurity in 1272.

Furthermore, within his allegory of love, Jean represents the personifications of False Seeming and Forced Abstinence as Mendicants. His other allegorical figures do not represent particular professions; these two alone are gratuitously labeled. Even the tolerant God of Love is horrified when they first appear before him (in Chap. 50). False Seeming, who need merely have represented the deceiver in love, is the son of Fraud and Hypocrisy, the father-to-be of Antichrist, and the type of the traitor. His traveling companion, Forced Abstinence, who might have represented no more than continence in love, is the mother-to-be of Antichrist (Chap. 66). When they set out to silence Evil Tongue (who might have thwarted the Lover's purpose), one is dressed as a Preaching Friar (Chap. 56), the other as a Béguine.

Jean makes clear the grounds of his opposition to the Preaching Friars (Dominicans) by allowing False Seeming to boast of his own faults (Chap. 52). The presence of Forced Abstinence ingeniously completes the satire. The term "abstinence" means the sexual continence vowed by members of a religious order. To be a true virtue, however, such continence should be voluntary and not constrained. Béguines belonged to a very loosely organized female order, and their vows were temporary; in the thirteenth century, they were widely criticized for their irregularity and occasionally condemned for heresy. Forced Abstinence thus belongs to the worst of all possible female orders and repudiates the basic ideals of the religious life.

Jean's satire of Mendicants has some historical basis. His satire of women, on the other hand, has been attributed to an unjustifiable, blind, and savage prejudice. On this sensitive subject Jean has met the familiar fate of the satirist, such as Juvenal, Swift, or Voltaire. When he reveals a vice, he is said to deny the existence of virtue; when he condemns an individual, he is accused of damning the entire community. Yet Jean's feelings towards womankind were perhaps much more charitable than those of his unreflecting contemporaries who, by a loose kind of logic, argued that Eve was responsible for the fall of Adam and therefore for the sacrifice of Christ, and that the daughters of Eve have ever since been responsible for the ills of mankind.

Jean's satire is undeniably devastating when the Friend and Genius in turn describe the woes of marriage and the Duenna reveals the wiles of a woman in love. But these are special pleadings. It is illuminating to compare them with one of their sources, Juvenal's *Sixth Satire*. Juvenal himself claims that there is absolutely no prospect for happiness in marriage because all women are evil. Jean's Friend says approximately the same, sometimes in the very words of Juvenal, when he attempts to help the Lover by explaining how women may be seduced. Yet, though his style is rhetorical and his method scholastic, a warm humanity underlies his argument. He admits the possibility of finding a woman "who is courteous, artless, wise, and good" (Chap. 39, l. 58). He recognizes the charm of an educated woman: "Time never will diminish her allure but ever will ameliorate her worth" (ll. 99–100). Flying in the face of contemporary assumptions, he eloquently insists on the necessity of equality between husband and wife. "True love cannot for long endure when . . . men treat their own wives like property" (Chap. 41, ll. 6, 8). Jean's satire thus appears to arise more from his thesis than from his heart.

The irreverence shown towards women in Jean's portion of *The Romance* arises from the author's conscious reaction against the humility of Guillaume's courtly lover. In Guillaume de Lorris' portion, the Rose is by convention entitled to demand complete feudal obedience from the Lover. According to Jean's thesis, however, a lover should not dance in attendance. Such behavior would be an intolerable misapplication of the true purpose of love. He should possess and fecundate. Traditionally, the courtly romances merely hint at the extent of their lovers' sexual joys and ignore the unromantic possibility of pregnancy. Scorning the courtly code and all its artifices, Jean in his unveiled allegory assures the reader that the Lover has consummated his purpose. Thus the Rose becomes the first important pregnant heroine in European literature. But in his bold *dénouement* Jean de Meun shows no irreverence to the Rose. At an earthly level she remains as sublime as Dante's Beatrice in Heaven. Cherished by her Lover, she is the vindicator of the Divine plan, and the justification of the author's Comedy of Love.

4. The Fame of *The Romance of the Rose*

The Romance was copied repeatedly in manuscript and, in its time, was probably one of the most widely distributed works of literature. More than two hundred manuscripts survive to the present day, and the book was put in print soon after the introduction of printing in Europe—probably as early as 1481.

Guillaume de Lorris' first part of *The Romance* won an immediate following even before Jean's continuation. The latter created a furore. Jean had in vain anticipated the chief objections when he apologized (in Chap. 70) for his satire of friars and of

women. For a time he even ran the danger of ecclesiastical condemnation. In 1277 Stephen Tempier, who as Bishop of Paris was
responsible for the orthodoxy of the University, denounced 219
propositions studied and discussed by the students in Arts. Among
these "manifest and execrable errors, nay, rather, false delusions
and insanities" appear several theses which seem to be supported
by Jean's characters, if not by the author himself. Three such are:
"Continence is not itself a virtue," "Total abstinence from the
work of the flesh corrupts virtue and the species," and "Unmixed
fornication insofar as between an unattached man and an unattached woman is not a sin."

Generally, Jean's work served as a stimulus to other writers,
even long after the code of courtly love and the scholastic speculations of the thirteenth century had been forgotten. Guillaume
de Deguilleville differs entirely in point of view from Jean de
Meun, but his *Pilgrimage of Human Life* (1330–1335) shows the
impress of *The Romance*. Chaucer translated *The Romance*, at
least in part. In *The Legend of Good Women*, Chaucer's God of
Love (a conservative) condemns *The Romance* as a heresy against
his law; but the poet himself was profoundly influenced by it.
False Seeming became Chaucer's enigmatic Pardoner in the
Canterbury Tales, and the Duenna was transformed into his incomparable Wife of Bath.

In France, during Chaucer's lifetime, Christine de Pisan prepared an *Epistle to the God of Love* (1399) as a spirited defence
of womankind against Jean's satire. Jean de Gerson, the anti-
scholastic chancellor of the University of Paris, in 1402 directed
a special tract against *The Romance*. In 1483 Jean Molinet wrote
a prose version of *The Romance* to which he added moralizations
intended to transform "the vicious to the virtuous."

In 1527 Clément Marot found it necessary to modernize the
now archaic language of *The Romance*. In the sixteenth century
the work was still popular and equally familiar to the ribald
Rabelais and the gracious Ronsard. It fell into obscurity in the
seventeenth century but was rescued by the antiquarians of the
eighteenth century and has been restored and interpreted by the

patient labors of the literary historians of the nineteenth and twentieth centuries.

This literary monument still survives, full-formed, complex, and vast, with all the vitality and mystery of its Gothic art. It is a unique and memorable work without which the course of Western culture would not have been the same.

5. ILLUSTRATIONS

The Romance appealed particularly to the aristocracy, and numerous expensively illuminated manuscript copies were made for such clients. The choice of passages for illustration remained relatively unchanged, each illuminator following his predecessor. The styles did, however, change from a simple, unadorned representation to one more elaborate. Backgrounds were more and more fully decorated, surrounding ornamentations were extended, perspective and landscape were introduced by Flemish artists of the fifteenth century, and style generally became increasingly realistic.

To provide some examples of the exquisite style of the fourteenth century, illuminations have been reproduced in the present work from three manuscripts belonging to the Pierpont Morgan Library in New York, all of which may have had royal patronage. The oldest of these is Morgan 324. It was illuminated in Paris *ca.* 1340–1350. The first page, which appears here as a frontispiece, is remarkably well preserved, and the reproduction, despite the loss of the original glowing colors, gives an excellent idea of the richness of such manuscripts. The heads inset around the frame suggest the potential readers—crowned rulers, bishops, and monastics. The sense of design is suggested by the delicate and varied backgrounds within each of the quarters of the upper page.

Morgan 132 was executed in France around 1380. It is a dainty volume, and the illuminations are appropriately delicate. The unadorned backgrounds and the gentle grisaille coloring emphasize the brilliant sharpness of the drawing. The positioning of the characters displays an astonishing command of space, as for instance when Dido and Phyllis (two separate examples in the text) are combined into one illumination, or when the soaring of Venus' chariot is suggested by the increasing size of the three trees underneath.

Morgan 245 was probably prepared for King Charles VI or some member of the royal family about 1415. The portrait of Jean de Meun, though stylized, is interesting in its representation of the author in what is presumably a Master's biretta. The majority of the illuminations (including those shown on pp. 42 and 444)are by the hand of an unknown but distinguished artist who is a master of realism, warmth, and shading. The sweeping lines of Galatea's green robe, with its golden embroidery (p. 444), is a reminder that Gothic art reached great heights not only in the vast spaces of cathedrals but also in the narrow compass of the miniature.

6. The Robbins Translation

The translation published here was the lifetime work of Harry Wolcott Robbins, who was born in Vershire, Vermont, in 1883, graduated from Brown University, took his doctorate under Professor Carleton Brown at the University of Minnesota in 1923, and became Professor of English that same year at Bucknell University and subsequently Head of the English Department.

Though he published numerous studies and texts, he left his translation unpublished when he died in 1954. By a fortunate coincidence, Professor Philip M. Withim of Bucknell drew the translation to my attention, and E. P. Dutton & Co. gladly undertook to publish it.

The translation is a brilliant achievement. The original poem is written in four-beat rhyming couplets, which cannot be readily converted into effective English verse. Professor Robbins chose the five-beat, unrhymed line of blank verse for his rendering, and was thus able to follow the involutions of the poet's argument without contortion or inaccuracy. He divided the verse into one hundred chapters, closing each one with a six-beat line.

The chapter divisions are not to be found in the original Old

French text but are convenient and logical and have been retained
here. For further convenience, line numbers have also been inserted. These do not, of course, coincide with the line numbers in
the original. The latter have been placed in brackets at the beginning of each chapter for those who wish to consult the Old
French. The translation has been revised in only a very few minor
details, all of which I hope would have been approved by Professor Robbins.

A transcript of the opening lines of the Old French as edited
by Langlois are here reproduced for comparison with Robbins'
rendering. These lines can also be read in the illustration which
serves as a frontispiece of this edition. (The latter contains some
scribal variations.)

> Maintes genz dient que en songes
> N'a se fables non e mençonges;
> Mais l'en puet teus songes songier
> Qui ne sont mie mençongier,
> Ainz sont après bien aparant;
> Si en puis bien traire a garant
> Un auctor qui ot non Macrobes,
> Qui ne tint pas songes a lobes,
> Ançois escrist l'avision
> Qui avint au roi Scipion.

The second half of the twentieth century seems to mark the
renaissance of translation. It is my belief that Harry Wolcott
Robbins will be recognized as one of the outstanding masters of
this flourishing art, for he has reopened the treasury of our literary
heritage.

CHARLES W. DUNN

New York University
Washington Square

SELECTIVE BIBLIOGRAPHY

EDITIONS

Le Roman de la Rose, ed. Ernest Langlois (Paris: Société des anciens textes français, 1914–1924.) 5 vols.
[Standard edition; invaluable notes on sources and parellels.]
Jean de Meun, *L'art de chevalerie*, ed. Ulysse Robert (Paris: SATF, 1897).
[Translation of Vegetius.]
——, "Boethius' De Consolatione," ed. V. L. Dedeck-Héry, *Mediaeval Studies*, XIV (1952), 165–275.
——, *Testament* and *Codicile*, in M. Méon, *Le Roman de la Rose* (Paris, 1814), IV, 1–116, 117–121.
——, *Traduction de la première épitre de Pierre Abélard*, ed. Charlotte Charrier (Paris, 1934).
[Jean de Meun's translations of Ailred and Giraldus are no longer extant.]

BIBLIOGRAPHY

R. Bossuat, *Manuel bibliographique de la littérature française du moyen âge* (Melun, 1951); *Supplement* (Paris, 1955).
Critical Bibliography of French Literature, ed. D. C. Cabeen: I, ed. U. T. Holmes (Syracuse, 1952).

STUDIES

Edmond Faral, "Le Roman de la Rose" *Revue des deux mondes*, XXXV (1926), 430–457.

M. M. Gorce, *Le Roman de la Rose* (Paris, 1933).
[Useful running commentary, particularly on scholastic elements.]

Alan M. F. Gunn, *The Mirror of Love: A Reinterpretation of "The Romance of the Rose"* (Lubbock, Texas, 1952).
[Comprehensive study; thorough analysis of rhetorical influences; exhaustive bibliography.]

Ernest Langlois, *Les manuscrits du Roman de la Rose* (Travaux et mémoires de l'Université de Lille, N. S., I, 7) (Lille, 1910).

———, *Origines et sources du Roman de la Rose* (Bibliothèque des écoles françaises d'Athènes et de Rome, 58) (Paris, 1891).

Charles Muscatine, "The Emergence of Psychological Allegory in Old French Romance," *PMLA*, LXVIII (1953), 1160–1182.

Gérard Paré, *Les idées et les lettres au XIIIe siècle* (Montreal, 1947).
[Basic study of Jean de Meun's scholasticism.]

Louis Thuasne, *Le Roman de la Rose* (Paris, 1929).
[Useful on later influence of *Roman*.]

CULTURAL BACKGROUND

E. Faral and Julia Bastin, ed. *Oeuvres complètes de Rutebeuf* (Paris, 1959). 2 vols.
[Rutebeuf wrote *ca.* 1249–*ca.* 1285 on topics also treated by Jean de Meun, particularly University and Mendicants. Important introduction; convenient references in index of proper names.]

Hastings Rashdall, *The Universities of Europe in the Middle Ages*, rev.edn., ed. F. M. Powicke and A. B. Emden (Oxford, 1936). 3 vols.
[See particularly vol. I for scholasticism and for University of Paris.]

Maurice de Wulf, *History of Medieval Philosophy*, trans. E. Messenger, 3rd edn. (London, 1935–1938). 2 vols.
[Useful guide.]

ILLUMINATIONS

Alfred Kuhn, "Die Illustration des Rosenromans," *Jahrbuch der*

kunsthistorischen Sammlungen des allerhöchsten Kaiser-hauses, XXXI (Vienna, 1913–1914), 1–66.
[Fundamental study of stylistic developments.]
Pierpont Morgan Library, *Descriptions of Manuscripts* (type-script) (New York, various dates).
[Contains authoritative accounts of MSS of *The Romance* in the Library: Nos. 48, 120, 132, 181, 185, 245, 324, 372, 503.]

THE ROMANCE OF THE ROSE

1. The Poet dreams a dream
[Old French original, lines 1–128]

MANY a man holds dreams to be but lies,
All fabulous; but there have been some dreams
No whit deceptive, as was later found.
Well might one cite Macrobius, who wrote
The story of the Dream of Scipio,
And was assured that dreams are ofttimes true.
But, if someone should wish to say or think
'Tis fond and foolish to believe that dreams
Foretell the future, he may call me fool.
10 Now, as for me, I have full confidence
That visions are significant to man
Of good and evil. Many dream at night
Obscure forecasts of imminent events.
    When I the age of twenty had attained—
The age when Love controls a young man's heart—
As I was wont, one night I went to bed
And soundly slept. But then there came a dream
Which much delighted me, it was so sweet.
No single thing which in that dream appeared
20 Has failed to find fulfillment in my life,
With which the vision well may be compared.
Now I'll recount this dream in verse, to make
Your hearts more gay, as Love commands and wills;
And if a man or maid shall ever ask

3

By what name I would christen the romance
Which now I start, I will this answer make:
"*The Romance of the Rose* it is, and it enfolds
Within its compass all the Art of Love."
The subject is both good and new. God grant
30 That she for whom I write with favor look
Upon my work, for she so worthy is
Of love that well may she be called the Rose.
    Five years or more have passed by now, I think,
Since in that month of May I dreamed this dream—
In that month amorous, that time of joy,
When all things living seem to take delight,
When one sees leafless neither bush nor hedge,
But each new raiment dons, when forest trees
Achieve fresh verdure, though they dry have been
40 While winter yet endured, when prideful Earth,
Forgetting all her winter poverty
Now that again she bathes herself in dew,
Exults to have a new-spun, gorgeous dress;
A hundred well-matched hues its fabric shows
In new-green grass, and flowers blue and white
And many divers colors justly prized.
The birds, long silent while the cold remained—
While changeful weather brought on winter storms—
Are glad in May because of skies serene,
50 And they perforce express their joyful hearts
By utterance of fitting minstrelsy.
Then nightingales contend to fill the air
With sound of melody, and then the lark
And popinjay with songs amuse themselves.
The young folk then their whole attention give
To suit the season fair and sweet with love
And happiness. Hard heart has he, indeed,
Who cannot learn to love at such a time,
When he these plaintive chants hears in the trees.
60   In this delightful month, when Love excites
All things, one night I, sleeping, had this dream.
Methought that it was full daylight.   I rose
In haste, put on my shoes and washed my hands,
Then took a silver needle from its case,

Dainty and neat, and threaded it with silk.
I yearned to wander far outside the town
To hear what songs the birds were singing there
In every bush, to welcome the new year.
Basting my sleeves in zigzags as I went,
70 I pleased myself, in spite of solitude.
Listening to the birds that took such pains
To chant among the new-bloom-laden boughs.
    Jolly and gay and full of happiness,
I neared a rippling river which I loved;
For I no nicer thing than that stream knew.
From out a hillside close thereby it flowed,
Descending full and free and clear and cold
As water from a fountain or well.
Though it was somewhat lesser than the Seine,
80 More broad it spread; a fairer I ne'er saw.
Upon the bank I sat, the scene to scan,
And with the view delight myself, and lave
My face in the refreshing water there;
And, as I bent, I saw the river floor
All paved and covered with bright gravel stones.
The wide, fair mead reached to the water's edge.
Calm and serene and temperate and clear
The morning was. I rose; and through the grass
Coasting along the bank I followed down the stream.

2. The Dreamer comes to a garden wall
[129–520]

WHEN I'd advanced a space along the bank,
I saw a garden, large and fair, enclosed
With battlemented wall, sculptured without
With many a figure and inscription neat.
Because of all the painted images
I will recall the wall, and will describe
The appearance of these figures, and will tell

As much of them as I remember now.
    Amidmost there I saw malignant Hate,
10 Who quarrelsome prime mover seemed in all
Contentions, and fulfilled with wickedness.
She was not well arrayed, but rather seemed
A frenzied dame, with dark and frowning face
And upturned nose, hideous and black with dirt.
Wrapped in a filthy towel was her head.
    Upon her left an equal figure stood
Close by; and, carved upon the stone above,
Her name I read. She was called Felony.
    Just at her right was stationed Villainy,
20 Who was so like her fellowimage carved
That in no feature could I difference see;
And she as wicked seemed—spiteful and proud
And evil-spoken. Well he knew his trade
Who could devise and paint the image so
That it seemed foul and churlish as alive,
Filled with injurious thoughts, a woman wont
But seldom to perform what she should do.
    Next her was painted greedy Covetousness,
Inciting men to take and never give,
30 But fill their money chests. The usurers
She tempts to lend to many, in desire
Of gaining and amassing property.
'Tis she impels to robbery the thieves
And harlots; and great pity 'tis, and sin,
For at the last the most of them are hanged.
'Tis she makes men purloin their neighbors' goods,
Deceive, miscount, embezzle, rob, and steal.
'Tis she makes all the tricksters and the scamps
Who, pleading by false technicality,
40 Too often strip of rightful heritage
Young men and maids. Knotty and bent her hands
Had grown, as was but right; for every day
Does Covetousness incite to larceny.
She cares for naught except within her net
To get her neighbors' wealth; this she holds dear.
    Another image, Avarice, I saw
Sitting by the side of Covetousness;

And she was ugly, dirty, weak, and lean,
Wasted and greener than a garden leek.
50 Such her complexion was, she seemed diseased,
Or like one famine fated, only fed
On bread concocted with strong, caustic lye.
Her shrunken limbs in rags were scarcely clothed;
Her seemingly dog-bitten cloak was torn,
Worn out, and poor—with older fragments patched.
Hard by her mantle hung from shaky pin;
It was of brunet cloth, not lined with fur—
Rather with sheepskin, shaggy, coarse, and black.
Her robe was ten years old, at least, for she
60 Would be the last to rush to get new clothes;
It weighed most heavily upon her mind
If each new dress she failed to wear out quite.
Even a costume threadbare, out of date,
She'd not, unless hard pressed, replace with new.
Her purse she clutched and hid within her hand
So tightly tied that long delay she made
Before a penny she could take therefrom
In case there was no help for it; she meant
That it for gain should open, not dispense.
70   Beside her sad, unsmiling Envy stood,
Who never in her life a thing enjoys
Unless it be to hear or see some ill
Or some discomfiture on good men fall;
For nothing moves her like mischance or harm.
They please her well; her heart has most delight
When she beholds someone of lineage high
Descend to shameful depths. When someone mounts
To honor by his prowess or his wit,
That sorely wounds her; when some good appears,
80 It well becomes her to be rancorous.
Envy displays so much of cruelty
That never she her loyalty will hold
To man or woman; and she has no kin,
How close soever, she will not desert.
She would not even wish her father well!
But you would know her malice dearly bought,
For in such torment great she always is,

And feels such woe when weal befalls a man,
Her felon heart seems breaking. Thus does God
90 Upon her sin a fitting vengeance take.
Envy will never let an hour go by
When all from her reproaches are secure.
I think, if Envy knew the very best
Of men who live near by or overseas,
She still would find some fault in him to blame;
And if he were so perfect in his wit
That she could never all his fame destroy,
Still would she try to lessen it at least
And by her words diminish his repute.
100 Now in that painting did I Envy note
To have an ugly look, a sidewise glance,
And never gaze direct, for face to face
She could not stare; but one eye in disdain
She closed. When anyone on whom she looked
Was loved or praised by others for good sense
Or gentleness or beauty, then with ire
She flamed, and seemed about to melt like wax.
    Close beside Envy, painted on the wall,
Was Sorrow, showing by her jaundiced hue.
110 That heavy dolor weighed upon her heart.
Not even Avarice looked so pale and lean
As she; for woe, distress, chagrin, and care
From which she ever suffered, night and day,
Had yellowed and emaciated her.
Such martyrdom no person born has known,
Nor felt such sad effects of ire, as she
Seemed to have felt; and no man, I believe,
Could please her e'er by doing anything.
Nor did she wish, at any rate, herself
120 To comfort or relieve from all the woe
That her heart knew. For any human help
Too much depressed, too deeply grieved was she.
Most dolorous she seemed, and had not failed
To scratch her cheeks; and, as if filled with rage,
In many places had she torn her robe,
Considering it as naught. Her hair, unbound,
Lay all about her neck, torn by her hands

Because of her unbounded spleen and grief.
Now you should know it for a fact that she
130 Wept most profoundly ever. There's no man
So hard of heart that, seeing her distress,
Would not profoundly pity her estate;
For she would beat and tear her breast, and smite
Her fists together most relentlessly.
So woebegone a wretch was she that all
Her thought was on her pain; she never knew
The joy of being fondled or embraced.
For you should know, in truth, that one in woe
Has no desire for caroling or dance;
140 Nor can she school herself, who lives in grief,
To merriment. <u>Joy is woe's opposite.</u>
   <u>Old Age was painted next to Sorrow there,</u>
<u>Shrunken at least a foot from what her height</u>
<u>Had been in youth.</u> She scarce could feed herself
For feebleness and years. Her beauty gone,
Ugly had she become. Her head was white
As if it had been floured. 'Twere no great loss
Were she to die, for shriveled were her limbs—
By time reduced almost to nothingness.
150 Much withered were her cheeks, that had been soft;
And wrinkled foul, that formerly were fair.
Her ears hung pendulous; her teeth were gone;
Years had so lamed her that she could not walk
Four fathoms' distance without aid of crutch.
<u>Time is forever fleeting, night and day,</u>
<u>Without sojourn, and taking no repose;</u>
But as he goes he steals away from us
So secretly that he appears to stand,
Although he never rests, nor stays his course;
160 So that no man can say that time is now.
Ask of some well-read clerk; ere he can think
Three times will Time already have passed by.
This never-lingering Time, who all day long
Is going on and never will return,
Resembles water that forever flows
But ne'er a drop comes back. There is no thing
So durable, not even iron itself,

That it can Time survive, who all devours
And wastes. He changes all—makes all things wax
170 With nourishment, and wane then in decay.
'Twas Time who made our fathers old, and kings
And emperors, and who will do as much
For you and me ere Death shall us demand.
This Time, who has the power to senescate
All things on earth, had so reduced Old Age,
It seemed to me that, willy-nilly, she
Had to her infancy again returned.
No power she had, and no more force or sense
Than yearling child, although she did appear
180 Like one who in her prime was sage and wise;
Henceforth she would be nothing but a sot.
Her body well protected was, and clothed
In furry mantle, warm against the cold
Which otherwise had wholly frozen her;
For all old folk feel chills habitually.

   The image standing next was well portrayed
To be a hypocrite, but she was named
Pope Holy. She it is who secretly
Contrives to take us unaware, and then
190 She does not hesitate at any ill.
Outwardly she appears a saint demure,
With simple, humble, pious person's face;
But under heaven there's no evil scheme
That she has never pondered in her heart.
The figure well her character did show,
Though she was of a candid countenance.
Well shod and clothed like good convent nun,
She held a psalter in her hand, and took
Much pains to make her feigned prayers to God
200 And call upon all male and female saints.
She was not gay or jolly, but she seemed
Attentive always to perform good works.
She wore a haircloth shirt, and she was lean,
As though with fasting weary, pale, half dead.
To her and to her like will be refused
Entrance to Paradise. The Gospel says
Such folk emaciate their cheeks for praise

Among mankind, and for vainglory lose
Their chance to enter Heaven and see God.
210   Last painted was the form of Poverty,
Who could not buy a rope to hang herself,
For she had not a penny in her purse;
Nor could she sell her clothes, for she was bare
As any worm, clad only in a sack
That fitted tight and was most poorly patched.
It served her for a mantle and a cloak,
But nothing else she had for covering.
I think that, if the weather had been bad,
She would have died of cold; for she did quake,
220 Clinging and cowering in a little coign,
Far from the others, like a mangy bitch.
Poverty-stricken folk, where'er they be,
Are always shamed and spited. Curse the hour
When poor men are conceived, to be ill fed,
To be ill shod, to be ill clothed—alas,
To be unloved and never to be raised
Into a place of profit or esteem!
    I scanned these images upon the wall
Full well, for as already I've explained
230 They stood out prominent in blue and gold.
High was the wall, and neatly built and squared.
Its bulk, in place of hedge, a garden fenced.
To which no low-born man had ever come,
For it was quite too fine a place for such.
Willingly would I have found a guide
Who, by means of ladder or of stile,
Might bring me therewithin; for so great joy
And such delight as in that place might be
Were seldom known to man, as I believe.
240 A generous and safe retreat for fowl
That garden was; ne'er was a place so rich
In trees bedight with songsters of all kinds;
For there were found three times as many birds
As there can be in all the rest of France.
The full accord of their most moving songs
Delicious was to hear. It would delight
The world; and, as for me, it brought such joy.

That when I heard it I had gladly paid
One hundred pounds to have had entry there
250 That I might the assembly (whom God save!)
Both see and hear. Warblers that were therein
Sang most enthusiastically their notes
In gracious, courteous, pleasing songs of love.
Most powerfully stirred by all their tunes,
I tried to think how I might entrance gain
Into the garden by some trick or scheme.
However, not a portal could I see,
Nor did I know what one might do to find
An opening or door into the place;
260 Nor was there anyone whom I might ask
To show the way, for I was all alone.
Distracted then, and anxious, I became
Until I finally bethought myself
That no fair garden ever was without
Some means of entry, either stile or gate.
Then hotfoot I set out to gird the wall
Of square-cut stone, and all the enclosure large.
A tiny wicket—narrow, fully barred—
At last I found; there was no other door.
270 For want of better, at this gate I promptly knocked.

3. The Dreamer enters the Garden of Mirth
[521–776]

FULL many a time I smote and struck the door
And listened for someone to let me in,
When finally the yoke-elm wicket gate
Was opened by a maiden mild and fair—
Yellow her hair as burnished brazen bowl—
Tender her flesh as that of new-hatched chick—
Radiant her forehead—gently arched
Her brows—as gray as falcon's her two eyes,
And spaced so well that flirts might envy her.

10 Her chin was dimpled. Mingled white and red
Was all her face—her breath sweet as perfume.
Of seemliest dimensions was her neck
In length and thickness—free from wen or spot;
A man might travel to Jerusalem
And find no maid with neck more fair and smooth
And soft to touch. Her throat was white as snow
Fresh fallen upon a branch. No one need seek
In any land a lady daintier,
With body better made or form more fair.
20 A graceful golden chaplet on her head
Was set than which no maiden ever had
One more becoming, chic, or better wrought.
Above the polished chaplet she had placed
A wreath of roses fresh from morning dew.
Her hair was tressed back most becomingly
With richest comb. Her hand a mirror bore.
Her fair, tight sleeves most carefully were laced.
White gloves protected her white hands from tan.
She wore a coat of rich green cloth of Ghent
30 All sewed with silk. It seemed from her attire
That she was little used to business.
When she was combed, adorned, and well arrayed,
Her daily task was done. A joyful time—
A year-long, carefree month of May—was hers,
Untroubled but by thoughts of fitting dress.
    When thus for me she had unlocked the gate,
Politely did I thank the radiant maid
And also asked her name and who she was.
She answered pleasantly, without disdain:
40 "All my companions call me Idleness;   IDLENESS
A woman rich and powerful am I.
Especially I'm blessed in one respect:
I have no care except to tress and comb
My hair, amuse myself, and take mine ease.
My dearest friend is Mirth, a genteel beau,
Who owns this garden planted full of trees
That he had brought especially for him
From that fair land where live the Saracens;
And, when the trees grew tall, he ordered made

50 The wall that, as you see, surrounds the whole,
   Together with the images outside,
   Which are not beautiful nor yet genteel,
   But dolorous and sad, as you've observed.
   To find diversion, Mirth oft seeks these shades
   With all his company, who live in joy
   And pleasure. Certainly he's now within,
   Listening to the songs of nightingale,
   Of wind thrush, and of many another bird.
   Here with his friends he joy and solace finds,
60 For never could he want more pleasant place
   Or one where he could more divert himself.
   The fairest folk that you'll find anywhere
   Are Mirth's companions, whom he keeps with him."
       When Idleness had told and I had heard
   Her tale most willingly, I said to her:
   "Dame Idleness, believe me when I say   THE DREAMER
   That since Sir Mirth, a generous gentleman,
   Is now within this garden with his friends,
   I hope the assembly may not so prevent
70 Me that I may not see them all today.
   I feel that I must meet them, for I think
   The company is courteous and well taught
   As well as fair." Without another word
   The gate by Idleness was opened wide;
   I entered then upon that garden fair.
       When once I was inside, my joyful heart
   Was filled with happiness and sweet content.
   You may right well believe I thought the place
   Was truly a terrestrial paradise,
80 For so delightful was the scenery
   That it looked heavenly; it seemed to me
   A better place than Eden for delight,
   So much the orchard did my senses please.
   The singing birds throughout the garden thronged:
   Here were the nightingales, and there the larks;
   Here were the starlings, and the jays were there;
   Here were the turtledoves, and there the wrens;
   Here were the goldfinches, and there the doves;
   Here were the thrushes, and the tomtits there.

90 New flocks from every side came constantly
   As others of the singing seemed to tire.
   The merle and mavis to surpass them all
   Seemed striving; elsewhere, in each tree and bush
   Where were their nests, parrots and other birds
   Delighted in the song. A service meet,
   As I have told you, all these birds performed;
   For such a song they sang as angels sing,
   And sang it, truly, to my great delight.
   No mortal man e'er heard a fairer tune.
100 So soft and sweetly pealed their melody
   That, if a man comparison should seek,
   It seemed no hymn of birds, but mermaids' song,
   Who for their voices clear, serene, and pure
   Are Sirens called. These birds were not unskilled
   Apprentices but tuneful journeymen,
   And to their craft they gave their greatest care.
   You may well know that, when I heard these tunes
   And saw the verdant place, I was most gay.
   Never so merry I—so glad of heart—
110 Until the day I knew that garden's charms!
   Then I perceived most plainly and well knew
   That Idleness had excellently served
   In placing me in midst of such delight.
   Well I resolved to be her faithful friend
   Because she oped for me the wooden gate.
       Henceforth, if I know how, I'll tell the tale
   Of what befell; and, first, what did Sir Mirth,
   And what the company he had, in brief
   I will recount; the garden then describe.
120 No man could list the whole in little space;
   But I will versify so orderly
   That none may have a chance to criticize.
       The birds kept on performing all their rites;
   Sweetly and pleasantly they sang of love
   And chanted sonnets courteously and well.
   In part songs joining, one sang high, one low.
   Their singing was beyond reproach; their notes
   With sweetness and contentment filled my heart.
       When I had listened for a little while

130 Unto the birds, I could no more refrain
    From going straight to see Sir Mirth himself.
    I much desired to know the state he kept
    And his entourage. Turning to the right
    And following a little path, with mint
    And fennel fringed, into a small retreat,
    Straightway I found Sir Mirth taking his ease.
    With him he had so fair a company
    That when I saw them I was quite amazed
    To think whence such fine people could have come;
140 For, truly, wingèd angels they did seem.
    No earth-born man had ever seen such folk.
    This noble company of which I speak
    Had ordered for themselves a caroling.
    A dame named Gladness led them in the tune;
    Most pleasantly and sweetly rang her voice.
    No one could more becomingly or well
    Produce such notes; she was just made for song.
    She had a voice that was both clear and pure;
    About her there was nothing rude, for she
150 Knew well the dance steps, and could keep good time
    The while she voiced her song. Ever the first
    Was she, by custom, to begin the tune;
    For music was the trade that she knew best
    Ever to practice most agreeably.
        Now see the carol go! Each man and maid
    Most daintily steps out with many a turn
    And farandole upon the tender grass.
    See there the flutists and the minstrel men,
    Performers on the viol! Now they sing
160 A rondelet, a tune from old Lorraine;
    For it has better songs than other lands.
    A troop of skillful jugglers thereabout
    Well played their parts, and girls with tambourines
    Danced jollily, and, finishing each tune,
    Threw high their instruments, and as these fell
    Caught each on finger tip, and never failed.
    Two graceful demoiselles in sheerest clothes,
    Their hair in coifferings alike arrayed,
    Most coyly tempted Mirth to join the dance.

170 Unutterably quaint their motions were:
Insinuatingly each one approached
The other, till, almost together clasped,
Each one her partner's darting lips just grazed
So that it seemed their kisses were exchanged.
I can't describe for you each lithesome glide
Their bodies made—but they knew how to dance!
Forever would I gladly have remained
So long as I could see these joyful folk
In caroling and dancing thus excel themselves.

4. The Dreamer meets the companions of Sir Mirth
[777–1278]

A WHILE I scanned the scene in all details
Until a winsome lady me espied;
Her name was Courtesy. May God forbid
She ever be but gallant, debonair!
She called to me, "Fair friend, why stand you still?   COURTESY
Come here and take a partner for this set,
If dancing with us may afford you joy."
With neither hesitation nor delay
I joined the throng; I was no whit abashed.
10 You may believe that when fair Courtesy
Asked me to join the dance and caroling
Most pleasing 'twas to me, who scarce had dared,
Though much I envied them, and greatly longed,
To join the band. But now, one of the crowd,
I covertly endeavored to observe
The faces and the forms of those who danced,
And also watched their fashions, manners, styles.
So now those who were there I will describe.
    Sir Mirth was fair and straight, of stature tall.
20 In no group could you find a finer man.
His face was white and rosy—apple-like—
Genteel and elegant his well-shaped mouth,

His gray-blue eyes, his finely chiseled nose,
His curling yellow hair. His shoulders broad,
His narrow waist, his nobly gracious form,
Compact in all its members, made one think
Of some great artist's portrait masterpiece.
Polite and agile and adroit was he;
You never saw one lighter on his feet.
30 He wore no beard or mustache, for the hair
Upon his face was still but tender down;
A youthful gentleman was he as yet.
Now he was clothed richly in samite cloak
Embroidered with the figures of fair birds
And ornamented all with beaten gold.
His coat was particolored and well slashed
And pinked in curious guise. His feet were shod
With shoes both slashed and laced most artfully.
For pleasure and for love a rosy wreath
40 His lady fair had set upon his head;
Most fitting and divine this crown appeared.
    Now do you know who his sweet mistress was—
The lady that did hate him least of all?
Her name was Gladness, she a singer gay
Who since she was but seven summers old
Had given him all her love. Now in the dance
Mirth held her by a finger; she held his.
Well did they suit each other—she a belle
And he a beau. Color of new-blown rose
50 Glowed in her flesh so tender smallest briar
Might scratch it, seemingly. Her forehead white
Was smooth and flawless over arching brows
Of brown that shaded joyous, smiling eyes
Seeming in constant contest with her mouth
Which should laugh first, and always they did win.
I know not what to say about her nose;
An artist could no daintier make of wax.
Her little lips were always pursed to kiss.
Her head was shining gold. But why should I
60 Go on to tell you any more of her?
That she'd a perfect form you may well guess.
Her hair was bound in finest gilded lace.

She wore a quite new orfray coronal.
Of chaplets twenty-nine at least I've seen
But never one more finely worked in silk.
Her body was adorned and richly clad
In gilded samite gown that matched the coat
Her lover wore, of which she was most proud.
    Upon the other side of Gladness stood
70 The God of Love, who at his own sweet will
Distributes amity. He lovers rules;
'Tis he abates the pride of men; 'tis he
Makes thralls of lords, puts ladies in their place
Whene'er he finds them puffed up with conceit.
Not knavish in his manner was the god,
And in his beauty there was much to praise.
I hesitate to tell you of his clothes,
For 'twas no silken robe he wore, but one
Made all of flowers worked with amorous art.
80 In lozenges and 'scutcheons, lions, birds,
Leopards were portrayed, and other beasts,
In every part. Of colors most diverse
Were flowers worked, blossoms in many a guise
Placed cunningly: the periwinkle blue,
The yellow flowers of broom, and violets.
No bloom exists that was not woven there
In indigo or yellow or in white.
The rose leaves that were interlaced with them
Were long and broad. He wore a rosy crown
90 Upon his head. A flock of nightingales
That flew above the crown would barely skim
The leaves. Now there were various birds about:
Besides the nightingales were popinjays
And orioles and larks. The God of Love
An angel seemed, descended from the sky.
    Love had with him Sweet Looks, a bachelor
Who customary fellow was to him;
And, gazing on the carolers, he held
Two Turkish bows belonging to the god.
100 One bow was made of bitter-fruited tree;
Knotted and gnarled it was at either end
And blacker than a wall. The other bow

Was made of slender, graceful, pliant stem,
Well shaped and polished smooth, and painted o'er,
For ornament, with maids and bachelors,
Glad faced and frolicsome, on every side.
With these two bows Sweet Looks, who seemed no knave,
Held for his master, five in either hand,
Ten arrows. Darts well feathered and well notched,
110 Cutting and hard and sharp enough to pierce,
Though golden pointed, did his right hand hold.
They were not made of iron or of steel,
But save for shafts and feathers were all gold.
The ends were tipped with hook-like golden barbs.
Sharpest and swiftest of these arrows five—
The one best feathered and the one most fair—
Was Beauty called; Simplicity was one
That sorer wounds, in my opinion;
Another one was Independence named,   *Franchise*
120 Feathered with valor and with courtesy;
The fourth, which bore the heaviest barb, and so
If shot from far could little damage do
But aimed from near at hand was dangerous,
Was called Companionship; the fifth and last,
Fair Seeming named, least grievous was of all,
But made the deepest wound, though him it hit
Could hope for speedy cure, for sovereign power
Its venom has to heal the wound it makes.
Five other arrows of quite different guise
130 He also held. They were of ugly iron;
Blacker than fiends in Hell, also, were they.
Pride was the first; the second, of like force,
Was Villainy, envenomed and made black
With felony; the third was christened Shame;
Despair and Faithlessness were fourth and fifth.
These arrows had a close relationship
And similarity; the hideous bow,
Crooked and knobby, fitly suited them,
And well enough it could such arrows shoot.
140 Opposing virtues had these arrows five
Against the others, but I will not tell
At present all their force and all their power.

However, ere my story finds an end,
I'll not forget their meaning to explain
And all the truth of what they signified.
    Now will I turn again unto my tale
And all the faces and the forms describe
Of those most noble folk there in the dance.
The God of Love seemed most attached to one
150 Of all the noble dames, and danced with her;
Her name was Beauty, like the arrow fair,
And she possessed the finest qualities.
She was not dark or brown, but rather bright,
And as the moon makes all the stars appear
Like feeble candles, so she dimmed the rest
Of that fair company. Her flesh was white
As fleur-de-lis, translucent as the dew.
She was as modest as a blushing bride;
She had no need to use an ogling glance.
160 Her form was straight and slender, and her face
Was clear and delicate. She sought no aid
From primping and adorning, powder, paint.
Her yellow hair—so long it touched her heels—
Her well-formed mouth and nose and cheeks and eyes—
With sweetness filled my heart. So help me God,
When I remember all her grace of limb,
It seems there's no such other in the world.
To summarize, she was both fair and young,
Neither too thin nor stout, neat and genteel,
170 Agreeable and pleasant, frank yet wise.
    Standing by Beauty's side I next saw Wealth,
A lady of great haughtiness and pride—
A stately dame. He who in word or deed
Should dare offend against herself or hers
Would hardy be and bold; for she can aid
Or hinder. Not today or yesterday
Was it first known that rich folk have great might
To bring to joy or grief. So high and low
To Wealth gave mighty honor; her to serve
180 Was all the care of those who sought her grace.
"My lady" was she called by each of them,
For all on earth are well within her power

And fear her. Many a traitor thronged her court,
And many an envier and flatterer.
These are the ones most careful to dispraise
And even blame those worthiest of love.
The flatterer, first to his victim's face,
In his deceit, will praise him, and beguile
The world with well-oiled tongue; but afterward,
190 Behind his back, his praises to the bone
He picks, that he may honored men debase
And dissipate the righteous one's repute.
With lying many flatterers have flayed
Full many a worthy man who would have been
In confidence at court, but by their wiles
Have banished been. May evil overtake
All envious flatterers; for honest men,
Such as we are, love not their way of life.
    Dame Wealth had on a robe of purple grain;
200 Consider it no deceit when now I say
That in this world none with it can compare
For beauty, richness, and becomingness;
With golden orfrays was the purple edged,
Each bearing portraiture of duke or king
Renowned in story; and about her neck
Most richly edged and collared was the gown
With band of gold, enameled and annealed.
And you should know that she had precious stones
More than enough, which brilliantly did flash
210 About her purple robe Wealth proudly wore
A gorgeous girdle buckled with a clasp
That bore a magic stone; for whosoe'er
Should wear this stone need fear no poisoning.
She could not die from any venom's power.
Well might such stone be prized; it would be worth
More than the treasures that are found at Rome
To any wealthy man. Another stone
The pendant of the precious buckle formed;
It could the toothache cure, and any man
220 Who, fasting, on it gazed would be assured
Of perfect sight all day, such was its power.
Upon the golden tissue there were studs

Of purest gold, each one of size and weight
That would be worth a besant at the least.
Dame Wealth upon her yellow tresses wore
A golden circlet; never was there seen,
As I believe, more fair. Set in the gold
Were precious stones, and he would be more skilled
Than I who could describe and estimate
230 The gems that in that sterling gold were set.
Rubies there were, sapphires and garnets fine,
And two-ounce emeralds; but in the front,
Set with skilled workmanship within a round,
There was a carbuncle so clear and bright
That, when the evening fell, a man at need
Might light his way by it at least a league.
Such brilliance had the stone that all the place
Shone with the glow about her face and head.

Holding him by the hand, Wealth led a youth
240 Most beautiful, who was her paramour.
He was a man who studied to maintain
An open house for hospitality.
Well dressed was he and shod; his stables good
Held many a priceless horse; and rather he
Had been accused of murder or of theft
Than that his stable should have housed a nag.
With Lady Wealth and her benevolence
To be acquainted he was therefore glad;
For ever in his mind was one thought fixed:
250 How he might sojourn most luxuriously;
And she would furnish him the wherewithal
For his expenditures as if she drew
Her money from a chest big as a barn.

Next Lady Largesse followed in the dance;
Well nurtured was she and well taught to spend
And to do honor. Alexander's kin
Was she, and never knew such joy as when
She could to someone say, "The thing is thine."
The wretched Avarice is not more quick
260 To take than Lady Largesse is to give;
God grants her such increase in all her goods
That she's ne'er able to bestow so much

That she has not more left. Much laud and praise
Has she, and fools and sages 'neath her sway
She holds by means of her unbounded gifts.
If any should her hate, I think that she
By serving them would make them all her friends;
Therefore she has the love of rich and poor.
Most foolish of all men is stingy lord;
270 No sin degrades the great like avarice.
No miser seignory or lands should win;
For he will have no friends to do his will.
Who wishes to be loved must not too dear
Hold his own treasure, but good will acquire
By generous gifts. Just as the magnet draws
The stubborn iron subtly to itself,
So gold and silver draw the hearts of men.
Largesse had on a new-made purple gown—
Sarcenet it was—and at the neck
280 The collar was unfastened; for this dame
Had just bestowed her brooch upon a friend.
However, this loose style became her well;
For now below her fair and well-formed face
Her neck was well displayed, and through the silk
Her skin showed white and clear and delicate.
    Dame Largesse, who so worthy was and wise,
For partner had a knight from overseas;
And Arthur, King of Britain, was his kin.
'Twas he that bore the brilliant gonfanon,
290 Insignium of glory. Great renown
Was his; of him do minstrels stories tell
Before both lords and kings. This knight had come
Late from a tournament where he maintained,
In many a joust and many a massed assault,
The honor of his lady. He had pierced
Fully many a buckled shield, and many a helm
Had he unseated, many a knight unhorsed,
By virtue of his valor and his strength.
    After all these did Franchise dancing come;
300 She was not a brunette, nor dull of hue,
But rather white as snow; her genteel nose
Was longer than the nose of Orléans.

Her gray eyes laughed; her eyebrows arched above;
Her yellow hair was long. Like turtledove's
Was her simplicity; her tender heart
Was debonair; she dared not say or do
To anyone a thing that was not meet.
If any man were dying for her love,
On him she would take pity, probably;
310 For such a rueful, pious, loving heart
She had that, lest he do a desperate deed,
She'd aid a man who suffered for her sake.
She wore a gabardine of finest wool—
A richer one in Arras you'd not find—
That was so finely sewed in every part
That at each point it was a perfect fit.
Franchise was very nicely dressed. No robe
So well becomes a maid as gabardine;
A woman more coquettish seems, and quaint,
320 In it than when she wears a common coat.
The gabardine, which was of white, proclaimed
That she who wore it was both pure and good.
    Side by side with her there danced a youth
Whose name I did not learn, but one who seemed
Genteel as if the son of Windsor's lord.
    Next her came Courtesy, much praised by all;
For she had neither folly nor conceit.
God bless her, she my invitation gave
To join the dance when first I reached the place!
330 She was not overnice or overbold,
But reasonable and wise; no insolence
E'er hindered her fair words and fairer deeds.
None misbespoken ever was by her;
She held no rancor against anyone.
A clear brunette was she, with shining face.
No lady of more pleasant grace I know;
Her form seemed that of empress or of queen.
    Holding her in the dance a young knight came,
Worthy and fair of speech, upon all men
340 Conferring honor. Fair and fine was he,
Well skilled feats of arms, well loved by her.
    Fair Idleness came afterward, and I

Secured her as a partner in the dance.
Already I've described her form and dress;
I'll say no more of them. She was the one
Who did me such a kindness at the gate
When, through the wicket, she admitted me
To see this flowering garden—these fine folk.
   The last that I remember of the band
350 Was <u>Youth, who in her clear and laughing face</u>
<u>Scarce showed the passage of twelve winter's time.</u>
She seemed still innocent—had yet no thought
Of evil or deceit—and gaiety
And joy were all her care; for well you know
That youthful creatures think but of delight.
   <u>Her sweetheart was so intimate with her</u>
That <u>they would kiss as often as they pleased,</u>
<u>And all the world might see their open love.</u>
They were no whit ashamed lest some might speak
360 Of them insinuating words; they let
All see them <u>kissing like two turtledoves.</u>
The boy was like the girl—both young and fair;
Well matched were they in age, as they were matched in heart.

5. The God of Love pursues the Dreamer
[1279–1438]

THUS danced those I have named and many more
Who of their consort were; all folk well taught,
Frank, and genteel they uniformly were.
When I had scanned the countenances fair
Of those who led the dance, I had the whim
<u>To search the garden farther and explore</u>
<u>The place, to examine all the trees found there:</u>
<u>The laurels, hazels, cedars, and the pines.</u>
   Just then the dance was ended; for the most
10 <u>Departed with their sweethearts to make love,</u>
<u>Shaded beneath the secret-keeping boughs.</u>

Foolish were he who envied not such life
As there they led! It lusty was, God knows!
He who might have a chance to live that way
Might well deprive himself of other boons;
For there's no better paradise on earth
Than any place where lover finds a maid
Responding freely to his heart's desire.
Straightway I wandered from the scene of love,
20 Amusing myself alone among the trees;
When suddenly the God of Love did call
To him Sweet Looks, who bore his weapons two.
No longer idle was the golden bow.
He was required to string it, and he did
Without delay; then with the arrows five,
Shining and strong and ready to be shot,
He handed it unto the God of Love,
Who, bow in hand, pursued me distantly.
Meant he to go so far as shoot at me?
30 Would God might guard me from a mortal wound!
Enjoying all the orchard, fancy free,
Unheedingly I went upon my way;
But still he followed, for in no one spot
Unto the garden's end did I make pause.
    The enclosure was a perfect measured square
As long as it was broad. Except some trees
That would have been too ugly for the place,
There is no fruitful one that was not there
In numbers, or at least in ones and twos.
40 Among the trees that I remember well
There were pomegranates, grateful to the sick,
And many fig trees, date palms, almond trees.
The nut trees were most plentiful of all,
Such as are in their seasons fully charged
With nutmegs not insipid nor yet sharp.
A man could find whatever tree he wished:
Licorice and gillyflower cloves,
A malagueta pepper tree, whose fruit
Is given the name of Grains of Paradise,
50 With many another most delightful spice,
Zodary, anis seed, and cinnamon,

That makes good eating when a meal is done.
   With all these foreign trees familiar grew
Those that bore loads of quinces, peaches, pears,
Chestnuts and other nuts, and medlars brown,
Apples, and plums that were both white and black,
Fresh vermilion cherries, hazel nuts,
Berries of beam tree, sorbs, and many more.
With lofty laurels and high pines the place
60 Was stocked, with cypress and with olive trees
That are so scarce as to be notable,
And great wide-branching elms, and hazels straight,
Hornbeams, beeches, aspens, and the ash,
Maple, and oak, and spruce. Why mention more?
There were so many trees of divers sorts
That should I try to name them all I'd find
The task a tiresome one. But you should know
That all these trees were spaced as was most fit,
Each from its neighbor distant fathoms five
70 Or six, and yet the branches were so long
And high that for defense against the heat
They knit together at the tops and kept
The sun from shining through upon the ground
And injuring the tender, growing grass.
   Roebuck and deer rambled about the lawns,
And many a squirrel climbed from tree to tree;
From out their burrows rabbits freely ran,
Of which there were not less than thirty kinds
That tourneyed on the dewy, verdant grass.
80 In places there were clear, refreshing springs,
Quite void of frogs and newts, and shaded cool,
From which by conduits almost numberless
Mirth had conveyed the water to small brooks
That made a soft and pleasant murmuring sound.
About the streamlets and the fountain brinks,
Beside the waters bright and frolicsome,
The grass was short and thick, where one might lie
Beside his sweetheart as upon a couch;
For, from the earth made soft and moist by springs,
90 Luxuriant grew the turf as one might wish.
The excellence of climate there produced,

Winter and summer, great supply of flowers
Embellishing the whole environment.
Most fair the violets, and fresh and new
The periwinkles bloomed, and other flowers
Were marvelously yellow, white, and red.
Exceeding quaint appeared the grassy mead,
As if enameled in a thousand hues
Or painted with the blooms, whose odors sweet
100 Perfumed the air. But I'll not bore you more
With long account of this delightful place.
'Tis better now that I should make an end;
For not all the beauty I recall,
Nor all the garden's sweet delightfulness.

Well, on I went, turning first right then left,
Till I had searched out and beheld each sight—
Experienced each charm the place possessed.
The God of Love followed me everywhere,
Spying continually, like hunter skilled
110 Who waits the time when he his quarry finds
In the best place to take the deadly stroke.
At last I reached the fairest spot of all
Where flowed a spring beneath a spreading pine.
Not since King Pepin's time or Charlemagne's
Has such a tree been seen; so high its crown
It towered o'er all others in the place.
Nature with cunning craftsmanship had set
The fountain that was underneath the tree
Within a marble verge, and on the stone
120 About the border, in small letters carved:
"Here t'was that Fair Narcissus wept himself to death."

6. The Poet tells the story of Narcissus
[1439–1614]

NARCISSUS was a youth whom Love once caught
Within his snare and caused such dole and woe

That in his grief he rendered up his ghost.
Now Echo, a fine lady, loved him more
Than any creature born, and was for him
So lovesick that she said she needs must die
If she had not his love. But of his own
Beauty he was so proud that hers he scorned,
And neither for her weeping nor her prayers
10 Would satisfy her passion. When she knew
Herself refused, she suffered so much pain
And anger, and she took it in such despite,
That hopelessly she pined away and died.
But just before the end she prayed to God,
And this was her request: that whom she'd found
Disloyal to her love, Narcissus' self
In his hard heart should someday tortured be
And burn with such a love that he would find
No joy in any thing; thus he might know
20 And comprehend what woe a loyal maid
Had felt when she so vilely was refused.
The prayer was reasonable, and therefore God
Ordained that she this recompense should have;
And so Narcissus, as one day by chance,
Returning from the hunt, tired with the chase
That up and down the hills had led him far,
He came upon that fountain clear and pure,
Beneath the shadow of the pine, and stopped
To quench the thirst that, with excessive heat
30 And great fatigue, had robbed him of his breath.
He gazed upon the fountain which the tree
Encircled with its reins and, kneeling down,
Prepared himself to drink a pleasant draft.
But in the limpid waters he perceived
Reflected nose and mouth and cheeks and eyes.
The sight dismayed him, and he found himself
By his own loveliness betrayed; for there
He saw the image of a comely youth.
Love knew how best to avenge the stubbornness
40 And pride Narcissus had displayed to him.
Well was he then requited, for the youth,
Enraptured, gazed upon the crystal spring

Until he fell in love with his own face;
And at the last he died for very woe.
That was the end of that; for when he knew
Such passion must go e'er unsatisfied,
Although he was entangled in Love's snare,
And that he never could sure comfort find
In any fashion or by any means,
50 He lost his reason in but little space,
For very ire, and died. And so he got
The just reward that he had merited
For his refusal of a maiden's love.
You ladies, who refuse to satisfy
Your lovers, this one's case should take to heart;
For, if you let your loyal sweethearts die,
God will know how to give you recompense.
    When this inscription had assured me well
That it was certainly the very spring
60 Of fair Narcissus, I withdrew a bit
Lest I like him might in its waters gaze;
For cowardly I felt when I recalled
The misadventure that occurred to him.
But then I thought that I assuredly
Might, without fear, into the waters look
Of that ill-omened spring; for my dismay   *pride*
Had been but foolishness. I then approached
And kneeled before the fountain to observe
How coursed the water o'er the pebbled floor
70 That bright as silver fine appeared to me.
'Twas the last word in fountains! None more fair
In all the world is found; for fresh and new
The water ever bubbled up in waves
In height and depth at least two fingers' breadth.
About it all the tender grass grew fine
And thick and lush, nourished by the spring;
And, since the source did not in winter fail,
The grass lived all the year and could not die.
    Two crystal stones within the fountain's depths
80 Attentively I noted. You will say
'Twas marvelous when I shall tell you why:
Whene'er the searching sun lets fall its rays

Into the fountain, and its depths they reach,
Then in the crystal stones do there appear
More than a hundred hues; for they become
Yellow and red and blue. So wonderful
Are they that by their power is all the place—
Flowers and trees, whate'er the garden holds—
Transfigured, as it seems. It is like this:

90 Just as a mirror will reflect each thing
That near is placed, and one therein can see
Both form and color without variance,
So do these crystals undistorted show
The garden's each detail to anyone
Who looks into the waters of the spring.
For, from whichever side one chance to look,
He sees one half the garden; if he turn
And from the other gaze, he sees the rest.
So there is nothing in the place so small
100 Or so enclosed and hid but that it shows
As if portrayed upon the crystal stones.

The Mirror Perilous it is, where proud
Narcissus saw his face and his gray eyes,
Because of which he soon lay on his bier.
There is no charm nor remedy for this;
Whatever thing appears before one's eyes,
While at these stones he looks, he straightway loves.
Many a valiant man has perished thence;
The wisest, worthiest, most experienced
110 Have there been trapped and taken unawares.
There a new furor falls to some men's lot;
There others see their resolution change;
There neither sense nor moderation holds
The mastery; there will to love is all;
There no man can take counsel for himself.
'Tis Cupid, Venus' son, there sows the seed
Which taints the fountain, and 'tis there he sets
His nets and snares to capture man and maid;
For Cupid hunts no other sort of bird.
120 By reason of the seed sown thereabout
This fountain has been called the Well of Love,
Of which full many an author tells in books

Of old romance; but never will you hear
Better explained the truth about the place
Than when I have exposed its mystery.
Long time it pleased me to remain to view
The fountain and the crystals that displayed
A hundred thousand things which there appeared.
But I remember it as sorry hour.
130 Alas, how often therefore have I sighed!
The mirrors me deceived. Had I but known
Their power and their force, I had not then
So close approached. I fell within the snare
That sorely has betrayed and caught full many a man.

7. The Dreamer falls in love with the Rose
[1615–1680]

AMONG the thousand things reflected there
I chose a full-charged rosebush in a plot
Encinctured with a hedge; and such desire
Then seized me that I had not failed to seek
The place where that rose heap was on display
Though Pavia or Paris had tempted me.
When I was thus o'ertaken by this rage,
Which many another better man has crazed,
Straightway I hurried toward the red rosebush;
10 And I can tell you that, when I approached
The blooms, the sweetness of their pleasant smell
Did so transfuse my being that as naught
Compared to it the perfume would have been
Within my entrails, had I been embalmed.
Had I not feared to be assailed or scorned,
One rose, at least, to handle and to smell,
I would have plucked; but I had heavy fear
Lest it might irk the owner of the place,
Who might thereafter cause me to repent.
20 What pile of ruddy roses was there seen,

More beautiful than any others known
Beneath the sky! Some only tiny buds
Still tightly closed—others more open were;
Yet others that belonged to later crop
Would follow in their season, all prepared
To open wide their petals. Who could hate
Such folded buds! For roses spreading wide
Within one day will surely all be gone;
But fresh the buds will still remain at least
30 Two days or three; so they allured me most.
Never in any place grew they more fair.
Most happy he who might succeed to pluck
A single one! Could I a chaplet have
Of such, I'd highly prize no other wealth.
    One of these buds I chose, so beautiful
That in comparison none of its mates
I prized at all; and I was well advised,
For such a color did illumine it—
So fine was its vermilion—that it seemed
40 That in it Nature had outdone herself;
For surely she could not more beauty give.
Four pairs of leaves had she in order set
About the bud with cunning workmanship.
The stalk was straight and upright as a cane,
And thereupon the bud was seated firm,
Not bending or inclined. Its odor spread,
The sweetness burdening the air about.
Now when I smelled the perfume so exhaled
I had no wish to go, but drew more near,
50 Intending to secure the tempting bud
If I dared stretch my hand; but briars sharp
And piercing kept me far away from it.
Pointed and scratching thistles, nettles, thorns
With hook-like barbs, prevented my advance
And made me fear to feel a doleful injury.

8. The God of Love makes the Lover his man
[1681–2010]

THE GOD OF LOVE, who, ever with bent bow
Had taken care to watch and follow me,
Beneath a fig tree lastly took his stand;
And when he saw that I had fixed my choice
Upon the bud that pleased me most of all
He quickly chose an arrow; nocking it,
He pulled the cord back to his ear. The bow
Was marvelously strong, and good his aim,
And when he shot at me the arrow pierced
10 My very heart, though entering by my eye.
Then such a chill seized me that since that day
I oft, remembering it, have quaked again
Beneath a doublet warm. Down to the ground
I fell supine; thus struck, my heart stopped dead;
It failed me, and I fainted quite away.
Long time I lay recovering from my swoon,
And when I gained my senses and my wits
I still was feeble, and supposed I'd lost
Great store of blood, but was surprised to find
20 The dart that pierced me drew no drop of gore;
The wound was dry. With both my hands I tried
To draw the arrow, though it made me groan,
And finally the feathered shaft came out.
But still the golden barb named Beauty stayed
Fixed in my heart, never to be removed.
I feel it yet, although I do not bleed.
Anxious and greatly troubled then was I
Because of double peril; I knew not
What I could say or do to ease my wound
30 Or find a doctor who with herb or root
Could offer unexpected remedy.
My heart still bade me strive to reach the bud—
Would have naught else. It seemed as if my life

Depended on possession of the Rose,
For certainly my pain was much relieved
But by its sight and smell and nothing more.
　　As I commenced to drag myself again
Toward the bud that did such sweet exhale,
The God of Love another arrow seized,
40 Headed with gold, and named Simplicity.
This is the second dart that many a man
And many a woman, too, has brought to Love.
When he perceived my close approach, he shot,
Without a warning, through my eye and heart,
This arrow, which was neither steel nor iron,
But one no man or woman born could draw;
For though with little effort I removed
The shaft, the arrowhead remains within.
Now know it for a truth that if I had
50 Great wish before to gain the crimson bud
Then was my longing doubled; for the more
My wound gave pain, the more desire increased
More closely to approach the little flower
That sweeter smelled than any violet.
Better for me had been a swift retreat,
But I could not deny my heart's command;
Where'er it led me I, perforce, must go.
But still the archer took the utmost pains
And strove to stop me. I could not escape
60 Without more woe. To overcome me quite
He sent another arrow to my heart.
This was named Courtesy; the wound it made
Was wide and deep; it stretched me in a faint
Beneath a branching olive tree near by.
Long time without a motion there I lay,
And when I stirred at last, my first attempt
Was to remove the arrow from my side.
Again the shaft came out and left the head,
Which wouldn't budge for all that I could do.
70 　　Anxious and sad in mind I took a seat.
Greatly the wounds tormented me, and urged
That to the bud, toward which so forcefully
I was attracted, I should drag myself;

Though ever anew the archer menaced me,
And scalded child should e'er hot water dread.
However, sheer necessity is strong.
Though thick as hail I'd seen a shower fall
Of square-cut rocks and stones pell-mell, yet Love,
Who all things else surpasses, gave to me
80 Such hardihood and such courageous heart
That willingly his bidding I'd obeyed.
Feeble as dying man, I raised myself
Upon my feet and forced my legs to walk.
Not for the archer would I quit the task
Of reaching the fair flower that drew my heart.
But there so many briars and thistles were,
And bramble bushes, that I failed to pass
The barrier and to the rose attain.
The best that I could do was close to stand
90 Beside the hedge of piercing thorns that hemmed
The rosary about. But of one thing
I got much joy: I was so near the bud
That I could smell the marvelous perfume
That it suffused—its beauty freely see.
And such reward I had of that delight
That in my joy my ills were half forgot.
My wounds seemed largely remedied and eased;
For never could I other pleasure find
Like to sojourning there, and night and day
100 Remaining near the place. When I had stayed
But little time, the God of Love, whose care
Was now to rack my heart, began anew
His dire assault. My mischief to increase,
He aimed another arrow at my side,
Which, entering below my breast, produced
Another wound. 'Twas called Companionship,
Than which there's nothing that more quickly quells
The scruples of a lady or a maid.
Now all the dolor of my wounds returned;
110 Three times successively I swooned away.
      Upon reviving, I complained and sighed
Because my pain increased and grew the worse
So that I had no hope of cure or help

And rather would have died than lived; for sure
It seemed that Love would lastly martyr me.
Yet, notwithstanding, I could not depart.
Meanwhile the god another arrow seized,
Fair Seeming named, most prized, and, as I think,
Most powerful of all to circumvent
120 Intended drawing back from Love's employ
By any lover who's afraid of pain.
Sharp is its point for piercing, and its edge
As cutting as a blade of razor steel;
But Love had with a precious unguent smeared
The point, lest too severely it should wound;
For he willed not that I should die, but wished
That I might some alleviation have
By means of grateful salve that brought relief.
With his own hands he had the ointment made
130 To comfort loyal lovers and dispel
Their woes the better. Wounded was my heart
With this last arrow that he shot at me,
But through the wound the remedy soon spread
And so restored my all-but-ebbing pulse.
I would have been in evil case and died
But for that balm. Then I withdrew the shaft,
Though, as before, the head remained within,
Anointed with the antidote for pain.
Thus were there buried well within my breast
140 Five arrowheads that could not be removed.
Although the ointment gave me much relief,
Nevertheless my wounds so sorely ached
That I was pale. This arrow had strange power
To mingle weal with woe; for well I knew
That it both hurt and healed. If agony
Was in the point, assuaging was the balm;
If one part stung me, yet the other soothed.
Thus while it helped, it at the same time harmed.
    Straightway with rapid step the God of Love
150 Approached me, and the while he came he cried:

                                    THE GOD OF LOVE

"Vassal, you now are seized; there's nothing here
To aid you in defense or toward escape.

In giving yourself up make no delay;
For the more willingly you abdicate
That much more quickly will you mercy gain.
He is a fool who with refusal thwarts
The one whom he should coax and supplicate.
Against my power no striving will avail.
Be well advised by me that foolish pride
160 Will gain you nothing; cede yourself as thrall
Calmly and with good grace, as I desire."

    I answered simply, "Sire, to you I give   THE LOVER
Myself most willingly; nor will I strive
To make resistance to your will. Please God
That I rebellious thoughts may never have
Against your rule. 'Twere neither just nor right.
Do what you please with me: or hang or slay.
My life is in your hands. I cannot swerve.
I cannot live a day against your will.
170 By you to weal and welfare I might mount
That by no other could I gain. Your hand,
Which thus has wounded me, must give me cure;
Make me your prisoner. I'll feel no ire
So long as I am saved from your disdain.
Of you so much that's good I've heard men say
That 'tis my wish to yield myself to you,
Completely in your service then to be,
Body and soul. If I perform your will,
Nothing can give me grief. But, furthermore,
180 I hope that at some time I may have grace
To gain that which I now so much desire.
I yield myself upon this covenant."

    At this I wished to kiss his foot, but he,
Taking me by the hand, thus made reply:
"Much do I love you, and I praise the speech   THE GOD OF LOVE
That you have made; never could such response
Come from a villainous, untutored man.
So largely have you gained by it that now,
For your advantage, it is my desire
190 That you should pay me homage, press my lips
Which no infamous man has ever touched.
No churl or villain did I ever kiss;

Rather he must be courteous and frank
That I thus make my man; though, without fail,
He must sore burdens bear in serving me.
But I the greatest honor do to you,
And you should most appreciative be
That you so good a master have, and lord
Of high renown; for Love the banner bears
200 And gonfanon of courtesy. So kind,
So frank, so gentle, and so mannerly
Is he that those who serve and honor him
Shall find that in their hearts cannot remain
Injustice, villainy, or base desire."
    At that, with clasped hands I became his man.
Most proud was I when his lips touched my mouth;
That was the act which gave me greatest joy.
Then he demanded hostages of me.

THE GOD OF LOVE

"From one and from another, friend," said he,
210 "I have received full many homages
In which I found myself deceived; with guile
False felons often have their oaths betrayed.
But they shall know how much it weighs with me;
If ever again I get them in my power,
Most dearly will I make them pay for it.
Now, since I love you, it is my desire
To be so very certain of your love
And so to league you to me that you ne'er
Will do that which you should not, or deny
220 Your covenant and promises to me.
'Twould be too bad if you should trick me—you
Who seem so honest."
                    Then I made reply,
"Sire, I know not why you ask of me   THE LOVER
Security and pledge; for you, in truth,
Must know that you have stolen my heart away
And seized it so that even if it wished
It could not act for me against your will.
This heart is yours; it is no longer mine;
For good or ill it does as you command.
230 No one can dispossess you of my heart;

O utrageux est qui plus demande

Lors a de samonere traute
Une petite clef bien faitte
Qui fu de fin or esmere
A ceste dist il fermeray
Ton cuer autre gatge ny veul
Soulz ceste clef sont my ioiel
Elle est maindre de ton doy maine
Mes elle est de grant auon dame
Et sy a mout grant proste
Lors la me toucha au coste
Et ferma mon cuer si souef

The God of Love locks the Lover's heart. *Morgan 245, f. 15v.*

You've set within it such a garrison
That by them it is guarded well and ruled.
Moreover, if you still have doubts, then lock
My heart and carry off the key in pawn."

THE GOD OF LOVE

    "Now, by my head, that's not unreasonable."
Responded Love. "I will agree to that.
Who has the heart within his power is lord
Of all the body. More to ask were harsh."
Then from his purse he took a little key
240 Made of refined gold. "With this," he said,
"I'll lock your heart, and ask no other pledge.
Under this key's protection are my gems.
I call it mistress of my treasury.
Though smaller than your little finger tip,
It has a mighty power." He touched my side
And locked my heart so gently that I scarce
Could feel the turning of the key that made it fast.

9. The Lover learns the Commandments of Love
[2011–2264]

THUS I did all he wished, and when past doubt
My loyalty was placed I said to him:
"My lord, to do your will is my desire;   THE LOVER
I pray you take my service graciously.
To me you owe it to maintain good faith.
'Tis not because of dastardy I speak,
For by no means do I your service fear;
But vain is servant's toil to do his best
If, when he offers him his services,
10 His master looks on him disdainfully."

THE GOD OF LOVE

    Love answered, "Now be not at all dismayed;
Since you have placed yourself among my train,

With favor I'll your services receive
And raise you to a high degree, unless
Misconduct forfeits you that place; but hope
For no great good within a little space.
Pain and delay you must a while endure.
Support and suffer the distress which now
Racks you with pain, for well I know the drug
20 That shall effect your cure; but hold yourself
In loyalty and I'll provide such balm
As shall your wounds make well. Yes, by my head!
Your cure I'll soon complete if you'll but serve
With willing heart, and follow night and day
All the commandments I true lovers give."

    "Sire," answered I, "before you leave this place,   THE LOVER
For God's sake, your commandments give to me.
'Tis my intention to preserve them all;
But, if I'm ignorant of them, I fear
30 I soon should wander from the proper path.
The more desirous am I now to learn,
Because I would misunderstand no point."

                                  THE GOD OF LOVE
    Said Love, "You've spoken very well. Now hear
And learn my rules. Schoolmasters lose their toil
When pupils, listening, give not their hearts
To treasuring up the counsels they receive."
    The God of Love then gave to me the charge
Which you are now to learn, and word by word
The ordinances he set forth of love.
40 Well are these points explained in my romance.
Whoso desires to love, let him attend;
For, from now on, my story will improve.
Most profitable 'twere to listen close,
For he who tells this tale his business knows.
The end of all this dream is very fine;
The substance of it is a novelty.
He who shall hear the story through and through
Quite well will understand the game of love,
Provided that he will the patience have
50 The dream's signification to await,
Which I expound in language of romance.

When you have heard my exposition through,
The meaning of the dream, which now is hid,
Shall be quite plain to you. I do not lie.
    "Beware of Villainy, above all things;   THE GOD OF LOVE
I'll have no backsliding in this respect
Unless you wish to be a renegade,"
Said Love. "All those who Villainy admire
Shall excommunicate and cursed be.
60 Why should I love her? Villainy breeds churls.
Villains are cruel and unpitying,
Unserviceable, and without friendliness.
    "Then guard yourself from telling what your hear
That better were untold; 'tis not the part
Of worthy men to gossip scandalously.
Notorious and hated was Sir Kay,
The Seneschal, just for his mockery;
While Sir Gawain for courtesy was praised.
As much of blame Sir Kay, the insolent,
70 Received because he cruel was and fell
And scandalous above all other knights.
    "Be reasonable to men both high and low—
Companionable, courteous, moderate—
And when you walk along the street take care
To be the first with customary bow;
Or, if another greets you first, be quick
To render back his greeting, nor be mute.
    "Then guard yourself against all ribaldry
And dirty speech; let not your lips unclose
80 To name a vulgar thing; no courteous man
I hold him who indulges in foul talk.
    "In ladies' service labor and take pains;
Honor and champion them; and if you hear
Calumnious or spiteful talk of them
Reprove the speaker; bid him hold his tongue.
Do what you can damsels and dames to please.
Let them hear you narrate most noble tales.
You'll gain a worthy reputation thus.
    "Then guard yourself from pride. If you judge well,
90 You'll find that it is but a foolish sin.
One stained with vanity can not apply

His heart to service or humility.
Pride nullifies the aim of lover's art.
   "The one who in Love's service would succeed
Genteelly should conduct himself and act.
Attainment of the ultimate in love
Is quite impossible in any case
For one who has no amiability.
But elegance in manners is not pride;
100 He who is mannerly will realize,
Unless he is a mere presumptuous fool,
That one's most valued who most lacks conceit.
   "Maintain yourself well as your purse can bear
In clothing and in haberdashery;
Good dress and well-selected ornaments
Improve a man immensely. Trust your clothes
Only to one who knows his business well,
Who can with skillfulness the sleeves adjust—
Make every seam produce a perfect fit.
110 Laced boots and shoes buy often, fresh and new,
Fitting so well that churls will marvel oft
How into them and out of them you get.
Your gloves, your belt, your purse should be of silk.
If you have not the means, restrain your taste;
But give yourself the best you can afford.
A coronet of blooms costs but a bit,
And roses at the time of Pentecost
Require no great outlay; such each may have.
Let no filth soil your body; wash your hands;
120 Scour well your teeth; and if there should appear
The slightest line of black beneath your nails
Never permit the blemish to remain.
Lace your sleeves and comb your hair, but try
No paint or other artificial aid—
Unsuitable e'en for a female's use,
Unless she be of ill repute, or such
As through misfortune must seek spurious love.
   "Then after this you must remember well
Forever to maintain your cheerfulness.
130 Dispose yourself to gladness and delight,
For Love cares nothing for a mournful man.

Love brings a very jolly malady
In midst of which one laughs and jokes and plays.
Lovers by turns feel torments first, then joys.
Lovesickness is a changeable disease:
One hour it bitter is, the next as sweet;
One hour the lover weeps, the next he sings;
Now he is glad, distracted next he groans.
If you know how to play a cheerful game,
140 With which you may amuse the company,
'Tis my command that you make use of it;
For everyone should do in every place
That which he knows will advantageous be,
Because by this he gets thanks, grace, and praise.
    "If you know that you're quick and lithe of limb,
Avoid no contests of agility;
If you look well on horseback, up and down
You ought to spur your steed; and if you know
How well to break a lance, you'll gain great praise;
150 You'll be much loved if you're expert in arms.
If you've a voice that's sweet and pure and clear,
Seek no excusal when you're asked to sing;
For well-sung song will furnish much delight.
'Tis advantageous that a bachelor
Should be expert in playing flute or viol;
By this and dancing he'll advance his cause.
    "Let no one think that you are miserly,
For such a reputation causes grief;
It is most fitting that a lover wise
160 Should give more freely from his treasury
Than any common simpleton or sot.
Naught of the lore of love the miser knows,
Whom giving does not please. From avarice
The one who wishes to progress in love
Must guard himself full well; for any swain
Who for a pleasant glance or winsome smile
Has given his heart entirely away
Ought well, after so rich a gift, his goods
Willingly to offer and bestow.
170   "Now shortly I'll review what I have said,
For best remembered are things briefly told:

Whoever wishes to make Love his lord
Must courteous be and wholly void of pride,
Gracious and merry, and in giving free.
    "Next I enjoin as penance, night and day,
Without repentance, that you think on Love,
Forever keeping ceaselessly in mind
The happy hour which has such joy in store.
That you may be a lover tried and true,
180 My wish and will are that your heart be fixed
In one sole place whence it can not depart
But whole and undivided there remain;
For no halfhearted service pleases me.
He who in many a place bestows his heart
Has but a little part to leave in each;
But of that man I never have a doubt
Who his whole heart deposits in one place.
When you have given your heart, then lend it not;
To lend what one has given is scandalous.
190 Unconditionally one should make
His gift, and thus a greater merit gain.
The bounty of a thing that's merely lent
Is paid for with a mere return of thanks;
But great should be the guerdon of free gift.
Give, then, not only freely but with grace;
For debonairly given gift is best.
Things given grudgingly are nothing worth at all."

10. The Lover learns the Pains of Love
[2265–2580]

"WHEN, as my sermoning advises you,   THE GOD OF LOVE
Your heart you have bestowed, there will befall
Adventures hard and heavy for Love's thane.
Often, when you're reminded of your love,
You'll find it necessary to depart
From company, lest they perceive your wound.

Then in your loneliness will come to you
Sighs and complaints, tremors and other ills.
Tormented will you be in many ways:
10 One hour you will be hot, another cold;
One hour you will be flushed, another pale;
No quartan fever that you ever had—
Nor quotidian either—could be worse.
The Pains of Love you will experience
Ere you recover thence; for times will come
When you will half forget yourself, bemused,
And long time stand like graven image mute
Which never budges, stirs, or even moves
Its foot, its hand, its finger, or its lips.
20 At last you will recover, with a start,
Your memory, reviving in a fright.
Like craven coward, from your heart you'll sigh;
For you should know all lovers act that way
When they have felt the woes that you will feel.

  "Then time 'twill be for you to recollect
The sweetheart that too long you've left alone,
And you'll exclaim, 'My God, how hard my lot   THE LOVER
That where my heart has gone I may not go!
Why did I send to her my heart alone?
30 Never I see, but always think, of her
Powerless to send my eyes to guide my heart,
I prize not what they see apart from it.
Ought they to linger here? No, let them go
To visit her for whom my spirit yearns.
Slothful am I far from my heart to stay.
God help me; I am nothing but a fool!
I'll go straightway; no longer will I wait.
Until I see her face, I'll ne'er have ease.'
You'll start upon your way in such a case   THE GOD OF LOVE
40 That often you will fail of your design
And waste your steps in vain; you will not find
Her whom you seek. Then naught there is to do
Except, mournful and pensive, to return.

  "Then will you be anew in sad estate.
To you will come cold shiverings and sighs,
And pains that prick more sharp than hedgehog's quills.

(Who doubts this fact, let him ask lovers true.)
But nothing will appease your soul. Again
You make assay to see, perchance, the one
50 On whose account you suffer so much care,
Hoping you may succeed by utmost pains.
Great diligence you'll willingly exert
To feast and satisfy your hungry eyes.
Her beauty with great joy will fill your soul;
But sight of her your heart will broil and fry.
The glowing coals of love will burst ablaze.
The more you gaze upon her whom you love,
The hotter will the fire engage your heart.
Sight is the grease that swells the amorous flame.
60 Each lover customarily pursues
The burning conflagration. Although scorched,
He hugs it closer; for its nature's such
As makes him contemplate his lady love
Although at sight of her he suffers pain.
The closer that he gets, the more he loves.
Sages and fools in this, at least, agree
That he who's next the fire will burn the most.
    "The more you see of her, the less you wish
Ever to leave her; but, when you must part,
70 Remembrance of her stays the livelong day
And the impression that you've been a fool
Not to have had the hardihood to speak,
But rather to have boobied by her side,
Awkward and dumb, and let the chance escape.
Well will you think that you have been remiss
Not to address the fair one ere you left.
Disadvantageous it will seem to you,
For if you had but gained a greeting fair
You would have valued it a hundred marks.
80 Bewailing then your fate you'll seek new chance
To wander in the street where you have seen
The lady whom you dared not interview.
Gladly, if possible, you'll seek her home;
All your meanderings and wanderings
Inevitably lead you to that place.
But from all men your purpose you'll conceal,

Seeking excuses other than the one
That makes you stroll near the attractive spot.
In such equivocation you are wise.

90 "If it should happen that you meet the fair
Where you can greet and have a word with her,
Then you will feel your color change; a chill
Will run through all your veins; and, when you try
To hold converse, your thoughts and words will fail.
Or, if you do succeed to start a speech,
Of every three words you'll say scarcely two,
So shameful your embarrassment will be.
No man so prudent lives that in such case
He'll not forget himself, unless he be
100 Pretended lover who but acts a part.
False lovers can their self-assurance keep
And undismayed say all that they desire.
Strong flatterers are they and traitors vile—
Felons who one thing think, another speak.

"When to an end your conversation comes,
Though you have not one word missaid, you'll think
You have been duped into forgetfulness
Of something special that you planned to say;
Then will your martyrdom begin again.
110 This is the struggle, this the sorry strife,
This is the battle that forever lasts.
Lovers will never gain all that they seek;
Always it fails them; never have they peace;
No consummation of the war there'll be
Until it is my will to call a truce.

"A thousand more annoyances at night
You'll have, and in your bed but small repose;
For, when you wish to sleep, there will commence
Tremblings, agitations, shivers, chills.
120 From one side to the other you will toss—
Lie on your stomach first, then on your back—
Like one with toothache seeking ease in vain.
Then will return the memory of her
Whose shape and semblance never had a peer.
I'll state a miracle that may occur:
Sometimes you'll dream that your beloved one,

Fair-eyed and naked quite, lies in your arms,
And yields herself companion to your love.
Then castles in the land of Spain you'll build,
130 And naught will please you but to fool yourself
With pleasant thoughts whose basis is a lie.
But e'en this fiction will not long remain,
And then you'll weep and thus make your complaint:
'Ye gods, have I but dreamed? What is this, then?   THE LOVER
Where do I lie? Whence came this thought to me?
Would it might come again—ten, twenty times
A day! It fed and filled my soul with joy
And happiness; but its departure kills.
Might I again experience that bliss
140 And be where I then thought I was, I vow
That willingly I would give my life.
Death could not grieve me should his summons come
While I lay clasped within my sweetheart's arms.
But I, tormented thus and grieved by love,
Constant complaint and loud lament must make.
However, if the God of Love would grant
That I might utterly enjoy my love,
Well purchased were my woe at such a price!
Alas! I ask too much. I am not wise
150 Such an outrageous bargain to demand.
A fool's request deserves a sharp rebuff;
Therefore I know not what I dare to say.
Many a greater and more worthy one
Than I has had in love less recompense
And thought himself well favored, nonetheless.
But, if a single kiss and nothing more
The fair one would allot to ease my pain,
Most rich reward I'd have for all my woe.
But now for me the future darkly looms;
160 Well may I hold myself a fool who dare
To set my heart upon so high a prize
That neither joy nor profit may I gain.
Yes, I'm a silly churl so to prefer
A look from her above another one's
Complete surrender. Should the gods me aid
To get, this instant, longed-for sight of her,

How soon should I be cured! Oh, help me, God!
Why does the dawn so long delay? I lie
Too long lamenting on this lonely couch
170 Where I no ease can have without my love.
Naught but annoyance 'tis to lie abed
When one can have no comfort or repose.
I'm troubled now, when I would fain arise,
Because the night has lingered all too long
And day breaks all too slowly in the east.
O Sun, for God's sake, haste; make no delay—
Speed the departure of the night obscure
Which, with its cares, has worn its welcome out!'

    "If I know aught of the distress of love,   THE GOD OF LOVE
180 I know that thus you'll waste away the night
And get but little rest. And when at length
You can no longer bear to lie awake,
You'll rise and dress yourself, put on your shoes,
And make your toilet ere you see the dawn.
Then furtively you'll seek, in rain or snow,
By shortest path, the mansion of your love,
Who, soundly sleeping still, scarce thinks of you.
By postern gate an hour you'll wait alone,
Hoping that perchance it may unclose;
190 But there you'll cool your heels in wind and sleet.
Then the front door you'll try, or elsewhere seek
Some unbarred window—any opening—
Where you may listen for some sound within
That may betoken who's asleep, who wakes.
And if by chance your sweetheart is the one
Who only is awake, I counsel you
To let her hear your groans and your complaints
That she may know that, troubled by her love,
You in your bed could find no more repose.
200 Unless her heart is hard, she should be touched
With pity for the one who bears such pain.

    "For love of that high sanctuary, then,
Because of which you're robbed of all your rest,
At your departure kiss the blessed door;
And, that no man may see you in the street
Before the house, take care to go away

While twilight lingers—ere the dawn is clear.
Such comings and such goings in the night,
Such wakings and such watchings, such complaints,
210 Make lovers' bodies thin beneath their clothes.
Of this yourself will an example be:
Love leaves true lovers neither flesh nor blood.
This fact helps one identify false churls
Who, wishing to betray ingenuous maids,
Attempting to deceive them, say they've lost
Completely their desire for meat and drink;
Yet ne'er an abby prior's more fat than they!
    "With one thing more I charge you, and command
That you your reputation make secure
220 For generosity, by many gifts
Bestowed upon the lady's serving maid,
That she may name you as a worthy man.
Hold dear and honor all your lady's friends;
Advantage may well come through them to you.
When those who have her confidence recount
How they have found you courteous, true, and kind,
Your love will prize you half as much again.
Depart not from your sweetheart's native land;
Or, if you must, by dire necessity,
230 Be sure to leave your heart as hostage there,
And plan a quick return; make absence brief.
Let her well know how long the hours seem
When you're away from her who guards your heart.
Now I have told you how and in what guise
Lovers should do my bidding; do it, then,
If you would lastly gain your pleasure with your love."

11. The Lover learns the Remedies for the Pains of Love
[2581–2764]

WHEN Love had thus commanded me, I said:
"Sir, how and by what means may I endure   THE LOVER

The evils you have just detailed to me?
They overwhelm my mind with grievous fear;
For how can any man live and support,
In every place and time, such sighs and griefs,
Such tears and cares, such burnings and such pains,
And so severe a strain? So help me God,
I marvel much that anyone could live,
10 Were he not made of steel, in such a hell."
    The God of Love, explaining, thus replied:

THE GOD OF LOVE

"No man has good unless he purchase it.
Fair friend, I swear this by my father's soul:
Things dearest paid for are the dearest prized,
And good seems best when it is bought with ill.
It's true that naught with lovers' woes compares.
No more than man can pump the ocean dry
Can story or romance love's griefs exhaust.
Yet lovers live as long as e'er they can;
20 To flee from Death each has a right good will!
The wretch immured in filthy dungeon dark,
Annoyed by vermin, eating barley bread
Or only oaten cake, dies not for that;
Hope gives him comfort, and he's confident
Some chance will offer freedom to him yet.
Like aspiration have the thralls of Love;
Though held in prison, they expect relief.
Hope so consoles them that with willing heart
They give themselves up thus to martyrdom.
30 Hope makes them bear such ills as none can tell
For sake of joys a hundred times more great.
It's Hope revives them, making them forget
Adversities they've suffered. Blest be Hope,
Who does the cause of lovers so advance!
Most courteous is Hope; she never lags
Six feet behind the valiant, till their end,
In spite of mischief or of peril dire.
Even the thief who feels the hangman's rope
By Hope is made still to expect reprieve.
40 This will I warrant: Hope will not depart
But ever succor you in your most need;

And with this Hope I give you three more gifts
That solace those who're caught within my net.
   "Sweet Thought, who e'er recalls what Hope accords,
Is first of those who comfort all my thralls.
Whene'er a lover weeps and sighs and groans
And is in torment, then Sweet Thought will come,
Within short space, to drive away his gloom,
Reminding him of all the joy that Hope
50 Has promised him, setting before his view
His sweetheart's laughing eyes, her saucy nose—
Neither too small nor large—her rose-red lips
Exhaling sweet perfume, and all her parts
The memory of which can pleasure give.
Then, doubling all his joy, a tender look
Or welcome kind or smile he will recall
Which his dear fair one has sometime bestowed.
Sweet Thought thus often calms the rage of love.
I willingly bestow on you this boon
60 As well as others, which if you refuse
You'll be ungrateful, for they're not less sweet.
   "The second gift is called Sweet Speech, who lends
To many a man and maid great comforting;
For lovers always long to talk of love.
Because of this a dame made up a song,
About her love, which I remember well:

     Whatever they may say, I joy to hear
     Men talk to me about my lover dear.

Well did she know what power in Sweet Speech lies;
70 For she had tested it in many a way.
I counsel you, therefore, to seek a friend,
Secret and sage, to whom you may reveal
Whate'er you wish, discovering your heart.
A great advantage you will gain by this;
For, when your malady gives you most pain,
You'll go to him for comfort, and converse,
You two alone, of her who has your heart—
Of her appearance, her sweet countenance,
Her beauty. Then you will recount the state

80 Of all your being, asking his advice—
What you may do, and how, to please your love.
If he who is your friend has set his mind
Upon some sweetheart, then his confidence
Is of most worth; for he of course will tell
His lady's name and what her station is,
And whether she's a widow or a maid.
So you will not suspect him of designs
Upon your lady, or have any fear
Of treachery; for you with him and he
90 With you will then have made an interchange
Of utmost trust. You'll know how sweet it is
To have a friend with whom your thoughts are safe.
When you have tested him, you'll feel well paid
To get such comforting as he can give.
  "My third gift is Sweet Sight, child of Regard,
Who stays away from those far from their loves,
So take my counsel and remain near yours.
Delicious to the taste of those who love,
The solace is that Sweet Sight offers them.
100 Delightful meetings have the eyes at morn
To which God shows the sanctuary blest
For sight of which they are most envious.
Nothing will seem mischance to them that day!
They fear no dust or rain or other grief.
And when the well-taught eyes gain such delight
They are too courteous to hide their joy
But rather wish with it to please the heart
And calm its woes; for such good messengers
Are lovers' eyes that to the heart straightway
110 They send the news of whatsoe'er they see,
And then in joy the heart forgets its grief
And all the gloom that troubled it before.
Just as the rising sun puts shades to rout,
So does Sweet Sight drive darkness from the heart
Which night and day lay languishing for love.
Heart nothing doubts when eyes have longed-for sight.
  "Now I've explained away your fears, I think;
For truthfully I've told you all the means
By which lovers are eased and kept from death,

120 And for your comfort now you know you have
　　At least Sweet Thought, Sweet Speech, Sweet Sight, and Hope.
　　It is my will that these shall be your guard
　　Till better aids you gain, for these, indeed,
　　Are but an earnest of the more that is to come."

12. Fair Welcome encourages the Lover
[2765–2822]

　　LOVE had no sooner shown me all his will
　　Than, ere I said a word, he vanished quite
　　And left me all amazed to be alone.
　　My wounds pained me again, and well I knew
　　That naught could cure them but the rosebud red
　　On which I'd set my heart and my desire.
　　For help I looked but to the God of Love,
　　Thinking that but through him I'd gain my Rose.
　　　The rose trees were preserved from trespassers
10 By means of hedges that I would have leaped
　　Most willingly to get the scented bud
　　But that I feared lest I should be accused,
　　And rightfully, of trying the Rose to steal.
　　While thus I hesitated by the hedge,
　　I saw approach a lusty bachelor
　　In whom was nothing one might criticize.
　　It was Fair Welcome, son of Courtesy,
　　Who, stepping from the path, thus friendly spoke:
　　"My dear, fair friend, don't let me interfere;　FAIR WELCOME
20 But, if you wish to smell the flowers' perfume,
　　O'erleap the hedge, and I will guarantee
　　That no disgrace or ill shall come therefrom,
　　Provided you yourself from folly guard.
　　Fear not to ask, if I can give you aid;
　　For I am at your service, and speak true."
　　"Sir, I accept your promise gratefully,"　　THE LOVER
　　In answer to Fair Welcome I replied,

"And for this goodness give the thanks deserved.
Your generosity impelled that speech;
30 Your service I'll return whene'er you please."
     Then through the thorns and briars, of which the hedge
Had quite enough, I made my troubled way,
Fair Welcome going with me in the quest.
I circled round the tree toward the flower
Which seemed to me best perfume to exhale.
I need not tell you how it suited me
That I was able to attain so near
That now I almost touched my budding vermeil Rose.

13. Danger frightens the Lover and drives away Fair Welcome
[2823–2970]

FAIR WELCOME'S cheer had helped me toward my Rose,
But a shameful churl named Danger there was hid,
Covered with grass and leaves, beside the tree
(He was the gardener who kept the blooms)
Ready to spy upon and to surprise
One who might stretch his hand to pick a bud.
He was not all alone; companions three
He had, named Evil Tongue and Shame and Fear.
Most powerful of all the three was Shame,
10 A female of a dubious ancestry.
Her mother's name was Reason, who ne'er lay
Beside the father, who was called Misdeed,
A creature foul and horrible to see,
Whose glance alone caused Shame to be conceived.
When God had suffered Shame to come to birth,
Assailed by sensualists was Chastity,
Who had been guardian of the buds and blooms
But now had need of aid—for Venus stole
Both day and night the roses and the buds—
20 And called on Reason for her daughter's help.

So Chastity, by Venus sorely vexed,
And quite disconsolate, obtained her wish;
For Reason lent her daughter, honest Shame,
An innocent. The better to protect
The roses, she had help at her command,
For Jealousy and Fear both went with her.
Then had the rose trees fourfold guard, combined
To stop the theft of roses and of buds.
My purpose had well sped had not these four
30 Kept watch of me. Fair Welcome was so frank
And generous that he took pains to aid
In everything he thought might comfort me.
Often he begged that I more near approach
The rose tree that was loaded full of blooms,
And even touch the bud. He gave me leave
To do whate'er he thought I wished to do.
He even plucked a neighbor leaf, and gave
It me because it grew so near the bud.
With that green leaf I decked my buttonhole;
40 And, knowing that Fair Welcome was my friend,
I confidently thought success assured.
    So I took courage, and Fair Welcome told
How Love enslaved me and upset my peace.
"Kind sir," I said, "I never will have joy   THE LOVER
Of anything but one; within my heart
Lies such a very heavy malady
That I could scarce explain the case to you
And not incur your scorn; the rather I
Would cut to pieces be with knives of steel
50 Than merit your ill will."
                              But he replied,
"Say what you will, I'll never angry be."   FAIR WELCOME
    Then I told all: "Fair sir, pray do not think   THE LOVER
That I would lie to you. The God of Love
Torments me so severely that he's made
Five wounds within my heart, whose ceaseless pain
Will last until I gain that best-shaped bud.
Naught else I wish; for it I live or die."
    Fair Welcome then seemed frightened, and he cried:
"You ask for that which ne'er may be attained. FAIR WELCOME

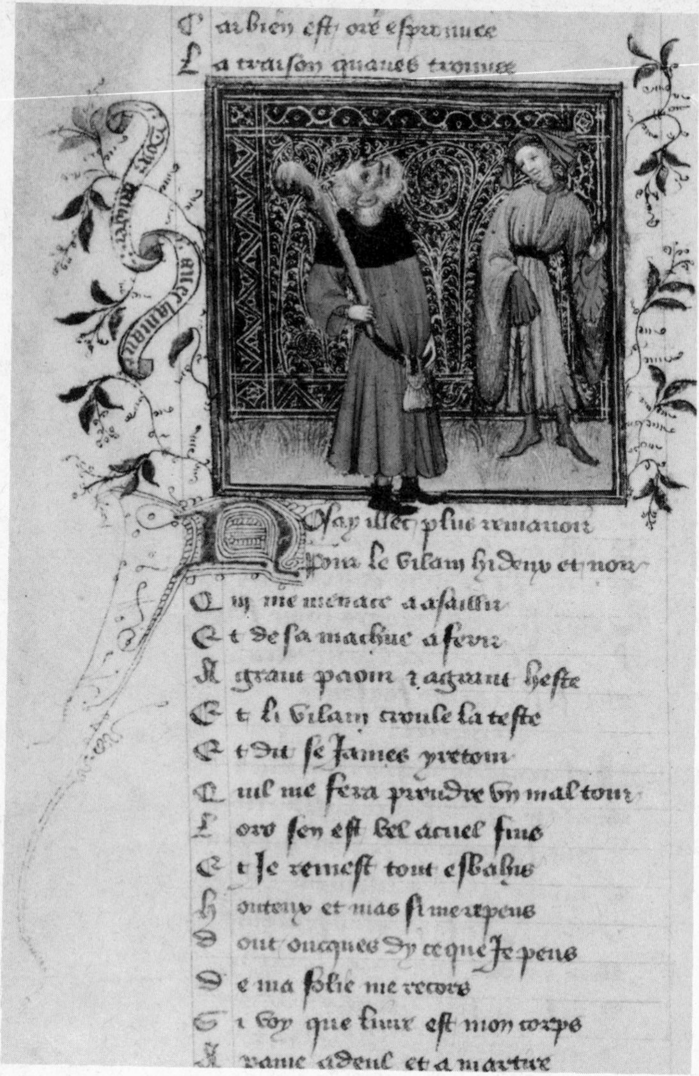

Danger shakes his head at the Lover. *Morgan 245, f. 22v.*

60 What! Would you shame me? You'd make me a fool
   Were you to pick a bud from off that tree.
   Where Nature placed the bud, there it must stay;
   It is not right that you should steal it thence.
   You are a villain with your rash demands.
   Let the bud grow into a perfect bloom.
   For no man living would I desecrate
   That rose tree, so much love have I for it."
      Danger then sprang from where he had lain hid;
   Hairy and black and great was he; his eyes
70 Were red as fire; his nose upturned; his face
   Most horrible. And maniac-like he cried:
   "Fair Welcome, why have you this gallant brought   DANGER
   So nigh the rose? As Christ my savior is,
   You do but ill. This man dishonors you.
   No one but you would suffer such disgrace,
   You who within these precincts brought the wretch!
   One is a villain who a villain serves.
   You thought to do a favor, but his thought
   Is, contrariwise, to pay you back with shame.
80 Flee, fellow, flee from hence! Small payment I
   Would take to kill you. Little do you know
   The one you tried so hard to succor here,
   Fair Welcome, who would now make you his dupe.
   Don't think to make me trust you any more,
   For well is proved the treason you'd assist."
      For fear of Danger I dared not remain
   There longer, since his black and hideous face
   Threatened attack, and made me hastily,
   And greatly frightened, leap back o'er the hedge.
90 Grimly he shook his head, and warning gave
   That if again he found me near the Rose
   I should be punished with a vengeance dire.
      Fair Welcome had made good his flight, and I,
   Astonished, shamed, and beaten, did repent
   Of what I'd said and done, recalling all
   My folly, and perceiving that I'd brought
   Upon my body martyrdom and grief.
   But that for which I had the greatest ire
   Was that I dared no more to pass the hedge.

100 No man knows ill who has not been in love!
    No other anguish can with that compare.
    Love had fulfilled his threat to give me pain.
    No heart can e'er conceive or tongue recount
    One quarter of my dolor. Scarcely stayed
    My soul within my body when I thought
    Upon my vermeil Rose, whom I must now desert.

14. Reason advises the Lover to abjure the God of Love
                    [2971–3098]

    LONG time I lingered near the place, distraught,
    Till Reason from her observation tower,
    On which she scans the country all about,
    Came forth, approaching nigh to where I stood.
    She's not too young or old, too tall or short,
    Too fat or lean. Her eyes like two stars shone.
    She wore a noble crown upon her head.
    A queen she might have been, but more did seem,
    To judge by her appearance and her face,
10 An angel come, perhaps, from Paradise.
    Nature could hardly frame a work so fair.
    'Twas God himself, unless the Scriptures lie,
    Who in his image and his likeness formed
    This godlike one, and her with power endowed
    To rescue men from rash and foolish acts,
    Provided that her counsel they'll believe.
    Reason addressed me as I madly wept:
    "Fair friend, your youth and folly brought this pain   REASON
    And this dismay, when on an ill-omened day
20 You yielded to the springtime's pleasant spell
    Which so bewitched your heart. 'Twas evil hour
    At which you came into that shady park
    Of which the key is kept by Idleness,
    Who ope'd the gate for you. One is a fool
    Who makes acquaintance with that tempting maid,

r poy que le cœur ne my part
Q uant de la rose me souuient
Q ue Je nay pas a mon talent

E n ce point ay qut preche esté
C rant q ainsi me bit maté
L a dame de la haute garde
Q ui de sa tour aual esgarde
R aison fu la dame appelee
L ors sest de sa tour aualee
G i est tout dont a moy benue
E lle nest ne vielle ne chanue
N e fu trop haulte ne trop basse

Reason warns the Lover against Love. *Morgan 245, f. 22v.*

Whose sweet companionship is perilous.
You've been deceived and brought to grief by her;
For had not Idleness conducted you
Into the garden that is named Delight
30 The God of Love had never seen you there.
Recover from your foolishness at once—
For foolishly you've acted—be on guard
That never more such counsel you accept,
By which you have been made to act the sot.
Unwise is he who would chastise himself!
But 'tis no wonder; men are fools in youth.
Now I should like to give you this advice:
Into oblivion consign that god
Who has so weakened, tortured, conquered you.
40 I see no other way to healthful cure;
For felon Danger lies in wait for you,
And you should wish to test his might no more.
Yet Danger's not to be compared with Shame,
My daughter, who the blooms defends and guards,
Aided by Fear, who surely is no fool,
But one whom all most surely should beware.
With these is Evil Tongue, who none permits
To touch the roses. Ere the deed is done,
He'll publish it abroad a hundredfold.
50 You're dealing with hardhearted customers!
Consider, then, which is the better plan:
To beat retreat or rashly persevere
In courses that will fill your life with pain.
   "Nothing but foolishness is this disease
Called love; 'twere better it were folly named.
A ne'er-do-well is every man in love;
No profitable task he undertakes.
He leaves his learning if he be a clerk;
Nor can he thrive in any other craft.
60 He pays more penance than a monk or friar.
The pain he feels is measureless; the joy
Comes but by chance and lives but a short life,
Only to fade away. How many a man
I've seen laboriously exert himself
Only to fail at last unutterably!

"It was not by my counsel that you gave
Yourself unto the God of Love; your heart—
Too fickle far—led to this foolishness.
Most easily you started in the game,
70 But hard 'twill be to issue out of it.
Cast aside love, which makes life valueless.
From day to day it will entrench itself
If you allow this folly to remain.
Now firmly seize the bits between your teeth;
Resist the guidance of your stubborn heart,
Against whose will you'll have to use some force.
You will be ditched if passion keep the reins."
    Then angrily I answered this rebuke:
"Madam, I beg you, stop this chastisement.   THE LOVER
80 You tell me that I should oppose my heart,
Which Love now dominates. But do you think
Love would consent that I the heart should rule
Which I have ceded to him utterly?
You counsel what can never come to pass.
Love has such domination o'er my heart
That to my wishes it no more responds.
His jurisdiction o'er it is so strong
That he has even locked it with a key.
Please let me be; in vain you waste your speech.
90 I'd rather die than that I should deserve
Love's charge of treason and of falsity.
I care not whether I be praised or blamed
For loving well. But her who chides I hate."
    Then Reason left, seeing her sermoning
Could not avail to turn me from my chosen course.

15. The Lover gains a Friend
[3099–3246]

FILLED with my grief and anger I remained,
Oft weeping, oft complaining that I knew

No remedy, until, remembering
That Love had said that I should seek some one,
To whom I might unburden all my care,
I from my torment found deliverance;
For I recalled such a companion true—
None ever better had—his name was Friend.
    I hastened to him and, as Love advised,
10 Explained the trap in which I found myself.
Of Danger I complained, who little lacked
Of eating me, and drove Fair Welcome off
When he heard me speak to him about the bud
For which I yearned—said I should dearly pay
If ever I should pass within the close.
When he had heard the truth, Friend soothed me thus:
    "Companion, be secure and not dismayed;   THE FRIEND
Long have I known this Danger, so well taught
To threaten, curse, and menace those who love.
20 Long time ago I proved that, if at first
One finds him such a felon, in the end
Quite other he becomes. I know him well.
He can be mollified with soft caress
Or supplication. Here's what you should do:
Beg that he pardon you for your misdeed,
Exchanging his malevolence for love
And amity; then make a covenant
That you'll do nothing that might anger him
From now henceforward. That will please him much.
30 Caress and flattery appease him best."
    With all this talk Friend somewhat solaced me
And gave me hardihood and heart to go
This villain Danger thus to pacify.
Shamefaced and anxious, to restore my peace
I went to Danger, nor o'erpassed the bounds
He'd set for me. I found him on his feet,
Apparently still savage and enraged,
And ready in his hand his thorny club.
With head bowed down, I him approached, and said:
40 "Mercy to beg of you, sir, have I come.   THE LOVER
It grieves me much that I have angered you;
And now I'm ready all amends to make

That you may ask of me; for it was Love,
From whom I never can my heart withdraw,
Who made me do the deed. Let never dawn
The day when I consent to anything
That might offend you. I'd endure disease
Rather than do what might displease your will.
May you have pity on me now, I beg!
50 Dismiss your wrath, which frightens me so much,
And I will swear and pledge my faith to you
That toward you I will so conduct myself
That ne'er a single fault will I commit,
Provided you'll agree to one request.
Naught else I ask of you save grace to love.
All of your other wishes I'll fulfill
If you will grant but this. When I thus beg,
It is not to deceive you that I seek
If you do not disturb me in my love;
60 For whomsoever it may please or grieve
I still must love, since 'tis my destiny.
But not for my whole weight in silver coins
Would I attempt to love in your despite."

　　Danger I found to be most surly, slow
My trespasses to pardon; but at length,
So much I sermoned him, he me forgave.
Briefly he spoke: "Your prayer does not displease,   DANGER
Nor will I make denial. I've no ire
Against you. What do I care how you love?
70 Your loving makes me neither cold nor hot!
Then love, provided that you keep yourself
Far from my roses. I'll ne'er menace you
Unless you pass the hedge."
　　　　　　　　　　　　So granted he
My boon; and I made haste to tell my Friend,
Who, like a good companion, did rejoice

THE FRIEND

When he had heard. "Now your affair goes well,"
He said. "Danger will now be debonair,
Who, though at first he arrogance displays,
Has been an aid to many a man. He'll rue
80 Your pain if he be taken in right mood.

Wait now in patience till you see your chance;
By suffrance one can conquer greatest ills."
　　Friend wished for my advancement as did I,
And comforted me sweetly as I left
To seek once more the hedge that Danger kept;
For I could brook no more delay at least
To see the bud that was my only joy.
Danger watched close lest I should break my vow;
But I, who feared his menace, had no wish
90 To misconduct myself—rather, took pains
Most faithfully his bidding to fulfill
To gain his friendship and conciliate
His ire. But long must I attend his grace,
And all my patience turned to blank despair.
I let him see that oft I wept and sighed
And made complaint that I so long should wait
At his command outside the rosary,
Whose bounds I dared not pass to seek the flower.
So did I act that my demeanor showed
100 Him certainly that I was thrall to Love,
Who drove me sadly; yet I nothing did
Which might seem treason or disloyalty.
Howe'er, no matter what complaint I made
Nor how he heard me agonize my grief,
Such was his cruelty he would not deign
To call his edict back or in the least relent.

16. Franchise and Pity intercede for the Lover
[3247-3356]

WHILE I was in such torment, there did come
Franchise and Pity, God-sent aid for me.
They tarried not, but straight to Danger went;
For both would gladly help me if they could,
Seeing my need. First Lady Franchise spoke,
(God bless her!) saying, "Danger, by God's love   FRANCHISE

You wrong this Lover whom you use so hard;
And, since I've never heard that he offends
Against you, you dishonor but yourself.
10 Should you blame him when he loves but perforce?
He suffers more than you in this affair,
For many pains he bears; nor will Love grant
The last repining. Were he to be burned,
He could not keep from love to save his life.
What gains you all this grievance and annoy?
Have you made war upon him but that he,
Your servant, shall esteem and fear you more?
Should you detest him for that Love has caught
Him in his net and makes him bow to you?
20 You ought to spare him more than you would spare
A more obstreperous wretch. 'Tis courtesy
To succor those beneath you; hard of heart
You'd be were you unbending when he begs."
      Then Pity said, " 'Tis true, austerity   PITY
O'ercomes humility; but, when it's pushed
Beyond all reason, sternness is a sin.
Therefore, Sir Danger, I request that you
No longer wage your war against this wight
Languishing here, yet steadfast in his love.
30 It's my opinion that you grieve him more
Than he deserves; too hard his penance is,
Since you've bereft him of Fair Welcome's stay,
Which was the thing he most depended on.
For every pain he had you've given him two!
He was maltreated and might well have died
When by Fair Welcome he was left alone.
Why do you contradict his every wish?
Love makes him suffer quite enough of ill;
He has such woe he can no more endure.
40 You'll gain naught from his further punishment;
Pray then, restore Fair Welcome to his side.
I join with Franchise in her powerful plea:
'Have mercy on the man, though he have sinned!'
Refuse not our request; most hard of heart
And tyrannous were he who heard the prayer
Which we two make, and never answered it."

Then Danger could resist no more, but felt
Convinced that he should mollify, and said:
"Ladies, I dare not veto your request;   DANGER
50 'Twould be too great discourtesy. I grant
That he Fair Welcome's comradeship may have,
Since 'tis your wish; I'll place no obstacle."
Soft-voiced Franchise then to Fair Welcome went
And courteously spoke, "Too far removed   FRANCHISE
Are you, Fair Welcome, from that courtier
Whom you disdain even to look upon.
Somber and sad is he, lacking your smiles.
Be amiable to him and do his will
If you'd enjoy my love; for you should know
60 That Pity and I have vanquished Danger's hate,
Which made you strangers."
                                        Then Fair Welcome said:
"If Danger has consented, then 'tis right   FAIR WELCOME
That I should do whatever you desire."
So Franchise brought Fair Welcome back to me.
Most sweetly did he greet me when we met.
If he had once been angry with me, now
He showed no whit of rancor, but appeared
More friendly than he'd ever been before.
He led me by the hand within the close
70 Whence Danger just before had banished me.
Now had I leave to go where'er I would;
Now was I raised from Hell to Paradise.
Fair Welcome, taking pains to grant each wish,
Now guided me throughout all the rosary.

17. The Lover succeeds in kissing the Rose
[3357–3498]

WHEN I approached the Rose, I found it grown
A little larger than it was before;
A little greater height the bush had gained.

But I was pleased that the unfolding flower
Had not yet spread so as to show the seed,
Which still was by the petals well concealed,
That stood up straight and with their tender folds
Hid well the grains with which the bud was filled.
And, thanked be God, the bud's maturer curves
10 Were better hued and comelier than before.
I was abashed, and marveled at the sight.
The fairer the bud, the more Love fettered me;
The happier I, the more I felt his chains.

Long time I lingered there when I had gained
Fair Welcome's love and good companionship;
And, when I found that he would not deny
His service or his solace, made request
For one thing that 'tis well to mention here.
"Fair sir," said I, "I have a great desire   THE LOVER
20 To gain a precious kiss from that sweet Rose;
And, if you're not displeased with my request,
I ask that boon. For God's sake, tell me now
If you'll permit the kiss; for certainly
Unless it please you I'll not think of it."

FAIR WELCOME
He made reply, "So help me God, dear friend,
If Chastity did not so frown on me,
I'd not deny you; but I am afraid
Of her, and would not act against her will.
She always tells me not to grant a kiss
30 To any lover who may ask for it;
For whosoever may a kiss attain
Can hardly be content with nothing more.
You know that one who has a kiss been given
Has gained the better and more pleasing half—
An earnest of the prize that he expects."

When I had heard Fair Welcome thus reply,
I begged no more, fearing to anger him.
One ne'er should press his friend immoderately
Nor agonize too much. The earliest stroke
40 Ne'er cuts the oak in two. One drinks no wine
Until the mash is squeezed within the press.
Long time my suit to gain the wished-for kiss

Had been delayed if Venus, e'er at war
With Chastity, had not supplied her aid.
She is the mother of the God of Love,
Who many a lover helps. In her right hand
She held the ruddy brand that has enflamed
Full many a lady's heart. She was so quaint
And wore such bright attire that she did seem
50 Goddess or fairy; by her ornaments
Well could one guess she was not any nun.
I'll not take time her clothing to describe—
Her golden headdress and her coverchief,
Her brooch, her girdle—I must not delay;
You know that she most richly was attired,
Though quite devoid of pride. Her way she made
To where Fair Welcome stood, and thus she spoke:
"Why so disdainful do you make yourself   VENUS
To this man when he begs a savory kiss?
60 It should not be denied him; for he serves
And loves, as you can see, in loyalty.
His beauty makes him worthy to be loved.
See how agreeable, fair, and genteel—
How sweet and frank he is to everyone;
And, what is better, he is young, not old.
There is no woman—not a high-born dame—
Whom I'd not call a fool him to refuse.
It will not cause his character to change
If you permit the kiss; 'twere good employ
70 For one who has so sweet a breath as he.
His mouth's not bad, but seems expressly made
For solace and delight; his lips are red;
His teeth are white and clean and undefiled.
It's my opinion that it would be right
To grant the kiss. Trust me, and give it him;
For to delay would be but to waste time."
    Fair Welcome felt the heat of Venus' brand,
And, such its power and hers, immediately
He granted me the boon I asked—a kiss.
80 Nor did I linger, but at once did take
A sweet and savory lipful from the Rose.
Let no man ask if then I felt delight!

My senses quickly were in perfume drowned
That purged my body from its pain, and soothed
The woes of love that had so bitter been.
Never before was I so much at ease.
Completely cured are all who kiss a flower
So pleasing and agreeable in smell.
The very memory of that caress
90 Henceforth will keep me from all sorrowing
And fill me with delight and joy, in spite
Of all I've suffered—all the woes I've had—
Since first I kissed the Rose. A little wind
Suffices to disturb the calmest sea;
So easily Love changes, never fixed—
One hour pours oil on waves, another raises storm.

18. Evil Tongue arouses Jealousy against the Lover
[3499–3796]

NOW rightly I should tell how Shame, by whom
I was much grieved, entered the strife, and how
The mighty walls and tower were raised, that long
The forces of the God of Love withstood.
No laziness shall make me interrupt
The full completion of this history
In hope that it may please a lady fair
(God bless her!) who may all my toil requite
Better than most, whenever she may wish.
10   Next Evil Tongue, who thinks or fancies wrong
In all affairs of lovers, and retails
All that he knows or weens, began to spy,
Between me and Fair Welcome, sweet accord.
Because he is old Scolding's son, and has
A dirty, bitter, biting gift of speech—
Her legacy—he could not hold his peace.
So Evil Tongue began to slander me,
Saying that ill relationship he'd seen

Betwixt me and Fair Welcome. Recklessly
20 The rascal talked of Courtesy's fair son
And me till he awakened Jealousy,
Who roused in fright when she the jangler heard.
Then to Fair Welcome did she run like mad
(In far Etampes or Meaux he'd better been!)
And thus assailed him: "Good-for-nothing boy,   JEALOUSY
Are you out of your wits to entertain
A youth of whom I have much ill report?
'Twould seem that all too lightly you believe
Palaver of a stranger. Don't expect
30 That I shall trust you more. You shall be bound
Or locked up in a tower, for certainly
I see no help for it. Shame's left you quite;
She's given you too much rope, nor taken pains
To guard you well. I've noted oftentimes
How she neglects her sister, Chastity,
And lets a lawless youth invade our realm
To bring disgrace on both myself and her."
    Fair Welcome knew not how to make reply;
He would have hidden himself but that we two
40 Were caught together there, to prove his guilt;
Though when I heard the scold start her attack
I took to flight, for quarrels bother me.
Then Shame came forward, showing in her face
She feared much to be taken in a fault.
In place of maiden wimple, veil she wore;
Humble and plain was she, like abbey nun.
Now much abashed, she spoke in accents low:
"For God's sake, dame, believe not Evil Tongue;   SHAME
A scandalmonger he, who lightly lies,
50 Deceiving many a worthy man. If he
Now blames Fair Welcome, it is nothing new.
He is accustomed to recount false tales
Of squires and demoiselles. Though I admit
Fair Welcome gives himself too long a leash
In gathering friends with whom he should not deal,
I certainly do not believe that he
Had least desire for foolishness or sin.
Indeed, 'tis true his mother, Courtesy,

Has taught him no affection to pretend
60 And surely not to show a foolish love.
Fair Welcome has no other wish or thought
Than to be full of jollity and fun
And to converse with hosts of genial friends.
Undoubtedly too easy I have been
With him, neglecting reprimand and guard;
For this I pardon beg. Disconsolate
Am I if I'm too soft to do what's best.
But I repent my folly, and I'll watch
Fair Welcome with due care from this time forth.
70 I'll never from this duty ask release."
"Ah, Shame," said Jealousy, "great fear have I   JEALOUSY
To be betrayed, for Lechery so reigns
That everyone's in danger of disgrace.
Nor groundless is my fear; Vice rules o'er all
And endlessly seems to increase his power.
Chastity no longer is secure
Even in cloister or in nunnery.
Hence I must with a stronger wall enclose
The roses and the rosary; no more
80 Shall they remain displayed to all men's sight,
For I can not depend upon your guard.
Now I perceive and know it for a fact:
'Best deputies deserve no confidence.'
If I'm not careful, scarce a year will pass
When I shall not be made to seem a fool.
Against that to provide is but good sense.
I'll close the road to those who come to spy
Upon my roses, making me their dupe.
I'll not be idle till a fortress's made
90 To enclose the rosary; and in the midst
A lofty tower shall be Fair Welcome's jail,
For fear of further treason. I will keep
So well his person that he'll have no power
To issue forth, companionship to have
With youths who flatter him with winning words,
Purposing but to bring him to disgrace.
Truant sots and fools too much have swarmed
About here in deceit; but, as I live,

Know this for truth: it was an evil hour
100 For him when first he granted them his smiles."
    At that came Fear, trembling and dismayed
And daring not to say a single word.
Since she perceived what ire her talking showed,
She stood apart till Jealousy withdrew.
Then Shame and Fear were left together there,
Shivering to their very buttock bones,
Till Fear, abashed, addressed her cousin Shame:
"Heavy it weighs upon my soul that we
Must bear the blame for what we have not done.
110 Many a time have May and April passed,
And we've had no reproach till Jealousy
Suspiciously heaped insult on abuse.
Let us immediately Danger seek
And show him well, and carefully explain,
That he has wrought great mischief not to guard
More warily the garden; far too much
He has allowed Fair Welcome openly
To work his will. He must amend his ways
Or necessarily flee from the land,
120 Since he could never brave the war for which
Mad Jealousy has provocation great
If she should likewise take his deeds amiss."
    At this agreement they arrived, and went
To Danger, who beneath a hawthorn lay.
The boor, in place of pillow for his head,
Was dozing on a biggish heap of hay
Till Shame awoke him, pitching into him
With chiding: "How then! By what evil chance
Are you asleep at such a time as this?
130 A fool were he who held you of more use
For guarding roses than some mutton tail.
Too lax and negligent are you, who should
Be strict, and harshly deal with everyone.
You foolishly Fair Welcome did allow
To introduce a man who gets us blamed.
You doze while we get undeserved rebuke.
Do you still sleep? Get up and mend the hedge,
And no exception make for anyone.

FEAR

SHAME

To side-step trouble little suits your name.
140 Fair Welcome's free and frank, but you should be
Savage and rude and harsh and insolent.
A courteous churl is an anomaly;
And, as I've oft heard quoted in reproof,
'No man can of a buzzard make a hawk.'
Who finds you debonair should think you mad.
With help and favor do you try to please?
You will be charged with cowardice if you
Henceforth shall have the name of being lax,
So readily believing flatterers."

150   Then Fear took up the word: "I'm much surprised   FEAR
That you're not wide-awake to mind your charge.
You soon for this may suffer; Jealousy
May fan her wrath, for she is proud and fell
And prompt to chide. Today she Shame assailed
And by her menace chased Fair Welcome off,
Declaring that she'll never rest until
She's walled him up alive. All this occurred
By your neglect, because you rigor lack.
I fear your heart has failed you; you'll pay dear
160 With grief and pain if Jealousy learns the truth."

    The churl his shock head raised. He shook himself,
Wrinkled his nose, and rubbed and rolled his eyes.
Hearing himself thus blamed, he showed his ire,
And thus he spoke: "If you think that I am licked,   DANGER
You give me cause for anger. If I've failed
To keep my charge, then I have lived too long;
Burn me alive if any man gets by.
The heart within my breast feels much chagrin
That any foot this place has ever trod.
170 I'd rather have two swords thrust through my breast.
That I have been a fool I plainly see;
But, for the sake of you two, I'll amend.
Never again will I be lax to guard
This place; if I catch anybody here,
He'll wish that he had stayed in Pavia.
I swear and vow, to the last day of my life
You ne'er again will think me recreant."

    Danger arose and fiercely looked about;

Seizing his club, he searched the rosary
180 For hole or gap or passageway to block.
Thenceforth the situation was reversed,
For Danger came to be more hard and fell
Than he was wont to be. I nearly died
Because I had aroused his anger so.
No longer could I feast my eyes upon
The sight for which I longed. My spirits drooped
At being from Fair Welcome so estranged.
You may believe my frame with shivers shook
When of the Rose I thought, which I at will
190 Had seen close by—when I recalled the kiss
Which through my being spread a balm so sweet
That I near fainted but still let me keep
Within my soul the savor of the Rose.
Know well that, when I realized that I
Must go away, I wished for death, not life.
Evil the hour when once I touched the bud
With eyes, with lips, with face, if ne'er again
The God of Love permit renewed caress!
My soul was fanned to flame with a desire
200 That was more great because I'd had a taste.
Then sighs and tears and sleeplessness returned—
Prickings and shivers, mournful thoughts, complaints.
My multitudinous pains put me in hell.
Accurst be Evil Tongue, whose lying lips
Purchased for me such store of bitter condiment!

19. Jealousy builds a castle in which to immure
Fair Welcome and the Rose
[3797–4058]

NOW it is time to tell what Jealousy,
Prompted by vile suspicion, brought to pass.
There was no mason that she did not hire,
No excavator, in the country 'round.

It cost a pretty penny, but they dug
A deep, wide moat about the rosary;
Beside the fosse a wall of square-cut stones
Was founded not on earth but solid rock;
Its massive fundament adjoined the moat,
10 And, narrowing to the top, it rose on high,
A mighty work; foursquare in shape it stood,
As long as broad, six hundred feet each way.
Side by side the turrets on it rose,
Securely battlemented with squared stones.
Four corner towers, strong to withstand attack,
Four portals, too, whose walls were thick and firm,
Were placed. These latter—one on either side
And one in front and one behind—at need
Defended easily against assault,
20 Would never fear a catapulted stone.
Portcullises there were to grieve a foe
And take and hold whoever ventured in.
    A master workman of such handicraft
Within the enclosure's very center raised
A donjon thick and high; no better keep
Could ever be. The walls would never crack
At stroke of any instrument of war;
For mortar mixed of lime and vinegar
Secured the native rock and made the tower
30 As strong as adamant. Built round in shape,
In all the world there was no tower more fine
Or better equipped within. About the keep
A bailey wall was built, and in between
The bailey and the keep were planted thick
The rose trees, plentifully bearing blooms.
Within the castle various instruments
Of war, like ballistas, one might observe;
And mangonels peered o'er the pinnacles;
An arbolast, 'gainst which no armor serves,
40 Peeped from each loophole of the lofty towers.
He'd play the fool who came too near that fort!
Enclosing all the moat, a lower wall
Assault by knights prevented until they
Had first their way thereto by battle won.

De ores est droit que ie vous die
La contenance Jalousie
Elle est en male souspeçon
Ou pais ne remest machon
Ne pronnyer quelle ne mant
Si fait fere au commencement
Entour les rosiers vns fosser
Qui cousteront deniers asser
Qui sont plus grant et plus parfont
Li machons sur les fosses font
Un grant mur de quarriaux taillez
Qui ne fut pas sur coulerz
Ains est fonde sur roche dure
Li fondemens tout a mesure
Iusquau ....

Jealousy's workmen secure the Rose against the Lover's advances. *Morgan 245, f. 29r.*

Jealousy arrayed a garrison
Within the castle that I have described.
'Twas Danger bore the key to the chief gate,
Which opened toward the east; with him he had
Full thirty wardens, by the best account.
50 Shame at the southern gateway stood on guard;
She was most sage, and many a sergeant had
Ready to do her will. Fear kept her watch
At the north gateway, which was on the left;
A great constabulary force she had,
But, were the gate unlocked, ne'er felt secure,
So seldom opened it; for if she heard
The noise of wind, or saw so many as two
Lone grasshoppers go issuing forth, she screamed
In panic for an hour. At the last gate
60 Had Evil Tongue (May God condemn his soul!)
His Norman mercenaries; but at night
He often visited the other three.
Each evening he would mount the battlements
And play his bagpipe, trumpet, horn, or shalms.
At one time he would sing descants and lays
And all the latest songs, to Cornish pipes;
Another time, accompanied with a flute,
Dispraising ladies, he would sing like this:

There is no maid who will not smile
70   When she hears tales of lechery.
The whores will paint, men to beguile;
    For all are full of treachery.
If the fool's not talking all the while,
    She's mistress of the ogling style.
There is no maid who will not smile
    When she hears tales of lechery.

Thus Evil Tongue, who will no woman spare,
Contrives to find in each some serious fault.
Jealousy (whom God confound!) then placed,
80 Within the tower round, her garrison,
Composed of all her friends most intimate.
Fair Welcome was imprisoned in the tower,
The door of which was barred 'gainst his escape.

An old beldame to spy upon him there
No other duty had but to keep watch
Lest he some folly might commit. No man
Could trick her with a gesture or a sign;
For there was no device she did not know,
Since in her youth she'd suffered all the pains
90 And joys that Love unto his servants gives.
Although Fair Welcome listened and kept still,
Fearing the hag, he could no motion make
So cautiously that she could not perceive
The thought behind his simple countenance;
For well she knew the ancient dance of love.

When Jealousy Fair Welcome had secured,
Walled up within the tower, she felt safe.
Her castle walls, which she perceived were strong,
Great comfort gave to her. She had no fear
100 That villains might purloin a rose or bud;
The rose trees now too stoutly were enclosed.
Sleeping or waking, she was undisturbed;
But I, without the wall, felt dole and pain.
If one could but conceive the life I led,
He could but pity me. Love set high price
Upon the goods that he had lent to me;
I thought that I had purchased them, but now
He charged me for them at a double rate.
The bargain galled me much more painfully,
110 Because of all the joy that I had lost,
Than if it never had been mine. But why
Do I continue telling you of this?
I'm like the husbandman who sows the seed
And joys when it grows fair and thick in stalk,
But ere he cuts the sheaves worse weather comes—
The season's bad—and evil clouds appear,
Just when the crop should ear, and kill the grain,
With all the hope the farmer had too soon.
I feared thus to have lost both pains and hopes.
120 Love had advanced my cause when I began
To give Fair Welcome greatest confidence;
Ready he seemed to join the game of love.
But so inconstant is love's God that he

Upset me in the hour when I believed
Myself about to ride triumphantly.
'Tis thus that Fortune lodges discontent
Within men's hearts one hour, but to caress
And flatter them the next. No, not an hour
Is passed without her change of countenance:
130 One minute she will smile, another frown.
She has a wheel she turns whene'er she will;
But half a turn upsets those at the top
To grovel in the mud, while those below
Are to the summit raised. Now was I one
Of those who are upset. Woe worth the day
When I first saw the fosses and the walls
Which I would dare not traverse if I could!
Fair Welcome being in jail, I had no joy
Or blessing; for the cure of all my pain
140 Rested with him and with the Rose enclosed
Within the walls, from which he must be freed
If Love were willing that I should be healed.
Never I'd wish by other means to have
Honor or blessing, health or happiness.

THE LOVER

"Alas, Fair Welcome, my sweet friend, though you
Be cast in prison, keep your heart for me;
For no price let that savage Jealousy
As she's enslaved your body chain your soul;
Though you without be punished, keep within
150 A heart as hard as diamond against
Her chastisement; in spirit keep your love
For me although your body pine in jail!
No punishment or evil treatment makes
A true heart leave its love. If Jealousy
Makes you endure annoyance and distress,
Strengthen your heart 'gainst her severity,
At least in thought, if you can't otherwise
Avenge yourself against the spite she shows.
Do this, and I will think myself well paid.
160 Now I'm distressed lest you should not do so,
But blame your dire imprisonment on me.
Yet surely 'twas no fault of mine, for I

Never revealed what should have hidden been.
Rather, so help me God, misfortune falls
More heavily on me than you; I pay
A greater penalty than man can tell.
Chagrin almost confounds me when I sense
My loss, which is so manifestly great.
My dread and dole will be, I think, my death.
170 Have I not cause to dread, when I perceive
The lying, envious traitors taking care
To injure me? Fair Welcome, I know well
That they are bent upon deceiving you
And by their stories bringing it to pass
That they'll be able, as it were, to lead
You by a halter! Mayhap they do now!
I know not how it comes, but blank dismay
So sorely troubles me that my heart fails.
If I lose your good will, I shall despair,
180 For elsewhere I can find no source of confidence."

Anonymous Conclusion
[Extra lines, 1–78]

"NO comfort can now aid me. Ah! My dear,   THE LOVER
He who might see you but one time each week
Would feel less pain; but by no road or path
Do I know how to gain one glimpse of you."
    While I felt such distress, I saw approach
<u>Dame Pity</u>, walking stately toward the tower,
Who many a sorrowing heart has made content.
She with these words began to comfort me:
"Friend, to console you and assuage your grief,   PITY
10 I've come into this orchard, and I bring
Fair Welcome, Beauty, Loyalty, Sweet Looks,
Simplicity. With difficulty great
We issued from that tower that rises high.
(But one of loyal heart should ne'er default
Though by his efforts he should lose his life.)
While Jealousy was sleeping, we contrived
To steal away. Great obstacles we found;
For Fear, who is so timid every day,
Had locked the gate, and wandered to and fro
20 Listening and spying everywhere;
And Evil Tongue knew scarcely what to do,
So much he was in doubt. The God of Love,
Who ever takes good care of all his own,
Opened the gate for us with greatest pains
In spite of Fear. If Evil Tongue had known,
We had no exit gained for all the world.

89

But Love, so fair and pretty, stole the keys
And let us out." As soon as they took seats
Beside me, all my dolor passed away.
30 Secretly Dame Beauty gave to me
The charming bud I prize with all my heart
With which to do whatever I might please,
And no one's contravention to be feared.
There at our ease we then took great delight;
The tender grass provided us a bed;
The rosebush petals fair made coverlets;
And all that night we nothing did but kiss
And satisfaction find in other joys.
But short enough the night appeared to me;
40 In early morning, when the dawn appeared,
We rose, much grieved the night had passed so soon.
Then Beauty had to take her rosebud back;
Unwillingly I had to give her up.
But, none the less, the blossom never closed
Against me, even when 'twas snatched away.
However, ere they left or said good-by,
Beauty approached shamefaced, and, laughing, said:
"Now Jealousy may spy and build his hedge   BEAUTY
Of eglantine as lofty as he likes,
50 For much he now has gained by that device!
Now fair, sweet lover, tell me what you think;
Has he not tired himself to death in vain?
His services have had their just reward.
See to it that you serve without deceit,
If you indeed would hold my service dear,
And always you'll be master of the bud
Even though it may not imprisoned be."
We separated then; I said good-by;
And gracefully they made their secret way
60 Back to the tower as straight as they could go.
Such was the very ending of my dream.

Jean de Meun

20. The Lover despairs
[4059–4220]

"CONFIDENCE being lost, I'm near despair; THE LOVER
But I will not give up—abandon Hope.
Worthless I'd be if Hope should fail me quite.
In this I should find comfort: that Love swore,
To make me better bear my ills, that Hope
Should be with me wherever I might go.
But what of that? What does it mean to me?
Though Hope be courteous and debonair,
She's never certain. Although she may be
10 Lady and mistress of all folk in love,
She puts them in great pain, and oft deceives
By promise false which she will never keep.
God help me, but this Hope is perilous;
For many a man in love depends on Hope
And trusts fulfillment that can never be.
Hope knows not what's to come; as little know
Her followers what they may count upon.
A fool is he who much on her depends;
For though she forms the fairest syllogism,
20 Fallacious may her whole conclusion be.
Ofttimes have I seen men by her deceived
Despite her wish that those who trust in her
May get the better of the bargain. Fool
Am I to blame her. Yet of what avail

Is her good will if she cure not my pain?
Mere promises are far too little aid;
Promise without performance buys no bread.
My luck has left me numberless denials.
Danger and Fear and Shame encumber me;
30 And Jealousy and Evil Tongue, who sting
And poison all their victims, with foul speech
Deliver me to saddest martyrdom.
Fair Welcome, who accepts my every thought
And knows that without him I soon shall die,
They hold in prison; but, to make more sure
My death, that foul Duenna, smelling old,
Guards him so close that he dares look at none.

     "From now my dolor will increase. 'Tis true
The God of Love presented me three gifts
40 In his great kindness, but I've lost them all:
Now Sweet Speech fails; Sweet Thought avails me not;
Sweet Sight has left me—so may God me guard!
Fair gifts they were, no doubt, but valueless
To me unless Fair Welcome shall escape,
Who is unjustly held. I think I'll die
For want of him, who'll ne'er get out alive.
What power can free him from such prison house?
Escape? But no; he cannot compass it!
In a crazy fit was I, at least half mad
50 When foolishly I made myself Love's man.
Shame on the schemes of Lady Idleness,
Who led me to it when she harbored me
Within the pretty orchard, at my prayer!
If she'd been wise, she had refused me then.
Not worth an apple is a fool's request;
Betimes he should be censured and reproved.
I was a fool, and yet she trusted me!
She worked my will too well, but ne'er increased
My welfare; rather brought me tears and grief.
60   "Well warned by Reason, mad I must have been
When I took not the advice she freely gave
And did not quit Love's service right away.
Reason was right to blame me when I lent
Myself to Love, incurring grievous woes.

I think I will repent. Repent? Alas!
How can I? False and traitorous I'd be!
Satan would seize me should I leave my lord
Besides abandoning Fair Welcome quite.
If he for doing me a friendly turn
70 Now languishes in Jealousy's strong tower,
Should I appear to hate him? Courtesy
He did me, certainly—so great a one
As scarce could be believed, when he allowed
My passage through the hedge to kiss the Rose.
I should not show ill will against a friend,
And truly I will not. So help me God,
No more complaints and clamors will you hear
Against the God of Love, or Idleness,
Or Hope, or friend Fair Welcome; all have been
80 Most gracious, and I've wronged them with complaints.
Naught's left save suffering and martyrdom
And waiting for relief that Love may send,
For I expect his mercy; I recall
He said, 'With favor I'll your services   THE GOD OF LOVE
Receive, and raise you to a high degree
Unless misconduct forfeits you that place;
But hope in little space for no great good.'

                                                 THE LOVER
    "These are the very words he used, which showed
He loved me tenderly; then naught remains
90 Except to serve him well, if I'd deserve
His favor, spite of any fault in me.
I'm sure no fault lies in the God of Love;
He fails no man. Then it must be my fault,
Though whence it comes I know not, and perhaps
Shall never know. Now Love may let me die—
Incur or else evade the consequence—
For he must work his will as best he can.
I'll ne'er achieve my purpose if I die;
But, if I live, I'll not without some aid;
100 And, if it be Love's will, who grieves me much,
My purpose to accomplish for me, then
No evil can aggrieve me, for I'm his.
Now wholly to his counsel should I bend,

As is his will, and interfere no more.
But, whatsoever shall encompass me,
I pray the God of Love to be benign
Unto Fair Welcome after I am gone,
Who, without my deserving, caused my death.
Meanwhile, since I cannot his burden bear,
110 To please him ere I die, as lovers do,
Without repentance I'll confession make
To you, Love, and declare my testament:
Unto Fair Welcome I bequeath my heart,
At death; I have no other legacy to leave."

21. Reason remonstrates with the Lover
[4221–4428]

WHILE I lamented thus my griefs aloud,
Knowing no doctor who my woes could heal,
Reason I saw returning straight to me,
Descending from her tower at my complaint.
"Fair friend," the sweet and gracious lady said,   REASON
"How goes the battle? Are you ready now
To leave off loving? Have you had enough?
What think you now of the effects of love?
Are they too bitter or too sweet for you?
10 Wise enough are you now to choose the means
Sufficient for your aid? Fine lord you serve,
Who has accepted and apprenticed you
And yet torments you ceaselessly. The day
You homage paid to him was evil starred.
You were a fool when you got into this;
You knew not with what lord you had to deal.
You'd never have been his if you had known.
You'd not have served a summer or a day
Or even an hour before you had renounced,
20 Without delay, his service and his love.
Do you yet know the man?"

                                  "Lady, I do!"   THE LOVER
          "That is not true!"   REASON
                              "It is!"   THE LOVER
                              "Why think you so?"   REASON
          "Because he said, 'You should be proud to have THE LOVER
So good a master, lord of such renown.' "
          "Know you no more of him than that?"   REASON
                                        "Not I,   THE LOVER
Except that he gave me his rules, and fled
More swift than eagle—left me in suspense."
          "Poor knowledge, certainly! But now I'll give   REASON
You better knowing of the one who brewed
30 Such agonizing drink for you that now
You're quite disfigured. No unfortunate
And caitiff wretch could greater burdens bear
Than you seem to have borne. 'Twere right that you
Know well the lord you serve, and when you do
You'll issue from the prison where you pine."
          "Lady, since he's my lord and I'm his liege,   THE LOVER
Most willingly my heart would hear and learn
His nature, if I found one who could teach."
          "Now, by my head, I'll undertake to show   REASON
40 You all your heart is ripe to understand.
Although the truth be not demonstrable,
I'll give it to you without fallacy.
Although uneducated, you shall learn;
Though inexperienced, you'll quickly grasp
That which can not be proved by syllogism.
This do I know about the God of Love:
No other means to end his dole but flight
Has any man who gives his heart to him;
Thus may you cut the knot that you have tied.
50 To hear me love describe now set your mind.
          "Love is a troubled peace, an amorous war—
A treasonous loyalty, disloyal faith—
A fear that's full of hope, a desperate trust—
A madman's logic, reasoned foolishness—
A pleasant peril in which one may drown—
A heavy burden that is light to bear—
Charybdis gracious, threatening overthrow—

A healthy sickness and most languorous health—
A famine swallowed up in gluttony—
60 A miserly sufficiency of gold—
A drunken thirst, a thirsty drunkenness—
A sadness gay, a frolicsomeness sad—
Contentment that is full of vain complaints—
A soft malignity, softness malign—
A bitter sweetness, a sweet-tasting gall—
A sinful pardon, and a pardoned sin—
A joyful pain—a pious felony—
A game of hazard, ne'er dependable—
A state at once too movable, too firm—
70 An infirm strength, a mighty feebleness
Which in its struggles moves the very world—
A foolish wisdom, a wise foolishness;
It is prosperity both glum and gay—
A laughter full of sighs and full of tears—
Laborious repose by day and night—
A happy Hell, a saddened Paradise—
A prison which delights its prisoners—
A springtime mantled yet with winter's snow—
A moth that feeds on frieze as well as silk,
80 For love lives just as well in coarsest clothes
As in a diaper material.
No man is found so highborn or so wise,
No man of such proved strength and hardiness,
No man of other qualities so good
That Love could never conquer him. The God
Of Love misleads them all; all go his way,
Except they be of evil life, cast out
By Genius, in that they have Nature wronged.
I have no care for these, but nevertheless
90 Would have no person love with such a flame
That in the end he must himself admit
Himself to be unhappy, cheated, grieved,
So much he has been fooled by Love. If now
You wish well to accomplish your escape,
From all Love's grievances to be well cured,
No better potion can you drink than flight;
No elsewise can you happiness enjoy.

Follow Love, and he will you pursue;
Avoid him, and away from you he'll flee."
100 When I'd heard Reason thus in vain debate,
I said, "My lady, I now know no more   THE LOVER
Than hitherto, that might deliver me.
Contrariwise, I understand no whit
(Although I know the lesson all by heart,
So that I can't forget it, having learned
It from you) that applies in fact to me.
Although you have so well this love described,
Praising and blaming it, you've not defined.
I pray that you'll a definition give
110 That I may understand what love may mean."
    "Right readily; I pray that you'll give heed.   REASON
If I know anything of love, it is
Imaginary illness freely spread   *gloss on oxymorons*
Between two persons of opposing sex,
Originating from disordered sight,
Producing great desire to hug and kiss
And seek enjoyment in a mutual lust.
Love cares for nothing but such ardent joys,
For delectation, not engendering,
120 Is all the end of love. Some men there are
Who value such a passion not at all
Yet feign themselves true lovers, and disdain
To love for love itself, but ladies mock
When they their bodies and their souls pretend
To give to those most apt to be deceived.
They swear to fictions till their lust's fulfilled;
Nor can you say that they deceive themselves,
For better 'tis to fool than to be fooled,
Especially when there's no other way.
130 Although no theologian, I know
That every man who with a woman lies
Should wish, as best he may, to procreate
The tenement for an immortal soul,
So that the race's succession may not fail
When he shall go his way to dusty death;
For when the parents die 'tis Nature's wish
That they leave children to perpetuate

Their likeness, and refill the void they've left.
Nature has made the task a pleasant one
140 So that the laborers may like the work
And not be bored and so avoid the job;
For some of them would never lift a tool
But for the pleasure that entices them.
Thus Nature subtly works. But none do right
Who more their pleasure than her ends intend.
What do they do who but of raptures think?
They give themselves as foolish serfs and thralls
Unto the hellish prince of all iniquity."

22. Reason contrasts Youth and Old Age
[4429–4628]

"THE root of vice is lust, as Cicero   REASON
Has written in his book upon Old Age,
Which he exalts and values more than Youth;
For Youth impels all men and maids to deeds
That jeopardize their bodies and their souls.
From shameful ills that curse posterity
They scarcely can escape with life and limb.
   "A man's to dissipation led by Youth,
And introduced to bad companionship
10 And lawless life and purposeless pursuits.
At last, fearful to keep that liberty
That Nature lent him, he to convent goes.
By caging himself there he thinks to catch
The bird of happiness in heaven, unless
He breaks his vows. But oftentimes the load
He finds too grievous, and deserts his cell;
Or, if he ends his life therein, by shame
Held to his vows, he stays against his will,
Living uneasily, lamenting oft
20 The freedom he has lost and can't regain,
Unless God's grace shall his misease efface,

Bestowing patience and obedience.
Youth leads a man to folly and debauch,
To ribaldry, outrage, and lechery,
To instability and quarreling
From which he scarce can extricate himself.
It is Delight, through Youth, her chamberlain,
Who leads in parlous paths the haltered mind
And body of one who sets his heart on joy;
30 For Youth is practiced in all evil schemes
And seeks to find no other work to do
But to entice and lead folk to Delight.

"But Age retrieves from folly. If you doubt,
Recall your youth or ask the older folk
Who've been Youth's victims and remember still
The perils they have passed, the follies done,
The foul desires they have been tempted with,
That have their strength diminished; and how Age,
Who now befriends them like companion good,
40 Recalls to right and leads them till the end.
But badly are Age's services received;
For no one loves or prizes Age enough,
That I know of, to want her for himself.
None to be old and near life's end desires.
The elders marvel and are quite amazed
When they awake their memories and think,
As think they must, of follies overpast,
Of the affairs in which they have escaped
Disgrace and scandal. If they've suffered shame,
50 They wonder how they managed to avoid
A greater loss in body, goods, or soul.

"Know you where Youth, whom many praise, resides?
While of propitious years, she serves Delight,
Who in return maintains Youth in her home.
Youth ministers to her so willingly
She dogs her every step, abandoning
Her body freely to Delight, nor would,
Without her, trouble to prolong her life.

"Do you know where Age lives? I'll tell you soon;
60 For there you'll go unless Death intervene
To lay you low in youth within his cave,

Which dark and somber is. Age has her home
Where Labor dwells with Grief, and both combine
To chain and fetter Age and torture her
And beat her till they bring her near to Death.
Such torments she endures till she repents.
Then tardily there comes the thought that Youth
Has evilly beguiled her, scattering
Her preterit for nothing, bringing her
70 Unto the present bald and most infirm,
And promising a future sans relief
From consequences of her wasted life,
Unless she shall do penance for the sins
That she committed in her youth, and gain
The sovereign good from which Youth parted her
When she made brief her days with vanities,
And never thought how short is time, that flies
Before a man can count or measure it.
    "However goes the game, both he and she—
80 And be she maid or wife—who would enjoy
Love's full delight should fruitful issue seek
And play their parts through to the very end.
I know some women fear to bear a child,
Counting it great mischance if they conceive;
But they, unless they're fools or ignorant
Or quite unruled by Shame, make no complaint.
Who set themselves unto the work of Love
Do so but for Delight, unless they be
Unworthy whores who sell themselves for coin
90 And whose vile life unfits them for all joy.
She who would yield herself for any price
Cannot be good. One should have naught to do
With any woman who her body sells.
Would one think woman held her body dear
Who willingly would flay herself alive?
Most wretchedly deceived is one who thinks
That such a woman loves him, just because
She smiles and feasts him, calling him her dear.
A beast like him deserves not such a name
100 Nor to be loved at all. No man should prize
A woman who but hopes to plunder him.

I say not that a woman may not wear
With pleasure and delight the jewelry
Her sweetheart freely gives or sends to her,
But that she should demand it not, for fear
That he will take it ill of her. And she
May freely give him presents in return.
The interchange alike of love and gifts
Unites their hearts more closely. I would have
110 Them do whatever well-bred lovers should
When they keep company. But let them guard
Against Love's follies, which enflame and burn
The heart, and let their love unselfish be;
For selfishness incites false hearts to greed.
True love should have its birth from noble heart, *gentilesse*
Not of the carnal will that masters men.
Carnal delight itself impersonates
That love which has so caught you in its net
That you can have no other wish or dream
120 Of good but your desire to gain the Rose.
But not two fingers' space is your advance
Toward the wished end; this mortifies your flesh
And robs you of your strength. A sorry guest
You entertained when first you harbored Love;
A sorry guest remains now in your house.
Therefore, 'tis my advice you turn him out
Before he robs you of all noble thoughts
That you should have. Let him no more remain!
Those who are drunk with love great mischief feel.
130 This will you know at last when you have spent
Your time, and wasted youth, in this sad sport.
If you shall live until you free yourself
Of love, you will lament the time you've lost,
But never can recover it again.
Yet to escape most fortunate you'd be;
For in the trap in which you now are caught
Many lose time and goods, body and mind and soul."

23. Reason expounds the higher love
[4629–4836]

THUS Reason preached, but Love set all at naught;
For though I heard the sermon word for word
I took no stock in it, so drawn was I
To Love, who still my every thought pursued
Like hunter, following me everywhere,
And ever kept my heart beneath his wing.
When he spied me thus sitting, as in church,
Out at one ear he shoveled from my head
Whate'er in at the other Reason pitched;
10 So she not only vainly spent her pains
But even angered me, till I replied:
"Madam, you would betray me; should I scorn   THE LOVER
All folk because the God of Love now frowns?
Shall I no more experience true love,
But live in hate? Truly, so help me God,
Then were I mortal sinner worse than thief!
Make no mistake! By one means must I win:
Either I'll love or hate. Perchance at last
I'll buy the hate more dear, though love be worth
20 No penny of my cash. 'Tis good advice
You give me now—that I should Love renounce.
He were a fool who'd disbelieve in you.
But you've recalled another kind of love,
Less known, perhaps, but sometimes entertained,
Which I've not heard you blame. If you'll define
This love to me, consider me a fool
If I pay ill attention to your words.
I'd learn, if I am able, at the least
The various kinds of loving, if you please."
30   "Certainly you would be but a fool,   REASON
Fair friend, if you cared not a straw for one
Who preaches to you for your good. I'm glad

To answer your request with all my skill,
Though I am doubtful if 'twill profit you.
   "Many and various are the kinds of love
Besides the one which has upset your sense.
You came to know that love in evil hour;
Please God you soon may drive it from your heart!
One kind of love is friendship, that unites
40 Two hearts so close in mutual accord
That no discord can interrupt their love,
Which seems like the benevolence of God.
'Twixt such friends there should be community,
In loving charity, of all their goods,
That no exception they may think to make.
Neither should hesitate in other's aid,
But be alike firm, loyal, ready, wise;
For wit is worthless without loyalty.
Whatever either one may dare to think
50 He should, as with himself, with his friend share
Securely, without fear to be betrayed.
Such custom should those have who'd be true friends.
No man can truly amiable be
Unless he is, in spite of Fortune, firm
And stable, that his friend, who's set his heart
On him, may find him e'er the same, in wealth
Or poverty. And if he see his friend
Decline in riches, he should never wait
Until he's asked to give his aid; for help
60 That must be begged for is too dearly bought
By one who's worthy of the name of friend.
   "Great shame it were for worthy man to beg;
And long he thinks and fears, is ill at ease,
Ere he will ask, ashamed to say his say,
Dreading refusal. But if he has found
A friend whose love he has already proved
A certainty, he'll tell both cares and joys
To such a one, whatever case arise,
And feel no shame. Why should he hesitate
70 With such a friend as I've described to you?
No third will learn the secret that he tells.
No reprimand he fears. To hold his tongue

The wise man better knows than do the fools
Who never silence keep. A friend will do
Whate'er he can to ease his friend's distress;
More readily he gives than that one takes.
Or, if one cannot grant his friend's request,
One feels more grief than he, and so one knows
The mastery of love. One bears his share
80 Of his friend's dolor, and one comforts him,
If each has equal share in other's love,
Well as one can; as one would share his joy.
    "In one of his discourses Tully says
That by the law of friendship one should grant
The honorable request of any friend,
Expecting him to do the same if asked
For anything that's reasonable and right.
There are but two exceptions to this rule:
No one should give his aid to take a life
90 Or bring disgrace upon an honored name.
In these two cases should a friend refrain,
But not refuse whatever else love ask.
Such love is not opposed to Reason's rule;
And 'tis my will you follow such a love,
Eschewing other kinds. All virtue this
Supports, but other love leads men to death.
    "Another, adverse, love will I describe,
As worthy to be blamed as this one praised;
cupidity It is feigned love in hearts that are diseased
100 With malady of direful covetousness.
So easily unbalanced is this love
That soon as it sees hope of profit lost
It fails and is extinguished, for true heart
Must love folk for themselves or not at all,
Rather than feign or flatter for reward.
Fortune-following love eclipses soon
As does the moon that falls into the shade
Of mother earth, which shadows and obscures,
Obstructing all the glory of the sun,
110 But, when the shadow passes, reassumes
Its former brightness from the solar rays.
So is vile love: first bright and then obscure.

As soon as Poverty's dark, hideous robe
Prevents the sight of Riches' golden glow,
Such love finds it convenient to depart,
But reillumines when wealth comes again.
It grows when riches grow, fails when they fail.
  "Such love alone do wealthy people gain,
Especially the avaricious ones
120 Who will not wash their hearts clean of the filth
And sin of greedy, burning covetousness.
No cuckold crowned with horns like tufted stag
Is half so silly as a rich old man
Who thinks that he is loved but for himself.
He who has ne'er another truly loved
Proclaims himself a fool if he suppose
That he's adored. He is more simple far
Than a fair-antlered deer. He who desires
True friends must friendly show himself.
130 One proves his love not when he clutches fast
His riches though he see his friends in need
And plans to keep his wealth till he depart
And hateful death fetter his mouth for good.
Rather he'd see himself torn limb from limb
Than share his wealth and see it melt away;
And so he cannot love, for in what heart
That lacks real pity can a friendship reign?
When man acts thus, one knows what is his state:
Blameworthy is the one who loves not, nor is loved." *one must love to be virtuous*

24. Reason describes the Wheel of Fortune
[4837-4974]

"NOW in our sermon we to Fortune come,   REASON
Of whom I'll tell a marvel you've ne'er heard.
You'll doubt me, but the statement's true, and found
Written in treatises: more profitable
To man bad fortune is than easy lot.

This paradox can easily be proved:
Fair fortune and a life of ease delude
With sweetest milk, like mothers, suckling men,
Seemingly only born to foster them
10 And give them jewels, honors, dignities,
High place and wealth, promised stability
Amidst all change—and feeding them with pride
In all the prosperousness of worldly rank.
When they mount high upon her fickle wheel,
They think their masterships have risen so much
That from their station proud they ne'er can fall.
She makes them think their friends infallible
And numberless, as they all come and go
About them, making them appear like lords,
20 Saying that they'd do anything for them,
E'en strip their own shirts off their backs, and shed
Blood from their veins them to defend and keep—
Be prompt to serve and follow all their lives.
Those hark'ning to such words are glorified,
And they believe them all like Gospel truth;
Yet soon they know 'twas guileful flattery,
When past recovery they've lost their wealth.
Then they see how their friends all act. If one
Out of a hundred sycophants remains,
30 Though all were relatives, they may thank God.
When Fortune makes her home with men, she starves
Their sense, but nourishes their ignorance.
    "Ill Fortune, on the other hand, when she
Upsets men's high estate and tumbles them
Low in the mire from off her turning wheel
And like a stepdame lays upon their hearts
A painful poultice, spent and thin, not strong
With vinegar, this teaches them the truth
That none should boast they're Fortune's favorites;
40 For no security they have. They learn
To know, when they have lost their wealth, what love
Those had for them who erstwhile were their friends;
For they whom then prosperity amazed
Are now astounded at adversity.
Seeing their patrons stripped, not one remains—

Not half of one!—but all depart and say
They never knew the poor unfortunate.
Nor do they stop at that, but everywhere
They scorn him, blame him, call him wretched fool.
50 Not even those who profited the most
Will say their folly lost his goods for him.
None will be found to help unless there are
True friends who have such noble hearts that they
Ne'er loved him for his wealth, and had no hope
Of profit. These defend and aid the man;
For Fortune has no influence on their hearts.
Eternal in his love is a true friend.
Friends' affection can't be cut in two—
Not even by drawn sword—excepting thus:
60 Man loses friends by anger, pride, reproach,
Or by revealing secrets he should keep,
Or by detraction—a foul, dolorous plague.
In cases of this kind will Friendship flee;
Naught else will injure her. But 'twould be strange
Were one true friend among a thousand found.
Since no amount of wealth can reach the price
Of one such friend—no value gain such height
That Friendship will not higher be—I say:
' 'Tis better to meet friends upon the road
70 Than to have cash in purse.' Misfortune shows,
When upon men it falls with sad mischance,
Most clearly who deserves the name of friend;
And such experience proves he's worth more
Than any wealthy man has in this world.
Thus is adversity of much more worth
Than is prosperity; for this provides
But ignorance, while knowledge comes from that.
Poverty such demonstration gives
As will distinguish true friends from the false.
80 One recognizes then, and understands,
What kind of friends they were when he was rich
Who offered him their bodies, souls, and goods.
Is any price too high for such advice?
Less had he been deceived if he had known!
From Poverty he's great advantage gained;

For it has made a wise man from a fool,
Which wealth had never done till lost by some mischance."

25. Reason defines true happiness
[4975–5182]

"WEALTH ne'er enriches truly one whose heart   REASON
Is set on money; sole sufficiency
Makes men live richly. One not worth two loaves
May be more rich and more at ease than he
Who has a hundred hogsheads full of wheat.
Suppose the latter is a merchant, torn
With care enough before his store is gained,
Then doubly, to increase and multiply;
Nor ever will he think to have enough,
10 However much he painfully acquires.
But happy he who asks but daily bread,
Lives on his income, finds it adequate,
And though his sole possession is a sou
Has little fear of losing it—knows well
That he can earn what he may need to eat,
Fitly to clothe himself, and mend his shoes.
If he fall ill and find all viands flat,
He knows he has no need of dainty food,
And recollects that diet is the cure
20 Most like to lead him on the road to health;
Or, anyway, a little will suffice.
Perhaps he thinks he never will be ill,
Or that the Hospital will care for him
In such a case, or that there's time enough
To ponder that when illness shall arrive.
Perhaps he finds some solace in the thought
That, if he nothing save for rainy day,
When frost or heat or hunger threatens death
He'll much more quickly get to Paradise,
30 Which he believes God has prepared for him

When he shall leave the exile of this world.
Pythagoras's *Verses Aureate*
Are famous for the phrasing of this thought:
'When from the body you depart, all free   PYTHAGORAS
You mount to Heaven, leaving worldliness
And living ever in pure deity.'
He is a fool who thinks the earth his home: REASON
Not even is the world one's native land,
As you may learn if you will ask the clerks
40 Who read the statements of Boethius
In *Consolation of Philosophy.*
(Who should translate it would do men much good!)
Happy is he who lives within his means
And nothing more desires, but ever thinks
That he is free from poverty. The book
Says, 'No man's wretched if he thinks he's not.'   BOETHIUS
It's as true of peasant as of knight or king.   REASON
Many a servant has a happy heart
Bearing his charcoal through the Place de Grève
50 Untroubled by the burden, since he works
In patience. He will hop and skip and jump
Toward Saint Marcel for his poor meal of tripe,
Nor ever hoard his pennyworth of wealth,
But in the tavern all his savings spend;
Then back to bear his burdens, not in pain
But in pure joy, for he has earned his bread
And ne'er is tempted to defraud or steal.
Returning to the tavern, he will drink
And live as live he should. Rich are all such,
60 Abundantly, in thinking they've enough;
God knows they're honester than usurers.
No usurer can actually be rich,
For covetousness makes him suffer want.
    "Whoever it displease to hear the truth,
I say no merchant ever lives at ease;
He has for life enlisted in the war
Of gain, and never will acquire enough.
Though what he has he fears to lose, he runs
After the remnant which he'll ne'er possess.
70 His only thought's to get his neighbor's goods.

As well he might tremendous effort make
To drink up at a draft the river Seine,
Which more supplies no matter how he drinks.
This is the anguish, this is the distress,
This is the greedy fire that ever burns,
This is the dolor, this the constant fight
That wounds his heart with fear of future want.
The more he gets, the more he seems to lack.
   "Doctor and lawyer both such fetters wear,
80 And, if they sell their skill for cash, they'll hang
By such a rope. The one would gladly see,
So sweet and pleasant does he find his gain,
Threescore in place of every invalid;
The other fain would have, for every suit,
Thirty at least or ten or twenty score,
So strongly he's by selfishness impelled.
As bad divines are who overrun the earth,
Preaching to gain favor, honor, wealth;
Their hearts feel like distress; they live in sin.
90 But worst are those who purchase their soul's death
By following Vainglory's treacherous path.
Deceived are such deceivers, for such priests
Are never profitable to themselves
Whatever good they may for others do;
For evil purpose, when it fails its end,
May yet produce a sermon that does good.
The hearers may a good example take
The while Vainglory damns the sermoner.
   "Leaving the Preachers, we'll of misers speak.
100 No love nor fear of God have they who hoard
More than they need of treasure in their chests
When out-of-doors they see the shivering poor
And starving hungry. God will make them pay.
Who lead such lives a triple vengeance feel:
The toil by which they wealth acquire; the fear
In which they ceaselessly their treasures guard;
The pain with which they leave them at the end.
In such a torment misers live and die.
All is from lack of love, so scarce on earth.
110 If such men loved, they would be loved again,

And perfect love would reign throughout the world.
No evil would be done; the more one had,
The more to those who were in want he'd give
Or lend for charity, not usury,
Provided their intentions were the best
And they were not with idleness attaint.
No poverty or wealth would then be seen
But where it was deserved, throughout the earth.
But so degenerate is all the world
120 That it has put up love for sale; no man
Loves but for his own profit, or for gift
Or service he may gain. E'en women sell
Themselves; may all such bargains have bad end!
    "Thus by Deceit are all on earth disgraced,
And goods once common portioned out to few,
Who, bound in chains by Avarice, submit
Their native freedom to vile servitude—
Slaves to the gold that in their coffers lies.
Themselves and not their goods are prisoners.
130 Such wretched, earthy toads are riches' slaves.
They cannot understand that wealth's no good
Except to spend; they think it's but to keep,
Which is not true. They never deign to use
But always hoard their cash. They may go hang,
For spite of all their pains it will be spent
When in the end they die and spendthrift heirs
Shall dissipate it all most joyfully;
Then little good of it the misers have.
Nor are they sure to keep it until then;
140 Tomorrow's rising sun may see it snatched away."

26. Reason discourses on Wealth and Justice
[5183–5588]

"RICHES are wronged by those who would divert   REASON
Them from their native use, which is to flow

Quick to the aid and succor of distress,
Not to be lent for usury; for God
Has furnished misers all that they keep hid.
Diverted from their destined functioning,
Riches avenge themselves upon such hosts.
Most shamefully they shadow, lurk, and draw
Three swords with which to pierce the hoarder's heart:
10 The first is toil by which the wealth's acquired;
The second, heartfelt fear of robbers' wiles,
Which ceaselessly dismays; the third is grief
That all must soon be left. As I have said,
Most miserably are misers self-deceived.
     "So, like a queen or highborn dame, does Wealth
Revenge herself on slaves who hold her fast.
Reposing herself in quiet peace, she makes
Those wretches lie awake with toil and care.
Close fettered at her feet she keeps them cowed
20 So that she has all honor, they all shame
Who languish in the torment of her rule.
No profit comes to one thus bound to her,
For she'll live on when he who dares not rouse
Her to activity shall end his life.
But valiant men will harness her and ride,
And make her gallop as they ply their spurs,
Wholeheartedly enjoying holiday.
They'll take example of old Daedalus,
Who formed the wings, by magic not by skill,
30 With which Icarus made the air his road.
So will they make Wealth wings with which to fly,
Who otherwise would but torment them so
That they'd no honor have nor praise by her.
Then they'll ne'er be reproved for avarice,
Inordinate desire, or covetous sin.
Rather they'll reputation get from Wealth
For courtesy that's known throughout the world,
For overflowing virtue, generous hearts,
Most grateful unto God, who generously
40 With His own goods did fill the world when He
Had made it. (Who but I e'er told you this?)
As Avarice her stench to heaven sends,

Free-handed, courteous Generosity
Sends up perfume. God hates the miserly
And damns them as uncouth idolaters—
Malodorous wretches—slaves unreasonable,
Although they think and say they only hoard
Their money as assurance against want.
    "O sweet terrestrial Wealth! Say, do you bless
50 Those folk who lock you up within their walls?
Do they not tremble all the more with fear
The more they get of you? State so unsure
Cannot be happiness. Should such a gift,
That can no calm assurance give, seem blest?
    "Perhaps someone who hears me rail at Wealth
May cite in refutation mighty lords
Who, as the common folk suppose, for praise
Of their nobility, take utmost pains
To hem themselves about with armèd men—
60 Five hundred or five thousand infantry—
And of their valor thus give evidence.
Quite contrary's the case, as God well knows:
It's grievous, haunting fear that prompts the show.
A beggar of La Grève more safely walks
Alone where'er he will, and e'en may dance
Among the thieves, unfearing their intent,
Than can a king in his fur-bordered robe
Bear with him all the treasure he's amassed
In gold and precious stones; for every thief,
70 Wherever he may go, will take his share,
And kill the king himself upon the spot
Lest he should have the robber caught and hanged.
The king's own strength is not two apples' worth
Greater than is the happy beggar's power;
But through his men he works. Oh, no; I lie!
They're not his men who own his seignory;
Though he's their lord, he must their freedom guard.
Rather he's theirs, for all his power depends
Upon his servants' will; if they remove
80 Their aid, which they may do whene'er they will,
The king remains alone. He has no claim
Upon the people's valor, wit, or might,

Nor on their bodies or their property.
Nature denies him this; they are not his.
Nor Fortune, be she e'er so debonair
To men, can more perform in giving things
Which Nature has denied, strive as she may."

 "Ah, madam, by the king of Heaven," I cried THE LOVER
"Tell me what things may certainly be mine,
90 Or if I can claim ought to be mine own."

 "Yes," she responded, "but not house nor land REASON
Nor robes nor rich adornments, worldly goods,
Nor any sort of furniture, but things
That better and more costly are by far:
What you within you have and know you have,
That ever will remain and never leave
To do another service; it is yours.
External goods are not worth anything
To you or any other man who lives.
100 You really own naught but what is within;
All other things are Fortune's property
Which she broadcasts or gathers at her will,
And gives or takes to make fools laugh or cry.
No wise man prizes aught that Fortune does;
Her turning wheel makes such nor glad nor glum.
Well may we doubt her instability.
Therefore the love of her is far from wise,
And most disgraceful in a man of wit;
Nor should it, easily eclipsed, delight.
110 By no means ought you set your heart on it;
Soil yourself never with so great a sin.
If ever you have called yourself a friend,
And yet have sinned in that you loved for gain,
You should be much disdained by all good men.
Believe me and be wise. The love I've named
You should renounce and leave as something vile.
I see also that you were splitting hairs
When you imputed malice to my lore,
Declaring that I give commands to hate.
120 What have I said that you interpret thus?"

 "All day you've urged, and haven't finished yet, THE LOVER
That I renounce my lord for some rude love

city of licentiousness - Dido, Augustine in youth

I know not what. To Carthage one might go
And search from west to east, from north to south,
And live until one's teeth fell out for age,
Scouring the earth with utmost diligence
Until all had been seen, and yet not find
The sort of love that you've described to me.
When gods of old before the giants fled,
130 And Chastity, Good Faith, and Law withdrew,
That love, I ween, was swept clean from the earth,
Or so dismayed it lost itself in flight.
Even ponderous Justice fled at last.
All left the world—they couldn't stand the wars—
To make their habitations in the skies,
Descending thenceforth but in miracles.
The gods were driven out by force of Fraud,
Who now with outrage holds their heritage.
    "Not even Tully, who took careful pains
140 To search all secret writings, could find out,
For all his ingenuity, that e'er
In all the ages since the world began
Have there been couples more than three or four
Who knew this perfect love; and I believe,
For never have I read of such a thing,
That fewer yet who lived in Tully's time
Proved by their words that they were such-like friends.
Am I more wise than Tully? I should be
A sottish fool were I to search for love
150 That is not to be found upon the earth.
Where should I look for what does not exist?
Can I fly with the cranes beyond the clouds
As did in truth the swan of Socrates?
I'll silent be; I've no such foolish hope.
The gods would think I threatened Paradise,
As did the giants once, and hurl their bolts
At me. Perhaps this is the end you seek;
'Twere, doubtless, in accord with your ill will."
    "Fair friend," said she, "now listen. If that love   REASON
160 Is unattainable, as well may be
In your case as in others, for your faults,
I'll tell you of another—no, the same

In different guise—which all men may attain.
It is a mere extension of true love,   *fin amor*
Embracing all mankind, not only one.
Participating in community
Of love, you may love all in general,
And love all loyally. Love the whole world
As you would one, with all-embracing love.
170 Be to all men what you'd have all men be
Golden Rule To you; do naught but what you would have done
To you again. If thus you show your love,
All will cry quits. This course you should pursue;
Without this trait no man should ever live.
Because unrighteous folk desert such love,
Justices are appointed on the earth
To be defense and refuge for the weak,
To punish and chastise the criminal,
And make him mend his ways who has renounced
180 True love, and wounds or kills his fellow man,
Or ravishes or robs or steals or harms
By false detraction or conspired complaint
Or other evil means, open or hid.
It is such men that Justice must control."

"Ah, lady, since you speak of Justice now,   THE LOVER
Who formerly was of so great renown,
For God's sake tell me something about her."

"Most willingly! Say what you wish to know."   REASON

                                                 THE LOVER
"Make judgment for me, then, 'twixt her and Love.
190 Which, as it seems to you, is worth the more?"
"To what species of love do you refer?"   REASON
"To that in whom you wish me to confide;   THE LOVER
I need not bring to bar the Love I know."

"Poor fool, believe that, if you will! In truth   REASON
The good love I describe has greater worth."
"Prove that."   THE LOVER

                 "I will most gladly. Of two things   REASON
Both profitable, proper, necessary,
The one that is most needed is worth more."

"Lady, you speak the truth."   THE LOVER

                 "You'll not deny,   REASON
200 Considering the nature of these two,

That needful and of profit is each one."

"That's true."   THE LOVER

        "The best of these most profit has?"   REASON

"That I agree."   THE LOVER

        "Then let me more recall: REASON
The love I praise, that springs from charity,
A greater necessity than justice is."

"Prove that ere you go on."   THE LOVER

        "Most willingly.   REASON
I say, without deceit, more necessary
And better is the thing that can suffice
All by itself to make one choose the best
210 Than that which needs extraneous aid. Can you
Deny me this?"

      "Why not? Make it more clear,   THE LOVER
That I may see that you're not tricking me.
Ere I agree, I'd an example have."

"My faith! You place on me a heavy task   REASON
With your demands for instances and proofs.
However, an example you shall have,
Since there's no other way to make you see.
If without aid a man could sail a boat
Better than you, you'd say he was more skilled?"

              THE LOVER

220 "Yes, dame; at least he'd better know the ropes."

"Take this, then, as sufficient simile.   REASON
If justice failed, then love would be enough
To lead men in a fair and perfect life
Without the aid of law; but, without love,
Justice could not. Therefore is love the best."

"Prove that to me."   THE LOVER

       "I will if you'll keep still!   REASON
Once Justice reigned, when Saturn was supreme;
But Jupiter the cullions of his sire
Cut off as they had been but sausages
230 (A cruel and hardhearted son was he!)
And flung them in the sea, whence Venus sprang,
Goddess of Love, as you may read in books.
If she came back to earth and was received
Today as once she was, there still were need

That men should love each other mutually
No matter how much justice they-observed;
For justice were destructive without love.
But were men joined in mutual love no wrong
Would any to another do; and vice
240 Thus banished, what of good could Justice do?"
    "Lady, I know not."   THE LOVER
                    "I believe you don't.   REASON
All the inhabitants of this fair world
Quiet and peacefully would live; no king
Nor prince they'd have—no bailiff or provost—
So honest they would be; judges would hear
No clamoring for justice. So I say
That justice is worth less than simple love.
Though Justice against Malice may prevail—
Mother of liberty—destroying Rule—
250 Yet, were the earth not soiled with crime and sin,
Mankind would have no use for judge or king.
Judges have proved most odiously that they
Ought first to judge themselves, since 'tis their wish
That men confide in them; and they should be
Both diligent and true, not negligent
Or covetous, pretentious, lax, or false
In doing right by all who make complaints.
But now they sell their judgments, and upset
All precedents; they tally, count, erase;
260 And poor folk pay—rob Peter to pay Paul.
Such judge who hangs a thief should hang himself,
If he would render judgment on the wrongs
And rapines that his misused power has often caused."

27. Reason narrates the story of Virginia
[5589–5794]

"OLD Titus Livius recounts the case   REASON
Of Appius, who well deserved to hang

For making his vile sergeant undertake
False cause by falser oath against a maid,
Virginia, child of Virginius.
Because he was not able to seduce
The girl, who hated him and lechery,
The ribald cried in open court, 'O judge,   SERGEANT
Give justice to me, for the maid is mine.
10 Against the world I'll prove she is my slave;
For, wheresoever she has been brought up,
She had her birth within my house. When young
Thence stolen, to Virginius she was given.
Now, Appius, I claim my slave again;
'Tis right that she should serve me, not this man
Who merely brought her up. If he deny
This charge, I'll prove it by good witnesses.'
Thus spoke the evil traitor, Appius' tool;   REASON
And ere Virginius could speak, who stood
20 Ready to confound his adversary,
The evil judge, without the least delay,
By heavy sentence made her Claudius' slave.
Now when Virginius, the noble knight,
Renowned as honest man, the judgment heard
And knew that he no longer could defend
His daughter from the lust of Appius,
But that she must her body yield to shame,
By resolution simply marvelous
Transforming the disgrace to tragedy
30 (If Titus Livius do not lie), for love
And not for hate his daughter's head cut off
And gave it to the judge before the court.
According to the story, this bad judge
Commanded that Virginius be seized
And led away, sentenced to hang and die.
But neither was he hanged nor killed; for when
The people knew the case they were so moved
With pity that they put a stop to that.
Then Appius was imprisoned for the crime,
40 And ere he came to trial he killed himself.
The plaintiff, Claudius, was then adjudged
Worthy of death. Virginius interposed,

Through pity, and procured him a reprieve,
Persuading folk to vote him banishment.
But the false witnesses were put to death.
    "Judges, in short, too oft commit outrage.
Read wise old Lucan's statement that no man
Has ever yet seen power and virtue joined.
But let such judges know, if they persist
50 And make no restitutions for the wrongs,
The everlasting Judge Omnipotent
In Hell among the devils will enchain
Them by their necks. I no exception make
Of king or prelate, judge of any kind,
Cleric or laic. They are honored not
That they may do such things; but without bribe
They should pursue to proper end each cause
That's brought to them, their portals opening wide
To every plaintiff, hearing personally
60 Every complaint, be it or wrong or right.
'Tis not for nothing that they honor have.
They should not be puffed up, but serve the folk
Who populate and fructify the land;
For they have sworn their oaths to do what's right,
As they should do. By them should live in peace
The honest folk, while they the bad pursue
And hang the robbers, if from out their hands
No other willingly such office takes;
For 'tis their function to see justice done.
70 On this should judges place their whole intent;
It is for this that they receive their pay,
And this they vowed when first they office took.
    "Now, if you've listened, you've had your request,
And I have given you proof that seems complete."
    "Lady," I said, "you've surely paid me well,   THE LOVER
And I should be appeased and give you thanks;
But one unseemly word I heard you use,
So wanton, it appears, that whoso would
Be minded to accuse and catch you up
80 Would find you destitute of all defense."
    Said she, "Well know I what you're thinking of.   REASON
Another time, whenever you may wish,

If you'll remind me, please, I'll make excuse."
"Yes, truly I'll remind you of that word,"   THE LOVER
Said I, "for keen my recollection is.
My master has forbidden that I speak
Of ribaldry, but I'll at least repeat
What I have heard, and name the word outright.
It's well to expose the folly that men speak;
90 And all the more, since wisdom you pretend,
Should I denounce and make you see your sin."
        "I'll listen; but I must forbid," said she,   REASON
"That you accuse me, moved thereto by hate.
I wonder how you dare say such a thing.
Do you not see that it's illogical
For you, escaping from one foolishness,
To fall into a greater or as great?
If I advise avoiding foolish love,
Must I therefore commend to enmity?
100 Do you recall what sage old Horace said:
'When fools escape one vice, they often turn   HORACE
To opposite extreme—no better off'?
He was no fool; and you should understand   REASON
Me to forbid no love except that kind
Which can but wound those folk who harbor it.
So if from drunkenness I should you warn,
I would not say you must not drink at all.
Such counsel were not worth a peppercorn.
If I advise against unthriftiness,
110 Well might I be considered imbecile
To counsel avarice, an equal sin.
I'm making no such argument to you."
        "Truly, you are!"   THE LOVER
                "Now, certainly, you lie!   REASON
Unflattering to you my words may be,
But when you try rebuttal of my points
You seem not to have read the ancient books,
For you're illogical in argument.
It is not thus that I have read of love;
Never my lips have said that man should hate.
120 Man finds a middle course in that calm love
Which strongly I uphold and try to teach.

" 'Tis natural love Dame Nature gives to beasts,
By which they bring their young to birth, and which
Provides these with their proper nourishment.
If natural love you wish me to define,
I'll say perpetuation of a race
By generation and by nourishment
Supplies the proper purpose of such love.
This love is common to all men and beasts.
130 However necessary such a love may be,
Its merit calls for neither praise nor blame;
Nature requires what's neither good nor bad.
'Twere blameworthy to break Dame Nature's laws;
To oppose her is no victory o'er vice.
What praise is due a hungry man who eats?
He merits blame if he forswears his food.
But I'll pass on; 'tis no such love you mean.
Far madder love than this you have embraced,
Which you'd best leave if you care for your good."

28. Reason offers her love
[5795–5920]

"NEVERTHELESS, I certainly advise   REASON
That you should not remain without a friend.
Why not take me—a gentlewoman fair
Worthy to serve the Emperor of Rome?
I'm willing; and, if me you will accept,
Do you know what my love is worth to you?
So much that you'll not want for anything
Which proper is, whatever may betide.
You'll find yourself so great a lord that ne'er
10 Was any greater known; and I will do
Whate'er you wish. Never too great desire
Can you conceive, if you will do my will;
And 'twere unfitting to do otherwise.
You'll have the great advantage of a friend

Of lineage that is beyond compare,
Daughter of God the Father, who conceived
And made me what I am. Regard this form,
And gaze in these clear eyes. No titled maid
E'er loved with such abandon as do I;
20 For I have from my father fullest leave
To love and to be loved, and not be blamed.
Nor need you fear reproach, for we shall have,
O'er both of us at once, my father's guard.
Does that sound good? Answer; what do you think?
That god who made you act so foolishly,
Knows he so well to pay his vassalage?
Does he give such good wage to those poor fools
Whose homage he accepts? Do not refuse
My offer; have a care, for maidens scorned
30 Are all too shamed and grieved, unwont to beg,
For which is Echo's case sufficient proof."

THE LOVER

"Your words are Greek to me. In language plain *ironic*
Tell me how 'tis you wish that I should serve."

REASON

"Let me serve you; but be my loyal friend.
Forsake the god who brought you to this pass.
Scorn Fortune's wheel, which is not worth a prune.
Be like old Socrates, who was so firm
And stable that in his prosperity
He ne'er rejoiced; nor grieved in indigence.
40 Good and ill fortune he in balance set
And found them like in weight. To no extreme
Of happiness or sorrow he gave way;
Nor glad nor sorry he, whate'er befell.
Solinus has well said he was the man
Apollo's oracle adjudged most wise.
Whate'er occurred, his face was always calm;
He was unmoved when hemlock doomed to drink
Because he'd not admit of many gods
But put his faith in one, and preached that man
50 By numerous deities should never swear.
Heraclitus, Diogenes refused
With equal courage to be cowed by woe
Or poverty—in resolution firm

Sustained mischances that occurred to them.
If you would serve me, do not otherwise.
By Fortune's turns however much abused
And tortured, guard lest you should be cast down.
He is no adversary good and strong
Who struggles not when Fortune seeks to beat
60 And with her cudgeling discomfit him.
He should defend himself most vigorously
And not give in; for Fortune faintly fights,
In palace or in dunghill, if opposed.
Who struggles well may win at the first blow.
Who fears her is not brave; who knows her strength
And knows his own should not be tripped by her
Unless he voluntarily falls down.
Disgraceful 'tis to see a man, who might
Defend himself, into the hangman's noose
70 Submit his head. No greater indolence
Could be than that he shows. It would be wrong
To waste regret on such a worthless one.
Take care, then, that you naught from her accept
Or help or honor; let her turn her wheel
Forever and a day without a rest,
Blindfolded, sitting in the midst of it.
She blinds the rich with honor and renown—
Others with poverty. But when she will
She takes back all her gifts. Great fool is he
80 Who finds in anything delight or grief,
For certainly he can defend himself
By power of will alone. Another thing
Most certain is: men say she is divine
And raise her to the skies, which is not right.
Nor rhyme nor reason gives her heavenly home;
Her house is perilous instead of being blest."

29. Reason describes the ambiguous Isle of Fortune
[5921–6182]

"AMIDST the deepest sea juts up an isle   REASON
Upon whose rocks the breakers ever beat,
Grumbling and quarreling at his defense.
Always at war with him, the billows strike
And, as they deal their blows, ofttimes succeed
In burying his head beneath the waves;
But then again the giant frees himself
Of all the water that has flooded him,
And, as the waves draw back, he lifts his head
10 And breathes again. But no one shape he keeps,
Transmuting and transforming his disguise,
His clothing changing e'er to something new.
Sometimes, when Zephyr rides the sea, he decks
His lifted head with grasses green, and flowers
Like heaven's flaming stars. Again he reaps,
With freezing sword, the flowerets and grass,
So that they die as soon as they are born
When cold Boreas blows his breath on them.
    "Ambiguous forest of amazing trees
20 Of strange varieties this rock supports.
Sterile are some and nothing ever bear,
Others delight in offering plenteous fruit;
Some never cease to be in flower, and some
Are naked quite of blooms; while some remain
Ever in leaf, some ne'er show foliage;
Some wither while the others flourish green;
If one tree raise his head, his neighbor trees
Incline to earth; and buds, that grow on some,
Are on some others blasted utterly.
30 Each tree there takes the form of other tree;
While stands the giant broom, the dwarf pine squats;
The laurel leaf that should be green is brown;

Barren the olive that should fecund be;
Willows, against their nature, bring forth fruit;
The elm excels the vine in bearing grapes.
There rarely chant the nightingales; but oft
The broad-faced screech owls make lament and cry,
Prophets of evil, messengers of grief.
　　"From different sources spring two neighbor streams,
40 Winter and summer flowing there, diverse
In flavor, color, form. Water from one
Is fine and pleasant, and so honeylike
That one who tastes it overdrinks himself
Yet cannot slake his thirst with all its charm;
The more he quaffs, the more he wants to drink.
None sips of it without becoming drunk,
Yet none can free himself from his desire.
The sweetness of the water so deceives
That those who try to stanch their thirst but wish
50 To fill themselves more full. They are so fain
That each of them becomes quite dropsical.
Most prettily this river flows along
And murmurs in a melody more sweet
Than that of timbrel or of tambourine.
Whoever sees the stream explores its course;
And many haste to enter it, but stop
Forthwith, as powerless to forge ahead.
They scarce can wet their feet, and hardly touch
The waters sweet, no matter how they try.
60 But if they drink not more than smallest sip
And savor its deliciousness, they plunge
All willingly within the deep profound.
Others rush headlong down to swim the stream;
They bathe themselves within its gulf, and shout
How much at ease they are; but one small wave
Carries them back till on the bank they lie,
Burning and heartsick at their ill success.
　　"Of the other river's nature now I'll tell.
Tenebrous are its waters sulphurous;
70 Like smoking chimney evilly it smells,
And scummy is its surface. It descends
Not softly but with such a hideous roar

That worse than awful thunderclap it splits,
With its reverberations, all the air.
Zephyr upon this stream, as I believe,
Ne'er blows, and ruffles not the ugly waves,
Nor moves the depths; but Boreas' doleful breath
Essays a contest, buffeting the flood,
And makes its vales and plains rise mountain high
80 Till wave fights wave, the river labors so.
Sighing and moaning on its bank, a crowd,
Shedding their tears, cease not a sad lament,
Dismayed that they must swim such threatening stream.
Those who wade in not more than belly deep
Are straightway swallowed up, by force o'erthrown,
Or by the fearful, hideous waves tossed back.
If many are recast upon the shore,
As many sink, quite swallowed by the flood;
And sucked down in the mud are most of these
90 So that no trace discloses where they went
And where they must remain forevermore.
This river twists and turns through many a gorge
Until its waters poisonous it pours
Into its sister stream, transforming quite
That one's sereneness with its filth and mud.
It spreads its pestilential waters there
And troubles the sweet stream with bitter bane.
Quickly the latter's worth is quite destroyed
And even its sweetness lost by its consort
100 With the great heat of its ill-smelling guest.
        "The home of Fortune on a hill is set,   *cf. Chaucer's*
Not on a level but on dangerous slope;   *House of Fame*
And it seems ever just about to fall
In crumbling ruin down. No rage of wind
Or tempest that may rise can it avoid,
But feels vexatious raids of many a storm.
Rarely does Zephyr, that soft, peerless breeze,
Temper with his sweet, peaceful breath the force
Of horrible assaults by harsher winds.
110 One half the hall stands high; the other, low.
It seems to dangle, slipping from its base.
Man never saw a more ambiguous house.

One part has gold and silver walls that shine,
And of like precious stuff is all the roof,
Gleaming with precious stones that are so bright
And magical they seem miraculous.
The other part has hand-thick walls of mud
And roof of straw. If one part proudly rears
Its height in beauty marvelous and fine,
120 The other grovels, feeble and debased,
With perforations making in its walls
Five hundred thousand crevices and gaps.
In this place 'tis that Fortune makes her home,
Unstable, changeable, and vagabond.
When she desires to be esteemed, she goes
Into the golden portion of her house
And lives there like a queen in her attire,
Appareled and adorned in trailing robes
Perfumed diversely, colored with fine dyes
130 Most suitable for silk and woolen goods,
Prepared from seeds and herbs and other things
Wherewith are tinted all such draperies
As rich folk wear to gain themselves most praise.
Fortune in this disguise cares not a straw
For any living man, but is so proud
When she beholds her body richly clothed
That there's no pride that's parallel to hers;
For, when she sees her honors and her wealth
And her incomparable majesty,
140 Not thinking how affairs may after fall,
Her folly mounts so high that she believes
No man or woman living has such worth.
Then she goes wandering throughout the house
With every turning of her fickle wheel
Until she comes into the viler part,
Feeble, decrepit, and about to fall,
Where, bending low and stumbling, she proceeds
As if she could not see. At last she falls,
Despoiling both her countenance and robe.
150 Orphaned of all her finery, she lies
Naked and stripped; and worthless now she seems,
All her resources have so wholly failed.

When she perceives her desperate quandary,
She makes a shameful bargain with her fate
And to the bordel goes to cool her heels,
Filled with despair and sighs, in floods of tears
To weep for all the honor she has lost
And the delight she had when richly dressed.
    "Since Fortune's so perverse that she upsets
160 Into the mire, dishonored and aggrieved,
Full many a worthy man, and sets on high
Unworthy ones, profusely granting them
Dignity, honor, power—which she withdraws
As oft—it seems she knows not her own mind.
Therefore the ancients represented her
With blindfold eyes. As sample of the pranks
Of Fortune, who debases worthy men
And ruins them, but honors evil ones,
Let me, although I've cited him before,
170 Remind you once again of Socrates,
The valiant man whom I have loved so much
And all whose deeds recall whose love again to me."

30. Reason relates how Fortune treated Seneca and Nero
[6183–6488]

"MANY a case of Fortune's spite I find,   REASON
But Seneca's and Nero's prove it best;
However, to avoid prolixity,
Let us abandon the particulars.
'Twould be too much to tell all Nero's deeds,
The cruel man who set all Rome afire
And foully put the senators to death
And, stonyhearted, sealed his brother's fate
And had his mother's womb anatomized
10 That he might see where he had been conceived,
And passed upon the beauty of her parts
As she dismembered lay, so stories go.

Ah, God! What a felonious judge was he!
For not a single tear fell from his eyes,
But for his stomach's sake he called for wine
And drank as he passed judgment on the corpse.
Moreover, he had lain with her before,
His sister raped, his body lent to men.
His good old teacher, Seneca, he doomed
20 To martyrdom, bidding him choose the means
By which he would prefer to end his life;
Who, seeing he could not escape his fate,
So powerful was the wretch, made this request:
'Since there's no help for it, prepare a bath   SENECA
In whose warm waters let my veins discharge
My blood, that unto God who formed my soul
(And who from other torment will defend)
It may return bravely and at peace.'
The emperor soon had the bath prepared,   REASON
30 True to his word, admitting no delay,
And in it had the worthy tutor bled
Until his flowing blood released his soul;
And no excuse had Nero for this crime
Except that, as a custom, from his youth
He had done reverence to Seneca
As pupil should to master. But he said:
'It is not fitting, and it shall not be   NERO
That anywhere I should do reverence
To any man, though he my father were,
40 Or teacher, now that I am emperor.'
Unable custom's force to overcome,   REASON
And since it irked him to do reverence
And in his master's presence to arise,
He doomed the noble man to meet his death.
It was this lawless king I have described
Who jurisdiction had o'er all of Rome
With its wide empire stretching from the north
Unto the south, and from the east to west.
    "If you have noted what I've said, you've learned
50 That riches, reverence, and dignity,
Honor, and strength, and all of Fortune's gifts
(For I except not one), are powerless

To change a man to virtuousness from vice—
To make him worthy to have wealth and rule.
If such men have in them hardheartedness,
Evil, or pride, the height to which they rise
Will soon display and emphasize their faults
More than would e'er have done their low estate,
Which could not nourish such deficiencies.
60 When they enlarge their power, they show their lust,
An evidence and proof they are not good
Or worthy to have honor, wealth, and rule.
      "There is a proverb which men oft repeat—
I call it foolish, but they count it true,
Misled by lack of learning—which declares:
'Manners are changed by honors.' But, in truth,
This is ill logic; honors do no harm,
But they give opportunity for proof
Of what the manners were a man had had
70 When in his low estate, and which he'd kept
As he pursued the road to prominence.
If such men are unpitying and proud
And cruel and malicious when raised high,
You may well know that they were so before,
And had appeared so had they had the power.
Therefore the name of power I'll not apply
To evil force; for well the Scripture says
All power comes from good, and evil deeds
Result from foolishness and lack of force.
80 Clearsighted men can see that evil's naught.
If unconvinced by such authority
(For possibly you'll think it is not good),
You may be quickly shown that naught can be
Impossible for God. But, truth to tell,
Not even God has power to do wrong.
Now if you're logical you will conclude,
Since God's omnipotent, yet powerless
To do a wrong, that wrong is naught that we
Believe to have the property of things,
90 As you can clearly see. A shadow has
No substance, but a simple lack of light;
So evil is no substance, but is lack

Of good in any creature that is bad.
Evil can add nothing to what is there.
The text that tells us all about this thing
Says further that the wicked are no men,
And weighty arguments brings up in proof.
But I'll not take the pains to give these points,
For you can find them written in the book.
100 Nevertheless, unless it troubles you,
I'll briefly state some of the reasoning:
Ill creatures tend the purpose to forsake
For which all were created, which we call
The purpose principal; in consequence
They are not of the order of mankind
Who do the things they were created for.
Therefore the wicked are as good as naught.

"Behold how Fortune makes all men despair,
Below in this terrestrial wilderness,
110 Choosing the very worst of them to rule
As lord and master over all mankind,
Condeming Seneca to such a death.
Wisely avoid her favors, then, for we
Are never certain of great happiness;
Therefore would I have you despise her grace
As nothing worth your heed. E'en Claudian,
The poet, pondering such facts, would blame
The gods, as if it were by their consent
That bad men mount so high and gain such rule
120 And riches; but himself refutes the charge
And shows the cause, by logic clear to all,
Absolving and excusing deity.
He thinks bad men to be allowed their power
That afterward may greater be their fall
And punishment; the higher the estate
Such men attain, the worse their overturn.

"If you perform the service I enjoin
And have explained, you'll never find a man
More rich than you. No envy will you feel,
130 However much your fortune may decline
With loss of friends, or bodily distress.
As soon as you accept me as your friend,

You'll patience have. Why linger sadly still?
I see your eyes distill the frequent tears
Like drops from an alembic forced by fire.
You're like a rag dragged through a dirty pond;
Now he would be a fool who called you man.
No one who ever used his mother wit
Appeared one half so wan and miserable.
140 The living Devil, enemy of faith,
Feeding his furnace hot, makes your eyes weep.
If you were wise, you would not be dismayed
At anything you ever undergo.
'Tis your good friend and master fans the flames—
The God of Love this sorrow brings to you—
And his acquaintance you have dearly bought.
It is not seemly for a man of sense,
Renowned for prowess, thus to shame himself.
Leave weeping to the children and the dames—
150 Creatures variable and feeble, too.
However Fortune comes, you should stand firm.
Think you her wheel will stop for great or small?
    "Nero, the emperor of whom I spoke,
Whose empire's boundaries stretched through the world,
In spite of honors gained, felt Fortune's turn.
Most miserable death did he receive,
So much the people hated him, they say.
Fearing to be attacked by them, he sent
To all his private friends, but none he found
160 Who thought they should give refuge to their king.
Then secretly and woefully he went
To knock upon their doors with his own hands.
No better but e'en worse was the result:
The more he knocked, the more they barred their gates,
Nor even gave him answer with a word.
Then, seeing he must hide, he safely sought
In orchard walled, with certain of his slaves,
And heard the cries of those who sought his life:
'Who has seen Nero? Where to find the wretch!'
170 But, though he heard, knew not what he should do.
So much abased that he despised himself,
Seeing no hope of aid, he begged his slaves

To slay him, or his suicide to help;
And so he killed himself, but first did ask
That they should let nobody find his head,
But burn his body quickly as they could
That it might not be found and recognized.
The ancient book of Suetonius
Called *The Twelve Caesars* tells of Nero's death.
180 (The author calls the faith of Christian sect
'False, new religion'—these the very words
Used by the infidel!) The Caesars' line
Ended with Nero. His foul deeds deserved
That with his death his dynasty should end.
Yet he so nobly reigned five years at first
That none could ask a better sovereign.
This hard, false king seemed pious and upright.
Once, when a death decree he had to sign
In court at Rome, he had the grace to say
190 That he would rather not have learned to write
Than to have signed the warrant. History
Recounts that he ruled fourteen years, and lived
Until the age of thirty-two. But pride
Incited felony, until so low
He fell from his great height, as I have told.
You understand that Fortune made him mount
To lofty state that thence his fall might greater be."

31. Reason recounts the story of Croesus and Phanie
[6489–6630]

"NO more could Croesus, Lydia's king, prevent   REASON
The rise and fall of Fortune's turning wheel.
Men put a bridle on his neck, and led
Him to his pyre, whence rain delivered him.
Seeing the fire extinguished, his foes gone,
And none remaining near the place, he fled
Unhindered by pursuit of enemies.

Once more he was the master of his land,
Once more was captured in another war,
10 And finally was hanged. But first this dream
He had: Two gods upon a tree appeared
And served him; Jupiter gave him a bath,
And Phoebus with a towel dried his limbs.
Unluckily relying on the dream,
He foolishly became puffed up with pride.
Phanie, his daughter, who was sage and wise
And knew how to interpret such a dream
When he had told it her, frankly replied:
'Dear father, doleful news this vision gives.   PHANIE
20 Fortune but mocks you; pride's not worth a cock:
By this dream you may understand that she
Intends that you shall on a gibbet hang;
And when with neither roof nor covering
You dangle, to the winds of heaven exposed,
The rain of Jupiter shall on you fall
And Phoebus' rays will dry your face and limbs.
To such an end you'll be by fortune brought,
Who gives her favors but to take them back,
And often brings the great to littleness—
30 The small to greatness—lording it o'er lords.
Why should I flatter? You're to hanging doomed.
Fortune will tie the halter round your neck,
Take from your head the lovely golden crown,
And give it to one whom you don't now fear.
Need I more clearly all the dream expound?
The sky that thunders and brings rain is Jove,
Who in your dream prepared the bath for you;
Phoebus, who held the towel, is the sun;
A gibbet by the tree was signified,
40 And you must surely tread the gallows plank.
No other meaning can I figure out.
Thus Fortune takes revenge upon the folk
Who show themselves as arrogant as you,
Maddened with pride. For many a worthy man
She has destroyed, and never cared a fig.
Loyalty and treachery are one
To her—and kingliness and low estate.

Like simple, careless girls at shuttlecock
She flings at random, here and there, her gifts—
50 Honor and dignity and wealth and power—
Careless on whom they fall. Her favors grow
As they're distributed, so that she throws
Them carelessly, as though they were but sand,
About the world, by ponds or prairies.
She counts none worth more than a tennis ball
Except Gentility, her daughter, friend
And cousin of Misfortune, whom she's like.
However much a man may try to win
This child of Fortune, she will not consent
60 Until he learns to cleanse his heart so well
That he becomes upright and courteous
And worthy; warlike bravery alone
Will never keep Gentility from flight
Before a man who's stained with villainy.
Gentility is noble; her I love
Because she will not enter villain hearts;
Therefore you'll flee from villainy, I hope.
My father dear, be not so proud and vain;
Be rather an example to the rich.
70 Keep winsome heart that's generous and fine
And full of pity for the poor. A king
Should ever thus be kind and debonair,
If he would have his people's amity,
Without which kings are worse than other folk.'
      "Thus Phanie pleaded. But a fool ne'er sees   REASON
In all his folly aught but soundest sense,
So much his silly heart confuses things.
Croesus abased himself no whit, but full
Of pride and folly thought that he was wise,
80 Howe'er outrageous he displayed himself.
'Daughter,' said he, 'it is most impolite   CROESUS
And wrong for you to sermon me like this.
I'm wiser than the one who chides me now.
Your mad interpretation of my dream
Is one great lie. Vision so fine as mine
Never such vile interpretation had.
A dream so noble, on which you have put

Such false significance, a literal   *ironic literalism*
Interpretation needs. I think we'll see
90 This as the outcome: Gods will come to me
And do me service, for they are my friends,
As I deserve, and as my vision shows.'
    "Now see how Fortune served the prideful king.   REASON
He could not save himself from gallows tree.
Does this not prove the instability
Of Fortune's wheel, when one can not prevent
Its turning even when he has been warned?
If you know anything of casuistry,
Which is as most authentic science held,
100 You must admit that when the mighty fall
The weak can strive against their fate only in vain."

32. Reason relates the story of Manfred
[6631–6900]

"IF you believe not ancient histories,   REASON
You may have proof from much more recent times
In new-fought battles excellent (that is,
As excellent as any fights can be).
Manfred, the king of Sicily, by force
And guile long peacefully held all the isle
Until at last the good Charles of Anjou,
Count of Provence, made war on him and won.
The latter still is king of Sicily
10 By providence divine; it is God's will,
For ever Charles observes the Christian faith.
He took away the lordship of that land,
And from the king his life, when on the field
Of the first battle, with well-tempered sword
Boldly he assailed and conquered him.
Astride his war horse proudly he made boast:
'You're checked and mated by one simple move
Of vagrant pawn in the middle of the board.'

"That other apt example need I cite
20 Of Conradin, his nephew, whom King Charles
Condemned to lose his head in spite of all
The German princes? Or the doleful fate
Of Henry, brother of the King of Spain,
Who, full of pride and treason, was condemned
To languish in a prison until death?
These two, like silly boys, lost rooks and knights
And pawns and bishops in their play, and last,
Fearing to lose themselves, resigned the game.
And yet, in fact, no mate need they have feared;
30 No check could have been given to either side
That fought without a king. The opposing force
In any chess game cannot check or mate,
Afoot or horseback, any pawn or knight,
Bishop or rook or queen. I tell the truth
As I recall the game. I'd not deceive
You if you knew it not. Most needful 'tis
That there should be a king to put in check
When all his force is captured, and alone
He stands with no refuge to which to flee,
40 Surrounded by victorious enemies
Who have reduced him to such poverty.
The miser and the prodigal both know,
As do all men, that there's no other way
To win at chess. This rule made Attalus,
Who by arithmetic devised the game;
And in the *Polycraticus* one reads
How good a game the author found in chess
As he by demonstration amply proved,
Digressing on the subject of this game
50 Instead of writing on arithmetic.

"However, fearing capture, these two fled.
Why say I capture? More they feared to die.
The game was badly played, at least by those
Who scorned their God and undertook the war
Against the fief of Holy Church. This doomed
Them to an opening without defense;
For by the first attack made in the game
The queen was taken, and the foolish king

Lost knights and bishops, castles, too, and pawns.
60 The queen was not, 'tis true, in person there,
But grieving wretchedly could not escape
Nor save herself, when finally she knew
That Manfred lay—head, feet, and hands all cold—
Mated and dead. Now when the good king heard
The other two had fled, he had them seized
And worked his will on them and many more
Copartners in their impious hardihood.

"This valiant king, whom men oft call a count,
Whose deeds I tell (may God defend and guard
70 And counsel him and his in body and soul
Each morn and evening, every day and night!)
Conquered the pride of all Marseilles, and took
The heads of all the greatest in the place
Ere he was given Sicily to rule,
Of which he's now crowned king, and vicar, too,
Of all the empire. But I'll say no more
Of him, for who would all his deeds recount
Must fill a ponderous volume with the work.

"You've seen these people who great honors had
80 And what their deeds have been. Is't not a fool
Who'd be assured of Fortune, when she thus
The foreheads of her favorites anoints
So fairly, and then stabs them from behind?
And you, who kissed the Rose and won such woe
As scarcely you are able to assuage,
Think you again to kiss, or ever have
Delight and ease? If so, you're insane, fool;
I swear it by my head. But, that this woe
No more may hold you, do but recollect
90 The tales of Manfred and of Conradin
And Henry; worse than Saracens they did,
Waging hot warfare 'gainst their mother church.
Recall the fate of dwellers in Marseilles,
Of Nero and of Croesus, mighty men
Of ancient times, who could not Fortune hold
For all the power they had. No freeborn man
Who prides himself upon his liberty
Should be unmindful of the sorry tale

Of how to slavery King Croesus came,
100 Of Hecuba's, the wife of Priam's, fate,
Of Sisigambis, mother of the king
Of Persia, great Darius—all these held
Kingdoms in their own right, and yet became
Mere slaves when Fortune was perverse to them.
      "Besides, I count it shame that you, who know
What writing signifies, and how to learn,
For all your study have forgot the page
Of Homer. What's your education worth?
You put your time on books of history
110 And then by negligence forget it all.
From all your study what will be the gain
If at most need you fail to grasp its sense?
Ever in your remembrance hold the sage,
A wise man should so cherish in his heart
All words of wisdom that they'll ne'er escape
Until death seizes him; for whoso knows,
And holds forevermore fast in his mind,
And learns how to appreciate his lore,
Will never be weighed down by what occurs
120 But always will hold firm against all chance
Adventures good or bad or soft or hard.
Besides, this text applies most generally
To all that Fortune does, as any man
Of good intelligence each day perceives.
'Tis strange that you, who've taken so much care
To study, never should have grasped this point.
But your insensate love has turned your head.
I'll tell a tale to make my meaning clear.
      "As Homer tells the story, Jupiter
130 Before the threshold of his mansion placed
Two tuns, filled full throughout the livelong year;
From one of these two tuns each person drinks
Who lives on earth—father or bachelor,
Maiden or mother, young, old, foul, or fair.
Fortune is hostess of the well-stocked inn,
Who draws absinthe or sugared wine in cups
And gives a drink to each one in the world;
To some the more, to some the less she grants.

No one there is who drinks not every day
140 From out these tuns a quart or pint or gill
Or many a gallon, as may please the jade,
Or but a palmful or the merest sip
That she may drop by drop put in their mouths,
Serving each well or ill as suits her mood.

   "No thinking man can feel such happiness
That he'll not find in midst of greatest ease
Something to trouble him; nor in his woe
Will he find nothing that can comfort give.
If he considers well his state, he'll find
150 Something of credit done or to be wrought,
Unless he fall into that hopeless pass
Which is the bane of sinners, far beyond
The help of study of philosophy.
What use for you to grumble, grieve, or groan?
Pluck up good heart; accept most patiently
What Fortune offers—good, bad, foul, or fair.
'Twere vain to tell of Fortune's risky wheel
The many turns—a game of pile and cross
That she so plans that victims never know,
160 Before they start, whether they'll win or lose.

   "Although I to the subject may return,
I'll pause a while to make you three requests,
For heartfelt wish comes crowding to my lips;
And if you shall refuse these honest prayers
Nothing prevents your bearing all the blame:
It's my desire that I may have your love,
That you henceforth the God of Love despise,
And that you trust in Fortune nevermore.
If you're too weak to bear this triple bond,
170 I'll lighten it to make it portable.
Fulfill my first request, and you shall be
Exempted from the others; if you well
My meaning comprehend, and are no fool,
Nor drunken, you should know and recollect
That whosoe'er conforms to Reason's law
Never will carnal love or Fortune prize.
Such was my true friend, Socrates—unmoved
By Fortune, and by Love ne'er set on fire.

Be like to him and wed your heart to mine;
180 It will suffice to fix it in my breast:
Observe how easy is my one demand;
Fulfill the first thing that I've asked of you
And I'll absolve you of the rest. No more
Keep your lips closed so tight. Respond! Will you do this?"

33. The Lover accuses Reason of lewdness
[6901–7230]

"DAME," said I, "I can do not otherwise   THE LOVER
Than serve my master, who can make me rich
One hundred thousand times more than you can.
If well I serve, he might grant me the Rose,
And then for nothing else would I have need.
Your Socrates I count not worth three peas,
However great; of him I'll hear no more.
Unto my master I'll return, and keep
His covenants, for that is fair and right.
10 Though he should guide my footsteps down to Hell,
I never could withhold from him my heart.
My heart? It is not mine; and nevermore
Will I impair my testament to him,
Or wish to do so, for another's love.
Unto Fair Welcome I have given my all;
I know my legacy by heart. I hear
Impatiently confession sans remorse.
I would not change my Rose for anything
You offer, and you ought to know my will.
20   "Besides, I hold you were not courteous
When you referred to cullions, for no maid   q. p. 117
In good society would use that word.
I know not how so fair and wise a dame
As you would dare to mention such a thing
Unless you found for it some term polite,
More seemly in a gentlewoman's speech.

Even the nurses who are often bold
And bawdy, when they give the children baths,
I've often seen undress and fondle them
30 And name those parts quite otherwise, I'm sure.
You know well what I mean, and if I lie."

Reason made answer to me smilingly:
"Fair friend, without disgrace I well may name   REASON
Quite openly and by the proper term
A thing that's nothing if it be not good.
Even of evil may I plainly speak;
Unless it tend to sin, I'm not ashamed.
But naught could make me have to do with sin,
For never in my life have I done wrong.
40 No sin is it to name such noble things,
In open text without resort to gloss,
As God the Father made in Paradise
With his own hands, and other instruments
Intended to perpetuate the race
Which without them had fallen in decay.
By his own will, and not in spite of it,
God made, for his transcendent purposes,
In order that the species might survive
By natural replenishment, these parts;
50 Unto the virile purse and staff he first
Entrusted generation's potency.
By birth the race is subject to demise,
But in decline provides for its rebirth;
With which provision God assures mankind
That it shall long endure and never fail.
So he provided also for dumb beasts
That, thus sustained, their species may remain;
For when one dies another takes his place."

Said I, "You're worse than ever; I perceive,   THE LOVER
60 By your lewd speech, you are a foolish bawd;
For though God may have made the things you name
He ne'er made words so full of ribaldry."

"Dear friend," sage Reason said, "no foolishness   REASON
Is valiance, nor was, nor e'er will be.
Say what you will, for you have time and space;
Nor should I, who but wish to gain your love

And favor, question it. I'll hear you out
And yet keep silence if you do no worse,
However much reproach you heap on me.
70 You'd like to make me answer foolishly,
But that I shall not do. 'Tis for your good
That I chastise you. I am not like you,
Nor would I start such villainous discourse.
As would to slander or to quarrel lead.
Be not displeased, but quarreling, 'tis true,
Is evil vengeance; slander's even worse.
Quite otherwise would I avenge myself
If vengeance I desired. By word or deed
If you offended me, I'd find a way
80 By deed or word to quietly reprove
And so chastise and teach you without blame
And without slandering you. If you refused
My good and true discourse, I'd have revenge
In other ways, by making my complaint
At proper time before the proper judge,
And he would see that I had equity.
Or by some other reasonable deed
I'd take some other honorable revenge.
I have no wish my neighbor to reprove
90 Or injure him or hold him up to scorn,
Whoever he may be, or good or bad.
Let each his burden bear, and as he will
Let each confess his faults or them conceal.
I urge him not. No folly would I do
Or say, could I avoid it. Silent tongue
May be small merit; but 'tis devilish
To utter things that better far were hid.
   "The tongue should bridled be, as Ptolemy
Early in his *Almagest* explains
100 In noble words: 'Most wise is he who strives   PTOLEMY
To hold his tongue save when he speaks of God.'
In such a case no utterance is too much;   REASON
We cannot too much praise our God, or vow
Ourselves too much to Him as sovereign lord,
Too much obey Him, too much fear His wrath,
Too much beg mercy, too much render thanks.

No man too much attention pays to this,
For always those who blessings have received
Should Him invoke. If you know Cato's book,
110 You will remember that he says the same;
There you'll find written that the highest worth
Is found in him who bridled keeps his tongue.
Then curb your speech, avoiding outrages
Of foolish talk, and you'll be wise and good.
A man does well the pagans to believe
If he from their wise words may gain great good.
  "One thing I'll tell you without ire or hate,
Without reproach or choler (foolishness
It were to anger you!), and this is it:
120 Saving your grace and peace, it seems to me,
Who love you and would have you silent now,
That you are much at fault when "ribald fool"
And other names you wrongly to me give;
Considering that my father, King of Heaven,
The courteous God, lacking all villainy,
From whom all goodness comes, has tutored me
And brought me up and taught me how to speak
(Nor do I think that I have badly learned);
And it is by His will that it's my use
130 To call things by their names, and properly,
Without a gloss, whenever I may please.
  "Now as to your injunction that I gloss,
I make response that God indeed has made
But has not named the things He did create.
Although He might have done so at the time
When He formed all that is upon the earth,
The names that they have now He ne'er assigned.
It was His will that I should choose the names,
Common and proper, as my pleasure bade,
140 Fitting to add to man's intelligence.
For this He gave his precious gift of speech.
You'll find authoritative proof of that,
For Plato in his school was wont to say
That speech was given to make us understand
And willingly to teach as well as learn.
In Plato's *Timaeus* you'll find the text

That I have metered here. He was no fool.
   "You make objection that I use a word
Which you call lewd. I ask you, before God,
150 If when I gave the names to all the things
I'd relics 'cullions,' cullions 'relics' called,
Would you who now so snap and bite at me,
Have said that 'relic' is a filthy word?
Cullion is a good word; I like the name—
Genitals and testicles as well.
No better named you'd find if you should try.
I made these words, who surely never did
Blameworthy thing. God, who is wise and sure,
Accepts as good whatever deed I do.
160 By the body of Saint Omer, dare I name
Improperly the works of God's own hand?
Should I compete with him? They must have names,
Else no one would know how to speak of them;
Therefore we give them such as men may speak.
If women never say such words in France,
It is through lack of custom; were they used,
The proper names would be acceptable,
And certainly their use would be no sin.
   "Custom is all-powerful, if I
170 Am any judge; new things often displease
Though they're found fair when custom sanctions them.
How many paraphrases women use,
In speaking of such parts, I do not know.
They call them purses, harness, torches, things,
And even pricks, as if they were like thorns;
But after they have been well introduced
They find them not so painful after all.
They call them what they like; it's naught to me
That they will not employ the proper names,
180 And 'tis not their example I'll observe
When I wish openly to nominate.
   "Within our schools you may learn many a thing
In parables that pleasant are to hear.
He'd be a fool who took them literally.
There was another meaning in the word
When I discoursed of cullions to you,

(margin note, left of lines 150–151:) Y. Pardon's Tale

Desiring briefly then to signify
Something quite other than the sense you got.
A man of understanding would have seen
190 The cloudy fable in a different light.
The truth that lay within had been most clear
If proper exposition it had had.
Recall Ovid's book *Integuments*,
And you will understand; for there you'll find
Much of the secret of philosophy,
Which will give you great profit and delight.
In profiting you will enjoyment gain,
And your enjoyment will be profitable;
For in the myths and fables of this sort
200 Philosophers their speculations hide.
'Tis thus they cover many a useful truth
Which you must see if you would comprehend.
But I've given you two words you understand
Quite literally, and should, without a gloss."
    "Lady, most easily whoever knows   THE LOVER
Our language will these words well apprehend;
They have no need of further commentary.   *cf. Croesus*
Now 'tis not my intention to explore
The sense of poets' fabling metaphors;
210 But, if I may be cured and merit have
In your employ, for which I hope reward,
I will expound continually such points
As may be fitting, that each man may see
Their meaning clearly. Hold yourself excused
For that first word you used, and other two
Employed thereafter, if, as you have said,
You use them properly. I'll take no pains
And waste no time in glossing them for you.
But, in God's mercy, censure not my love!
220 It's my own lookout if I am a fool.
I took good care of one thing to be sure:
That I was acting wisely when I swore
Allegiance to my lord. If now I'm mad,
Regard me not. Whatever may befall,
I'm vowed to Love—in service to my Rose.
No other will I ever give my heart.

I could not keep my word if I to you
My love should promise, for I must deceive
You or him to whom I tendered it
230 Ere you proposed your covenant to me.
But often have I told you that no thought
I have for others than my longed-for Rose.
Now oft by your reiterated words
You irk me so that my thoughts fly away
And tempt me to achieve escape by flight
Unless you'll quiet keep; for still my heart
Is in attendance on another one."
    When Reason heard this speech, she turned aside
And left me pensive—lonely—most disconsolate.

34. The Lover's Friend takes Reason's place
[7231–7524]

THEN of my friend I thought, and it seemed best
That I bestir myself and seek him out,
Whatever care and pain it might involve.
But God led him to me, and when he saw
That dolor pricked my heart he quickly said:
"What's this, fair friend, that's torturing you so?   THE FRIEND
Some mischief has befallen. What's the news?"
    "So help me God, 'tis neither fair nor foul."   THE LOVER
    "Recount it all."   THE FRIEND
                    And so I told to him
10 The tale that I've already told to you.
When I had finished; he exclaimed, "By God,   THE FRIEND
You've Danger pacified and kissed the Rose.
If you Fair Welcome had but made your own,
You would have had no cause for drearihood;
But, since he was so loyal to your cause
That he procured the kiss that you received,
No prison will long keep him from your side.
However, it behooves you to behave

More prudently if you'd achieve your end.
20 But you may comfort take from this idea:
Fair Welcome will be rescued from the keep
In which he is confined for love of you."

 "Alas!" said I, "too strong an enemy   THE LOVER
He'd have if he had none but Evil Tongue,
Who against me incited all the rest.
I'd not been caught unless the fool had blabbed.
Gladly had Fear and Shame concealed the act;
Not even Danger would have told on me.
All three were keeping still when that great boor
30 Summoned the devils as Fair Welcome paled
At Jealousy's lament (an evil voice
That old girl has!); the more's the pity, too,
That I incontinent at once did flee.
Then were walls mortared that now hold the sweet.
O Friend, without your aid I were but dead!"

 Then spoke my Friend like one well schooled in love:
"Companion, do not be disconsolate;   THE FRIEND
Comfort yourself with your idolatry.
Give loyal service to the God of Love
40 Unceasingly; both night and day be true.
'Twere shame if he should find you recreant
And have to own himself so much deceived
When he, who ne'er has loyal friend forsworn,
Received your homage. Do what he commands;
Keep all his precepts. Never willingly,
However he delays, will he desert
One who his ordinances well observes.
However Fortune may make her awards,
Think of your service to the God of Love.
50 On him be all your thought; such thought is sweet.
Therefore too great a folly it would be
To leave him who has ne'er abandoned you.
Besides, he has you tethered with his leash;
And, since you can't escape, you must submit.

 "Now I will tell you what you ought to do:
Forbear a while to go to see the tower;
Let not by night or day a sight or sound
Betray your presence there until this storm

Has overpassed. At least be seen no more,
60 As has your custom been, about the gates
Or near the walls, no matter what you wish.
And if chance bring you there, pretend, at least,
That for Fair Welcome you have no concern.
And if from far away you him behold
At crenelet or window, look on him
But covertly, though with a pitying eye.
If he perceive you, he will happy be,
Though spying eyes may make him leave his place
With neither look nor sign, unless perhaps
70 Some secret gesture he contrive to make.
Perchance he'll close his window when he sees
You speak to others, though athwart the chinks
He'll feast his eyes on you while you remain,
Unless his guard shall drag him from the place.
   "Take special care that Evil Tongue beholds
You not; but, if he does, salute him fair;
And be not moved to look with hate or wrath.
If elsewhere you should meet him, show no spite;
A wise man ever covers up his ire.
80 Good work it is deceivers to deceive;
Know well that thus wise lovers all should do.
Pretend to serve and honor Evil Tongue
And all his race, though they would you destroy.
Offer them heart and body, goods and aid.
They say, and it is true, as I believe:
'Cunning 'gainst cunning,' for it is no sin
To cheat a rascal who is cheating you.
Such a deceiving wretch is Evil Tongue.
From scalawag remove a syllable
90 And scaly still remains; a scaly thief
He is, as you can very well perceive;
And he deserves to have no other name,
For folks he robs of their good name, which he
Can never render back. Much better hanged
Were he than all the other larceners
Who steal I care not how great store of pence.
One of these penny thieves, red-handed caught
Robbing a hen roost or a farmer's barn,

At least four times his theft's compelled to pay
100 According to the laws; but Evil Tongue
By his vile, spiteful tales does so much harm
That once the word has left his cursed throat
No power has he to give repute again,
If by his libel it has been destroyed.
He can extinguish not one single word.
    " 'Twere well that Evil Tongue should be appeased,
As oft men kiss the hand they fain would burn.
Would that to Tarsus were the villain sent,
Where he might tell what lies he could contrive,
110 Provided that no lovers suffered wrong!
At least 'twere a good deed to stop his mouth
So that no more detraction he may spread.
This Evil Tongue you should, and all his folks
(God guard them not!), deceive by treachery,
By flattery and coaxing blandishment,
By adulation and servility,
By false dissimulation and by ruse,
By bowing and by greeting; for a man
Does well to pet a dog till he gets past.
120 Most surely you will bring his care to naught
If Evil Tongue you can at least persuade
That you've lost all desire to steal the bud
Which he believes he has secured from you.
    "Treat likewise that old hag, Fair Welcome's guard
(Whom may hell-fire destroy!), the pessimist
Who feels such savage rage at others' joy,
Who is so cruel and so gluttonous
That she wants everything; though she would find
Her share no less if she let all partake.
130 Foolish is he who grudges happiness;
One candle in a lantern can give light
To many men and yet have plenty left.
This simile is clear to all but fools.
So, if these villains should have need of you,
Serve them as best you can. Show courtesy;
It is a thing most prized. But let them not
Suspect that you but practice to deceive.
Thus you should act. With arm about his neck,

By flattery and by cajolery,
140 One leads his enemy to hang or drown,
If otherwise he can't achieve his end.
In this case I can guarantee and swear
There is no other means; they are so strong
That open war would mean only defeat.
    "Then it behooves you to approach the rest,
If you are able, offering them gifts:
Bonnets adorned with bandelets of flowers,
Purses and veils and other little things,
Fashionable, well made, and in good taste.
150 If you've the means without impoverishment
To make such gifts, they should be thus appeased.
Then emphasize the travail, pain, and woe
You've suffered from the love that's led you there.
Or, if you cannot give, make promises.
However small the chance they'll be fulfilled,
No hesitation show in making them.
Rather than be o'ercome in argument,
Make strongest oaths—hypothecate your faith.
'Twere advantageous in their sight to weep;
160 The higher wisdom counsels show of tears.
Before them, with clasped hands, on bended knees,
Show them some hot drops from your humid eyes
Trickling down your cheeks—a piteous sight!
Scorn not the power of grief to influence men.
    "However, if your tears refuse to flow,
Be not afraid to secretly employ
Saliva or a juice of any kind
Which may your eyelids well humidify;
Or by the aid of onions or of leeks
170 You may shed tears as often as you wish.
Thus many a crafty lover has contrived
To loose the leash by which he has been led,
Playing upon the sympathy of dames
Till from his neck they quite removed the rope.
Many by such device have seemed to weep
Who never felt love's force; and many a maid
Has been deceived by such pretended tears.
Weeping may soften even jailors' hearts

Unless they see 'tis false. In such a case
180 No mercy for you would they ever have.
In vain you then would look for sympathy;
The gates would never ope for you again.
If you should fail by such means to approach,
Select a trusty messenger to send
With word or letter; in the latter case
Sign not your proper name, for secrecy.
Better call her Fair Sir and him Sweet Dame,
As if he were a lady, she a man;
For many a thief has read a lover's script,
190 Unknown to the inditer, and exposed
The lovers' secrets, ruining their joy.
If you confide in children, you'll be duped;
They make ill messengers, for they delight
To brag and of their own importance boast,
Revealing all to those who flatter them;
Or through their ignorance they play the fool,
Publishing what they know, unless they're sly.
　"These jailers, you will find, have pitying hearts,
Provided they will deign to take your gifts,
200 They'll not deceive you; and you may be sure
That they'll accept the presents that you bring.
When once they've taken them, the business's done;
For even as a lure at night or morn
Will make the sparrow hawk come back to hand,
So will the lover's gifts gain grace for him
From chatelaines whom thus he fully vanquishes."

35. The Friend predicts that the Lover will succeed by bribery and deceit
[7525–7794]

"IF it should happen that you find guards stern　　THE FRIEND
And not to be moved by either gifts or prayers
Or tears or any means that you may try,

And they by haughty words or acts severe
Reject all your advances, cursing you,
Then courteously take your leave of them
And let them fry in their own fat; no cheese
Of autumn ever was more quickly cooked
Than they will be. If from them you depart,
They'll make pursuit, which will be to your gain.
A churlish heart is often arrogant;
The more one begs of such, the less he gets;
The more one serves, the more he is despised.
But Pride is soon abased when left alone;
Once conquered, Pride seeks to conciliate.
Foul becomes fair when Pride sees suitors leave.
   "The mariner who sails upon the seas,
Searching for many a savage land unknown,
Although he steers but by a single star
Relies not always on a single sail
To win his port through tempest and through storm.
So must the heart that ever loves but one
Rely not always on a single means,
But sometimes flee, at other times pursue,
As best may help him to enjoy his love.
   "This should be clear, and I'll no more expound
A text that you may well depend upon:
'Twere well to make your prayer unto these three.
He risks but little who expends but words
Which may avail to soothe their arrogance.
They will accept or else reject your prayer;
You cannot lose more than the time you spend.
A meek petition scarce should raise their ire;
Refusing it may even mend their mood.
Who ever heard of one so villainous
That he could not be flattered by appeal?
Though they may silent be, they can but think
That they are now important, grand, and great,
Possessing all good traits, since they are sought
By suitors of your sort, however speed
The suit. If all goes well, you'll surely win;
If ill, why then you need but comfort take
And try again; and if, as it may hap,

10 ... 20 ... 30 ... 40

You fail, and well disguise the pain you feel,
The better chance you'll have next time you try.
  "But do not tell the jailers at the first
That your design is to deflower the Rose;   *
Pretend you feel naught but platonic love.
Now rest assured that they can be o'ercome;
50 They'll not repel you if you treat them right.
Nothing will be refused. Take my advice:
Don't pain yourself to multiply your prayers
If things go wrong; for they may vaunt themselves
For probity if they are not seduced,
But they'll not say a word if they give in.
  "They're all alike: however stiff they seem,
They'll ask for bribes that are not offered them,
Or serve for nothing if they are not pressed.
But suitors too precipitate with gifts
60 May so awaken avarice that they'll raise
The price of roses most inordinately.
Expecting thus to gain advantage, they
Gain naught but disadvantage; without bribe
The jailers had accomplished all they wished
If no advance request had been preferred.
Or, if they wished to let themselves for hire,
The fee had been but small. If 'mongst themselves
All suitors could arrange to give no gifts
And make no prayers to guardians, ere long,
70 Seeing their roses wither, they'd give in.
Such folk as sell their bodies please me ill;
In no such traffic could I take delight.
But, nonetheless, you must avoid delay;
Solicit them, extend to them the net
By which you hope to snare your prey. Beware
Of sloth that might allow your rivals time
To gather—one or two or three or four
Or fifty dozen in as many weeks.
If you delay too long, the guards may turn
80 To other customers; and they may buy.
No man expects a maid to beg his love;
Too much upon his beauty he relies
If such should be his hope. But whosoe'er

Would see his cause advancing from the start
Must never fear to risk his lady's scorn,
Regardless of how cold and proud she seems.
If only he his craft will wisely steer,
He'll see it reach its haven in good time.
Thus act, companion, when you deal with guards,
90 But when you find them gruff, make no requests.
Approach them when you see they're light of heart;
Avoid them when you know they're out of sorts,
Unless you wish to brave the bitterness
That's born of jealousy which hurts your cause
Although it might have conquered them for you.
    "If you succeed so far that privately
You interview them without fear of spies,
Fair Welcome may from out his prison break,
Where he so long is suffering for you,
100 And smile upon you as he well knows how.
(To gentlemen he can complaisant be.)
Then will your time have come to pluck the Rose.
Even if Danger should the scandal spread,
Or Shame and Fear complain about the deed,
You'll find they will but feeble struggle make
And laxly feign defense, and, struggling, yield,
As you will by their conduct soon perceive.
Consider them not worth an empty rind
As you see Fear all of a tremble then,
110 And Shame blush red, and Danger's knees give way,
And all three moan and make most dire complaint.
Lay hands upon your Rose with might and main;
And prove yourself a man when with the time
The place and the occasion both agree.
Nothing, perhaps, will please them more than force
Employed by one who understands its use.
There's many a one whose nature's so perverse
That what she dares not give she'll yield to strength
And feign that what she would permit and wish
120 Has ravished been from her against her will.
Know well that such a one might sorely grieve
If her trumped-up defenses should succeed,
No matter how much joy she might pretend.

"Fear not their hate, no matter how they scold—
No matter how infuriate they seem.
But if by their plain speech you realize
That they are truly wroth, and vigorously
Defend the castle, then withdraw your hand;
Give in, cry mercy, and attend the time
130 When these three porters who obstruct your path
Shall leave you with Fair Welcome all alone,
Who may vouchsafe complete success for you.
This is the way you should conduct yourself
Toward them: as worthy, valiant, and wise.

"Observe Fair Welcome and his attitude;
Conform yourself to his psychology.
If he seem venerable and serious,
Take care that you solemnity preserve;
If he's facetious, show naïveté;
140 If he is gay, display glad countenance;
If he is angry, share his bitterness;
If he laughs, laugh; and if he weeps, lament.
Praise what he praises (then he'll trust in you);
Love whom he loves, and blame each one he blames.
Each hour take pains to follow all his moods.

"Think you that any gracious-hearted dame
Would love a petulant and foolish boy
Who like an idiot would rave all night
And sing till morning that she found him fair
150 And how her love for him destroyed her peace?
She'd fear defamement's notoriety
If he cared not who knew about their love.
Passions sung in the streets are quickly known.
She'd be a fool to give her heart to him.

"When wise man talks of love to foolish girl,
He'll never turn her head with sage display;
Let him ne'er think his lore will profit him.
He should employ a style equal with hers
Or else he will be shamed, for she will think
160 That he's a cheat, a fox, a sorcerer.
Quickly the fool will leave him for a man
Who lowers himself to her, the worthy one
Reject, and pick the worst of all the crowd.

She incubates and nourishes her love
Like to the she-wolf so degenerate
As to select the evilest of the pack.
   "If with Fair Welcome you should play at chess
Or dice or tables or some other game,
Play poorly so that he may always win.
170 Upon whatever game, lose all you stake;
Boast of your losses and make light of them.
So shall you gain the mastery in play.
Praise his behavior, countenance, and dress.
Serve him with all your skill; so serve your cause.
If he would sit, bring him a stool or chair;
If you see fall on him a speck of dust,
Remove it straightway though it be but small;
Protect his robe from trailing in the dirt.
In brief, do whatsoe'er you think would please.
180 If you thus act, you need fear no repulse;
But to your goal, as I have said, you'll surely win."

36. The Lover revolts against the Friend's advice
[7795–7884]

THE LOVER

"SWEET Friend," said I, "what's this you say to me?
No man but some false hypocrite would do
Such deviltry; no greater was e'er broached.
Would you have me these false and servile folk
Honor and serve? Except Fair Welcome, all
Within the tower are only false and base.
Is this your counsel? Traitor would I be
If I should take it and deception play.
Now let me tell you this: when I aspire
10 To see what they are up to, I'll defy
Them to their faces—leastwise Evil Tongue,
Who has so troubled me. Ere I him trick,
I'll say that he must quell the storm he's raised,

Or, if he please, that he must make amends
Or on myself I will amendment take
And beat him well or at the least complain
Before some justice who will aid my cause."

THE FRIEND

"My Friend," he answered, "well it were to wage
An open warfare thus, but Evil Tongue
20 Is not a frank opponent in a war.
He's too deceitful; when he hates a man
Or woman, he tells lies behind their backs.
May God shame such a traitor as is he!
It is but right that he should be betrayed.
'Fie,' say I, 'on such traitors!' Faithless they,
And so I'll put none of my trust in them.
With lips and teeth such villains falsely smile
While they bear basest hate within their hearts.
Such folk I like not; let them go their way,
30 And I'll go mine. Who betrays such does right,
Though it should bring him to his death, if he
Could get no other honorable revenge.
    "Think you that if you should complain of him
You'd stop his lying? You could never prove
Your case, nor get sufficient witnesses.
Or, should you win, you could not silence him.
The more you logic use, the more he'll lie;
Less would you gain than you would lose by it.
You'd but succeed in publishing abroad
40 The slander, and establishing your shame.
Whoever thinks a libel to abate
By argument does but increase its force.
Petitioning abatement of the blame,
Or punishment of it, would do no good;
I swear by God 'twould not diminish it.
Expecting that he'll make you due amends
Is just as vain, unless I'm very wrong.
I'd not accept amends from him though they
Were offered; rather would I pardon him.
50 If you defied him, by the saints I swear
That soon you'd see Fair Welcome put in chains,
Or burned in fire, or in a river drowned,

Or so confined that you'd see him no more.
Then more you'd grieve than ever Charlemagne
For Roland did lament at Roncesvalles
When he was killed by treacherous Ganelon."

　　"I'd not like that. The devil take the wretch!　　THE LOVER
He's spilled the beans for me. I'd see him hanged!"

　　"Now don't excite yourself to hanging yet;　　THE FRIEND
60 'Tis not your office; you are not a judge.
Accept my plan, and study to deceive;
A better vengeance on him then you'll take."

　　"Your counsel, Friend, I see I must accept;　　THE LOVER
From your advice I will no more revolt.
If you have any skill to find a way
By which more easily the fort may be
O'erwhelmed, I'll gladly listen if you will expound."

37. The Friend explains Mad Largesse's means
of access to Fair Welcome
[7885–7960]

"I KNOW a path that's pleasant and secure,　　THE FRIEND
But most uneasy for a poor man's tread.
Without accepting my advice, the rich
May find a speedy way to seize the keep
And overthrow the stronghold to its base
And open thus all doors to quick access
And capture all the guardians of the place,
Who'd not defend themselves or say one word.
The path's called Giving Much, and it was made
10 By Mad Largesse, who's ruined many a man.
Too well I know the path, for I have been
A pilgrim on it now more than a year
And but two days ago returned from it.
Leave Largesse on the right—turn to the left—
And without much sole leather wear you'll come,
Within a bow shot, by a well-trod road,

To where you'll see the walls begin to quake
And portals open wide all by themselves
And towers and turrets tremble to the ground,
20 No matter how secure they were before.
The gates could not be forced more easily
If all their guardians were lying dead.
Approached by this path, not a castle wall
Is harder to subdue than cake to cut.
A weaker force will serve to do the deed
Than needed Charles the Great to conquer Maine.

    "No poor man enters by this path, I know;
Alone he can but fail, and with a guide
Who's indigent also he'll not succeed.
30 But one who has a guide who has been there,
As I have been, will soon the pathway learn
As well as I, than whom none better know.
Now, if you like, you soon shall take this way,
For 'tis not hard if you the riches have
To stand a big expense; but as for me
The very entrance to the path's denied
By Poverty, who bars the way. I spent
Whate'er I had, what I from others got;
I cheated all my creditors, for I
40 Could not have paid a single one of them
Though I had been condemned to drown or hang.
Then Poverty proclaimed, 'Come here no more   POVERTY
If you have not the wherewithal to spend.'

    " 'Twill be most difficult to enter there   THE FRIEND
If Wealth conduct you not; and she'll refuse
To leave with you when she has got you in.
Though she accompany you on the way,
She will desert you ere you can return.
Be sure of this: if you make entry thus
50 You'll make your exit neither day nor night
Except dragged forth by Poverty's stern hand,
Which has full many a lover sorely grieved.
Mad Largesse stays within, whose only thought
Is fixed on play and other wild expense
As if she drew upon barnfuls of cash

Without account or reckoning of cost—
Without a thought of how short time her hoard might last."

38. The Friend expounds the Pains of Poverty
[7961–8188]

"IN quite a different style lives Poverty;   THE FRIEND
Depressed by shame and misery, she feels
Her heart too much afflicted by disgrace,
So much she has to beg and be refused.
However she may try, she'll not escape
The universal blame for all her works.
She is unloved, and vilified by all.
One never thinks of her except to plan
His actions so that he may her avoid.
10 Naught can so grieve a man as falling in
With Poverty; this debtors know full well
Who've spent their all and fear a gallows end.
Full well one knows this who is forced to beg
And suffer much ere folk will give him aid;
And one who's felt the joy of love should know
This just as well; for Ovid truly says,
'Poor men have not wherewith to pasture love.'   OVID
    "Poverty makes a man despair and hate   THE FRIEND
And live a martyr till he lose his mind.
20 For Heaven's sake, from such fate guard yourself!
Compel your mind to accept my words as true.
Know well that I have tested what I say;
Experience has proved in my own case
All that I've told you in this sermoning.
Better I know the depths of poverty—
I who have felt its shame and woe—than you,
Fair friend, who never have encountered it.
Believe in me; I say this for your good;
Blessed is he who learns by others' woe.

30   "I formerly was known as valiant man,
    Loved by my friends when freely I could spend—
    So freely that I was accounted rich.
    Now I am poor through waste of Mad Largesse,
    Who brought me to such great distress that I
    Have scarce enough to drink or aught to eat
    Or clothes or shoes to wear, so Poverty
    Has mastered me and robbed me of my friends.
    Know well, companion, they all disappeared
    As soon as Fortune put me in this case;
40 Or all but one who now remains alone.
    Thus Fortune robbed me, helped by Poverty,
    Who came with her. Yet should I say she stole
    When she but took what properly was hers?
    For all I know, if they'd been truly mine
    They never would have left me just for her.
    She did no wrong when her own friends she took.
    Little I knew that they were really hers;
    I thought I'd bought them—body, soul, and goods—
    But not a cent's worth of them did I own
50 When it came to the pinch. When they perceived
    My state, these friends of nothing thought but flight.
    All mocked me when I fell 'neath Fortune's wheel,
    Turned upside down, depressed by Poverty.
    No whit should I complain, for she had done
    Me greater courtesy than I deserved,
    Mine eyes she has anointed with such balm
    That all around me I can plainly see
    More clearly than a lynx, who'd not perceive
    What I have seen were it before his eyes.
60 This ointment made me confident and sure
    What kind of friends they were that Poverty
    Removed some twenty of. Ah, no! I lie;
    Four hundred fifty did she take away.
    But Fortune straightway in their stead bestowed
    The open-faced, true love of one real friend
    Whom I had never known, had Poverty
    Not introduced him when he learned my need.
    Soon as he knew my state, he running came;
    As far as possible he gave me aid,

70 Offering me what he had to end my care.

THE FRIEND'S FRIEND

'My friend,' said he, 'assure yourself you own
My body and my goods as much as I.
Take without asking leave. How much? Take all
If all you need. Of Fortune's many gifts
No friend from friend a single plum withholds.
Take even the gifts that Nature gave to me.
Since we first met, we've known each other well;
Our very hearts are joined, and we have found
And proved ourselves good friends, a fact unknown
80 Until it's proved. What's mine I hold as yours.
So powerful you'll find the bonds of love,
For your behoof you may surrender me
As pledge or hostage—sell my goods for bail.'

   "Nor did my friend stop short with promises;   THE FRIEND
To prove himself sincere, he forced on me
His having, and I shamed and silent stood,
Unwilling even to reach out my hand,
Like needy wretch whose shame has shut his lips
So that he dares not tell his direful state
90 But tries to cover up—keep to himself—
The poverty he feels, that none may know,
And puts up a good front. So then did I.

   "That not all do so I remember well;
Some able-bodied Mendicants intrude
Where'er they please, by means of flattery.
They show their hardihood to all they meet
Outside; but, once within, they well conceal
Their nature, to deceive the ones who give.
They say they're poor, and so fat pickings get;
100 Their treasuries great heaps of farthings hold.
Enough of these; for I could say so much
That it might go with me from bad to worse,
Since always such-like hypocrites detest
The truth that's to their disadvantage told.

   "Alas that e'er my foolish heart had placed
Upon such friends its trust! I was betrayed
By my weak mind—and generally despised,
Hated, defamed, without my least desert

Or any reason but the loss I've named.
110 I had no friend to whom to turn but you,
Who never lost your love, but more attached
Your heart became to mine, as it will be,
So I believe, forever, if God please;
For never will I cease from loving you.
Though my terrestrial companionship
You'll lose, when on the latest day Death comes
To claim his right, my body, he'll ne'er touch
Us save in our corporeal estate
And in its appertaining substances.
120 We both may die more soon than either hopes,
For death will separate the best of friends;
But probably we'll not together die.
Long as I live I'll keep your memory.
   "The story tells how sadly Theseus grieved
When Pirithous was dead; he loved him so
He followed him to Hell, for in his heart
The friend still lived whom best he'd loved on earth.
   "But Poverty does worse than Death; she bites
And both the body and the soul torments,
130 Not for a single hour, but for so long
As either one remains. She urges men
To theft and perjury and other crimes
Which hit them hard and condemnation bring.
This, Death will never do, but rescues men
From everything, and at her coming stops
All earthly torment, howsoever great,
And, in a single hour, ends all their grief.
Therefore, fair friend, hold in your memory
Great Solomon, King of Jerusalem,
140 From whom one learns full many a goodly thing.
He said—now note it well—'Beware, my son,   SOLOMON
Of poverty the days of all your life.'
And in his book the reason thus he gives,
'Far better 'tis to die than to be poor
In this terrestrial life.' By poverty   THE FRIEND
He doubtless means the suffering that comes
From indigence which so annoys its hosts
That never so despised a folk I've seen

As those we term the poor. The very laws
150 Declare that they are barred as witnesses—
Put poverty upon a par with infamy!"

39. The Friend explains how gifts engender love
[8189–8354]

"A THING unbeautiful is poverty—   THE FRIEND
Yet I dare say that if you have a store
Of coin and jewels, and will give of these
As many as you promise, you may pluck
Roses and buds, no matter how well kept.
You may not wealthy be, but don't be close
Or miserly; give gladly fair, small gifts
That won't impoverish you unreasonably.
If they should do that, you would fare but ill;
10 Many would mock and few would pardon you
For having paid for goods more than they're worth.
    "He's well advised who offers of fresh fruits
Presents in baskets or in napery.
Don't overlook such things as mulberries,
Strawberries, cherries, quinces, apples, pears,
Barberries, peaches, plums, and beam-tree fruit,
And grafted medlars, prunes, and nectarines,
Raspberries, chestnuts, figs, and purple grapes.
Be sure they're fresh and ripe; and, if you buy
20 In nearby markets, say they come from far,
Presented to you by one of your friends.
Give roses red, primroses, violets,
In season, fairly placed in basketry.
Remember, presents take away their spite
From evil tongues, and silence calumny.
Though some may know of donors something bad,
They'll say of the donation naught but good.
Many a reputation by fair gifts
Has been sustained that else had fallen low.
30 Many a prebendage has been secured
By gifts of food and wine. Trust what I say:

Good gifts give testimony of good lives;
He's noble thought to be who nobly lives.
Presents cause givers gain and takers loss;
These forfeit freedom when to those they're bound.
What shall I say in summary? By gifts
One wins the favor of both men and gods.
 "Companion, hark to what I now advise:
Know well that, if you'll do what I have said,
40 When you the mighty castle shall assail,
The God of Love will never fail to keep
His promises to you; Venus and he
Will so attack the jailers that the fort
Shall fall. However strongly she's shut up,
You'll then be able to secure your Rose.
 "But when you have attained your end, there's need
Of mastership, wisely and well to guard
Your conquest if you would enjoy it long;
For no less valor is required to keep
50 And well defend what once has been acquired
Than to attain, by whatsoever means.
One would be right to call himself a wretch
Who by his own fault loses what he loves.
Most high and worthy is the mother wit
To know well how to keep a woman's heart
And lose no share in it, especially
When God has been so gracious as to give
One who is courteous, artless, wise, and good—
One who'd not sell but gladly gives her love.
60 No woman e'er made love a merchandise
Except a harlot proved; there's no real love
Found in a woman who will sell herself.
Beware of such; may hell-fire burn feigned love!
 "Yet are most women covetous of gain,
And gluttonous to swallow and consume
Until there naught remains to those who claim
Themselves their lovers, loyal in their love.
Old Juvenal tells us of Iberine
That she more willingly would lose an eye
70 Than trust one man to satisfy her lust;
One man would not suffice to feed her flame.

No woman is so ardent in desire
To keep her sweetheart and his love that she
Would not despoil and into torment bring
Her dearest lover. See what others do
Who give themselves to men for gifts they get.
No woman can you find who will not try
What men are in her power thus to prove;
This one intent is common to them all.
80 This is the rule that Juvenal lays down;
But it is not infallible, for he
Of evil women this harsh judgment makes.
   "This is what you should do if she you love
Is true in heart and innocent in face:
A man who's innocent and debonair—
Who is not careless where he sets his heart—
Will not be too impressed with face and form,
But will assure himself of character
Founded on art and science; beauty's self
90 Too short a time remains, as well he knows
Who's learned the workings of effect and cause.
Beauty is like the flowers of the mead
Whose vesper song's soon sung—no sooner blown
Than they begin to wither and decay.
   "She who an education has acquired
Will make a fitting helpmeet for a man
Long as she lives on earth, and at the end
She'll better be than at the first she was.
Time never will diminish her allure,
100 But ever will ameliorate her worth.
Any man of high intelligence,
Who wisely acts, should be much loved and prized.
Conversely, every woman takes delight
When she gives her devotion to a man
Who shows her proof that he is wise and good.
   "Someone may ask if it is not worth while
To make and send to charm and hold his love
Fair verses, motets, ballads, chansonettes.
Alas, one gains not much from such pursuit—
110 He need not pain himself to poetize—
Perhaps the poem's praised, but that is all.

But ample purse, filled and weighed down with gold,
Will make them run to him with open arms
When ladies see him draw and open it;
Their desperation has become so great
That they pursue naught but full pocketbooks.
Once, to be sure, 'twas different; times are getting worse."

40. The Friend contrasts the present with the Golden Age
[8355–8454]

"WRITINGS that emphasize degeneracy   THE FRIEND
Prove that in our first parents' early days
Loyal and true was love—not mercenary.
Most precious was that glorious Golden Age!
Men were not greedy for fine clothes or food.
They gathered acorns in the woods for bread;
In place of fish and flesh, they searched the glades,
Thickets, hills, and plains for fruits and nuts:
Apples and pears, chestnuts and mulberries,
10 Sloes and the seed pods of the eglantine,
Red strawberries, and blackberries and haws.
As vegetables, peas and beans and herbs
And roots they had. They gathered heads of grain.
The grapes that grew upon the fields they picked,
Nor put them in the wine press or the vat.
Abundantly on honey they could feast;
It fairly dripped from stores within the oaks.
No claret or spiced honey wine they drank
Nor any mixture—only water pure.
20   "No plowing was then needed by the soil,
But by God's care it foisoned by itself,
Providing all the comforts that men wished.
They ate no pike or salmon; and they wore
But shaggy skins, or made their clothes of wool
Just as it came from off the backs of sheep.
Nor did they dye it scarlet, green, or blue.

The cottages grouped in their villages
Were roofed with broom or branches, or with leaves;
Or else they made their homes in earthly caves.
30 Sometimes they refuge took among the rocks
Or in the hollow trunks of mighty trees,
When tempests made them fear the stormy blasts
And warned them that for safety they must flee.
At evening when they wished to go to sleep
In place of beds they brought into their homes
Great heaps of moss or leaves, or sheaves of grass.
    "Whene'er as if 'twere everlasting spring
The wind had been appeased, and soft and sweet
The weather had become, with pleasant breeze,
40 So that each morning every bird essayed
In his own language to salute the dawn,
All this inspired their hearts with joyous love.
    "Then Zephyrus and Flora, his fair wife,
The goddess and the lady of the flowers,
Enlarged the little buds of opening blooms
Which such new splendor gave to springing grass
In every field and wood that you had thought
That earth had into competition gone
With heaven to see which should be better starred,
50 So proud it seemed to be of all its flowers.
'Tis from these two the blossoms take their birth;
They recognize no other parentage,
For he and she together sow the seeds
Throughout the earth, and give the flowers form
And all the hues with which they are made fair—
The blossoms prized by maidens and young men
Delighting in fair chaplets made for love—
And very fine and great their true love is.
    "Upon such beds as I've described to you,
60 Free from all thought of harlotry or rape,
Those who were pleased to play the game of love
With kisses and embraces would unite.
In groves the verdant trees stretched out their limbs,
Protecting thus the lovers from the sun
With curtains and pavilions made of leaves.
There carried on their play and caroling

And lazy pleasantries this folk secure,
Void of all care except to lead their lives
In frank and joyous amiability.
70 Not yet had king or prince brought despotism
To pinch and rob the folk. All equals were.
Not yet for private property they strove.
Well did they know this saying is no lie
Or foolishness: 'There's no companionship
'Twixt Love and Seignory.' Whom Love unites
Either's supremacy will quickly separate."

41. The Friend tells how a Jealous Husband abuses his wife
[8455–8744]

"ONE sees some marriages in which the man   THE FRIEND
Thinks it the part of wisdom to chastise
And beat his wife, to make her live in fear,
Saying that she is silly or a fool,
Staying too late at dances, meeting men.
True love cannot for long endure when such
Reciprocal annoyances exist
And men treat their own wives like property,
Accusing them: 'Your levity's too great;   JEALOUS HUSBAND
10 You act too foolish. When I go to work,
You dance and frolic, and you play such games
And sing such siren songs you seem debauched.
God give you a bad week in recompense!
When I must go to Frisia or to Rome
To carry on my business, you become
At once so impudent—I know it well,
For there's somebody who keeps track of you—
That gossip of it runs throughout the town.
Then when folks ask you why you dress so well
20 Where'er you go, you answer mockingly,
"Aha! Oho! 'Tis for my husband's sake."   THE WIFE
For me! Alas! I'm wretched, weary, sad!   JEALOUS HUSBAND

Who knows my labor at the forge or loom,
Or if I live or die? No wonder 'twere
If men with mutton bladder banged my face.
When I've not punished you enough, you think
That I'm not worth a button, and you brag
That this is so. Small honor 'tis to me,
For everybody knows your boasts are lies,
30 For me? Alas! For me? What irony!
I've cramped my hand into an evil glove.
Most cruelly did I deceive myself
When at our wedding I believed your vows.
Is it for me that you amuse yourself?
Is it for me you lead so gay a life?
Whom do you think that you're deceiving now?
I never thought to see such dressing up
As that with which you waken the desires
Of ribald lechers (who the harlots chase)
40 When they accompany you on the streets
And spy and ogle your bold-faced display.
Whose chestnuts am I pulling from the fire?
Who could deceive me more than you deceive?
I'm only your protection from the rain,
Which you hug close when you have need of it.
Beneath this wimple and this cloak you seem
As turtledove or pigeon innocent.
You care not whether it is long or short
When it's but I who's wrapped in it with you.
50 No matter how good-natured I may be,
But for my shame, for four cents I would beat
You well, and see if I could mar your pride.
You know that I'm displeased to see in you
Signs of flirtatiousness at dance or ball
When you are dancing with another man.
Besides, I can't conceal my jealousy
Of what's between you and that bachelor,
Green-hatted Robichon, who at your beck
Comes quickly as if you shared property.
60 You cannot stay away from him. You two
Seem ever fluting on one set of pipes.
I don't know what you find to talk about

That such reciprocal amusement gives.
To see you carry on so shamelessly
Must necessarily incite my rage.
By God, who lies not, if again you talk
With him, I'll give you wherewithal to blanch
Your face or make it black and blue. By heavens,
Unless you leave this dissipated life,
70 Such blows I'll give, so hard I'll slap your cheeks,
Which all the libertines now think so sweet,
That you'll be coy and quiet for a while.
Without me never shall you leave the house
Though I must clamp on you an iron ring
To make you slave at home as you deserve.
'Tis deviltry makes you so intimate
With ribalds full of flattery, whom you
Should never recognize. Was it for them
Or for myself that I affianced you?
80 Do you think that you can deserve my love
When with whoremasters you associate?
Think you their minds would have such bawdy thoughts
Unless they found you bawdy in your turn?
I have no faith in such a dirty drab!
      " 'The devil 'twas that made me marry you!
Would that I Theophrastus had believed
And never wed! He thinks a man a sot
Who joins himself in wedlock with a wife,
Be she or foul or fair or poor or rich;
90 For in his noble book called *Aureole*,
Which should be studied in the schools, he says,
And I believe it true, that such a man
Too grievous life will lead, filled full of pain,
Of labor, quarrels, danger, and reproach
Caused by a silly woman's foolish pride
And the demands and the complaints she makes,
Occasions for which she never fails to find.
Hard it will be to curb her foolish will
And guard her from herself. If she be poor,
100 Her clothing, shoes, and food will be great charge.
If she be rich, he may avoid expense,
But he will suffer from her proud disdain,

Her arrogance, and her presumptuousnesss.
If she be fair, all men will her besiege,
Flatter, pursue, attack, torment, engage—
Make battle for her, study to assist,
Flock round her making prayers, her favor seek,
So covetous of her that in the end
They'll manage so that it small wonder were
110 If her defenses, thus beset, should fall.
  If she be foul, she'll try to please them all;
And how can one do this and yet be safe?
She guards a jewel all are fighting for—
Which every man desires who glimpses it.
No one on earth can everybody fight
And safely guard a thing that all men wish.
  " 'Had she not been the best of wives in Greece,
The suitors who besieged Penelope
Had won their point and conquered even her.
120   " 'King Tarquin's son so gained his end when he
Ravished by force the chaste Lucretia,
Though, to be sure, she therefore killed herself.
Nowise, as Titus Livius says, could sire
Or husband, or her other relatives,
However much they sought to save her life,
Keep her from suicide before their eyes.
Much did they beg her to forsake her grief.
Wisely they spoke. Her husband, notably,
Gave pious comfort, freely pardoned her,
130 Said and did everything he could to prove
By logic that her body had not sinned,
Since never had her heart desired the act;
For when the will consents not there's no sin.
But she maintained her mourning, and kept hid
Beneath her robe a knife which no one saw
Until she drew it forth to kill herself.
Boldly she answered, "Though you pardon me,   LUCRETIA
Fair sirs, for that foul sin that weighs me down,
Myself I cannot pardon, nor sustain
140 The shame." Then, full of agony, she struck JEALOUS HUSBAND
And cleft her heart in twain, falling to earth
Before them all; but ere she died she prayed

That they would labor to avenge her death.
This case procured enactment of that law
By which all women were thenceforth assured
That death should be the punishment for rape.
Proud Tarquin and his sons, to exile sent,
Died miserably. After this ill event
No Roman wished to have him king at Rome.
150   " 'But no Lucretia lives in Rome today,
And no Penelope in all of Greece;
Indeed, if one should search the entire world,
He'd hardly find a woman of this kind.
The pagans say no woman guards herself
Against the attack of a determined man.
'Twere hard to find exception to this rule.
Indeed, there's many a one offers herself
When she's aware no man solicits her.
     " 'Most inconsistent is the wont of men
160 When they would marry; often I'm amazed
That such a risky custom they should use.
Whence comes their foolishness I do not know,
Unless from madness or insanity.
I never see a man who buys a mare
Act so unwisely as to close the deal
Without observing her unblanketed.
If she is covered, he will strip her bare
That he may see her parts and try her out.
But one will take a wife without such test,
170 All unaware of solace or regret,
For better or for worse, without a chance
Of finding faults in her, provided that
She no displeasure give before they're wed.
But when the knot is tied, her spite appears;
Then first does she reveal the vice she has;
Then first the fool perceives her evil tricks
When late repentance will avail him not.
No matter, therefore, how much care he takes,
There's scarce a husband, but he be a sot,
180 Who, once he's married, finds no discontent.
     " 'A virtuous maid! By Saint Denis I swear
She's rarer than the phoenix. He who weds

Afflicts himself with many a hard mischance
And fear and care, as says Valerius.
More rare than is the phoenix, did I say?
If I say that she's rarer than white crows,
However fair their body seem, 'twould be
More just comparison. But ne'ertheless,
Lest any living man assert that I
190 Seem too severely to assail the sex,
I'll modify my statement. He who'd find
A virtuous woman—secular or nun—
Much labor must expend upon his search.
Such birds are scattered thinly o'er the earth;
You are more apt to find a Negro swan.
This is confirmed by Juvenal, who says:
"If ever you should find a woman chaste,   JUVENAL
Go kneel within the temple, bow and pray
To Jupiter; take pains to sacrifice
200 A gilded cow to Juno, his famed wife."
For no more marvelous adventure came   JEALOUS HUSBAND
Ever to living creature in this world.
   " 'Valerius is not ashamed to ask
To what end thinks the fool that he will come
Who either in this land or overseas
Makes love to evil women, who abound
Thicker than flies, or bees about a hive.
Who trust in such frail twigs lose body and soul.
Valerius, who grieved when he perceived
210 That Rufinus, his friend, would take a wife,
Spoke these hard words: "May God omnipotent   VALERIUS
Forbid that e'er you're caught within the net
Of woman, who is powerful to crush
All things by her destructive artifice!"

JEALOUS HUSBAND
   " 'And Juvenal wrote likewise to his friend
Posthumus, when the latter wished to wed:
"You wish to marry? Can't you find for sale   JUVENAL
A rope or halter—any kind of cord?
Can you not jump from open window high,
220 Or fall into the river from a bridge?
What Fury leads you to endure such woe and pain?' "

42. The Jealous Husband tells the story of Héloïse and Abélard
[8745–8956]

JEALOUS HUSBAND

" 'THE king who first gave laws unto the Greeks,
Phoroneus, unto his brother said,
While lying on his deathbed: "If I knew   PHORONEUS
You'd never wed, I could most happy die."
Leontius asked the reason. He replied:
"All husbands prove by sad experience
The truth of my opinion, which you'll know
Right well if e'er you dare to take a wife."
    " 'In turn confesses Peter Abélard,   JEALOUS HUSBAND
10 Who loved the abbess of the Paraclete,
That Héloïse wished never to agree
That he should take her for his wedded wife.
She was a wise, well-educated maid,
Well loved and loving, yet with arguments
She taught her lover wedlock to avoid.
Her letters pointed out how hard are found
The circumstances of a wedded life,
No matter how discreet the wife may be.
Not only had she read and studied books
20 But learned of woman's nature in herself.
That he should love her she made her demand
But also that he'd claim no other right
Than what was granted freely, of good grace,
Without supremacy or mastership;
That he might study freely, without tie
Though hers, while she, in science not unversed,
Pursued her studies, too. She said at least
Their joys would be more pleasing when they met,
Their solace would by absence be increased.
30 But he, as he has writ for us to read,

Loved her so much that he must marry her
Against her good advice; whence came mischance.
No sooner had they joined in this accord
Than she was, as a nun, at Argenteuil
Immured; and he, at Paris caught one night
Abed, was made emasculate by foes,
Living thenceforth in shame and impotence.
A monk of Saint Denis he then became,
And later abbot of another house;
40 And then, we're told in his biography,
He built the famous abbey, Paraclete,
Of which the former nun, his Héloïse,
Was abbess made. And she herself recounts
In writing, unashamed, that she so loved
Him that she called him master and her lord.
Some say her letters show insanity,
But marvelous are many things she wrote,
Which one who reads attentively may find,
And which she sent especially to him
50 E'en after she had donned the abbess' robe.
She writes, "If e'en the Emperor of Rome,   HÉLOÏSE
In whose subjection everyone should be,
Should ever wish to take me as his wife
And make me foremost lady in the world
(I call on God to witness what I say),
I'd rather be your mistress than crowned queen."
But, by my soul, I scarcely can believe   JEALOUS HUSBAND
That such another woman ever lived.
It was her education, I suppose,   absurd
                                                   moralitas
60 That taught her how she best could hold in curb
Her woman's nature; and, if Abélard
Had trusted her, he had not come to grief.
  " 'Marriage is but an evil bond. Help me,
Saint Julian, who aids all wanderers,
Saint Leonard, who the prisoners unchains
When they, repentant, make appeal to him!
'Twere better on my wedding day I'd hanged
Than married one who shows such coquetry
That her deceit will bring me to my grave.
70 By Virgin Mary's son, what good to me

Is all this bravery, this costly dress,
All the expense that makes you vain and proud
But only vexes me and gives me grief?
The more your long and sweeping train you swing,
In which you take such pride, the more I rave.
What profit have I in such luxury?
However much you others please with them,
You give me but annoyance with your clothes.
If I desire with you to take delight,
80 The things you wear are always in the way;
You're so dressed up in your encumberments
That, thanks to them, I never gain my end.
I never can succeed to hold you close;
Such turnings and such twistings you perform
That always you escape from my embrace.
You ward me off with arms and hips and legs.
I don't know why it is, but plainly see
That all my amorousness and offered bliss
Are most distasteful—please you not at all.
90 At night when I'm abed and share my couch
With you, as every man does with his wife,
Then you, indeed, must needs undress yourself;
And what good then are all your clothes to me?
In bed you nothing wear upon your head,
Upon your naked body and your limbs,
Except, perhaps, a linen nightcap white,
Bedecked with ribbon bows of green or blue
To give protection to your coiffured hair.
Then all your dresses and your costly furs
100 Wave in the air all night upon a rail.
Except to sell or pawn, they're naught to me.
No wonder that you see me so enraged,
Dying of ire that I can't rid myself
Of trumpery that bothers me all day
And adds not to my pleasure in the night.
How profit I from it unpawned, unsold?
As for yourself, if I must tell the truth,
You're not worth one whit more because of it
Either in sense or good companionship,
110 Or even in attractiveness, by God!

If someone to confound me should respond,
"Fine feathers make fine birds, and ornaments
Women's and maidens' beauty oft improve!"
I'd answer him most shortly that he lied.
The beauty of whatever thing is fair—
Be it a violet, be it a rose,
Be it a fleur-de-lis or silken gown—
As I in Scripture read, stays in itself
And to the one who wears it ne'er transfers.
120 You women should perceive that all your lives
You'll have no beauty but that given at birth.
Of goodness I will make the same remark.
Exemplification makes my meaning plain:
A dungheap covered o'er with silk or flowers,
No matter how made neat or how disguised,
Remains a dunghill still, and smells the same.
And should you say, "Though it be foul within,   THE WIFE
Without it looks much better than before;
So, too, the ladies dress that they may seem
130 More fair, or that their foulness may be hid,"
My faith, the only answer I could give   JEALOUS HUSBAND
Is that one so deceived is surely blind
To all but outward show, ignores the heart,
Alone upon a fair impression trusts
That from his fooled imagination comes,
Unable to discern 'twixt lie and truth,
And, ignorant, succumbs to sophistry.
If men had lynx's eyes and were more wise,
To them no woman would appear more fair
140 Because of sable mantle or rich cloak
Or panniers or guimpes or headdresses
Or pelisses or finest linen gowns
Or jewelry or other ornaments
Or bonnets trimmed with floral novelties
Or simpering expression on her face
Or any superficial brilliancy
Which makes her seem most like a work of art.
Than Alcibiades no one more fair
Could be in figure or in coloring,
150 So well had Nature formed him; but within

That wise and worthy man, Boethius,
Says one would find that he was far too foul.
He Aristotle cites, and quotes his words
That one would see this had he eye of lynx,
Whose vision is so piercing and so clear
That he sees plainly everything, inside and out.' "

43. The Jealous Husband recalls the war between
Beauty and Chastity
[8957–9078]

" ' 'TIS said that Beauty ne'er in any age   JEALOUS HUSBAND
Has been at peace with Chastity; their war
Remains so fierce that in no song or tale
Have I e'er heard that they are in accord.
Their strife is mortal; neither yields a foot
Of ground which her opponent might secure
To aid her victory. But so unmatched
Are they that Chastity, for her own part,
Whether she attacks or makes defense,
10 To strike or ward possesses such small skill
That ever she acknowledges defeat,
For she is powerless 'gainst Beauty's force.
E'en Ugliness, her handmaiden, who owes
Service and honor, does not love or prize
Her mistress, but pursues her from the house
And chases her with high-uplifted mace
That is so powerful and weighs so much
That 'tis a wonder that her lady lives
A single hour. So Chastity's assailed
20 On either side, and is so badly served,
Securing succor from no single source,
That from the lonely struggle she takes flight.
If she'd a sword by its neck to wage the war,
She'd hardly dare to fight for hopeless cause,
Knowing so little, and opposed so much.

" 'Curses upon the traitor, Ugliness,
Who her pursues whom she should most defend!
She should have hidden her beneath her shirt
Next to the skin, were there no other way.
30 Beauty, moreover, is as much to blame,
Who ought to love her and procure her peace,
If that would please her; or employ her power
To that good end when she gave up the fight;
Or even, were she courteous, wise, and good,
Bring homage to her, not disgrace and shame.
Now Vergil gives authority for this;
In his sixth book he quotes the Sibyl's words
That one will not be damned who chaste life lives.

" 'I swear by God, who is of Heaven king,
40 That every dame who wishes to be fair
And paints her face that she may seem to be,
Admiring the reflection in her glass,
Taking great care with ornaments and clothes,
Is willing to make war on Chastity,
Who of such enemies has many a one.
Throughout the abbeys and the nunneries
They've sworn against her; none are so immured
That they do not hate Chastity so much
That they attempt to shame her if they can.
50 Homage to Venus all the women pay,
Regardless of the profit or the loss,
Painting and primping to deceive the men
Who watch them as they trail about the streets
To see and to be seen, and rouse desire
Of fornication in the lookers-on.
To dances and to church alike they wear
Their finery, which surely they'd not do
Did they not hope the men who see them there
Would thus be pleased—more quickly be seduced.
60 To tell the truth, they shame the deity.
Like crazy fools they are, who're not content
With that degree of beauty God bestowed.
Each one must crown her head with silk and gold
Or floral wreath in which she takes much pride
As simpering she shows herself in town.

By means of which the cursed unfortunate
Most vilely lowers herself when things more vile
Than she herself she puts upon her head,
Her beauty to increase or to perfect.
70 Thus she despises God, considering
Him insufficient in His handiwork;
And in her foolish heart she thinks the Lord,
When He bestowed what beauty she may boast,
Was negligent and gave her an affront.
She borrows beauty from the earth and flowers
And other things of little worth, which God
In viler form than hers has edified.
   " 'Undoubtedly this is as true of men
If we to gain more beauty chaplets make,
80 Or other frippery, to magnify
The beauty God has given. We insult
Him when we show ourselves unsatisfied
With that which he accords the human race
Us to exalt above all creatures else.
I have no use for such frivolity;
Sufficient clothes to guard me from the heat
And cold alone I wish. God helping me,
I can protect myself from wind and storm.
My woolen, lined with lambskin, is as good
90 As any finer fabric furred with squirrel skin.' "

44. The Jealous Husband recounts how women have deceived men
[9079–9360]

JEALOUS HUSBAND

" 'I WASTE my money when I buy for you
Expensive clothes dyed red or blue or green,
Adorned with squirrel fur or ermine lined,
In which you make parade with swish and smirk,
Trailing them through the mud and dust alike

With no regard for either me or God.
And then at night, when naked in my bed
You lie beside me, you must not be touched;
For when I want to take you in my arms,
10 A kiss or other solace to procure,
You cool my heat with looks as black as hell,
And spite of all my efforts turn your back.
Then you pretend you're ill, and sigh and groan,
And so impede my efforts that I fail,
Nor try again for fear of like success,
Not even in the morning when I wake.
But much I wonder if your lovers fail
When in their arms they take you fully clothed,
If when you play with them you twist and turn—
20 By day vex them as you vex me by night!
I don't believe your practice that would be
When you go tripping through the garden lanes
Or singing through the fields with traitors vile
Who, though the green grass glistens wet with dew,
Chase after you, who are my wedded wife,
Voicing among themselves contempt of me:
'Here's how we trick the dirty, jealous wretch!'
May wolves devour the flesh, dogs gnaw the bones
Of those by whom I am so cuckolded.
30 Foul woman, ribald hussy, lecherous bitch,
By you and your vile ways I'm put to shame.
May you not live one year beyond the day
When you bestowed your body on such curs!
Your lechery has leagued me with the band
Of cuckolds whom Saint Arnold dominates,
From whom no married man can e'er escape,
In my opinion. Though a million eyes
He had to guard and spy upon his wife,
If she's assailable, and freely gives
40 Herself, no guard can make a wanton safe.
If it should happen that her purpose fail
While yet the will thereto is strong, she'll know
How to accomplish it, for wish will find a way.
   " 'Cold comfort gives us Juvenal, who says
Stupration is the least of women's sins,

Whose nature urges them to greater crimes.
We read how mothers-in-law cooked poison broth
For daughters' husbands, and with spells and charms
Worked many other mighty deviltries
50 Unthinkable, which I cannot rehearse.
  " 'All women are, have been, and e'er will be,
In thought if not in deed, unvirtuous;
Though some may hesitate to do the act,
None can restrain their wish. All women have
This great advantage: they their purpose hold.
Scolding and beating will not change their minds;
He'd rule their bodies who could rule their wills.
Let's talk no more of things that ne'er can be!
  " 'So help me fair, sweet God, the King of Heaven,
60 What can I do against this ribald crew
Who wrong me so and put me to such shame?
What do they care for all the threats I make?
They'd beat or kill me if I tried to fight,
For they are felon outlaws bold enough
To work all ill; voluptuous and proud,
Foolish and strong, they prize me not a fig;
For youth enflames them, filling them with fire,
And stimulates their hearts to risky deeds.
So light and volatile are all their thoughts
70 That each a Roland thinks himself to be
If not a Samson or a Hercules.
It matters not which of the latter two,
For, as we read, they were alike in strength.
According to the author Solinus,
The last-named one was seven feet in height,
The greatest size attainable by man.
Many a labor did he undertake;
Twelve dreadful monsters did he overcome
But never gained the thirteenth victory,
80 For Deianira, who had been his love,
Jealous of Iole, whose love he was,
Sent him the poison shirt that ate his flesh.
Thus Hercules, so valorous and strong,
Was conquered by a woman. Samson, too,
Who no more than ten apples feared ten men,

While he still had his hair, was overcome
When it was by his wife, Delilah, cut.
" 'But I'm a fool to talk. You will repeat
Me word for word when next you meet your friends,
90 And you may have those ribalds beat my head
Or break my legs or 'twixt my shoulders stab
If e'er I let you talk with them again.
However, if I hear that you have blabbed,
Unless they hold my arms or steal my club,
I'll break your ribs before that comes to pass.
No relative or neighbor shall prevent
The deed—not even all your lecherous friends.
Alas! Why were we ever introduced?
Woe worth the evil hour when I was born!
100 You think me vile; and yet those stinking dogs
Who flatter and caress you, you make lords
And masters of the body that belongs
Alone to him who should your seignor be,
Who keeps you, feeds you, clothes you, buys you shoes.
You make me but a coparticipant
With those who give you naught but shameful name!
The honor that you fail to guard they steal,
When in your arms you clasp them. To your face
They say they love you, but behind your back
110 They call you whore. Then, after meeting you,
They get together, they exchange their tales,
The worst they can invent, of how the game
Went with each one. I may as well confess
That all their boasts most probably are true.
When to their will you offer up yourself,
They need small skill to bring you to the point.
There's no resistance in you when the crowd
Sees fit lewdly to spank and rummage you.
Of them and of the pleasure that they get
120 I must confess that I some envy feel;
But you should know what I most emphasize:
That it is not your body nor the thrills
It gives them that attracts them all to you,
But rather jeweled buttons, golden clasps,
Rich gowns and mantles, that like crazy fool

I let you wear. For when you go to balls
With all your crowd of silly satellites
I stay at home like any drunken sot
While on your back you wear a hundred pounds
130 In worth of gold and silver, and demand
That I dress you in camelot and furs;
While I myself in care and anger pine,
So much your conduct irks and vexes me.
　　" 'What good to me are all your orfrays fine,
The gilded bands and headdresses you wear,
The coronets of decorated gold,
Your ivory mirror, and your golden ring,
Carved and enameled with such costly skill,
The fair and finely polished golden crown
140 Which so enraged me, the jewelry,
The sapphires, rubies, emeralds, and pearls
Which make you proud and of such seeming worth?
What good to me is all such gewgaw trash
As golden clasp beset with precious stones
That calls attention to your neck and breast,
Or silver-threaded cinctures for your waist,
Whose buckles cost their weight in pearls or gold?
You're shod so finely that you lift your skirts,
Oft as you can, to show the men your feet.
150 So help me Saint Thibaud, within three days
I'll sell this trash, and then you will be crushed;
For, lacking it, you'll be considered vile!
God's body, but I'll give you different clothes:
A woolen dress and mantle, hempen scarf,
Not fine but coarse, and mayhap woven ill
Or torn and mended, spite of your complaints!
And do you know what belt shall bind your waist?
A plain white leather one without a clasp.
Of my old gaiters you can make laced shoes;
160 If they're too ample, stuff them out with rags.
I'll take away all these deceitful clothes
That lead to fornication and naught else,
And then you'll go no more to show yourself
And lure the ribalds to adultery.
　　" 'Now tell me truly, who bought you that dress

Which you appeared in at the dance last week?
I never gave it. In what love affair
Did you receive it as a prize? You swore
By Saint Denis and holy Filibert
170 And by Saint Peter 'twas your mother's gift,
Who sent it to you out of love for me,
As you gave me to understand, that I
Might save my money while she spend her own.
If those are not the very words you used,
I'll see her burned alive, the dirty whore,
Old prostitute, vile bawd, and sorceress—
And you along with her, as you deserve.
To ask the truth of her were labor lost—
Not worth a marble the replies I'd get—
180 For worthless as her daughter is your dame.
You've been in consultation, I know;
Your hearts are bells with single clapper rung;
And well I see on which foot you both limp.
With that old, dirty, painted, debauchee
You're in complete accord. In former days
She twisted the same halter you now twirl;
So many roads she's traveled that she's been
Bitten by many dogs, until at last
Her force is spent so that she's nothing worth,
190 And so she plays the procuress for you.
She comes here three or four days every week
And on new pilgrimages leads you forth,
As she pretends according to her wont.
But I know all the secret of that trick.
She promenades you as one would a nag
Which he desires to sell; she preys on men
And teaches you to prey upon them too.
Do you think I am ignorant of this?
What holds me back from breaking all your bones,
200 As if you were a pullet or a pye,
And putting to good use a pestle or a spit?' "

45. The Friend tells how the Jealous Husband beats his wife
[9361–9492]

"THEN suddenly the husband seizes her,   THE FRIEND
Sweating with rage, and by the hair he drags
Her madly through the house from room to room,
And rudely shakes her, tearing out her locks,
More furiously than lion fights a bear
In wrath accusing and belaboring her.
So evil is his temper that no vow
Of hers will he in exculpation take;
Rather he strikes and beats and thumps and spanks,
10 While she, lamenting, fills the air with cries
And screams that through the windows and the doors
Attract the neighbors, who surround the house
And hear the husband speak his mind and scold,
Until they think the two of them are fools
And separate them with the utmost pains,
Succeeding only when he's lost his breath.

"When o'er this scene of turmoil and abuse
She ponders, and recalls the serenade
Her lover played for her the night before,
20 Think you she loves her husband more for this?
She wishes he were in Romania
Or far-off Meaux. I think I may assert
She'll never wish to love the man again.
'Tis true that she may make pretense of love;
But could he climb on high without a fall,
Or fly into the clouds above, and view
The deeds of man on earth, and muse thereon
At leisure, he would know his dangerous case
And by what wiles his wife protects herself.
30 If after that she shares her bed with him
He runs much risk, for, sleeping or awake,
Great fear attends him lest she take revenge

And have him stabbed or poisoned; or at least
Her tricks will make him lead a dangerous life,
Or she'll desert him for another love.
When women's heads are turned, they lose all shame
And sense of honor. As 'tis truly said,
They're unintelligent in love or hate.
Valerius calls them bold in artifice
40 And all too studious to give annoy.

    "Comrade, this silly, foolish wretch, whose flesh
Is as to wolves delivered, so he's filled
With doubt, may an éxample be to you.
He masters thus his wife, who should not be
Supreme, but his companion and his peer,
As they have been united by the law;
And he should be, in turn, companion, too,
And not her lord and master. Do you think,
When he torments her thus and makes her life
50 In such misease, and her unequal holds,
That he can please her and retain her love?
Whatever she may say, no woman likes
A husband who demands supremacy.
Love dies when seignory exalts its head;
Love cannot live or last except in hearts
That are emancipated, frank, and free.
And so 'tis rarely seen that those who love
Before their marriage can affection keep;
For he who formerly to be her slave
60 Had sworn, and said his passion was pure love,
Now thinks himself her master and her lord."

    "Was he a slave?"   THE LOVER
          " 'Tis true."   THE FRIEND
                                 THE LOVER
             "And in what way?"
    "In that she did not beg, but ordered him: THE FRIEND
'Jump, friend, and get me something,' and he'd jump
At her command, and fetch it without fail.
Whate'er she said, he'd do as he was bid;
To give her pleasure was his only wish.
But when they're married, as I have described,
Then Fortune's wheel has turned. (He lives in vain

70 Who does not learn this truth before he dies.)
Now he who lately served but orders gives
That she shall wait on him like any slave—
Holds her in check, and makes her give account
To him of all she does, though once he said
She was his mistress! Now she may complain
Her evil case when she is treated thus
By him whom she supposed to be the best
And worthiest of men that she could find
In all the earth, who now but balks her will.
80 She knows no one to whom she can confide
Her fear when at her throat her master stares
In such a way as he ne'er stared before.
Most evilly her husband's changed his tune,
And now she has to dance a different jig.
The game's become so strange and ominous,
When thus he's changed the dice for her, that she
Could not enjoy it if she dared to play.
How can she sing the praise of such a man?
If she does not obey, he will complain
90 And, in his anger, call her ugly names.
Before his wrath she's like a deadly enemy."

46. The Friend describes the decline in human happiness
[9493–9678]

"COMRADE, the ancients for each other bore   THE FRIEND
True friendliness, living their lives in peace,
With neither villainy nor servitude
Nor other yokes; nor had they freedom sold
For all of Araby's or Phrygia's wealth.
The bargain had been bad at any rate.
They made no pilgrimages—never left
Their native shores in search of foreign lands.
Not yet had Jason passed beyond the seas;
10 And he was first to compass such a feat

When he his ships assembled for the search
Of fabled golden fleece. But when they saw
The sailing ships make war against the waves,
Neptune and Triton fell into a rage,
As Doris did, and all her daughters, too.
They thought they were by magic ruse betrayed,
They were so fearful when they saw the ships
Skimming the ocean at the sailors' will.
Our first forefathers never mounted ship.
20 What seemed worth seeking they found on the land.
Equally rich, they lived in loyal love;
And, since by nature each was loved by each,
They led in peace their simple, pleasant lives.
Love then depended not on simony,
For no one of his friend demanded aught.
    "But then Deceit came charging, lance at rest,
And Sin and Evil Chance—Contentment's foes.
In state came Pride (she scorns equality)
With Covetousness, Envy, Avarice,
30 And all the other vices. Poverty
They brought from Hell, where she had lived so long
That none on earth knew anything of her;
For in this world she ne'er had been before.
Evil the early day when she appeared,
For her arrival was the worst of all!
Uneasy Poverty brought Theft, her son,
Who quickly to the gibbet found his way—
Thinking to aid his mother—and some day
Will hang, for Poverty can give no aid;
40 Nor can Faint Heart, his father, whose distress
At the event left him in sorry state;
Nor can the maid Laverna, guide of thieves,
Goddess and governess, who hides the crimes
Of night, and covers treacheries with mist,
So that they are not manifest, indeed,
Until investigation finds them out,
Arrests are made, and in the end all's proved.
She has no pity when one thrusts his neck
Within the noose, nor will she then go bail
50 Even for one she knows repents his deed.

"Soon as these cursed fiends, with fury fired,
Seeing men lead such lives, o'erran the earth
With Envy, Anger, Slander, Grief, and Hate,
And Discontent, sowing discord and war,
Men held gold dear, and so they flayed the earth—
Drew from her entrails, from her ancient caves,
Metals and precious stones which all desired;
For Avarice and Covetousness fixed
Within their hearts the urge to gather wealth.
60 One strove to gain; another sought to keep;
Neither would spend while he remained alive,
But, if no mishap fell, preserved his goods
For his executors and heirs at death;
And none would care enough to voice regret,
But all would say it was his proper end.
When once the fiends had thus seduced the folk
And led each one astray, they all forsook
Their former life, becoming cozeners,
Nor ever after left their evil deeds.
70 Then they established private real estate—
Apportioned out the land, and verges fixed,
And even fought about the boundaries,
Each taking what he could, the powerful
Obtaining necessarily the most.
But while these went about their enterprise
The lazy, who remained at home, despoiled
The caverns where the rich had stored their wealth.
    "Then all agreed that one they'd find to guard
The homes, and seize the thieves, and be a judge
80 Of all complaints, nor opposition fear.
So they assembled to elect a king.
They chose a sturdy peasant, big of bone,
The largest limbed and tallest that there was,
To be of all the seignor and the prince.
He promised that he justice would dispense
And guard their homes, if individually
They would contribute means for him to live.
It was agreed, as books and records tell;
And for a time he that position kept.
90 But the malicious thieves, assembling oft

To steal the goods when they saw him alone,
Sound beatings gave him. Once again the folk
Assembled and agreed to pay a tax
Which should provide retainers for the prince.
They gave him large apportionment of land,
Tribute, and income. Thus the kings of earth,
And princes, had their origin, 'tis said
In ancient books. We should most grateful be,
And give great praise and thanks unto the men
100 Who wrote them; for 'tis only by their scripts
That we have knowledge of the ancients' deeds.
    "Then men amassed great treasuries of gold
And precious stones and silver. They stamped coins
From both these metals, malleable and rare.
Vessels and buttons, clasps and rings they made,
And purses also from the costly ores.
From iron hard they armor forged: their knives,
Long swords and poleaxes and coats of mail
And daggers—fought their neighbors with all these.
110 Then towers and escarpments they must make,
And walls of quarried stone to hem their towns,
Their castles, and their gated palaces;
For every rich man trembled in his fear
Lest all the gold he'd gathered should be lost—
Stolen by craft or carried off by force.
Much did their woes increase in that sad hour
When not a wretch could longer be assured
Of that which formerly had been as free
As sun and air; so were men bound to wealth
120 That avarice made them appropriate
All that they could, till one man was more rich
Than twenty should be. No good came from that!
    "Certainly I'd not two buttons give
For such base gluttons; little would I care,
No matter how much happiness they lacked.
Let them or love or hate, or sell their love!
And yet it is too bad, and cause for grief,
When clear-eyed ladies, fair and frolicsome,
Who should a loyal love preserve and prize,
130 Descend into such slavery; a thing

Too foul it is to hear that they should sell
Their all-too-noble bodies for the love of gold."

47. The Friend teaches the Lover the art of love
[9679–10014]

"HOWE'ER the matter fall, let gallants guard THE FRIEND
Lest they learn ill the arts and sciences
That would secure, and if need were, defend
Them and their ladies from abandonment.
Such arts uplift above the fear of grief.
So let each strive my counsel to retain
Ever in mind. If e'er he thinks or knows
His lady, be she young or old, desires
To seek another friend, or has secured
10 New love already, let him not reproach
Or blame the acquisition or the wish.
Amiably let him pursue his course
Nor scold nor chide; or even further go
To make estrangement less: if he her find
E'en in the very act, let him pretend
That he is blind, or simple as an ox,
And never look that way—make her believe
That he has not detected anything.
If someone send his love a billet-doux,
20 He should not intercept it or attempt
To read it or search out their secrets there.
He ne'er should wish to contravene her will,
But make her welcome when she reaches home
After a walk upon the street, and smile
Wherever she may wish to go, as if
He centered all his will in her desires;
For women never like to be restrained.
    "Follow this counsel and what more I'll give,
Which should be writ in books for men to read:
30 You who would seek to gain a lady's grace

Must set her free to come and go at will
And never try to hamper her with rules.
Be she your mistress or your wife, you lose
Her love as soon as you make an attempt
To check her liberty to come and go.
If man or woman come to you with tales
About your lady, saying what they've seen,
Never believe a word of it—assert
That they are foolish to report such news.

40 It never could have been so chaste a wife,
Always respectable above reproach,
That they have seen; therefore you can't believe
That she would ever do a thing like that.

"Even her vices one must not reproach—
Much less, to punish, lay his hands on her.
For he who'd beat his wife in hopes to make
Her love him better, when again he tries
Her to conciliate, will find his task
As hard as that of one who beats a cat

50 To tame her, then attempts to call her back
To put her collar on; if puss gets loose,
In vain will be attempts at catching her.

"Though it be she who scolds or beats her spouse,
He must take care that his heart does not change.
He must not take revenge for words or blows
Or even nails that scratch him to the quick,
But rather give her thanks and e'en assert
That willingly he'd live such martyrdom
Forever could he only be assured

60 That she delighted in his services—
Better to die than be divorced from her!

"If it should chance that he the quarrel starts
Because she has been too censorious
And cruel in her frowns and menaces,
Let him look well, before he leaves her side,
That he buy peace, that he make love to her,
Especially if he lacks property;
For his advantages will then be least.
A poor man quickly finds he's left alone

70 Unless he bows before his lady's will.

He must live cautiously—humbly endure
Without a semblance of ill will or ire
Whate'er he sees or hears her say or do;
While in like case a richer man would care
Less than two peas, and well might scold and rage
In all the pride of his authority.
    "If one should wish to seek a second love
And yet not lose the first, when he presents
His latest sweetheart with a handkerchief,
80 Scarf or headdress, ring or fan or belt
Or jewel set with dainty workmanship;
Let him take care the other knows it not.
Cruel would be her agony at heart
If she the other saw such presents wear,
And nothing would avail to comfort her.
Then let him ne'er allow his second love
To go with him into the selfsame place
Where with the first it was his wont to go
And where perchance they'd meet. If that should hap,
90 And she should find him with her there, no ruse
Would help him to escape. No ancient boar
Could bristle half so fiercely when by dogs
He is attacked; no lioness, beset
By hunters while she give her cublings suck,
Could be more fierce and fell; no snake whose tail
Some wayfarer has trod upon (no joke
It is for him!) could be more venomous
Than wife who finds her spouse with someone else.
Body and soul aflame, she flashes fire;
100 And even though she never should surprise
The two together in a proven fault,
She well may feel an equal jealousy
Because she thinks or knows she is deceived.
Howe'er it goes, whether she knows or thinks,
<u>Let him be bold to disavow the crime</u>
<u>And even swear with oaths she knows are false.</u>
If he can so contrive with blandishments
That she will join him in the game of love
At once and on the spot, her plaints will cease.
110   "If, on the other hand, she agonize

And so assail him that he must confess,
Let him no longer try to make defense;
But if he can compel her to believe
That though he struggled hard to overcome
The temptress' wiles, his efforts were in vain.
Moreover, he'll assure her that her watch
Has been so strict—he's been confined so close—
That never have they had the slightest chance
Till this time their conjunction to complete.
120 Let him then promise, swear, and make his oath
That he in future will behave so well
That never will there come to her a word
Reproaching him; or, if she should again
Have reason to suspect him, willingly
He'll let her kill him or drive him quite mad.
    "He'd rather that the naughty renegade,
Her rival, should be drowned, than that again
She bring him to the pass where they were caught.
If it should happen that she sent for him
130 Again, he would not go at her command;
Nor would he let her come, could he prevent,
To any place where he might later be.
    "Then let him tenderly embrace his love,
Kiss and caress her, give her comforting,
And beg her mercy for his sad misdeed
That never will committed be again.
He'll swear that he is truly sorrowful
And ready any penance to perform
That she may be desirous to enjoin
140 When she has pardoned him. Then let him urge,
If he would be forgiven for stolen joys,
That she herself should satisfy his need.
Let him give her no cause to fear his boasts.
Vile shame it is that many a one defames
With false and feigned stories the good name
Of many a lady he has ne'er possessed.
Such are not courteous or worth-while men,
But ones whose failing hearts impede success.
A villain vice is vaunting; he who brags
150 Is worse than fool; the wise man who succeeds

Conceals the fact. Love's treasures are best hid
From all but faithful friend who'll quiet keep;
To him the sweetheart's boons may be revealed.
    "If his loved one fall ill, a man will strive,
And rightly, to be serviceable to her
That later he may in her favor be.
Let no discomfort keep him from her then,
But let her see him bending o'er her couch
With streaming eyes and reassuring kiss
160 And vows of pilgrimages he will make
To distant shrines if God permit her cure.
If he is wise, he'll bring her food she likes
And never any bitter medicines
Or anything but what is good and sweet.
Let him tell tales of pleasant lies composed:
How all last night upon his lonely couch
He slept but little and lay waking long;
But when he dozed he dreamed that in his arms
All night, restored and well, she naked lay
170 Solacing him with lavishment of love
And her delightful charms till it was day.
This fable, or the like, he'll tell to her.
    "So far I've told in verse how lover should
His lady serve, in sickness or in health,
If he'd deserve her favors and her love,
And in them both continue. He who fails
To do what he should do will find love quenched.
No man can be so sure of womankind,
Or know his lady well enough, to feel,
180 How loyal e'er she be and waverless—
However firmly fixed her heart may be—
That he can hold her, with his utmost care,
Better than by the tail he'd hold an eel
Caught in the Seine, so that it could not move
Or get away as soon as it was caught.
That creature cannot be so wholly tamed
That it's not ever ready to escape;
No one can cope with all its various shifts.
    "I say not that there are no women good
190 Who fix restraint by virtue on their lives;

But only that, although I've tested them,
I've found none such. Not even Solomon,
Who well knew how to try them, could find one;
For he himself affirms he never saw
A woman steadfast. If with greatest pains
Your search should find one, seize and hold her fast;
In her you'll have a sweetheart who's so choice
That she'll belong entirely to you.
If she has no desire to gad about
200 And gain a lover elsewhere, and no man
Comes seeking her, she'll keep her chastity.

     "Before I leave this subject, I will add
Just one brief word which will apply to each
Maiden, or fair or foul, whose love you seek.
Remember to observe and hold most dear
This my command: Give her to understand
That you against her can make no defense
So much abashed are you, and overcome
By her desert and beauty. There's no maid
210 Good, bad, young, old, religious, secular—
Not even a nun, chaste in both body and soul—
Who'll not delight to hear her beauty praised.
No matter though she be considered foul,
Swear that she is more lovely than a fay,
And say it with assurance. She'll believe
You easily; for each one thinks herself
Sufficiently possessed of loveliness,
However ugly she may be, to gain
A lover. Every gallant gentleman,
220 If he as courtier would have success,
Should be thus diligent to hold his love
And hesitate her follies to reprove.

     "A lady hates most to be criticized;
For she considers that instinctively
She knows how she should play her part, and needs
For her vocation no one's tutelage.
Unless he wish his lady to displease,
No man dispraises anything she does.
Just as a cat by nature knows the art
230 Of catching mice, nor can be taught to change—

For kittens e'er are with that science born
And need no schooling—so do womenkind
Most foolishly believe they always know
By native instinct that which they should do,
Whether it's wrong or right, or good or bad,
Or what you will; so they correction hate.
Their science from no master will they learn;
They're born with it and can forget no part.
He who would teach will ne'er enjoy their love.

240   "Companion, thus it is with your sweet Rose,
So precious that you'd never substitute
For her whatever treasure you might have,
If you could gain her. When at last you win
Her favors, as your hope predicts you will,
And all your joy is finally complete,
Guard her as such a flower should guarded be,
And you'll enjoy a love beyond compare.
In forty cities you'll not find her peer."

   "Tis true," said I; "there is not in the world   THE LOVER
250 One whose possession was and is so sweet!"
   My Friend consoled me thus; in his advice
I set great store, and verily believe
That he knows more than Reason in this case.
And ere he finished his discourse, which I
Found so agreeable, Sweet Thought returned;
Sweet Speech also, who afterward remained
And scarcely from that day e'er left my side.
But they brought not Sweet Sight; nor could I blame
Their failure, for I knew they did the best they could.

48. The Lover goes to seek Fair Welcome
[10015–10306]

THEN to my Friend I bade adieu, and left
With happy heart, traversing all the mead
Brilliant with flowers and grass, and listening

To sweetest birds that chanted newest songs;
Their pleasing music filled my heart with joy.
One thing my Friend had told me gave me grief:
He said I must avoid and circle 'round
The castle, nor seek pleasure near its towers.
I knew not if I could that counsel keep,
10 For by desire I was e'er toward it led.

   Avoiding then the right-hand path, I took
The left-hand one, to seek the nearest way,
Which I was fain to find, that in most haste,
Unless a stronger force should interfere,
I might Fair Welcome, frank and debonair
And lovely, rescue from his prison house.
Should I soon see the all-enclosing walls
Crumble like o'erdone cake, and every gate
Fly open, leaving nothing to oppose,
20 If then ingression I should fail to gain,
A devil in my paunch I'd surely have!
And I would bet a hundred thousand pounds
Fair Welcome should be freed, you may be sure,
Could I but manage to traverse the road.
But from the fort a distance I must stay,
Though not too far, as I may promise you.

   Musing upon my budding Rose, I found
Hard by a fountain clear, in pleasant spot,
An honorable and most exalted dame,
30 Genteel of figure, beautiful of face,
Sitting beneath an elm beside her friend.
His name I know not; Wealth the lady was
Who guarded most majestically the gate,
Though she indeed did not blockade the path.
Soon as I saw them, I inclined my head
In salutation; they returned my bow
Most promptly, but that did me little good.
However, I asked them if that were the road
Of Too-Much-Giving. Promptly Wealth replied
40 In somewhat haughty words, "This is the path,   WEALTH
And I am she who guards it."

                              "God preserve   THE LOVER
You, lady," I replied. "If 'twill not weigh

Too much upon your conscience, please consent
That I may go into that castle new
That Jealousy has just erected there."
      "Vassal," said she, "that cannot be as yet;   WEALTH
I know you not at all. Since you're not one
Of my acquaintance, you're not welcome here.
Perhaps ten years may pass ere you by me
50 Will be admitted; and none enters here,
Though he from Amiens or Paris were,
Unless he be my friend. I grant ingress
To all who know me and who wish to lead
Awhile a pleasant life of dance and song
And balladry, which no sage need begrudge.
Within they're entertained with farandole,
With merrymaking and with morris dance,
With viols, tambours, and the latest songs,
With games of chess and backgammon and dice,
60 With most exotic and delightful feasts.
Ancient duennas there join man with maid,
And these explore the gardens, fields, and groves,
Wanton as popinjays; then to the baths
They go together and together bathe
In pools provided, to the chambers nigh,
Where, with flowery wreaths upon their heads,
They lie in Mad Largesse's hostelry.
'Tis true that he impoverishes them,
And bleeds them till they scarcely can revive,
70 So high his prices are—so dear he sells
Accommodations and all services.
So harsh his tribute, they must sell their lands
Ere they contrive to pay the bill in full.
Most joyful are they when I lead them there,
But Poverty conducts them from the place,
Cold, trembling, all but bare. The entrance mine,
But hers the exit, I have no concern
With those who leave, however learned and wise.
They may go to the devil when they're broke!
80 Yet I'll not say I can't be reconciled
With them again, if they can raise more cash,
Though hard the task may be. Oft as they wish

I'll introduce them; when they have the price,
I'll never be too tired to let them in.
The one who most repentant is at first
Will in the end frequent the place the most,
Although they cannot face me without shame.
Little they lack of giving up their lives,
So angry they become, so much aggrieved.
90 I always flee from those who flee from me.
    "I warn you well that later you'll repent
If e'er you set your foot upon this path.
No captive bear's so wretched and so cowed
When flogged, as you will be if you proceed.
If you in Poverty's dominion come,
She'll make you linger long on bed of straw
And hay until you lastly starve to death.
Famine was formerly her chamberer,
And served so well with ardent fervency
100 That Poverty repaid her with her lore,
Teaching her all her malice, making her
Mistress and nurse of ugly-featured Theft,
Nourishing him with milk from her own breasts
Because she had no pap to feed him on.
Her land, you know, is neither sand nor loam,
For Famine dwells upon a stony field
Where neither tree nor bush nor grain will grow,
In far-off Scotland, country marble cold.
Finding no trees or grain, she digs the herbs
110 With hard and sharpened nails and teeth, but finds
Them growing sparse, thin-sown among the stones.
    "If you'd have me describe her, 'tis soon done:
Great need has she of oaten bread; she's tall
And thin and feeble and worn out; her hair
Is ragged; bleared her deep-set eyes; her face
Dry-lipped and pale; her jowls besmeared with dirt;
Her entrails one can see through her thin skin;
Marrowless, her bones stick from her flanks;
She has no belly but the cavity
120 Where it should be—it is a pit so deep
Her very breasts seem pendent from her spine.
Her knees lack roundness, and her hollow toes

And heels as lean are, angular and thin,
As if there were no flesh upon her bones,
So tightly are they pinched in meagerness.
  "The fruitful goddess Ceres never finds
The way to Famine's home to sprout the grain;
Nor guides Triptolemus his dragons there.
The Fates decree that ever separate
130 Sad Famine and the harvest goddess stay.
But soon enough will Poverty contrive
To lead you there if you're held in her grasp
When you persist in going to that place
Where you can loaf as much as is your wont;
For men reach Poverty by other paths
Than that which here I guard: a lazy life
And slothful brings a man to her as well.
If it should please you to pursue the road
I guard to wretched, spiteful Poverty,
140 You may well fail when you assail the fort;
But Famine will your next-door neighbor be.
Better than if she had a parchment map
She knows the way to Famine as by heart.
And so attentive and so courteous
Is Famine to her lady, Poverty,
Whom she nor loves nor prizes, although she,
However stripped and wretched, still contrives
Her handmaid to sustain, that Famine comes
Each day to see her and with her to sit
150 And kiss her with one hand beneath her chin,
No matter how distasteful be the act.
She grabs Theft by the ear, if he's asleep,
And wakes him, bending o'er him in distress,
Saying that by his craft alone may they
The wherewithal to save their lives procure.
Faint Heart with Theft and Famine is agreed,
But always thinks about the hangman's rope
Which makes his every hair to stand on end
In fear lest he should see his offspring hang
160 Because someone has caught him in his sin.
Enter not by this path; seek other ways.
You've served too little to deserve my love."

"Lady, I swear I'd gladly win your love,"   THE LOVER
Said I, "if I were able, that I might
Your pathway enter to release my friend,
Fair Welcome, who's imprisoned in the tower.
Grant me that favor, if it may you please."

"I heard your first request," said she, "and know   WEALTH
You've not sold all your forest, large and small.
170 A beech you have retained, and you're no fool;
For without fuel none can hope to live
Who would pursue the enterprise of love.
Those in such madness think they are most wise;
And yet they do not live, but rather die,
As long as in their torment they remain.
This rage and madness cannot be called life.
Reason knows well your case but could not turn
You from your folly. When you'd not believe
Her words, you fooled yourself most cruelly.
180 Ere Reason came, nothing could hold you back;
Nor can my words restrain you; for you prize
Them not at all now you have fallen in love.
No lover half appreciates my worth,
But each makes haste to dissipate the goods
That I allot him—flings them everywhere.
Where, in the devil's name, could one procure
What lovers spend? Depart, and let me be!"
  Seeing that I could nothing get from her,
I stayed no longer but departed thence;
190 And with her stylish lover she remained.
Pensive I wandered through the garden fair,
Which was so rich and precious, as you've heard.
My thoughts were elsewhere; it gave little joy.
In every place, at every time, I mused
How I might better serve without deceit.
I would avoid commission of a fault
So that I might no reputation lose.
My heart the counsel treasured and held fast
That Friend had given me: that I should try,
200 Wheree'r he were, to honor Evil Tongue.
I set myself to serve, and homage pay
As best I could to all my enemies.

Whether I'd gain their favor I knew not;
But what I could I felt compelled to do,
Not daring to approach the castle walls
As I had done could I have had my way.
Thus did I sorry penance, sadly torn
In conscience, as God knows; for what I did
Was quite another thing from what I wished.
210 Ne'er had I such duplicity in mind
As then when my intentions double were.
To gain my ends I felt I had to be
A traitor, though before I ne'er that name deserved.

49. The God of Love pardons the Lover for listening to Reason, and promises aid
[10307–10438]

NOW when the God of Love had proved me well
And always seen me show such loyalty
To him as was my duty, he appeared,
Smiling at my grief, and placed his hand
Upon my head and asked if his commands
Had all been kept, and how my case now stood
With that fair Rose who had my heart entranced.
Though he omniscient is, he asked all this.
Said he, "Have all the laws which I impose   THE GOD OF LOVE
10 Upon true lovers, and on none besides,
From which they never must depart, been kept?"
   "I know not, sir, but I have done my best."   THE LOVER
                                          THE GOD OF LOVE
   "That's right, but you are far too changeable;
Your heart's not stable, filled with wretched doubt.
Well know I all the truth: the other day
You wished to leave me; little lacked it then
That you gave up my homage; and you made
Of me and Idleness most dire complaints.
You said the lore of Hope uncertain is;

20 You called my service foolish; you agreed
   With Reason. Were you not a wicked man?"
      "Pardon me, sir; I grant that I have been.   THE LOVER
   But please remember that I never fled
   One step, but ever did your least behest
   As it behooves true lovers e'er to do.
   Reason considered me as most unwise,
   And therefore evilly she scolded me
   In lengthy sermon, thinking she could wean
   Me from your service if to me she preached.
30 I ne'er believed her, but (I will not lie)
   So well she argued that I had some doubts—
   No more than that. Reason shall never move
   My will to go against your mild commands,
   Please God, whatever may occur to me,
   As long as my heart remains attached to you,
   As it will be till it's torn from my breast.
   I know I was most palpably a fool
   To think of her or give her audience.
   For that I beg your pardon. 'Tis my will
40 So to amend my life as to conform
   To what it may e'er please you to command—
   Never again to follow Reason's words,
   But always in your service live and die.
   Naught can erase your laws out of my heart.
   May Atropos cut off my thread of life
   If I do aught but that which you enjoin!
   I'll take upon myself the pleasant work
   Of Venus, which gives, doubtless, more delight
   Than any other. Then, when my end comes,
50 And friends beweep my death, they'll say of me,
   'Appropriately thus you die, fair friend;   THE LOVER'S FRIENDS
   For truly, without fail, you ever led,
   While yet within your body lived its soul,
   A life agreeing well with this, your death.'"

                                    THE GOD OF LOVE
      "Now you speak wisely, by my head. I see
   That all my trust in you is well sustained.
   No renegade are you or faithless wretch
   Who me renounces when he gains his end.

Your heart is pure. You wisely sail your ship,
60 And to good port 'twill come. I pardon you
Not for a ransom, only for your prayer;
For neither gold nor silver do I wish.
But in confession I'd have you repeat,
Ere I accord with you, all the commands
And prohibitions, numbering ten, I gave.
Recite them; if you've well remembered all,
'Twill not be that you've thrown a double ace."

"I'll do it gladly. Villainy I must shun;   THE LOVER
No scandal spread; no dirty stories tell;
70 Greetings give promptly, and the same return;
To honor ladies ever must I strive;
Though shunning pride, keep neat, be well behaved
And jolly, liberal, and true in love."

THE GOD OF LOVE

"You know your lesson well; now, by my faith,
I doubt no more. But tell me how you fare."

"My heart is nearly dead with heavy grief."   THE LOVER

THE GOD OF LOVE

"But do you not possess three comforters?"

"No; for Sweet Sight is absent, he who knew   THE LOVER
So well to cure my grief with soothing balm.
80 All three took flight, but two returned to me."

"Have you not Hope?"   THE GOD OF LOVE

THE LOVER

"Yes, sire, she left me not
Disconsolate; for, once secured, she stays
Long after."

THE GOD OF LOVE

"And Fair Welcome; where is he?"

THE LOVER

"That sweet, frank friend I loved so much is held
In prison."

"Be not frantic or dismayed;   THE GOD OF LOVE
By my two eyes I swear you shall have more
Than you have had, according to your wish.
Since you have served me loyally, I'll send
My forces quickly to assault the fort.
90 Agile and strong my minions are, and free

Shall be Fair Welcome ere they end the coming siege."

50. The God of Love summons his barons and proposes a war to rescue Fair Welcome
[10439–10680]

THE God of Love, awaiting neither time
Nor fitting place, summoned his baronage
By letters begging or commanding them
To meet in parliament. They all appeared
Without excuse, ready to do his will
As each was able. I will name them all
Disorderly, as best befits my verse.
   Dame Idleness, the garden keeper came
Beneath the biggest banner; Noble Heart
10 Came next with Wealth and Franchise and Largesse,
Hardihood, Pity, Honor, Courtesy,
Gladness, Simplicity, Companionship,
Youth, Mirth, Security, and Fond Delight,
Humility and Patience, Jollity,
Hidewell and Beauty and Forced Abstinence,
Who led False Seeming, who'd not come alone.
These were the chieftains who their forces led
With willing hearts. Only Forced Abstinence
Feigned readiness; False Seeming, too, appeared,
20 Whate'er he did, to have fraud in his heart.
   False Seeming, who men's hearts appropriates,
Was son of Fraud and old Hypocrisy.
The shameful villainess who nourished him,
Giving him suck. This dirty Pharisee
Deceives full many a land, her rotten heart
Hiding beneath Religion's snowy cloak.
When Love saw him, his mind was much disturbed.

THE GOD OF LOVE

"What's this?" he asked. "Is it a dream? Tell me

Into my presence by whose leave you come."

30 Forced Abstinence then took False Seeming's hand

FORCED ABSTINENCE

And said, "I pray that you'll not be displeased,
But I brought him along. He comforts me,
Sustains me, does me honor, gives me ease.
I might of hunger die except for him,
So blame me not. I wish he might be loved
And called a worthy and a saintly man,
Although he loves men not. I am his love
And he the friend I keep for company."

"So be it," said the God of Love; and then   THE GOD OF LOVE
40 He briefly spoke to the assembled band:
"I've called you here to conquer Jealousy,
Who brings our lovers into martyrdom
And builds and holds in my despite her fort,
Which sorely irks my heart. So fortified
Is it that fiercely we shall have to strive
Ere we may take it; and I sadly grieve
That she Fair Welcome has immured therein,
Who helped our friends so much. I'm in bad case
If he cannot be rescued. At the death
50 Of old Tibullus, who well recognized
My qualities, I bow and arrow broke,
My ragged quiver dragged, and my poor wings,
All rumpled, to his tomb, so much I grieved—
So badly was I broken up with woe.
Venus so wept for him she nearly died;
No one there was but must for pity weep;
No rein or bridle could restrain our tears.
Catullus, Gallus, Ovid served us well;
They knew the art of love, but they are dead.
60 See William de Lorris, who's doomed to die,
Unless I rescue him, of pain and woe
This Jealousy, his adversary, deals.
Most willingly, he counsels me in this,
As is but right, for he's entirely mine,
And 'tis for him we are assembled here
By guile or force Fair Welcome to release.
He says he is unwise; but it would be

Great shame should I my faithful servant lose
When I both can and ought to succor him
70 Who shows great merit in his loyalty.
Therefore, as best I may, I will besiege
The mighty castle, and prepare assault
To break the walls and tower. Then will he serve
Me further. A *Romance* will he begin,
In which all my commands will find a place,
And write to where he has the Lover say
To him who guiltless now in prison lies:
'Dismay so troubles me that my heart fails. WILLIAM DE LORRIS
If I lose your good will I shall despair;
80 For elsewhere I can find no confidence—'
Here William will break off to sleep his last,   THE GOD OF LOVE
And may his tomb be filled with myrrh and balm,
With aloes and with incense, he's so served
And praised me. Then Jean Chopinel shall come,
Joyous of heart, agile and sound of limb,
Who shall be born at Meun upon the Loire,
Who'll serve me all his life in feast and fast;
And he will be a very prudent man,
By neither avarice nor envy marred.
90 For Reason, who my ointments hates and blames
Although they smell more sweet than any balm,
He shall have little use. And should it chance
That he somehow should fail in anything
(For there's no sinless man; each has his stain),
His heart shall always be so true to me
That ever when he knows himself at fault
Sooner or later he'll repent his crime;
For he'll not trick me, but hold me so dear
That he will wish to finish the *Romance*
100 If time and place permit. Where William stops,
After his death will Jean take up the tale,
Following a lapse of more than forty years,
And he shall say in fear and hopelessness
Because of that mischance that made him lose
Fair Welcome's kindness, which before he'd had,
'Confidence being lost, I'm near despair . . .'   JEAN DE MEUN
And all the other words, whate'er they be,   THE GOD OF LOVE

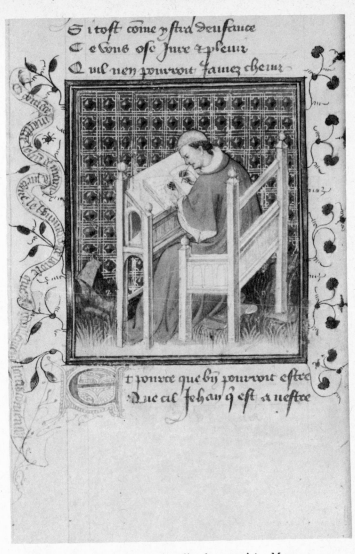

Jean de Meun (a conventionalized portrait). *Morgan 245,*
f. *77v.*

Foolish or wise, till he have plucked the bloom
From off the rosebush fair in flower and leaf
110 And shall have gained his beauteous vermeil Rose,
And 'twill be day, and from the dream he'll wake,
Then he'll the allegory so expound
That nothing shall remain unmanifest.

"If those two now could give me their advice,
They'd do so promptly; but the one cannot—
The other is not here; he's not yet born.
Of so great moment is this whole affair
That certainly if I fly not to him
And read him your decree when he is born,
120 Or at the latest ere he has grown up,
I swear to you and give you guarantee
He'll ne'er be able to complete the task.

"Lest it should happen that the unborn Jean
Should be, perhaps, prevented (which would be
A shame, a loss, a cause of dire lament
To all the lovers he might benefit),
I pray Lucina, deity of birth,
He may be born without disfigurement
Or weakness, so that he may have long life.
130 When he is weaned, and Jupiter him holds
Within his arms and offers him a drink
From those two tuns he has—one clear and sweet,
The other turbid, bitterer than soot
Or than the sea—when he's in cradle placed—
I'll spread my wings o'er him and sing him songs,
So much I'll love him. I'll teach him my art
That he may spread my doctrine in the speech
Of France in places where assemblies meet
Throughout the kingdom, and in all the squares.
140 Then those who hear will never die of love
And its sweet woes, for they'll believe in him;
And, rightly read, his book shall have such worth
That all men living should give it the name
Mirror for Lovers. Reading its contents good,
They'll no more trust in Reason, recreant wretch.

"Of you, my counselors, I now ask aid;
With clasped hands I beseech that you will help

And comfort William de Lorris in grief,
For well he's borne himself in my regard;
150 And, if I did not pray for him, I ought
Most certainly to ask your aid for Jean—
At least that he may easily endite.
I prophesy that he will come to birth;
Then this advantage you should give to him.
Moreover, aid all others who may come
Devotedly to follow my commands,
Which they will find inscribed within his book,
That they may overcome the tricks and guile
Of Jealousy, and all the castles raze
160 That she may dare to build. Advise me, then,
What we should do—how order best our hosts
Where we may strike most quickly to destroy."
Thus spoke the God of Love; his speech was well received.

51. Love's barons plan the war
[10681–10886]

THE barons met in council when Love's speech
Was ended. Various plans they offered then;
And divers ones of them diversely spoke.
But after discord they agreement reached,
Which they reported to their lord, and said:
"Unanimously, sire, we're in accord,   THE BARONS
Excepting Wealth, who has by oath affirmed
That she the castle never will assail
Or strike one stroke with dart or lance or ax
10 Or any other weapon, whate'er men say.
She scorns our enterprise, and leaves our ranks,
So much she holds this Lover in despite
And blames him that he never held her dear.
Toward him she takes this attitude of hate,
Which she declares she'll keep, because the man
Wished never to amass a treasury.

Not otherwise he failed—this his sole crime.
Day before yesterday, she says, he asked
To tread the path that Too-Much-Giving's called,
20 And with a flattering speech he made his prayer;
But she denied him for his poverty.
Nor has he since then managed to obtain
A single penny he can call his own,
Or so she says. When we had heard her speech,
We came to an agreement without her.

     "False Seeming and Forced Abstinence we plan
To send with all their forces to assault
The postern gate that Evil Tongue defends
With all his Normans, whom may hell-fire burn!
30 Largesse and Courtesy with them shall wend
To show their hardihood against the hag
Who holds Fair Welcome in subjection dire.
Delight and Hidewell go to murder Shame;
Gathering their hosts, they will assault her gate.
Security and Hardihood, to Fear
Opposed, will attack with all their forces one
That never has acquired the taste for flight.
Franchise and Pity offer their assault
To Danger. Thus your army's ordered well
40 If each one can accomplish his intent,
The castle will be shattered every whit.
But still, your mother Venus should be there;
For she is very wise, and knows love's way
So well that, lacking her, no strategy
Can perfect be in either plan or deed.
'Twere well you called her to amend our lack."

                                        THE GOD OF LOVE

     "My lords, the goddess who gave birth to me,
My lady and my mistress, will not do
All my desire, and is not at my call;
50 Though, when it pleases her, her custom 'tis
To come and aid me to attain my ends.
But I'm unwilling now to trouble her.
She is my mother, whom from infancy
I've treated with great reverence and awe;
For if a child his parents ne'er respects,

How can he give them fitting recompense?
Yet we can summon her as last resort.
If she be nigh, I know she'll come so fast
That none can stop her. Venus is a dame
60 Of mighty prowess, who full many a tower
Well worth a thousand besants has cast down
Without my help. Though I the credit had,
I never entered there. When Love's away,
With such a conquest he is never pleased.
Whate'er men say, it seems no other thing
Than meretriciousness. Who buys a horse
And pays a hundred pounds for it is quit;
He nor the merchant owes the other aught.
So I call not a sale by name of gift;
70 It merits no gratuity, e'en thanks.
Seller and buyer part in equity.
Buying and selling love is not like this;
For when the buyer's horse is in his stall
He has it yet to sell, perhaps with gain,
Or at the worst he'll not completely lose,
For though the horse may die he'll have its skin,
Which is worth something. If he likes the horse
And keeps it as his courser, he will be
Still master of the beast. But worse affair
80 Is every purchase that's through Venus made;
For, whatsoever care he takes, a man
Will lose the gold he pays and what he buys.
The seller gets the price and keeps the goods;
The buyer loses all. He cannot pay
A sum that's high enough to win control.
Not all his favors and his prayers prevent
Whatever stranger comes in his despite—
Be he a Roman, Breton, Englishman—
From the enjoyment of his merchandise,
90 Whether he pays a little or pays much
Or, giving nothing, gains by flattery.
Would you consider such a merchant wise?
No; rather miserable and wretched fool
Who, knowing what he does, yet loses all
Whene'er he buys, in spite of all his care.

'Tis true my mother is not wont to pay;
She's not so simple as to have that vice.
But men pay her, who afterward regret
Their bargains when they're pinched by Poverty,
100 Disciples of Dame Wealth though they may be,
Who loves me well whene'er my will is hers.
    "To make assurance doubly sure, I'll swear
Not by Saint Venus my progenitress
Alone—by Saturn, too, her ancient sire,
Although his wedded wife gave her not birth—
And by the faith I to my brothers owe,
Though no man knows their fathers, so diverse
Are they with whom my mother has been joined—
I swear by the infernal river Styx,
110 And if I lie may I a year abstain
From drinking piment; for you know the use
Of gods who are forsworn: to drink no wine
Until a year has passed. I've sworn enough;
If such an oath I break, I'm in bad case.
But never shall you me perfidious find,
And Wealth shall dearly pay for her default,
Unless she arm herself with sword or pike.
Since she disdains me, sad for her will be
The day's dawn when the tower and the fort
120 Shall both together tremble to their fall.
When next I get a rich man in my grasp,
You'll see me squeeze him so that not a pound
Or mark will he retain when I am through.
I'll make his every penny fly, unless
A golden fountain floods his barns. Our maids
Shall pluck him till he has to sell his lands
To buy new plumes, if his defenses fail.
    "It is the poor men who make me their lord;
Though they're unable to make me a feast,
130 I've no despite for them. No good man has.
Wealth is most avid and most gluttonous;
She chases, kicks, and quite outrages them.
But better lovers they than grasping rich
And stingy misers, by my father's faith!
More serviceable they—more loyal, too!

Their hearts and their good will suffice for me.
They think of me, and I must think of them.
I'd honor them if I were God of Wealth
Instead of God of Love. I feel their plaints.
140 Him must I succor who has worked for me;
For should he, lovesick, die, I'd most unloving seem."

52. The God of Love accepts the service of False Seeming, who recounts his deceits
[10887–11222]

"ALL that you have recounted is most true,"   THE BARONS
The barons said. "Well may you keep the oath,
As right ànd just and proper, that you've made
Against the rich. They certainly will be
But fools if they pay homage to you now.
You'll never be forsworn nor cease to drink
Your piment with the gods, nor suffer shame.
Ladies into whose clutches rich men fall
For them will stinging pepper pulverize
10 Until they shall bewail their fate. The dames
Will be so courteous that they'll discharge
Your vow; you will no better vicars need.
Don't fear that you will not be recompensed.
Don't interfere with them; they'll talk until
Their dupes cannot tell black from white. Such tales
They will recount, and make such bold requests,
With most disgraceful acts of flattery,
With kisses and embraces, smacks, and pats,
That, if they are acceded to, the men
20 Will not retain even the residence
From which they first the furniture have sold.
    "Give your commands; be it or right or wrong,
We will perform whatever is your wish.
But, sir, False Seeming fears to come more near—
Because you hate him, thinks he may be shamed—

And so we pray you to abate your ire
And welcome him into your barony
With Abstinence, his friend. This is our wish."

THE GOD OF LOVE

    "My faith," said Love, "I grant that he may be
30 Henceforth one of my court. Let him come nigh."
False Seeming thither ran, and Love went on:
"False Seeming, you may now become my man
By swearing that you'll succor all our friends
And grieve them never, but afford relief,
And ever will afflict our enemies.
The bail and bond are yours, and you shall be
Our King of Ribalds; thus the court ordains.
'Tis true you are a thief and traitor vile—
A hundred thousand times you've been forsworn—
40 But yet, to chase our doubts, in audience
Inform our people, by some general sign
At least, where they can find you easily
If they have need of you—how recognize
You then, for knowing you demands some skill.
Tell us where it will be you'll make your haunt."

    "Sire, I have many mansions so diverse   FALSE SEEMING
That if you please to grant me this respite
I'd much prefer to name them not to you
Lest I incriminate and shame myself.
50 If my companions knew I had disclosed
Their secrets, they would hurt and harry me,
If aught about their cruelty I know.
Opposed to them is truth, which they'd not hear,
But rather everywhere they'd silence keep.
Too much of evil treatment I might get
If I should say of them a single word
That is not sweet and pleasing to their ears.
A speech that pricks them rouses them to rage,
They are so cruel in their wickedness,
60 Although 'twere the Evangelist himself
Who reprimanded them for their ill deeds.
I know if I a single secret tell
Your court could not so hide my evidence
That they'd not learn of it or late or soon.

I have no fear of good men, who would take
Naught that I say to heart, as touching them;
For if they did, suspicion would alight
On them that Fraud and false Hypocrisy,
By whom I was begotten and brought up,
70 Had also some connection with their lives."

THE GOD OF LOVE

   "Fine job they did when they engendered you!"
Said Love. "Great benefit to them it was!
Better might they have brought the Devil to birth.
But just the same, however that may be,
It's necessary that you name your homes
At once, without mistake, that all may hear.
Give explanation of your way of life as well;
To hide it longer from us is unwise.
Discover likewise, now you're one of us,
80 What are your deeds—how is it that you work.
If beaten just because you tell the truth,
Which you're not used to do, you will not be
The first to suffer so."

                    "If it please you,   FALSE SEEMING
I have so great desire to do your will
That I'll fulfill it though I die therefor."
   False Seeming, no more tarrying, began
His speech as follows, to the audience:
"Hear me, O barons, as I now declare   FALSE SEEMING
That he who would False Seeming find may go
90 To cloister or to secular abode.
I live in both, preferring neither place,
But more in one than in the other dwell.
In short, I stay where I can best keep hid.
Concealment is most sure 'neath humble dress.
Religious folk more covert are than lay.
I'll not defame religion or those blame
Who in whatever habit follow it
In humble loyalty, though ne'ertheless
E'en these I will confess I cannot love.
100   "I speak of false, felonious priests and nuns—
Malicious ones who would the habit wear
But never would subdue their evil hearts.

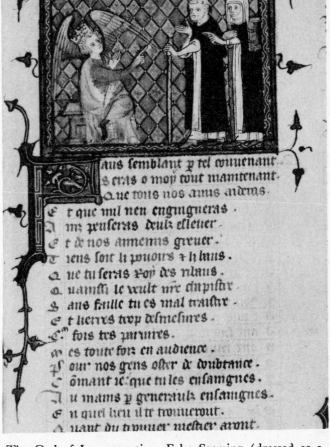

aus semblant p̃ tel conuenant
Seras o moy tout maintenant.
Que tous nos amis aidons.

E t que nul nen engingueras .
A uis penseras deulz elleuer
E t de nos anneniis greuer.
T iens soit li pouoirs τ li bíus .
Q ue tu seras roy des ribaus.
Q uamsti le veult n̄re empistr̃
S ans faille tu es mal traistre .
E t lierres trop desmesures .
Ꝑm̃ fois tres parj̃ures .
A es toute fors en audience .
Ꝑ our nos gens oster de doubtance .
C omant icelque tu les ensaignes .
A u mains p̃ generaulz ensaignes.
E n quel lieu il tr̃ trouueront .
Q uant du trouuer mestier aront .

The God of Love questions False Seeming (dressed as a
Preaching Friar) and Forced Abstinence (dressed as a
Béguine). *Morgan 324, f. 74r.*

Charitable are true religious folk;
You'll find no one of them who pity lacks.
They humbly live and have no trace of pride.
I would not dwell with such; or, if I must,
I'd make pretense. I could assume their clothes;
But I would rather let myself be hanged
Than leave my purpose, whate'er cheer I make.
110 "With those who're tricky, proud, astute, I live—
With those who covet worldly reverence—
With those who needs of other men exploit—
With those who highest salaries pursue—
With those who purchase the acquaintanceship
Of men of worldly power, and follow them—
With those who, though they poverty pretend,
Drink precious wine and eat delicious food—
With those who preach the boon of poverty,
Yet fish for gold with mighty nets and seines.
120 An evil catch they'll compass, by my head!
Neither religious are such folk nor pure;
Fallacious is the logic of their claim:
'Religious garment makes religious man.'
Such argument's not worth a privet knife.
'A monk's not made by his habiliments.'
So high they have the hair trimmed on their heads
And shaved with razor argumentative,
Wielded by Fraud, who thirteen cuts has made,
That no one knows a way to answer them;
130 No one can such a close distinction make
That he would dare to say a single word.
But wheresoe'er I go, howe'er I act,
Naught I pursue but fraud; just as the cat,
Sir Tybert, only thinks of rats and mice,
So do I think of nothing but of guile.
You'd not know whom I live with by my clothes,
Nor by my words, so soft and mild are they.
You'll see me in my works, unless you're blind.
The one whose promise is unlike his deed
140 Will surely dupe you, whate'er robe he wears,
Whoever he may be—woman or man,
Learned or lewd, knight, squire, lady, or maid."

As thus False Seeming spoke, the God of Love
Again addressed him, breaking off his speech,
As though he were a liar or a fool,

THE GOD OF LOVE

"What's this, you fiend, have you quite lost your head?
Who are these folks you cite? Can one of them find
Religion in a secular abode?"

FALSE SEEMING

"Yes, sire; 'twould be too bad if worldly clothes
150 Should mean their wearers all must lose their souls;
It follows not at all they live bad lives.
Holy religion thrives in colored clothes;
Many a virgin, many a glorious saint,
Religious and devout, have men seen die,
Who all their lives had worn the common dress;
Yet ne'ertheless they all were canonized.
Many a one of such I could adduce.
The saints in churches—those to whom we pray—
Chaste virgins, married wives who brought to birth
160 Full many a noble child—were almost all
Such as in worldly clothing lived and died;
Yet they are saints and saints will always be.
Eleven thousand virgins who in heaven
Their tapers bear before the Lord himself
(Their festivals are held in every church)
Were taken in their secular attire
When they received the boon of martyrdom;
Yet they are now no whit the worse for that.
Habiliment nor gives nor takes away;
170 Good thoughts produce good hearts and worthy deeds
Which show religion, which is rightly this.
Sir Isengrin, the wolf, who donned the skin
Of Don Belin, the ram, as sable robe,
Refrained not from devouring the sheep
Because he joined with them in this disguise.
No whit the less he drank his victims' blood,
But rather more, for they were so deceived
They could not recognize their mortal foe
But followed him e'en when he tried to flee.
180   "If there are but a few of such-like wolves

Among your new apostles, Holy Church,
You're badly off; your city is assailed
By knights of your own table, and your rule
Is sadly in decline. If those who've sworn
You to defend are leading the attack,
Who against them will give you guarantee?
You will be taken ere you feel one stroke
Of trepeget or mangonel, or see
A single banner flaunted in the wind.
190 If you're not rescued, they'll o'errun your land.
Then you must give permission, not commands;
Or, if you do, no force can rescue you.
Their tributary you will then become
In making peace—accepting it from them—
Unless (what's worse) they master everything.
Well know they how to circumvent you now:
By day they man, by night they mine your walls.
Root other plants, if you would gather fruit,
Without delay. But now I'll hold my peace
200 Upon this point, which I'll no longer urge,
If I may pass it o'er, lest I you tire.
    "But I will make a covenant with you
To aid your friends who keep me company,
But they will die if they'll not me receive.
And they must likewise treat my paramour,
Or never, God forbid, achieve their ends.
I am a traitor and adjudged a thief
By God. Perjured I am most certainly;
But till it is accomplished scarcely known
210 Is the conclusion that I'm aiming at.
Many I've killed who ne'er perceived my guile;
And this shall happen many a time again.
If any man suspects me, and is wise,
Let him take care, or 'twill be just too bad.
    "The more deceit, the harder 'tis to see.
Old Proteus, who changed, oft as he wished,
His shape, knew not so much deceitfulness
And guile as I; for ne'er in any town
Have I been recognized, though seen and heard
220 There many times before. For I know well

The way to make my habits strange appear.
Now I wear one, next to another change:
Now knight, now prelate, canon now, now monk,
Now clerk, now master, student now, now priest;
Now I'm a castellan, now forester—
In every occupation I engage—
Now prince, now page—I every language know—
Now old and gray, next hour I'm young again;
Now I am Robbie called, now Robbins named;
230 Now I'm Franciscan, now Dominican.
    "Many another guise do I assume
To follow in the footsteps of my love,
This lady who is named Feigned Abstinence,
Who gives me solace and companionship—
To please her and accomplish her desires.
In women's clothes now am I maid, now dame;
Sometimes I am religious—anchorite,
Abbess, novitiate, probationer,
Or prioress or nun. But everywhere
240 I'm turning all religion inside out.
I take the straw, but let the kernels lie.
I ask no more than just to wear the robe
To fool the folk whom I am living with.
What more's to say? In whatsoever guise
Best pleases me I muffle up myself.
My tune is changeable. My words and deeds
To one another but a slight resemblance have."

53. False Seeming explains how the friars outwit priests
[Interpolation: 1–98]

"BY means of dispensations I persuade   FALSE SEEMING
The entire world to fall within my grasp;
No prelate can invalidate my power
To hear confession, absolution give,
To everybody, wheresoe'er he's found;

That is, I know of no one but the Pope,
Who on our order made this settlement
That ne'er a priest should dare to criticize
Or grouch against my fellows. Well have I
10 Shut up their mouths. But they have spied upon
My moves, so I am not so well received
By them as I might wish; for I have tricked
Them all too much. However it may go,
I little care, for I have got the cash
And all the gilding that they hoped to get.
So much I've labored, so much have I preached,
So much they've given me, so much I've grabbed
From foolish men and women everywhere,
That now I lead the jolly life, and scorn
20 The simpleness of prelates and of priests
Who but too greatly fear my snares and traps.
No one of them can be compared to me,
But none of them can realize this fact.
Thus I bring all about as is my wish
By my dissimulation and my feints.
Although, according to the scripture, each
Should to confession go before a priest
One time a year, before the sacrament
He takes (for this is ordered by the Pope,
30 Whose statute yet exempts each one of us,
Who go there only if we can deceive),
Much better can we manage the affair,
For we have been allowed a privilege
Relieving them of many a grievous load.
  "We never hold our counsel about this
But multiply the powers that the Pope
Has given us, so that a man who's sinned
Can tell the priest as follows, if he likes:
'In this confessional I can assert   THE SINNER
40 That he to whom I have confessed my sins
Has from their consequences freed me quite;
He has absolved me from the vice I knew
Had sullied me. Now 'tis not my intent
To make a new confession, or repeat
The other one; so you can mark me paid

And, howsoe'er you like it, call it quits;
For, though you swore the contrary, I have
No fear of any prelate—any priest—
Who may attempt to force me to confess
50 Otherwise than as it pleases me.
I have had someone else to whom to plead.
You cannot scare or bother me so much
That I will feel I am compelled to make
Confession twice, unless, indeed, I wish
A twofold absolution to receive.
The first was quite enough for me, so you
The second may as well relinquish now.
I am released, and I may well assert
That you can scarcely free me any more;
60 For he who has released me is the one
Who is omnipotent o'er every bond.
If you should dare to force me, and I go
To make complaint, no just imperial judge,
Official, king, or prelate would hand down
Against me a decision in the case.
I'll make complaint to no one else besides
My new confessor, who is good. His name's
Not Brother Wolfing, either, and he'll be
Greatly incensed at one who'd call him by
70 That name, and most impatient he'd remain
Till he'd exacted cruel punishment.
At least he'd exercise his fullest power,
And not for God's own sake would he relax.

" 'But Brother Wolf, who eats up everything,
However lucky people were before,
Will dare to swear an oath and shut your mouths,
Well knowing how he may subsist on you;
For he has means by which to get you caught
So that you never can escape from him
80 Without disgrace and shame, unless you give
Him liberally of your goods and cash.
He will not be so senseless and absurd
As not to have his bulls conveyed from Rome
As summonses to all of you, at will,
To fetch you two days' journey at the cost

Of toil and trouble. Documents so forged
To serve his purpose cover much more ground
Than most authentic, ordinary ones,
And are so ethical that they apply
90 Never to more than eight persons at once.
Credentials he may show are valueless,
Though they're addressed to those in every place
Who have the power to uphold the law.
But he has for your law no least concern,
He is so powerful in high affairs.
So energetically he'll operate
With you that for no prayer will he desist,
Nor yet for lack of cash, of which he has,
Hidden in his attic, goodly store;
100 For Property serves as his seneschal
And is in acquisition bright and keen,
And Purchase is his brother by right birth,
Who is not less desirous to acquire,
But rather more, and has amassed great wealth,
By which he mounts so high that he surmounts
All others. May God help me, and Saint James,
If you at Easter do not offer me
The body of Our Lord, I'll leave you flat,
And make you no more trouble; but I'll go
110 To take the sacrament from him, for I
Out of your jurisdiction can escape
The moment I make up my mind to leave.'

FALSE SEEMING

"Thus may the one confess who would forsake
His priest; and, if the latter dare object,
I am prepared to bring the priest to trial
And make him lose his church. If folk but knew
Of such confession all the consequence,
No priest would longer have the chance to learn
The consciences of those beneath his charge."

54. False Seeming explains his tricks and
denounces mendicancy
[11223–11406]

FALSE SEEMING would have ended his discourse,
Though no annoyance showed the God of Love
But rather gave him this encouragement:
"Tell us, all shame aside, explicitly   THE GOD OF LOVE
How you, a holy hermit, as your clothes
Denote, engage in such disgraceful tricks?"
    "That's what I seem, but I'm a hypocrite."   FALSE SEEMING
    "You go about advising abstinence."   THE GOD OF LOVE
    "True! But with finest food and wine I fill   FALSE SEEMING
10 My paunch, as is befitting a divine."
    "Yet poverty you preach!"   THE GOD OF LOVE
                                            FALSE SEEMING
                        "But wealth has power;
And, howsoe'er I feign that I am poor,
I make no point of being really so.
One hundred thousand times would I prefer
The friendship of the King of France to that
Of any poor man, though he were as good.
When I see naked beggars quake with cold,
On stinking dunghills making plaint and moan,
I intermeddle not in their affairs.
20 If they are carried to the Hospital,
They go uncomforted by me; for they
Who are not worth an oyster will not feed
My mouth with any alms. What can he give
Who after eating licks his very knife?
Much more agreeable and wise it is
To go to visit some rich usurer;
I comfort him in hope to get his gold.
If evil death should make an end of him,
I'd gladly convoy him unto his grave.

30 If I'm reproved because I leave the poor
Alone, know you how then I make excuse?
I by my cloak let it be understood
That rich men are more sinful than the poor
And I must counsel those in greatest need.
However, souls endure as great a loss
From poverty as from excess of wealth;
One and the other rob it equally.
Riches and poverty are both extremes;
Sufficiency's the mean where virtue lives.

40 In Proverbs, chapter thirty, Solomon
Delivers us a text upon this point:
'Guard me, O God, by thine omnipotence   SOLOMON
From riches and from beggary alike';
For if a rich man thinks too much of wealth   FALSE SEEMING
So he upon this folly sets his heart
That his Creator he forgets. So how
Can one fight poverty and sin at once?
A liar and a thief he needs must be,
Or God lied when he suffered Solomon

50 To pen for him the text you here have read.
I swear that there is written in no book,
At least not in the Bible that we have,
That Christ or His apostles when on earth
Were ever seen to beg their bread; for they
Would not be mendicants for anything.
Thus taught the masters of divinity
In Paris formerly. Custodians
Of souls, God's shepherds, might enforce demands,
In fullness of their power, but never beg.

60 After the crucifixion of their Lord,
Disciples to their manual toil returned;
And, by their labor, nothing more or less,
They patiently procured their sustenance,
Living in huts—not palaces or halls—
And gave the poor whate'er surplus they had.
    "An able-bodied man should gain his bread
By labor manual and corporal,
Unless he ample patrimony have,
However much he wishes to serve God

70 And be religious. This should all men do
Save in some cases which I now recall
And will recount to you when I have time.
The Scriptures say that one should further go
And sell his all and work for livelihood
If perfect in his virtue he would be.
The lazy loafer who haunts others' boards
Is a deceiver, living but by lies.
Nor can he reasonably excuse himself
On grounds that he must pray; for it is right,
80 At all events, that he God's service leave
To make provision for his various needs:
To eat, to sleep, and other things to do.
Our orisons may rest while we're at work;
The truthful Scriptures all agree in this.

"Justinian, who wrote the ancient codes,
Forbids that any able-bodied man
In any manner stoop to beg his bread,
Provided he can find a means of gain.
Rather than countenance such evil ways,
90 One should such villain hale before the court
And see him flogged. One acts not as he should
Who thus accepts an alms, unless he have
A license that abates the penalty.
I don't see how such license can be got
Unless a prince has been deceived, or how
He rightfully can have the power to grant.
I say not this in order to define
The power of princes; I no question make
Whether their sway extends to such a case.
100 I should not get myself mixed up in this;
But, by the letter of the law, I think
That one who eats the alms which ought to go
To people spent and feeble, naked, poor,
Covered with sores and old, unfit to earn
Their bread because they are too weak to work,
His own damnation eats, depriving them,
Unless Adam's Creator has told lies.

"Remember, when Christ told the rich young man
To sell his goods, give alms, and follow Him,

110 He meant not he should in His service live
By beggary. That was not His intent.
Rather that he should labor with his hands
He meant, and follow Jesus in good works.
Saint Paul bid the apostles to procure
Necessities of life by their own toil.
Mendicancy he banned when thus he said:
'Work with your hands; on no one else depend.'
He'd not have one of them demand an alms
From those they preached to, nor the gospel sell.
120 He feared their asking would to taking turn;
For there are many donors in this world
Who give, to tell the truth, because ashamed
To make refusal; or because they wish
To rid themselves of precatory bores.
If but solicitation to escape
They make their gift, what can it profit them?
They lose the merit and the gift itself.
The men who heard the preaching of Saint Paul
Begged him for God's sake to accept their gifts;
130 However, he'd not reach his hand for them,
But gain his livelihood by his own manual toil."

55. False Seeming explains what mendicancy is permissible,
and reveals his true nature
[11407–12014]

THE GOD OF LOVE

"TELL me," said Love, "how able-bodied man
Who'd follow God religiously can live
When he's sold all and given it to the poor
And would devote his time to prayer, not work.
Can he contrive to do it?"

                    "Yes."   FALSE SEEMING
                                       THE GOD OF LOVE
                    "Then how?"

"He can avoid all mendicancy, and live   FALSE SEEMING
If he will enter, as the Scripture says,
The abbey that his own goods have endowed,
Like those of Canons Regular, or those
10 Of White or Black Monks, or the Hospitalers
Or Templars (more examples I'll not give).
Many a monk first works and then tells beads.
Since discord, I remember, there has been
About the mendicants' estate, I'll tell
In brief how one may beg who lacks the means
To feed himself. The cases, one by one,
You'll hear, so that you can repeat them all
To spite felonious scandal; for the truth
Will ever try to hide behind some quoin.
20 Though I, who've never dared to plow such field
Before, may suffer for the tale I tell.
    "These are the special cases: if a man
So beastly is that he has learned no trade
And yet desires to leave his ignorance,
He well may beg till he has learned a craft,
And, without vagrancy, thus gain his bread;
If one's too young or old or sick to work,
He legally may beg his livelihood;
Or if a man of gentle family
30 Has been brought up to live too soft a life
We ought to pity him with charity
And let him beg rather than starve to death;
Or e'en a man who has the skill and strength
And will to toil, and gladly would find work,
When there is no demand for what he does,
May beg to satisfy necessity;
Or if the income from his work be small
And insufficient to sustain his life,
He then may beg to supplement his wage,
40 Going from door to door to seek his bread;
Or if he will engage in chivalry
And guard our faith in arms, or otherwise,
As by the composition of a book,
If poverty then grieves him he may well
Resort to begging to supply his needs

Till he can work again; but then he must
With force corporeal, not spiritual,
Perform his labor. That's no metaphor!
In all these cases, and in others like,
50 If other reasonable ones you find
Besides those I have offered here to you,
A man may beg to live—not otherwise—
Unless I've been misled by Saint Amour,
Who used to preach and lecture on this point
And argue it at Paris with divines.

   "May I ne'er drink of wine or eat of bread
If in this truth the University
And all the people there who heard him talk
Were not in full accord with him. No man
60 Who this denies will find excuse with God.
Let grumblers grumble, let the scoffers scoff,
I'll this assert though I should lose my life
Or like Saint Paul unjustly go to jail
Or from the realm be banished without cause
As was the teacher, William of Saint Amour,
Exiled by envious Hypocrisy.
My mother's plot it was that drove away
This valiant man because he taught the truth.
My mother he offended far too much,
70 When later he wrote his biography,
Saying I should forsake mendicancy
And labor if I had no other means.
Did he think me befuddled? I hate work.
I've naught to do with labor; it's too hard.
Better I like to pray before the folk
And 'neath my mother's mantle hide my sin."

                                        THE GOD OF LOVE

   "You devil, dare you say such words to me?"
   "What, sir?"   FALSE SEEMING

                                        THE GOD OF LOVE

        "Your speech confesses perfidy.
Fear you not God?"

                        "Most certainly I don't.   FALSE SEEMING
80 A man who fears his God can scarce attain,
Here in this world, to any great estate.

The good, who evil shun, and honestly
Maintain themselves as he would have them do
On their own means, will lastly come to beg
Of others bread, imbibing great misease,
Than which nothing exists that I hate more.
But see what heaps of gold the usurers,
The bankers, coiners, beadles, magistrates,
Provosts, and bailiffs have in treasuries.
90 They well-nigh all exist by knavery,
Like wolves devouring folk of little means
Who still must bow to them. They all despoil
The poor; not one of them himself restrains.
Scalding them not, they pluck the birds alive,
Of the plumes make their adornments, suck them dry.
The stronger rob the weaker ones; but I,
Wearing my simple robe, the cozeners
And cozened cozen—rob robbers and robbed.
    "By my chicanery I gain and keep
100 A treasure great in weight as well as size
That cannot waste away. With it I build
A palace where I taste of all delights
Companions and bedfellows can supply
Or tables loaded down with entremets.
I'd never wish for other life than this.
My gold and silver multiply meanwhile,
For ere my treasury can emptied be,
Abundantly the coins roll in again.
Do you not think I make my bears dance well?
110 Acquisition is my only care;
Better than my tithings is my graft.
At risk of scourge or death, unceasingly,
I'll venture anywhere to hear confess
A king, duke, baron, count, or emperor.
But 'twere a shame to shrive the indigent,
Unless for other reason. I love not
Such shriving; for the poor I have no care.
Their situation's neither fair nor fine.
The empresses and queens, the duchesses,
120 The countesses and wives of palatines,
The abbesses and Béguines, bailies' wives,

The ladies, and the bourgeoise rich and proud,
The nuns and maidens—wealthy ones or fair—
Without my counsel never will depart
Whether I find them nude or richly dressed.
For the salvation of their souls, I ask
Of lord and lady and their servants all
About their wealth, about the lives they lead.
Into their heads I put a firm belief
130 That their own parish priests are only beasts
Compared to my companions and to me.
Yet I'm in league with these same filthy dogs,
To whom the people's secrets I reveal,
Withholding nothing; they in turn disclose
Whate'er they know to me—so I know all.
   "That you may know the rascals who deceive
People continually, I will quote
Saint Matthew's gospel, chapter twenty-three,
Where we may read, 'Now sit in Moses' seat   ST. MATTHEW
140 (The gloss says 'tis the Older Testament)
The Scribes and Pharisees (the Scriptures call
Them men of falsehood and cursed hypocrites).
Do what they say, but act not as they act;
For though they're not remiss with good advice
They have no mind to practice what they preach.
The foolish man they bind with grievous loads
Which he upon his shoulders cannot bear;
But they'll not aid with e'en a finger's touch.' "
   "Why not?"   THE GOD OF LOVE
                       FALSE SEEMING
     "They do not want to, by my faith!
150 They know the porters' shoulders often ache;
                     ST. MATTHEW
They would avoid such pain. 'They do good works
But to be seen by men; and they enlarge
Their garments' hems and their phylacteries;
They love, at table and in synagogues,
The highest and most honorable seats;
And in the streets (the proud and haughty rogues!)
To hear men call them Rabbi as they pass.'
(This should not be, for it is most opposed   FALSE SEEMING

To Scripture, which reveals their wickedness.)
160 "Against opponents still another plan
We have: we hate them all with deadly hate
And all unite against them. Whom one hates
We all detest and strive to overthrow.
If we see one prevail with certain folk
To gain a prebend or some other place
Of worldly honor, we attempt to find
The ladder which enabled him to mount.
The better to discomfit him, and shame,
We stuff his patron's ears with scandal false;
170 For we have not a bit of love for him.
So we dismount him from the steps he mounts,
And cut him off, and steal his friends away.
Until they're lost, he'll nothing know of it;
For we'd be blamed if openly we worked,
And we might miss our aim. If he but knew
Our ill intent, he would defend himself;
And we might be well punished for our sin.
     "If one of us has done some good, we say
It was the work of all. Though it were feigned
180 And he but boasted to have helped advance
Some worthy man, we all claim partnership
And say he was promoted by our aid.
To have the people's praise, by flattery
We letters get from influential men
Who to our excellence will testify,
So that the people commonly believe
That we have all the virtues in the world;
And, though we always feign that we are poor,
We are, however much we make complaint,
190 The non-possessors that possess all things.
     "I intermeddle in diplomacy,
Settle estates, make peace and marriages,
As envoy or attorney sometimes act,
Hold inquests, going beyond my true employ.
But my most pleasant enterprise it is
To intermix in other folks' affairs.
If any business you should have with those
With whom I mingle, place it in my hands;

It will be done as soon as it's explained.
200 If you serve me, my service you deserve.
But he who'd chastise me will lose my grace
At once. I neither love nor prize the man
By whom I am reproved for anything.
I'll reprehend the others, one and all;
But will not listen, in my turn, to blame.
Though scourging others, I've no taste for it.
     "I've little love for hermitages, woods,
And deserts. Wilderness and hut and lodge
I leave to John the Baptist; too remote
210 Are they from burgs and cities where I build
My castles and my palaces and halls
To which a man at full speed may retreat
And say that he's renounced the worldly life.
There I immerse myself in worldliness
And bathe and swim and dive and take my ease
Better than any fish that swims with fin.
One of the slaves of Antichrist am I—
Those wretches who, the Scripture says, are clad
In saintly robes, but live in wickedness.
220   "Pious lambs we seem outside, but we,
Inside, are ravening wolves. We overrun
The land and sea, make war on all the world,
And fain would rule the life of every man.
If of a castle or a town we hear
Where there's a bugger rumored to reside,
Though from Milan he were, which has the blame
For such; or if a man assuredly
Take usury or sell on terms, so mad
He is for gain; or if one lecherous be;
230 Or if a provost or an officer
Of simony or theft should be accused;
Or prelate lead too jovial a life;
Or priest possess a mistress; or a bawd
Or pimp or brothel wench open a stew;
Or anyone's accused of any vice
For which he ought to answer to a judge—
By all the saints to whom a man may pray,
Unless with feasts he make a good defense,

With lampreys, luces, salmons, and with eels
240 (If they are to be purchased in his town),
With tarts and custards, basketfuls of cheese
(Which is the finest jewel of them all),
With Cailloux pears, capons, and fatted geese
(Which tickle gullets well); unless he serve
Us promptly with a roebuck or a hare
Larded upon a spit, or at the least
A loin of pork—he'll feel a length of cord
By which the folk will drag him to the stake
(And then we'll hear him yelling loud enough
250 At least a league away), or in a cell
He'll be immured for life, or otherwise
Get greater punishment than he deserves—
Unless he has provided for us well.
But if he has the wit to build a tower,
I care not of what stone, or if 'twere built
With neither square nor compass out of wood,
Turf, or material of other kind;
Provided that he shall amass within
An ample store of worldly goods, and mount
260 An arbalest upon it, fit to hurl
To either side, and to the front and back,
Upon us, thick as hail, such ball and shot
As I have said, his good name to redeem,
And from great mangonels whole barrels throw,
And tuns, of wine, and heavy sacks of gold—
Then shall he find himself delivered soon.
But if he cannot find such pittances
Let him lay sophistry and lies aside
And study how to find equivalents
270 If he would hope to win to our good grace;
Or such false witness we'll against him bear
That if he's not condemned to burn alive
He'll pay a penance far worse than the doles.
These wretched traitors, full of dire deceit,
You'll never recognize in their array;
If you would guard against them, scan their deeds.
  "Did not the University well guard
The key of Christianity, our faith

Beyond all recognition had been marred
280 When in the year twelve hundred fifty-four
(No man now living will gainsay my words)
With bad intent there published was a book
The Devil must have written. I speak truth.
The Everlasting Gospel it was called,
And by its title page we were informed
It was transmitted by the Holy Ghost
(Though it was worthy only to be burned).
In Paris there no woman was, nor man,
Within the square in front of Notre Dame
290 Who could not get the book if he desired
To copy it; and in it he would find
Such blasphemous comparisons as this:

EVERLASTING GOSPEL

'As much as does the sun surpass the moon
In value for its gift of heat and light,
Because the latter is more faint and dull—
Much as the shell by kernel is surpassed'
(Think not that I am joking; on my soul
I swear that I am quoting accurately!)
'So does this gospel that old book surpass
300 That bears the names of four evangelists
Of Jesus Christ.' Unless I make mistake,   FALSE SEEMING
A host of such comparisons were there.
    "The University had been asleep,
But at the noise about the book awoke
And raised its head; nor did it slumber more
But armed itself and was prepared to fight
Soon as it saw this monster horrible
Ready to take the field. Then to the judge
The book was borne; but authors of the work
310 Regained it by a desperate attack
And hid it promptly; for full well they knew
There was no explanation and no gloss
That would suffice against the champions
Who would attack the cursed words there writ.
What has become of it I do not know,
Or what the end will be; but it behooves
Its champions to secure more strong defense.

"So now we wait for antichrist to come,
And all together hold to him; for those
320 Who do not so will surely lose their lives.
By the deceit in which we cloak ourselves,
We will incite the people against them
And bring them to destruction by the sword
Or other means; since they'll not follow us
According to what's written in the book,
The words of which have this significance:
'John can display no strength while Peter rules.'
This is the bark of sense which hides the pith
Of meaning, which I'll now expound to you.
330 By Peter's meant the clergy secular
And Pope, who keep the law of Jesus Christ,
Against all foes maintaining it as guards.
By John are meant the friars, who say no law
But their *Eternal Gospel* should be kept,
Which by the Holy Ghost has been sent down
To guide all men upon the heavenly path.
The powers of John they teach to be the grace
By which they boast the sinners to convert
And make them turn to God. Within this book
340 Are many other deviltries ordained
And authorized against the law of Rome,
Upholding antichrist, as I there read.
They soon will give commands to kill the folk
Who hold to Peter, but they'll never have
The force to beat down Peter's law, I swear
(In spite of all their murder and assault),
So that enough shall not remain alive
Who will maintain it ever, till at last
All shall accept it, and that law shall fall
350 Which they pretend is signified by John.
I'll tell you little more—the story's long—
If that book had prevailed, I would have been
More secure, though I still have some friends
Who'd gladly see me placed in high estate.

"My lord and father, Fraud, is emperor—
My mother empress—of the entire world.
Spite of the Holy Ghost our lineage reigns

In every powerful kingdom. It is right
That we should rule who all the world seduce
360 And know so well how to deceive mankind
That none perceive our guile, or if they do
They dare not let the truth be known. Such men
As fear my brethren more than they fear God
Risk wrath divine; they're not good champions,
Surely, who fear such feigning, dodge the risk
Which might from making accusation come.
God will refuse to hear such men, in truth;
He'll turn away His face and punish them.
Howe'er it goes with such, we do not care,
370 Since men esteem us, think we are so good
That howsoe'er censorious we be
No man reproves us. Whom should they exalt
But us, who ever pray in all men's sight,
Whatever we may do behind their backs?
    "What greater folly's known than to extol
And love the chevaliers and noblemen
Who look so elegant in well-made clothes?
If they're such men as they appear—as clean
As is their dress—and if their words and deeds
380 Accord—is it not cause for shame and grief?
Curse them, if they will not be hypocrites!
Most certainly, such folk we do not love;
But Béguins with their faces delicate
And pale shaded by wide brimmèd hats,
Who mantles wear of gray, bedaubed with dung,
Great boots like quail-traps, and bewrinkled hose!
Are these within whose hands a prince should place
His lands in war or peace; to let such misrule
If to great honor he aspires to come?
390 Though they be other than they seem, they thus
Secure all worldly grace; and therefore I
Hasten to join with them in tricks and fraud.
I will not therefore say men should despise
A humble cloak that does not cover pride.
No one should hate the poor man for the dress
He wears; but God cares not two straws for those
Who say they've left the world, yet still enjoy

All kinds of earthly glory and delights.
Who could excuse such Béguin? Hypocrites
400 Who join the orders—say they've left the world—
And then seek worldly ease—grow fat on it—
Are like the dog who is so gluttonous
That to his vomit he returns. But I
Would not dare lie to you unless I felt
That you perceived it not, for you would have
The lie within your fist; though certainly
I'd not abandon falseness as a sin
If I could quite outwit and baffle you.
Therefore you'd better be upon your guard."
410   The God of Love smiled at this strange discourse,
And all the barons laughed, amazed, and cried:
"Behold a servant whom a man may trust!"   THE BARONS

                                                THE GOD OF LOVE
    Said Love, "False Seeming, since you've been advanced
To such great power within my court that you
Are there the King of Ribalds, tell me, now,
Will you uphold for me my covenants?"

                                                FALSE SEEMING
    "Yes, sir; I swear to you and pledge my oath
That never had your ancestors or sire
A slave more loyal than I'll be to you."

                                                THE GOD OF LOVE
420   "How can that be? Your nature would forbid!"

                                                FALSE SEEMING
    "Best take your chance of that; if pledge you ask,
You'll never be assured though I should give
A hostage, testimonial, or proof.
I call yourself to witness that no man
Can pluck a wolf out of his hide unless
He flay him first, no matter how he beat
And pummel him. Think you because I wear
A simple robe I'd not deceive and trick?
Many great evils 'neath that I've performed.
430 Never, by God, shall I my heart restrain;
For why should I my evil deeds renounce
Because I have a coy and simple face?
Forced Abstinence, my very dearest friend,

Has need of my protection; she had been
Hard used and almost dead were't not for me.
Let us—both her and me—pursue our course."
   "So be it; I'll believe you without pledge,"   THE GOD OF LOVE
Said Love. And then the rascal knelt to him
And thanked him, showing treason in his face.
440 Though white without, he was entirely black within.

56. False Seeming and Forced Abstinence go as envoys
to Evil Tongue
[12015–12360]

THEN was there naught to do but form the troops.
Love loudly called, "Delay not the assault!"   THE GOD OF LOVE
Full of ardor, he quickly sallied forth.
   Now at the mighty castle they've arrived,
From which they swear they never will depart
Until it's taken or they all are dead.
Their forces in four battles they divide
To make attack at once against four gates
Whose guards are far from slothful, ill, or dead;
10 But, rather, strong and eager for the fray.
   Now I'll tell in what guise went Abstinence,
False Seeming partnering her, to Evil Tongue.
A conference between the two was held
About how best they might their ends attain—
Whether to go disguised or openly.
On this decision they accorded soon:
That they should go in the array of folk—
Good, pious, saintly—who make pilgrimage.
Immediately Forced Abstinence appeared
20 Like Béguine clothed in robe of cameline,
With coverchief of white upon her head.
Her psalter she forgot not, nor her beads,
Which hung upon a lace of whitest silk.
She never bought them, for they were the gift

Of one who called her daughter, though a friar;
She paid him visits much more frequently
Than any other of her nunnery,
And often he would visit her in turn
And many charming sermons preach to her.
30 He never let False Seeming interfere
With frequent shrivings that he gave to her;
Confession heard he so devotedly
That often their two heads were in one hood.
  I should consider her of figure fair,
But somewhat pale of face. The lustful bitch
The horse resembled in the Apocalypse
That signifies the evil people, tinged
With pale hypocrisy; he shows no hue
Upon his body but the white of death.
40 Such jaundiced color Abstinence displayed.
Her face seemed proof she her condition rued.
Theft was the pilgrim staff she had from Fraud
As gift; it was embrowned with doleful smoke—
And full of cares her scrip. Upon her way
She went when she had thus prepared herself.
  False Seeming, for his part, was well equipped.
As if to try it out, he wore the cloak
Of Preaching Friar. He seemed to have no pride.
Peaceful and mild he in appearance was,
50 With simple, pious look upon his face.
A Bible hung suspended from his neck.
Squireless he went; but, as he weakness feigned,
He carried, to support his limbs, the crutch
Of Treason; and a sharp steel razor slipped
Into his sleeve; 'twas made at Cut Throat's forge.
  So forth they went, and Evil Tongue approached,
Who, watching wayfarers, sat at his gate.
He saw them come, as humbly they drew nigh
And bowed to him with mock humility.
60 Abstinence came close and curtsied low,
And afterward False Seeming made salute.
In turn, and quite unmoved, he greeted them.
He had no doubt or fear, because he thought
He recognized their faces when he looked,

For well with Abstinence he was acquaint,
Though he knew not Constraint. He little guessed
Her feigned and thievish life was now but forced,
But rather thought she came of her free will.
However, she now came quite otherwise;
70 For, if she willingly began the game,
That will had failed her ere she reached the end.
   False Seeming he examined with more care,
But knew him not for False. False as he was,
His falseness could not well be recognized;
For Seeming covered up his falsity.
Though you before had known the knave now dressed
In this attire, you would have taken oath
By Heaven's Eternal King, that he, who once
Had led the dance as jolly Robin, now
80 Was quite transformed into a Jacobin.
   But surely Jacobins are honest men;
Most evilly their order were disgraced
If all of them were charlatans like him.
So with the Carmelites and Cordeliers—
Fat and big bellied though they all may be—
The brothers who wear sacks, and all the rest;
No one of them seems aught but honest man.
But no good consequence can you conclude
From mere appearances in arguments
90 That men may make, if there is any fault
In entity; you'll sophistry perceive
That quite invalidates the consequence,
If you can penetrate duplicity.
   When as they should these pilgrims had come near
To Evil Tongue, they laid their harness by
And sat beside him as he said to them:

EVIL TONGUE

"Come here, now; tell me all the news you know,
And what occasion brings you to my home."

FORCED ABSTINENCE

Forced Abstinence replied, "Fair gentleman,
100 We come as pilgrims pure, with hearts devout,
To do our penance. Almost all the way
We've come afoot; all dusty are our heels.

About this erring world we both are sent
To set a good example and to preach
And fish for souls; we want no other catch.
As we have been accustomed, in God's name
Shelter we seek of you; and for your good,
Unless it would displease you, we'd recite
A fitting sermon in a few brief words."

110 　Then answered Evil Tongue, "Such as it is,   EVIL TONGUE
My shelter shall not be denied to you.
Take it, and preach whatever you may wish;
I'll listen to it, whatsoe'er it be."

FORCED ABSTINENCE

　　"Gramercy, sire," said Abstinence, and then
She thus began her speech: "The virtue first
And greatest that a mortal man may have
By acquisition or inheritance
Is to restrain his tongue. That, every wight
Should strive to do, for it is better far
120 That he say nothing than some evil word.
And those who listen to him willingly
Are not good men, nor have they fear of God.
Above all other sins this sin taints you;
You lately told a lie about a youth
Who here repaired, and 'twas an evil act.
You said that he sought nothing here at all
But to seduce Fair Welcome. 'Twas not true,
But rather 'twas hyperbole, perhaps.
Now he no longer comes and goes; perchance
130 You'll never see him more. And yet immured
Is still Fair Welcome, who throughout the week
Was wont to play his merriest games with you
Without one evil thought, but now dares not
Give solace to himself. The youth who here
Came to enjoy himself you've had chased hence.
What is it moves you to annoy him thus
But your bad mind that thinks up all these lies?
What moves you but your foolish eloquence
That rages, screams, and scolds, and makes a row,
140 Puts blame on folks, dishonors them, then grieves
With accusations which have no support

Except appearances that you've contrived?
I dare to tell you openly that truth
Is not what it appears; it is a sin
To forge a lie that brings one to reproof.
This you know well, which makes the matter worse.
However, naught the Lover cares for this;
He would not give an acorn how things went.
You may know well that he intends no wrong,
150 For if he did he'd come and go at will;
No reason would detain him. As it is,
He cares so little that he comes not here
Except by chance, and less than others do.
Yet tirelessly you're watching, lance at rest,
Here at the gate for him. May you, you fool,
Fool all your time away! You stay awake
Both day and night for naught; for naught you slave.
For Jealousy, attentive as she is
To you, will ne'er repay you for your toil.
160 Fair Welcome gets the worst of it, for he
Remains in pledge though he has had no loan;
Imprisoned though he's made no forfeiture,
Like felon wretch he languishes and weeps.
If never you've committed other sin
In all the world but that wrong you did him,
It would be only just—don't take it hard—
That men should dispossess you of your post,
Thrust you in prison, chain you up in irons.
Unless you shall repent of all your sin,
170 You will be doomed to go to hell's backside."
        Cried Evil Tongue, "Now certainly you lie.   EVIL TONGUE
Ill come are you! Did I but take you in
To hear your insults and your injuries?
'Twas evil chance you took me for a clown.
Now you who give the lie to me may seek
A lodging place elsewhere. The two of you
Are sorcerers come here to do me wrong
And put me to shame because I tell the truth.
Go you about now seeking this to do?
180 May God confound me—devils take my soul—
If, but ten days before this tower was built,

That varlet came not here, as I was told
And so repeated it, and kissed the Rose.
What more he did with her I do not know.
If 'twere not true, why was it told to me?
What I have said, by God, I will repeat;
And I don't think I lie. I'll trumpet it
To all my neighbors, how he came and went."

FALSE SEEMING

    Then spoke False Seeming, "All's not gospel truth
190 That's rumored in the town; be you not deaf,
And I will prove that all the tales are lies.
You certainly know well that no man loves
With all his heart one who speaks ill of him,
Though he be poor of wit, if he's informed.
It's just as true, if I have read aright,
That men are fond of visiting the place
Where live their sweethearts. Take this Lover, now,
Who loves and honors you and calls you oft
His most dear friend, and when he meets you shows
200 A fair and friendly face, salutes you well,
Yet never bores you with solicitude,
For others come far oftener than he—
You know, were he enamored of the Rose,
That he would come, you'd often see him here
And catch him in the act. He could not stay
Away though he risked being burned alive.
Things have not come unto that pass with him,
So you may know that it's not in his mind.
Fair Welcome's no more guilty, though he has
210 Ill payment for his innocence. By God,
If those two really wished, they'd pluck the Rose
In spite of you. As for this youth you wrong—
Who loves you well, you know—if he were bent
To steal the Rose, you'd learn it soon enough.
Not one day more he'd love you—call you friend—
But lie awake at night to plan assault
To break your castle. Were't as you surmise,
Someone had told him; he would know it all.
Or he himself would guess, since he's denied
220 Access that formerly he had, the truth.

But now his actions are quite different,
And so I say you utterly deserve
The pains of hell, since you've served him so ill."
    False Seeming thus the matter proved to him
So well that he knew not how to respond—
At any rate in such light saw the case
That he was near repentance when he said:
    "By God, it well might be. I hold you both,   EVIL TONGUE
False Seeming and Forced Abstinence, as wise.
230 You're both good teachers and of one mind seem.
What would you counsel me that I should do?"

                           FALSE SEEMING

    False Seeming answered, "You must here be shrived;
Confess to me no more than this one sin
Of which you now repent; for I'm a priest
In orders; I have all the world in charge
To shrive the mightiest of men there be
Long as the world shall last. No curate priest,
Sworn to his church, has such great power as I;
I swear by Our High Dame. One hundred times
240 More pity than your parish priest have I
Upon your soul, though he were your close friend.
Moreover, I a great advantage have:
No prelate is one half so wise or learned
As I, a doctor of divinity.
A piece ago I taught theology.
The best men known on earth have chosen me,
Both for my learning and for my good sense,
As their confessor. If you'd now be shrived,
And banish this one sin, not mentioning
250 The rest of them, my absolution you shall have."

57. False Seeming kills Evil Tongue and enters the castle with Forced Abstinence
[12361–12540]

TRULY repentant now kneeled Evil Tongue,
Humble confession of his crime to make.
False Seeming promptly seized him by the throat;
With his two fists he choked and strangled him,
Bereaving him fore'er of power of speech.
Then, with his razor, he cut out his tongue.
Only in this way did they end his life
And so achieve their purpose with the host.
This done, they pitched his corpse into the fosse.
10 The now-unguarded door they quickly broke;
They went within and found the Norman guard
All sleeping, for they'd drunk at will such wine
As I have never poured; they'd even swilled
So much that they all lay upon their backs.
Drunken and sleeping, all were strangled there.
No more they'll be in any shape to lie.
    Now came Largesse and Courtesy in haste
Within the gate. In silence, secretly,
The four assembled there. The harridan
20 Who was Fair Welcome's guard awhile before,
And had seen nothing of the butchery,
The four now saw down from the tower descend
And move about the courtyard. On her head
Above her wimple now, in place of veil,
She wore a hood. Against her ran the four
And hastily assailed her. When she saw
Resistance to all four would be in vain,

THE DUENNA

She thus exclaimed, "My faith! You seem good folk,
Valiant and courteous; then tell me, pray,
30 Without more fuss, what 'tis you're seeking here.

I'm sure 'twas not to take me prisoner."

"To take you, sweet and gentle mother! No;   THE FOUR
We do not come to take you prisoner,
But just to see you, and, if you agree,
To offer to your sweet authority,
Quite freely, both our bodies and our goods,
So far as they're worth while; and never you
Shall find us wanting. If you please, sweet dame,
Who never have been otherwise than sweet,
40 We come to beg that you'll with favor look
On a request that you cannot take ill:
Namely, that he who languishes within,
Fair Welcome, be released to play with us
So little while as scarce will soil his shoes;
Or grant, at least, that he may say a word
Unto the Lover, so that mutually
Each may the other comfort. At small cost
To you you'd furnish solace great to them,
And he would be your liegeman and your slave
50 With whom you could do anything you wished:
Torture, sell, or hang. It's a good thing
To gain a friend. See here these gems, this fan,
These buttons which he sends you as a gift;
Not to make mention of the ornament
Which he will give you soon. He has a heart
That's courteous and free and generous.
He'll surely be no trouble great to you,
For well he loves you; and you'll not be blamed
Because of him, for he's most mum and sly.
60 We beg that you permit him to come here
Without abuse, and that you him conceal;
By doing so you'll surely save his life.
And now this chaplet made of flowers new
We beg you give Fair Welcome as from him,
And comfort him and give him fair salute,
Which will be worth more than a hundred marks."

THE DUENNA

"God help me!" cried the dame, "I'd do it well
If I were sure that Jealousy'd not know,
And that I'd never get the blame for it;

70 But that bad scandalmonger, Evil Tongue,
Is far too talkative. He is the guard
Engaged by Jealousy to spy on us.
There's no preventing him from publishing,
By shouts and cries, whatever he may know,
In fact whate'er he thinks, or what invents
When he knows no one whom he can traduce.
I'd not defend him were he damned to hang,
But if the thief this matter should reveal
To Jealousy, I should be badly shamed."

80   Said they, "You need have no more fear of him;   THE FOUR
He will not spy nor listen any more
In any way, for out there he lies dead
With gaping throat, not cradled on a bier
But in the ditch. He'll never come to life,
Unless by sorcery, those two again
To slander. He will ne'er accuse them more
Unless the Devil work a miracle
With charm or philter."

                    Then replied the dame,
"In that case, I'll no more refuse your prayer.   THE DUENNA
90 But let the swain make haste. I'll gain access
For him, but let there be no insolence.
Let him come secretly when I make sign,
And not remain too long. Let him guard well
Himself and his, that no man him perceive.
Let him do nothing that he should not do,
Though he may talk as much as he may wish."

    "Lady," said they, "it doubtless will be so."   THE FOUR
Each thanked her, and with that their work was done.
    False Seeming, howsoever that might be,
100 Thought otherwise, and muttered to himself:
"If he for whom we undertook this task,   FALSE SEEMING
Since he his thoughts of love will not renounce,
Would trust to me, if you would not accord,
Not by a long way would you then succeed,
In my opinion, in preventing him
From entering and reconnoitering,
If he found time and place. Not every time
Do shepherds see the wolf that steals their sheep

Beneath their very roof, however well
110 They may have guarded them out in the fields.
Sometime you'd go to church, as yesterday,
When you remained so long; and Jealousy,
Who tricks him so, would walk outside the town
Perhaps, or find occasion to depart.
In secret then, or in the night, he'd come
Up through the garden, lighted by no torch,
And all alone, unless his Friend were there,
Who'd keep a watch for him at his request.
Unless the place were lighted by the moon,
120 Whose shining beams have many a lover scathed,
He'd lead him quickly, with encouragement,
Since well he knows the precincts of the place,
To some point where, descending by a rope,
He'd enter by a window. Thus he'd come,
And thus he'd go away. Then would descend
Fair Welcome to the garden, where he'd wait
The Lover's coming. Or he would have fled
From the enclosure, where he's captive been
For many days, and come to meet the youth
130 And talk to him, provided that the swain
Had been unable to invade him.
Or when you slept, if he saw time and chance,
Perhaps he'd leave the door unlocked for him,
And then the Lover would approach the Rose
Of which he thinks so much, and pluck its bloom,
Unfearing interruption, if the rest
He could discomfit in some other way."
    Now as for me, who stood not far away,
I thought that thus I should accomplish it.
140 No fear felt I of further handicap
If the old hag her convoy to me gave,
And if she would not I should enter there
When best I saw my chance, as had devised
False Seeming; for I held his counsel to be good.

58. The Duenna acts as go-between for the Lover
and Fair Welcome
[12541–12760]

NO more delay the harridan then made,
But to Fair Welcome, at a trot, returned,
Who in the prison, much against his will,
Still suffered from his long imprisonment.
She entered by the gateway of the tower,
And joyously she hastened up the stairs
As fast as trembling limbs would her permit.
From room to room she sought him, and at last
She found him leaning o'er the battlement,
10 Pensive and sad and mournful, ill at ease
With his confinement. Thus she cheered him up:
"Fair son," said she, "it moves me much to find   THE DUENNA
You so low-spirited. Tell me, I pray,
What are your thoughts. If I can counsel give,
Never will I abuse your confidence."
     Fair Welcome did not dare to make complaint
Or tell the whys and wherefores of his mood;
For he knew not if she spoke true or lied.
Thus insecure, he disavowed his thoughts;
20 His heart warned him to put no trust in her.
Trembling and fearful, he dared heave no sigh,
So much he'd always feared the vile old crone.
He wished to guard himself from treachery,
Which he much feared; so he did not disclose
His great uneasiness; but with a face
And manner of pretended happiness
He strove to reconcile himself to her.
"My most dear lady, certainly," said he,   FAIR WELCOME
"However much you lay it to my charge,
30 I'm not low-spirited, except that you
So long have kept away. Unwillingly

I stay here in your absence, for my love
Of you is great. Where have you been so long?"

THE DUENNA

"Where? By my head, I soon will let you know,
And from the knowledge you will gain great joy
If valiant or wise you claim to be.
A gallant, the most courteous in the world,
In whom all pleasing graciousness abounds,
Whom I just now saw passing through the street,
40 A thousand times salutes you, and by me
He sends to you this chaplet; and he says
That he would like to see you, that he'll have
No day of health or any wish to live
Unless by your good will. He says, 'My God   THE LOVER
And good Saint Faith preserve my life, unless
I can succeed in pleasing him when once
At leisure I've conversed with him a while!'
For you and no one else he loves his life.   THE DUENNA
If by that means he could do anything
50 That might be pleasing to you, he would walk
Stark naked all the way to Pavia.
He cares not what becomes of him, unless
You will consent to have him call on you."

Fair Welcome straightway asked who this might be
Who thus desired to see him, ere he took
The present, for he felt some little fear
That from such source it came that he'd not wish
To keep it. Without further tale, the dame
Revealed the truth to him: "It is that youth   THE DUENNA
60 Of whom you've heard so much, whom you know well,
Because of whom but lately Evil Tongue,
Who is no more, brought you to so much grief
When great detraction he heaped up on you.
Oh, never may his soul see Paradise!
Full many a good man he's made desolate;
But now the Devil has him, for he's dead.
Forever we're delivered; we've escaped;
We need not care two apples for him now;
And even could he come again to life
70 He could not grieve us, howsoe'er he blamed,

For I know more than he has ever known.
Believe me, then, and take and wear this wreath;
Give him that much of comfort, at the least.
You need not doubt he loves you with true love,
With love without a flaw; or, if he had
Other intention, I perceived it not.
I think we both may give him confidence.
If he asks anything he should not seek,
Most easily you can deny his will.
80 If he brews folly, he must drink the brew.
But he's no fool; the rather, he is wise.
Never an insult will be given by him,
And that is why I love and prize him so.
He'll not be so discourteous as to ask
A thing it were not fitting you should grant.
Loyal above all living men is he,
As all his company, and I myself,
Have always testified. He's well brought up
And mannerly; no man of woman born
90 Has ever any evil of him heard
Save that which Evil Tongue has said him.
But now all that is in oblivion;
Even I have almost forgotten it,
And all that I remember of his words
Is that they were most foolish and most false.
The Lover would have killed him, certainly,
If he had known what Evil Tongue has said;
For he is bold and hardy. In this land
There's not another one can match his worth,
100 His heart's so full of true nobility.
King Arthur's bounty cannot his exceed—
Nor even Alexander's—could he spend
So much of gold and silver as was theirs.
Howe'er well they knew how to give their gold,
He'd give a hundred times more than they gave.
So good a heart he has, he'd daze the world
If his possessions were so plentiful.
He needs no lessons in munificence.
Therefore, I beg you, take this chaplet now,
110 Whose flowers smell more sweet than any balm."

a gueirs ny gnaignissie
n lonc aler mon escient
q'l y entrust en espient
S il en eust et temps z leu
E en ne voit ins touds le leu
A ms prent bien ou tort la bde
T out les gart len ples herbz
v ne heure a lissez an montier
v os y demourastes mlt hier
J alousie qui si le gule
z alast espor lors de la vile
o u q soit convient il ql aille
J l vemst lors en repostaille
u par nuit deuers les costs
S eul sanz chatele z saz tortis
S e niert danu sil le gaitast
S enseuet len amonestast
z par confort le condunst
o ms q la bune ne buisist
C ar la bune p son der luize
S eut as amas maintes fotz nuire
o ul entrast ples fenestres
Q'l seet bien de lostel les estres
P ar vne corde il saualast
A msi y vemst et alast
B elacueil espor descendist
E s countils on al latendist
o n sen souut hors du ppris
o n tenu lauez niait tour ps
z vemst au varlet parler
S il aluy ne prust aler
o u quil endorm w'scenst
S e teps z leu auoir prust
L es huis entrouuers li laissast

A msi du louio saprestast
L is mis amas q tant y pense
z le cueillist lors saz deffense
S i veust par autre matire
L es autres portiers desofrir
rie qui Lamant prile
g uenirs long nestoire
d apensay quant le servie
S e la vielle me veult zduire
C e ne me doit giuner ne nuire
z sel ne veult gi enterray
P ar la ou mier mon pît vray
S i co faux semblat lor veuse
d u tout metng a co veuse
oment la vielle maqrese
p ourhate alamat sa querele
E t presente z robes chapel
X telacueil le donts et bel

L a vielle leue plus
ne seiourne
L enot a brlac sen tourne
Q' la tour oultre so gir garde
C ar bien se souffust de tel gre

The Duenna gives the imprisoned Fair Welcome a chaplet from the Lover. *Morgan 132, f. 91v.*

"My faith, I fear that I'll be blamed for it,"   FAIR WELCOME
Fair Welcome cried, trembling in every limb,
Sighing and shaking, blushing, turning pale,
And losing countenance. She thrust the gift
Upon him, almost forcing him to take,
Although he dared not reach his hand for it,
But said, the better to excuse himself,
That 'twould become him better to refuse
Than that, 'twere known, how'er he liked the gift.
120 "The chaplet's very beautiful," he said,   FAIR WELCOME
"But better 'twere for me that all my clothes
Were burned to ashes than that I should dare
Accept a gift that's sent to me by him.
Suppose I take it, what could we then say
To Jealousy, who is so quarrelsome?
Well know I that she'd be enraged with ire—
She'd strip my head of flowers, one by one,
Then kill me—if she knew they came from him;
Or I'd be seized and still more closely bound
130 Than ever in my life I've been before;
Or if I could escape her and take flight,
Where could I any place of refuge find?
You'd see me buried while I still had life
If after such retreat I should be caught.
I think there'd be pursuit; and I'd be seized
In midst of flight, there'd be such hue and cry.
I'll not accept the gift."
                              "Oh, yes, you will;   THE DUENNA
It will involve you in no blame or loss."

                                        FAIR WELCOME
"But what if she should ask me whence it came?"

                                          THE DUENNA
140   "You've more than twenty answers you can make."
        "But what could I reply to her demand?   FAIR WELCOME
Whence shall I say I got it, if she scolds?
If I don't tell the truth, I must tell lies;
And, if she found me out, I swear to you
'Twere better I should dead than living be."

                                          THE DUENNA
    "What shall you say? If you've no better tale,

Tell her it came from me. I've such renown
That you need no shame or fear of blame
For taking anything I give to you."
150   Fair Welcome said no more, but felt assured
And placed the wreath upon his golden hair.
The old crone laughed, and swore upon her soul,
Her body, bones, and skin, that he'd ne'er had
A headdress that became him half so well.
Fair Welcome then admired it in his glass
And often it surveyed to see how well
It looked on him. Now the Duenna saw
That none except the two were in the place,
So gracefully she took her seat by him
160   And thus began to preach: "Fair Welcome dear,   THE DUENNA
How much I love you! For you are so sweet
And of such worth! My joyous days are gone,
But yours are still to come. I scarce sustain
My limbs with cane or crutch; while you're still young
And careless what you do. But well I know
That late or soon, whenever it may be,
You'll pass amidst the flame that scorches all—   *thus Wife of*
You'll plunge into the(bath)where Venus makes   *Bath*
All women bathe. I know you'll feel her brand.
170   Now I advise that you prepare yourself
By listening to the teaching that I'll give
Before you take that bath; it's perilous
For youths to bathe there who have not been taught.
But, if you follow straight the advice I give,
You will arrive most safely in your port at last."

59. The Duenna tells Fair Welcome the story of her life
           [12761–12986]

"BELIEVE me, if at your age I had known,   THE DUENNA
As well as I know now, the game of Love,
It had been well. I had great beauty then,
But now, when I survey my worn-out face

And see its wrinkles, I but sigh and groan;
For I recall my former loveliness,
Which then so agitated all the swains,
And how I led them such a merry chase
That 'twas no wonder that they felt Love's wounds.
10 Then had my beauty such a great renown
Throughout the land that there was such a crowd
Within my house as ne'er was seen before.
Much knocking at my door each eve was heard,
Which went unanswered when I, hard of heart,
Oft found it inconvenient to admit
Another, when already company
I had. That started trouble more than once,
On which account most angry I became.
Often the riot even broke my door.
20 And ere the combatants would separate
They sometimes lost their limbs and even lives.
Envy and hatred made the contests worse.
If master Algus, best of reckoners,
Had cared to come with his ten numerals,
With which he numbers and computes all things,
However much he deigned to multiply,
He could not calculate the total sum
Of those great conflicts. Though I then was strong
And lively, and in silver sterlings had
30 A thousand pounds more than I now possess,
I managed my affairs most wretchedly.
    "I was a fair, young, silly fool; and had
No training in the school of Love, where's taught
The theory. The practice well I knew;
Throughout my life I've had experience
That's made me wise, so now I know the game
Up to the final bout. It were not right
That I should fail to teach you what I know,
Since I have made so much experiment.
40 He who to young folk counsel gives does well.
It is no wonder that you know of it
Less than a quarter of an ell, for you
Have yet a yellow beak; you're still unfledged,
While I have graduated from my course

And know the science to the very end;
I could uphold a lectureship on love.
The lore of age should not be shunned or scorned;
In it experience and sense one finds.
Full many a man has found that in the end,
50 However much he may have paid for it,
He's gained but judgment and experience.
    "When once, with no small labor, I'd achieved
Some wit and practice, many a valiant man
Who fell into my snares I fooled and held;
I was deceived, upon the other hand,
Before I ever learned to know myself.
Grievous misfortune 'twas I learned so late!
For by that time I was beyond my youth;
My door, that once oft opened, night and day,
60 Now ever to its threshold closely clung.
'No one has come today or yesterday;
Alas, poor wretch, in sorrow I must live,'
Was then my thought. My heart was cleft with grief.
When thus I saw my door so idly hang—
And I myself as idle all the while—
I could not stand the shame, and wished to leave.
How could I stay to see those handsome swains,
Who formerly had been my dearest guests,
Who loved me so they thought they ne'er could leave,
70 Now pass me by and look at me askance?
E'en those who once had loved me most would skip
Me by as though I were not worth an egg.
They called me 'wrinkled crone,' and even worse,
Before they had beyond my hearing passed.
    "My gentle friend, no one, however wise,
However schooled in grief, could understand
What dolor held my heart when I recalled
The lovely words, the sweet felicity,
The soft delights, the kisses savory,
80 Embraces more delightful than all else,
Which flew away so fast. Did I say flew?
'Tis true; they did, and never to return!
I'd better been imprisoned in a tower
Forever than to have been so early born.

God! To what care brought me those same fair gifts
When they deserted me! And what was left
Of them, what torment did it cause to me!
Unfortunate, why were you born so soon?
    "Thus I complain; and is there one but you,
90 Whom I so dearly love, to hear my plaint?
How otherwise can I revenge myself
Except by teaching you my principles?
Fair son, my tutelage is to this end:
That, when you shall be learnèd, you shall take
Vengeance for me upon the whoremongers;
For when that time shall come, so may God please,
You will remember all my sermoning
Which you'll retain by reason of your age
That gives you great advantage to this end.
100 For Plato says, 'It is a well-known fact   PLATO
That more retentive is the memory
Of things it learns in youth, whatever be
The nature of the learning that it gains.'
    "Certainly, dearest son, beloved youth,   THE DUENNA
If I were young like you, no pen could write
The vengeance I would take upon my foes.
Wherever I might come, I'd miracles,
The like of which were never heard before,
Perform upon those ribalds who despised
110 And slandered me, and of so little worth
Considered me that basely they passed by,
Vying with one another in their pride,
And giving me no pity or reprieve.
Do you know what I'd do to them, now God
Has given me the lore of which I spoke?
I'd eat them out of house and home, and press
Upon them so their faults and errancies
That they would come to be the food of worms
And lie all naked on manure piles,
120 Especially the ones who loved me first,
With loyal hearts, they said, and took such pains
Most willingly to serve and honor me.
If I were able, there should not remain
To them what might be worth a garlic clove

That I'd not have within my purse, and they
Should all be left in cruel poverty;
Stamping in lively rage they'd follow me.
   "Regrets are vain; what's gone is not to come.
What do they care for all the threats I make?
130 My wrinkled face has now no hold on them;
And long ago the ribalds told me so
When first their love to detestation turned.
Then could I naught but weep; I now rejoice;
When musing on the past that is no more,
I am delighted with my thoughts; my limbs
New vigor feel when good times I recall,
And all the jolly life that pleased my heart.
Rejuvenated all my body seems
When recollections come into my mind.
140 When I remember every little fact,
It does me all the good in the world. At least
I had my fun, however much deceived.
A damsel is not indolent who leads
A life of joy, especially if she
Knows how to make expense and gain by it.
   "Then to this countryside I came, and met
Your lady, who engaged me to maintain
Your guardianship within these castle walls.
May God, who's guard and father of us all,
150 Grant that I do my duty! So I'll do
Most certainly if you behave yourself.
Since Nature's granted you a marvelous,
Surpassing beauty, risky were the task
If also you'd not learned good sense and wit
And gallantry and grace. Since place and time
Now serve us well and we need not to fear
To be disturbed in saying what we wish
A little better than we're used to do,
To counsel you I'll say what's on my mind;
160 Although my words be few, be not surprised.
I'll tell you in advance, 'tis not my wish
To set your thoughts on love; but, if your will
Is strong to intermeddle in such things,
I'll gladly show you all the roads and paths

That once I trod before my beauty fled."
  The woman sighed and ceased, that she might know
Fair Welcome's answer; but her wait was short;
For, when she saw him well disposed to hear,
What she might say, and silence still to hold,
170 As she prepared her purpose to pursue,
She thought, "There's no denying that the one
Who will not say a word assents to all;
Since willingly he listens, I may dare proceed."

60. The Duenna teaches Fair Welcome her theory of love
            [12987–13172]

THEN, like the false and servile crone she was,
She recommenced her prating, with the thought
That by her doctrines she might cozen me
To fool myself with honey licked from thorns,
Advising him that he should call me Friend
Though no true love on me he did bestow.
But he remembered all and told it me;
Though certainly, had he been what she thought,
He had betrayed me. Spite of all she said,
10 Fair Welcome never worked such treachery.
He gave his solemn oath and word for that,
And also he assured me other ways.
  "Most fair, sweet son—exquisite, tender flesh— THE DUENNA
I'll teach you all the games of Love, that you,
When you have learned them, cannot be deceived.
Conform yourself unto my art, for none
Not well informed can fail to lose his all.
Now strive to hear and understand and keep
All that I say within your memory,
20 For I know all the history of love.
  "Fair son, whoso would taste the joys of love—
Its pleasant pains that are so bittersweet—
Must know the laws of Love, but not Love's self.
All these I'd teach you, did I not perceive
That you by nature have all that you need

In heaping measure. If you count them well,
Of those that you must know the number's ten;
But he is foolish who the last two heeds,
For they're not worth a counterfeited cent.
30 Devote yourself, then, to the other eight,
For he who would observe the latter two
But fools himself and loses all his pains.
These two should not be taught in any school;
Any professor who would lover teach
That he should have a generous heart, and yet
Bestow it in a single place, would lay
Too great a burden on the neophyte.
The text is false; the doctrine is untrue.
The son of Venus lies in teaching this;
40 No one should credit either him or her.
Dearly he'll pay who follows their advice,
As will appear before I make an end.
    "Fair son, be never prodigal in love;
Bestow your heart on no one specially,
But many places have where it may be.
Don't either lend or give it quite away,
But sell it only for the highest price
At auction, and take care that he who buys
Secures no bargain. It were better far
50 That you should burn or hang or drown yourself
Than he should have your love who nothing gives.
Above all else remember these two points:
Take with an open hand, but close your fist
When 'tis your turn to give. Great foolishness
It is to give, except by way of lure,
When one can see it would be profitable,
Or hope for some repayment of the gift
That would be better than the price he'd get.
Such gifts I grant you well. 'Tis wise to give
60 When giving will but multiply the gain.
He who is certain of his usury
Will not repent the loan; that I agree.
    "Now, next, as to the bow and arrows five
Which are so full of finest qualities
And shoot so subtly, you know all their use

Better than Love himself, the archer skilled.
He cannot draw the golden bow, fair son,
As well as you, who many a time have shot
Its arrows, though you have not always known
70 Just where the shot would strike; for when one shoots
At random someone may receive the stroke
Who by the archer had not been perceived.
But he who should your manners well regard
Would see that you so well can bend and draw
That you have really nothing left to learn.
You may be able, then, someone to wound
Whose conquest will, please God, be profitable.

     "I do not need to speak of your attire—
The gowns and garnishments that you should wear
80 To make yourself seem better than you are.
It's not important to repeat that song
About the image of Pygmalion,
Which you must know by heart, since you have heard
Me oft repeat it as we took our ease.
From it you've learned more of appareling
Than oxen know of plowing. There's no need
To give you counsel in such things as that.
If this will not suffice, you'll hear me say,
If you will listen to me presently,
90 Some things from which you may a lesson take.
This much I'll tell you: if you wish to choose
As friend a fair young man who prizes you,
Although you set your heart on him, beware
Lest you should love him all too fervently.
Love others prudently; I'll find for you
Enough from whom great gain can be amassed.
'Tis well to make acquaintance of rich men
Whose hearts are neither miserly nor close,
If you but know how you may dig their gold.
100   "Fair Welcome may gain whatsoe'er he please
Provided he give each to understand
That he would not accept another friend—
Not for a thousand marks of finest gold—
And swear that, if another he'd allowed
To gain the Rose which is so much desired,

He had been loaded down with gold and gems;
But that so faithful is his loyal heart
That not another shall extend his hand
To pluck the Rose, except the favored one.
110 Though they a thousand were, to each he'd say:
'God fail me if I should apportion her!'
So he should swear and pledge his faith, nor fear
If he perjures himself; for God but smiles
On such an oath, and lightly pardons it.
   "When lovers swear false oaths, great Jupiter
And all the gods laugh loudly. They themselves
Commit their perjuries when they're in love.
When Jupiter would reassure his wife,
Queen Juno, he pronounced the highest oath,
120 Swearing by river Styx, yet falsely lied.
When such examples gods to lovers give,
They should the latter much assurance lend
Falsely to swear by temples, shrines, and saints.
And so, God love me, he is but a fool
Who would believe a lover on his oath;
Lovers have hearts that are too changeable.
Unstable are the young; and, oftentimes,
The old folks, too, will break their faith and vows.
   "You know 'tis true the master of the fair
130 Takes toll from all; and he who fails to grind
At one mill seeks another, lickety-clip;
And at great peril forages the mouse
Who has for refuge but a single hole.
Just so a woman, mistress of all marts,
Who makes her bargains in pursuit of gain,
Should take her toll from all; she were a fool,
As she herself should on reflection know,
If she did not desire more friends than one.
I swear by Saint Lifard of Meun that she
140 Who all her love would in one sole place lay
Has badly served her heart, confining it
Bereft of all its freedom. She deserves
Enough of grief and pain who but one man
Takes care to love. If he to comfort her
Should fail, she then would have no comforter.

Such are the ones who suffer most default
Because their hearts to one man they entrust;
Misfortune they must feel and suffer woe
When they are left deserted in the bitter end."

61. The Duenna tells the stories of Dido, Phyllis, Oenone, and Medea
[13173-13280]

"UNTO no happy end can woman come   THE DUENNA
In such a way. Aeneas' love to keep
Did Dido strive in vain, though she was queen
Of Carthage, and the great advantage had
That she had succored him with food and clothes
When he was but a wretched fugitive
From that fair land of Troy where he was born.
She honored his companions for the love
She bore to him, and had his ships repaired
10 To be of service and to please him well.
To hold his love she offered him herself,
Her wealth, her city; he in turn took oath—
Gave promises and firm assurances—
That he was hers, as he would always be,
And never would desert her. But small joy
She had of him. The traitor fled away
Over the sea in ships, without good-by.
Because of this the fair one lost her life
When, on the morrow, in her chamber, she
20 With her own hand committed suicide,
Using the sword that he had given her.
Still mindful of the friend whose love she'd lost,
She stood the sword upright upon its hilt
And, standing naked, placed the naked point
Between her breasts and fell upon the blade.
Great pity 'twas to see that deed performed;
Hard would the man have been who did not feel

Compassion when he saw Queen Dido fair
Impaled throughout her body on the sword,
30 Such grief she had because she had been tricked.
  "Phyllis awaited Demophon so long
That, when she knew he'd broken vows and faith
Because he came not when he said he would,
She hanged herself.

                    "And how did Paris serve
Oenone, who had given him her soul
And body when he offered her his love?
Too soon he rendered back to her the gift
When with his knife he carved, in place of scroll,
Upon a tree that grew upon a bank,
40 In little letters hardly worth a tart,
That Xanthus would return unto its source
Sooner than he would leave her. It would seem
That Xanthus must have soon reversed its flow!
For Helen promptly he deserted her,
Leaving the letters carved on poplar bark.
  "Was not Medea treacherously betrayed
By Jason, who had sworn to keep his faith
With her until his death, but soon proved false
After she had delivered him by charms
50 So that he suffered neither burn nor wound
From those fire-breathing bulls who came to rend
And cremate him, and after she had drugged
The dragon so that he could not awake
From out the sleep profound that she produced—
And after she had caused the earth-born knights,
Warlike and fierce, who would have Jason killed
After he threw the stone into their midst,
Each other to engage, each other kill—
And after she had helped him gain the fleece
60 By means of her concoctions and her arts—
And after she restored to youth his sire,
Old Aeson, that she might have better hold
On Jason? She demanded naught of him
Save that he love her as he once had done
And recognize the merits she possessed
And better keep the faith he swore to her.

Dido and Phyllis kill themselves when betrayed by love.
Morgan, 132, f. 97r.

The evil traitor, liar, recreant, knave
Then left her—she in sorrow and in rage
Strangled the children she had borne for him;
70 When she perceived the truth her mind gave way,
Maternal tenderness abandoned her,
And she performed a deed far worse than those
That bitter stepdames have been guilty of.
  "I know a thousand tales like this to tell,
But far too long the narrative would be.
In brief, these ribalds say they give their hearts
To many a maid, but trick and cheat them all;
Therefore should woman trick the men in turn
And never give her heart to one alone.
80 She's but a fool who does so; she should have
A host of friends, and strive to please them all,
So, if she can, to give them all misease,
If she lack graces, she must some acquire.
Most haughty she should be to those who try
The most to gain her love by serving her.
The ones who of her loving set least store
Are those she must work hardest to attract
By learning games and songs, by trying hard
To shun dispute and clamor when they are about."

62. The Duenna tells Fair Welcome
how women gain men's love
[13281–13846]

"IF it should chance a woman is not fair,   THE DUENNA
She should make up her lacks with dainty dress—
Its elegance offsets her ugliness.
If she should lose her hair—the saddest sight—
Because it falls too soon from her blond head,
Or else because of some great malady
She finds it needful to cut short her curls,
Diminishing her beauty by the act,

Or else because some angry ribald tears   *hair and lechery*
10 Her hair in anger, leaving not enough
To form a braid, then she must soon procure
The hair of someone who has lately died,
Or else she must make pads of yellow silk
To tuck beneath her few remaining locks.
Above her ears such towering horns she'll wear
As never buck nor stag nor unicorn
Could boast if he should dare to match with her;
And if she should have need to dye her hair,
There's many an herb with which it may be tinged,
20 For root and bark and stem and leaf and fruit
Possess the qualities of medicines.

"If she is pale and finds this cause of grief,
Moist unguents in her chamber in a box
She should provide, and always by herself,
In secret, can her color be renewed.
Let her take care that not a lover sees
Or knows her use of such a subterfuge.
Too sad mischance might well result from that.
If her neck's beautiful, and white her throat,
30 She should instruct her dressmaker to cut
Her robe so low that half a foot of skin
Shows fair and clean behind and in the front,
Thus so much more attracting all the men.
If she should think her shoulders are too large
To be most pleasing at a dance or ball,
Then she should wear a dress of thinnest lawn,
In which her figure will appear less gross.
If she have hands that are not smooth and fair
But rough or calloused, she should care for them,
40 All blemishes removing with a pin,
Or hiding scabs and blisters in her gloves.
If she have breasts that are too large and full,
Napkin or kerchief she should bind about
Her body, knotting it or sewing fast,
To hold them close against her chest; and then
She may enjoy herself at any dance.

"A maid should keep her Venus' chamber clean;
If she would be considered well brought up,

No spiderwebs will she allow about
50 That she'll not burn or scrub or scour away;
Nor leave a soapy puddle in the place.

"If she has ugly feet, they are well shod;
A leg too large is clothed in finest silk.
In brief, if she's aware of any flaw,
She'll cover it unless she is a fool.

"If her breath's bad, it should not be too hard
To hold her peace until she's breakfasted,
Or at the least to turn her mouth away,
That people's noses it may not approach.

60 "When she's amused, she always smiles so well
That she discloses dimples in her cheeks;
She neither opens wide her jaws to laugh,
Nor closes them too tight in simpering.
A woman ne'er should laugh with open mouth;
Her lips must cover and conceal her teeth;
For if too wide a gulf appears, it looks
As though her face were slit—it's no fair sight—
And if she have not even, well-shaped teeth,
But ugly, crooked ones, she'll be less prized
70 Should she let them appear in laugh or smile.

"Important is her manner when in tears,
But every woman is expert enough
In lachrymation in whatever place;
For, even though men do to them no wrong
Nor give them grief or shame, their ready tears
Are always at their call. All women weep
In whatsoever fashion pleases them.
A man should never be too much disturbed
Though women's tears he sees fall thick as rain;
80 For ne'er she rains such tears or shows such grief
Or such chagrin, except for trickery.
Naught but a ruse the tears of women are;
'Tis not with grief that they are most concerned,
But with the thought how they can best conceal,
By what they say or do, what's in their minds.

"Fit manners should she have when she's at meat;
But ere she takes her seat she should appear
Often outside the door and let all know

How busy she has been about the meal.
90 Hither and thither she should go and come,
And be the last of all to take her place,
Although the company may have to wait.
When she is seated, finally, she looks
To see that each one properly is served;
Before them all she breaks and passes bread.
To gain his grace, she chooses some one friend
To eat with her, serves him with leg or wing
Or cuts him some fine bit of beef or pork,
Or fish or flesh—whatever there may be.
100 She'll not be stingy if he will accept.
She should not wet her fingers in the sauce
Beyond the joint, nor soil her lips with soup,
With garlic, or fat meat; nor pile a heap
Of food and then convey it to her mouth.
With tips of fingers she should handle bits
That she should dip in sauce, white, yellow, or green,
And very carefully the mouthful lift,
That on her breast no bit of pepper falls,
Or soup or gravy. Then so gracefully
110 She should her goblet quaff that not a drop
She spills upon her clothes, for far too rude
Or gluttonous men might consider her
If they should see such accident occur.
The common cup should not approach her lips
While yet there is some food within her chops;
And ere she drinks she wipes her mouth so clean
That on her lips no speck of grease adheres,
At least not on her upper lip, for then
Globules of it might float upon the wine,
120 Which would be most disgusting and not neat.
However thirsty she may be, she drinks
A little at a time; she never drains
A goblet at a draft, nor e'en a cup,
But often sips, lest others she incite
To say that with a glutton's throat she gulps;
Deliciously the drink should trickle down.
She should not suck the goblet's brim too much,
As nursemaids often do, so gluttonous

cf. Prioress in CT

And boorish that they pour into their throats
130 The wine as crudely as if into a barrel,
And swallow such great mouthfuls at one time
That they are overcome and dazed with drink.
A lady should beware of drunkenness,
For not a man or woman while in drink
Could ever keep a secret; just as soon
As she intoxicated has become,
She babbles everything that's in her mind.
A drunken woman is without defense,
And prey to any man, when she has done
140 Such mischief to herself. She should not sleep
At table; 'tis a most uncomely thing,
And many a mishap has occurred to those
Who thus have dozed. 'Tis not good sense to sleep
In places that are meant for waking hours;
Thus napping, many folk have come to grief,
For, falling on their faces, sides, or backs,
They've broken arms or ribs or even heads.
A woman who thus feels beset with sleep
The fate of Palinurus should recall,
150 Who steered Aeneas' ship, and steered it well
So long as he contrived to keep awake,
But, when at last he was with sleep o'erwhelmed,
Losing the tiller, he fell overboard,
And drowned before his shipmates' very eyes,
Who long lamented, afterward, his death.
    "A maid should take good care that not too long
She waits before she plays the game of love,
For 'tis quite possible thus to delay
Until no one will offer her his hand.
160 While she enjoys her youth, she should pursue
The joys of love; for, when old age assaults,
She'll have no further part in lovers' bouts.
The woman who is wise will pluck the fruit
While she is in the flower of her age.
The more, unfortunate, she loses time,
The more will pass the savor of love's joys.
If she despise the counsel that I give
But for the common profit, she'll repent

When age shall wither all her loveliness.
170 But well I know wise women will believe
And keep the rules I give; and they will say
Full many a paternoster for my soul
When I am dead, because I teach them now
And comfort them; for well I know my words
In many a school will be hereafter read.

"Most fair, sweet son, I know that if you live
You'll willingly inscribe within a book,
Without omission, all my tutoring,
And when you leave me, please God, you will teach
180 And be professor of the art, like me.
In spite of what all chancellors may say,
I give you license for your lectureship,
To school your pupils in the upper halls
And lower rooms, in gardens, fields, and woods,
Beneath pavilions, under tapestries,
In garrets, wardrobes, pantries, or in stables,
If you cannot more pleasant places find,
Provided that my precepts you'll expound
When you have mastered and committed them.

190 "A woman should against seclusion guard;
The more she stays at home, the less she's seen,
And so the less her loveliness is sought—
The less men covet and solicit her.
To church she oft should go, and visits pay,
Attend all weddings, all processions see,
View festivals, and plays, and carolings.
Cupid and Venus at such times keep school,
And for their pupils celebrate high mass.

"But in her mirror she should first observe
200 If she is well attired; and, when she feels
That all is perfect, through the streets she'll go
With most seductive motion, not too stiff
Nor yet too much relaxed, not low, or high,
But moving gracefully throughout the crowd.
So nobly sway her shoulders and her hips
That men no motion could believe more fair.
Genteelly she can walk in fine, small shoes
Which she's had fashioned so becomingly

That without wrinkle they will fit her feet.
210   "If she wears dress that trails upon the ground
Or near the pavement hangs, at front or sides
She lifts it slightly, as to feel the air,
Or as to give a chance for freer tread;
But she takes care thus to disclose her foot,
That its fair form the passers-by may see.

  "In case she wears a mantle, it should hang
So that it may not interfere too much
With seeing the fair body it protects;
And, that her form the better may appear,
220 As well as what she wears beneath her cloak
(Which neither thick nor thin should be, but gilt
With silver thread-work and with little pearls),
Not to forget the alms purse all should see,
She frequently in both her hands will seize
Her cloak, and, stretching wide her arms, stand still,
Whether the road be dry or deep with mud,
Reminding one of the brilliant, feathered wheel
That peacocks fashion when they spread their tails.
She'll know how best to do this if her cloak
230 Have lining gray or green or of what hue
She may have chosen, and she thus will show
Her figure openly to all who gaze.

  "If less than beautiful her face should be,
If she is wise, she'll often turn her head
To show her precious, golden-gleaming locks,
Plaited above her comely neck behind;
Most pleasing is the beauty of the hair.

  "With care should women always imitate
The wolf when she desires to steal a sheep.
240 That she may fail not, and be sure of one,
A thousand she assails; she never knows,
Before she has him caught, which one she'll get.
A woman everywhere should spread her nets
To capture all the men; she cannot tell
With whom she will find grace. That at the least
She may succeed in drawing to herself
But one of them, she'll try to hook them all;
Then it can scarcely chance that none she'll find,

Among the many thousand fools there are,
250 Who'll rub her flanks for her. She should find more
Than one, for art is nature's greatest aid.
   "If several she should get upon her hook
Who wish to place her on the spit, she guards,
Howe'er the contest goes, that in one hour
She make appointment with but one of them;
For, if a number should together come,
They'd think themselves deceived, and all might leave.
She might be shamed, and at the least she'd lose
The presents they would bring; whereas her care
260 Should be to leave to none of them the means
Of living well, and bring them one and all
To such great poverty that each will die
Most wretchedly in debt and leave her rich;
Whate'er she's failed to get will then be lost.
   "She need not worry o'er a poor man's love,
For such a one is nothing worth to her;
Though Ovid 'twere or Homer, he would have
The value of two goblets at the most.
Nor should she strive to win a stranger's love,
270 For, as in many an inn he eats and sleeps,
As shifty as his body is his heart.
I counsel not to love a traveler,
But, in his sojourn, if he offer gems
Or money, she may put them in her box
And then his pleasure she may well fulfill
Immediately—or she may make him wait.
   "A woman never should as lover take
A man of too great elegance, or one
Who boasts of beauty; pride has all his heart.
280 Doubt not that one who's satisfied with self
Deserves the wrath of God. Thus Ptolemy,
By whom was science greatly loved, has said,
Such men have not the power truly to love,
So bitter and so evil are their hearts;
What they profess to one they say to all.
Many a woman's by such man deceived
But that he may despoil and plunder her.
Complaints I've heard from many thus seduced.

"If promisers, sincere or false, appear
290 And swear that they will link their lives to hers
To gain her love, a woman may in turn
Give promises to them; but let her guard
Lest she should put herself within their power,
Unless she first gets good return in cash.

"If one sends her a letter, she should note
Whether he writes deceivingly, or shows,
Writing wholeheartedly, intentions good.
After a little time she'll write in turn,
But not without delay; for negligence
300 Oft teases lovers on, but not for long.

"When she shall hear the lover press his suit,
She should not haste to offer him her love
Nor all deny; but him in balance hold,
That he may fearful be, yet have some hope.
When he the harder begs, she has him caught
So firmly that she need not grant her love
But, while she still defends herself with force
And ingenuity, she fans his faith.
Then by degrees she lets her fears subside
310 And seems to weaken till he treaty makes
And they are in accord. But as she yields
She knows enough of guileful tricks to swear
By God and all the male and female saints
That, howsoever much solicited,
She ne'er before has yielded to a man.
'This is the consummation,' she will say,   THE WOMAN
'And by the faith I owe the Pope in Rome
I swear that now I give myself to you
Not for the presents you have given me
320 But for true love alone. I'd do this thing
For not another man in all the world,
However great he seemed, for any gift.
Many a valiant man has courted me,
And I've refused them all. But now I think
You have bewitched me with your evil chant.'
And then still further to deceive the fool   THE DUENNA
She clasps him tight and gives him many a kiss.
"But, if she'll heed my counsel, she will pay

Attention to no thing except her price.
330 To the last feather should she pluck her friend,
Unless she is a simpleton or fool;
For she who best knows how to strip the gull
Will much the better of the bargain have.
The thing that's dearest bought is dearest held;
But what men get for nothing they despise,
And value it less than they would a shuck;
And if they lose it they are not disturbed.
At least their irritation's not so great
As for the loss of things that cost them dear.
340   "But plundering a lover needs some skill:
A woman's varlets and her chambermaid,
Her nurse and sister, and her mother, too,
Unless she's foolish, many presents need
Before they will consent to aid the cause.
The lover should present them robes or cloaks,
Or gloves or mittens, which they'll pounce upon
Like kites that ravish all that they can seize.
In no way can he from their hands escape
Until he's given cash and gems to them,
350 As if he played the game with worthless chips,
And his last sou is spent. The booty goes
Most quickly when 'tis plucked by many hands.

                                                          ATTENTANTS
   "From time to time they'll say, 'Sir, don't you see
How much your lady needs a costume new?
You are the one to give it. Can you let
Her suffer such a lack? Now, by Saint Giles,
If she would do the will of one who lives
Right in this village, she might dress like queen
And ride with great equipment. By Our Dame,
360 Why do you wait so long to order it?
'Tis shameful you should leave her suffering.'
And she, no matter how much she is pleased,   THE DUENNA
Should bid them cease, because, perhaps she'll say,
He may be straitened by so many gifts.
   "But if she sees that he his gifts perceives
To be more numerous than he should give
And that he's deeply grieved at the amount

Which he must furnish her, then she'll relax
Her prayers for costly gifts, and rather beg
370 A loan from him, which she swears she'll repay
On whatsoever day he please to name.
But I'd forbid return of anything.

"Then if another friend revisit her
(Of whom she certainly should several have,
And all should claim as friends, although she trusts
Her heart to none of them), then she'll complain,
If she is wise, that her best gown's in pawn,
Held in security upon a loan,
The interest on which mounts day by day,
380 On which account she feels anxiety
And is so brokenhearted she can do
Nothing to please him till she has her pledge.
If he's a foolish youth—mere source of cash—
He'll thrust his hand at once into his purse
Or give his note to get the sum she needs
To free from pawn her robe, which really needs
No freeing, for it's locked within some chest
Out of his sight. To her it matters not
If he should search her closet and her press
390 Better to be convinced. She gets the cash.

"A similar deception serves a third:
She asks of him a wimple or a dress
Or silver girdle; then some cash to spend.
If he has no gold with him, but declares,
To comfort her, that he'll tomorrow bring,
Unless he suffers loss of hand or foot,
All that she asks, then let her ears be deaf.
Let her believe him not; these are but lies.

"Far too expert in lying are all men.
400 The debauchees have sworn to me more oaths
To fortify their lies, in former days,
Than there are saints in Heaven. If he can't pay,
Then let him borrow for a trifling fee,
Or go away, elsewhere to find his fun.

"Unless she is a fool, she'll make a show
Of cowardice, when she her friend receives,
By trembling and displaying signs of fear,

Distraction, and most dire anxiety;
And she should make him clearly understand
410 The risk she runs for him when she beguiles
Her husband, parents, or her guardians.
She'll say that if her deed should come to light,
Which she is willing to do secretly,
'Twould be the death of her, beyond a doubt,
And swear he must not long remain with her
If he'd not have her slain before his eyes.
When she's bespelled him thus, he's sure to stay.

      "She should make note when next he's due to come,
And through the window, if there's none to spy,
420 Let her receive him, though the door would serve,
And swear that she is ruined and nigh dead,
And that there nothing would be left of him
If anyone should know he was within;
For no sharp-pointed weapon would avail—
No helm or hauberk, spear or battle club,
No hutch or closet, and no secret room—
To save their bodies from dismemberment.

      "Then ought the dame to sigh and seem displeased,
Assailing him and trampling him roughshod,
430 Accusing him of having stayed so long
Away from her for reasons of his own;
That in his lodgings he some other friend
Is keeping, whom he much prefers to her,
Because of whom his love has turned to hate
And she's betrayed; and that she well might call
Herself deserted—loving but unloved.
When he shall hear these words, his foolish brain
Will falsely think she loves him loyally,
Since far more jealous she has shown herself
440 Than Vulcan was of Venus, when his wife
He found with Mars in proved adultery.
After the fool had watched them all too well,
Within the net that he had forged of brass
He held them both in painful bonds confined,
Conjoined and close united in the game of Love."

63. The Duenna tells the story of Vulcan, Venus, and Mars
[13847–14186]

"SO soon as Vulcan, who was but a sot,   THE DUENNA
Had captured Mars and Venus in the net
That he had placed about their bed (more fool
Was he to dare to venture such a trick,
For little worldly wisdom has a man
Who thinks his wife belongs to him alone!)
In haste he called the gods, who laughed and joked
When they perceived the victims in such case.
Most of the gods at once were set on fire
10 By Venus' loveliness, as she made plaint
And her chagrin revealed, ashamed and grieved,
As well she might, so captured and disgraced;
For never had there been a like disgrace.
Yet 'twas no wonder that she gave herself
To Mars, for Vulcan was so foul and black—
Face, hands, and throat—with charcoal from his forge,
That he could not by Venus be beloved,
However much he claimed her as his wife.
Had it been Absalom with tresses blond
20 Or Paris, son of Priam, King of Troy,
She had not been complaisant, for she knew
Too well the game all women love to play.
    "Women are freeborn; they've restricted been
By law, that takes away the liberty
That Nature gave them. Nature's not so fond,
As we should see if her intent we scanned,
That Margot she would bring into the world
Solely for Robichon, nor Robichon
Solely for Agnes, Margot, or Perette.
30 Rather, fair son, we're made, beyond a doubt,
All women for all men, and all the men
For all the women, interchangeably;

So that, when they're affianced and espoused
And seized by law intended to prevent
Dissentions, bickerings, and violence,
And to assist in bringing up the ones
Of whom they both together have the care,
Then dames and women, whosoe'er they are,
Ugly or fair, feel forced in various ways
40 To summon back the freedom that they've lost.
So far as in them lies, they will maintain
Their liberty, from which full many an ill
Comes and will come and has come formerly.
Well could I name ten evils—yes, or more—
But I pass over them. I should be tired,
And you'd be bored, before I numbered them.
However, when in former times one saw
The woman who most pleased him, on the spot
He'd seize her, if no stronger man than he
50 Took her away from him; and, if he pleased,
When his desire was satisfied, he'd leave.
Thence murders came and homes were broken up
Until, upon the counsel of the wise,
The marriage institution was ordained.
If Horace you'd believe—and he wrote well
And truly, for he was a poet sage—
I'd cite him here for you, for dame discreet
Need have no shame authorities to quote:
Before the time of Helen many fights
60 Broke out because of women, and there died
In greatest suffering the men who fought
For them, whose very names are now unknown,
For they're not found in books. Not first was she,
Nor will she be the last, for whom great wars
Came and will come among the men who loved
And e'er will love, of whom full many a one
Has sacrificed his body and his soul
And will so long as e'er the world shall last.
Regard, then, Nature; and, that you may see
70 More clearly what a wondrous power she has,
Many examples can I give to you
Which literally apparent make the fact.

"The bird that's captured in the forest green,
Shut in a cage and nourished carefully,
And fed delicious food, may seem to sing
With happy heart, in your opinion;
And yet it longs to be among the boughs
Out in the woods, which naturally it loves,
And howsoever well it may be fed
80 Would much prefer to flit among the trees.
Ever it pines and struggles to get free.
With all the ardor which fulfills its heart
It treads its food beneath its feet, and seeks
Throughout its cage, in greatest agony,
To find some door or other opening
Through which it may escape into the woods.
Know well that every damosel or dame,
Whatever her environment may be,
Has the inclination naturally
90 To long and search for roadways and for paths
By which to come into that liberty
Which all of them forever wish to have.
  "I tell you it is so with everyone
Who in a cloister takes his place, for he
Will afterward to such repentance come
That scarce he fails to hang himself for grief.
He's inwardly tormented; he complains;
He lamentation makes. The one desire
That wells up in him is to hit upon
100 Some stratagem by which he may regain
The freedom that he's lost. His will's unchanged,
Spite of whatever habit he may don
And of whatever refuge he may seek.
  "It is a foolish fish that swims within
The narrow opening of a net, and finds,
When he desires to go the way he came,
In spite of all his efforts, no escape.
While he remains a hopeless prisoner,
The others, who remain outside the net,
110 Crowd round, on seeing him, and think that he
Diverts himself in pleasure and great joy.
They watch him circle, seemingly content,

*cf. Boethius.
cf. Squire's Tale*

And note especially that he therein
Has food aplenty, such as each would like,
And so they gladly would their entry make.
They swim and wheel about, and push and search
So much that finally they find the hole,
And in they dart; but when they realize
That once within they're taken and confined
120 Forever, then they scarcely can refrain
From wishing to regain their liberty.
But that's impossible; more surely caught
Are they than if behooked upon a line.
Till death shall free them, there they'll live in woe.
   "Just such a life does young man seek who takes
The monkish vow; he'll never learn to make
Shoes large enough, or cowl, or broad-brimmed hat
To hide what Nature's planted in his heart.
He's badly served, and might as well be dead,
130 When he gives up his former free estate,
Unless he makes, by great humility,
A virtue of necessity. When she
Fulfills his heart with thoughts of freedom lost,
Dame Nature does not lie; for Horace says,
And well he knew what such words signified,
'Who against Nature to defend himself   HORACE
Should seize a fork to thrust her forth would find
She'd soon be back again.' That I know well.   THE DUENNA
The cloth will never make her hesitate,
140 For Nature e're recurs. Why stress the point?
Each creature to its nature will return,
Nor can relinquish it for violence
Or force or covenant. This should excuse
Venus' desire to practice unrestraint,
And all the dames who play the game of Love
No matter how much hedged with marriage vows.
Nature surpasses tutelage in power;
She is too strong for them, and makes them wish
Ever to strain toward greater liberty.
150   "Fair son, if one should take a cat brought up
Never to see a male or female rat
Or even mouse, and long time feed him well,

With most attentive care, delicious food,
And then allow a mouse to come in sight,
And let the cat escape, naught could prevent
The cat from running fast to seize its prey.
It matters not how hungry he may be;
His most attractive food he'll leave for it.
No penalty that man may e'er impose
160 Can with a peaceful treaty end their feud.
 "If one knew how to rear a new-foaled colt
So that he never even saw a mare
Until he was a full-grown steed, and fit
For saddle and for stirrup, and then brought
A mare in sight, he'd hear the stallion neigh
And see him run to jennet to encounter,
If not restrained. Not only does the black
Seek black as mate, but white and gray and brown,
If not retarded by the bit and rein.
170 He will assail them all, and only looks
To see if he can find them disengaged
Where he can mount their backs and cover them.
So, too, a chestnut mare, if unrestrained,
Will come arunning to a chestnut steed
Or one that's gray or tawny, as she may please.
The first she finds is he she'll make her mate,
For she, in turn, will no espial plan
Except to find a stallion that's free.
 "And what I say of horses—gray or brown—
180 And mares, of bull and cow, of ram and ewe
Is that (doubt not, fair son) each one desires
To seek a mate; and every female longs
For every male, and each gives free consent.
The natural appetite is just the same,
Upon my soul, in every maid and man,
Though law impose some moderate restraint.
Moderate, I say! It seems too much,
For when the marriage law together joins
A man and maid it would forbid them both,
190 At least so long as t'other partner lives,
To have the others who are not their mates.
But ne'ertheless they're tempted to enjoy

Free will, and well I know that but one thing
Will hold them to their vows, if even that:
'Tis fear of punishment restrains the one,
And shame the other. Nature's influence
Is just the same in them as in the beasts.
Thereof I've had experience myself,
For always I have taken greatest pains
200 To be beloved by all the men I knew;
Had it not been for fear of shame, which curbs
And halters many a heart, when through the streets
I sauntered—and I'd always go attired
With ornaments the like of which ne'er wore
The finest doll—and when the youths, who pleased
Me greatly, tender glances on me cast
(Good God! what tremors seized me when their looks
Were turned my way!), I gladly had received
As many as I pleased, or all of them,
210 And one by one I had embraced them all
Had I been equal to the task. It seemed
To me that all were willing, if they could,
To play their part with me. I'll not except
Prelate or canon, burgess, knight, or monk,
Cleric or layman, erudite or fool,
Provided he was still of virile age.
If they had thought it needful, when they sought
My love, they would have from religion leaped;
But had they known my mind, which held such thoughts
220 As are but common to all womankind,
They never would have had a lurking doubt.
And I believe, if some of them had dared,
They had annulled their marriages for me.
They surely had forgotten all their vows
Had they in private held me in their arms.
No one of them had thought of his estate,
His faith, or his religion, save some fool
Who might have been so manacled by Love
That he adored his sweetheart loyally.
230 He probably had called it quits with me
And turned to her for whom he'd take no price.
By God and by Saint Amand, I believe

The lovers of that sort are very rare.
However, if the rest would talk with me
But long enough, whatever they might say
Of lies or truth, I would inflame each one,
Whate'er he were—a layman or a monk,
Cinctured with leather red or with a cord;
And whatsoever chaperon he wore,
240 He'd take his joy with me did he but think
That 'twas my will or that I would permit.
Thus Nature governs us, incites our hearts
To take their pleasure. Venus, then, deserved
But little blame when she enamored Mars.

"When Venus was disclosed in Mars' embrace,
Most willingly had many of the gods
Been laughed at by the others, being found
In Mars' position; while two thousand marks
Had Vulcan given not to have revealed
250 To common knowledge what the lovers did,
For when the pair he thus exposed to shame
Perceived that everybody knew their case
They afterward performed with open doors
The acts that they kept secret formerly,
Nor ever felt the stigma of the deed;
And then the gods the tale told far and wide
Until it was well known throughout the heavens.
As things grew worse and worse, Vulcan in rage
Perceived that he could find no remedy;
260 And, as the story goes, that it had been
Better than set the net about the bed
To suffer silently and make pretense
That he knew nothing of the whole affair,
And not to be disturbed, if he would have
The favors of Venus, who then had more complaisant been."

64. The Duenna concludes her exposition of love and
the story of her life
[14187–14546]

"THE moral of this tale is that a man   THE DUENNA
Should take good care how he spies on his wife
Or friend and by his foolish trickery
Discovers her in any open lapse;
For he should know that worse she will become
When once her fault is proved; nor will he have
From her obedience or friendliness
When once he's caught her, moved by jealousy.
Than jealousy, which burns and fills with care
10 The jealous one, there's no more foolish vice;
But she with feigned complaint will oft pretend
To jealousy, thus to deceive the fool.
The more she hoodwinks him, the more he burns.
And, if he deign not to excuse himself,
But, to increase her anger, says 'tis true
That he another mistress entertains,
Let him beware if she refuse to scold.
'Twill have more meaning than may there appear
If he's procured himself another friend
20 And she cares not a button, so she says,
How much the ribald plays the whoremaster;
And if she make pretense that he in turn
Believes, because she cannot love renounce,
That she has wished to find another friend,
And that she does it to get rid of him
From whom she's willing now to be divorced,
For certainly from him she is estranged;

                                                    THE HUSBAND
And if he says, 'You've wronged me far too much—
I must revenge myself for your misdeeds—
30 Since you have made me cuckold. I will serve

You with a drink from out the self-same cup—'
Then worse than ever will become his case,   THE DUENNA
If still he loves her, for he can expect
No further consolation from her love.
None feels the flames of love within his breast
Like him who fears he may be cuckolded.

    "Just at this point appears the chambermaid
With fearful face, and says, 'Alas! we're lost;   THE MAID
My master, or some other man, has come—
40 He's entering our courtyard even now.'
The wife must interrupt the work in hand   THE DUENNA
And run away; but first she hides the youth
In stable, barn, or even rabbit hutch,
Where he must stay until she calls for him
When she returns. Thus he who had such joy
At coming gladly would be gone, I think,
So much he now feels terror and despair.

    "Then if it prove to be another friend
To whom she's given untimely rendezvous,
50 However dear the first one be to her,
Let her at no deception hesitate,
But lead the second comer to her room,
Grant him her favors soon, but let him know
That he can not remain, on which account
Heavy of heart and angry he will be,
For plainly will the lady say to him:
'This is no time to stay; my husband's here   THE WIFE
And cousins four, so help me, Saint Germain.
When at some other time you please to come,
60 I'll do whatever you may wish me to;
But with that promise you must be content.
Now I must go, for they're awaiting me.'
Then she will hurry him outside the house   THE DUENNA
That she may thenceforth nothing have to fear.

    "Then to the first the woman should return
That in discomfort he may not remain
Too long; she would not have him too displeased.
So she recomforts him and calls him out
From his imprisonment, and bids him come
70 To bed with her, and takes him in her arms.

But let her guard lest he unfearful lie,
And let her make him clearly understand
That she's too bold and foolish; let her swear
That by her father's soul she buys his love
Too dearly when she such great chances takes,
And let her say that she's no more secure
Than those who sport in vineyards and in fields.
All this she does because secure delight
Less pleasant is, and counted of less worth.
80   "When they've together lain all night, and yet
He stays until he sees the daylight clear,
Let her take care lest for another bout
She preparations make before she's drawn
The shades at all the windows, that the room
May be but dimly lit; for, if she have
Some spot or blemish on her body, he
Must nothing know of it. If he should spy
Some filthiness that marred her pulchritude,
He'd soon be on his way, and take to flight
90   Like frightened cur with tail between his legs.
This were a most embarrassing disgrace!
   "Whenever on the sea of love they swim,
Each one should play his part so skillfully
That, both together, they will have one joy
Rather than partial, separate delights;
And both should strive to reach a common goal.
Neither should let the other swim alone,
Nor leave the sport till they in unison
Arrive at port. 'Tis this makes joy complete.
100 If she feels no delight, she still should feign
Enjoyment, giving all the evidence
Of joy she knows is most appropriate,
That he may think she gratefully accepts
Attentions worthless as a nut to her.
   "If he is able to persuade the dame
That free from interruption they would be
If she should come some time to where he lives,
Then on the day she undertakes to go
Let her delay a little, thus to fan
110 His amorous desire for her embrace.

The game of love is such that when deferred
It's more delightful than when promptly played.
Less appetite has he who has his will.

"When to his house she comes, and is received
Most lovingly, then she should let him know
That she so fears her husband's jealousy
That she is all atremble and alarmed,
Most sorely doubting that she can escape
Scolding or beating when she shall return.
120 But howsoever much she may lament,
And whether she shall lie or tell the truth,
Assuredly the fright she should pretend,
Accepting his assuagement anxiously,
And thus enhance the joys of dalliance.

"In case she finds no chance to go to him
And dares not entertain him at her house
Because her jealous husband keeps close watch,
Then should she, if she can, make drunk her spouse
If of no better plan she can conceive;
130 And if the wine have no effect on him,
She may employ a pound or more of herbs
Which without danger he may eat or drink.
Then will he sleep so sound he'll let them do
Whatever they may wish; he can't oppose.

"If she has servants, she will send them forth,
One here, one there, or win them with small gifts
So that they'll help her to receive her friend;
Or, if she fears them, she may make them drunk.

"Or, if she please, she'll to her husband say:
140 'With I know not what illness I'm afire—   THE WIFE
Apostema or fever or the gout—
That runs through all my body; needs must I
Go to the public bath. Our two bathtubs
Will not suffice; we have no steaming box,
And what I really need's a thermic bath.'
After the jealous wretch has thought awhile,   THE DUENNA
Ungraciously, perhaps, he'll give her leave.
Then with some neighbor or her chambermaid,
Who's in her confidence, and who will have
150 Some friend herself the dame may know about,

She'll to the baths repair; but she'll not seek
The swimming pool or tub bath, but will couch
There with her lover, if it seem not good
To them to bathe together. He'll be there
If of her destination he's informed.

    "No man can keep a woman under guard
If for her honor she has no respect,
Though it were Argus' self who kept the watch
And spied upon her with his hundred eyes,
160 Of which half kept awake while t'others slept
Until he lost his head by Jove's command
When Mercury was sent to cut it off
Because by Juno he had been ordained
To see that Jove no assignations kept
With Io, whom the ruler of the gods
Had changed from lovely maid into a cow—
And then his watch was worthless. He's a fool
Who strives to safeguard such a worthless thing.

    "But let no woman be so great a sot
170 As to believe, whatever clerks may say,
Or laymen, that by magic, sorcery,
Enchantment, necromancy, or by charm,
Though Balenus should help with all his lore,
She may compel a man to fall in love
With her or hate another for her sake.
Medea's incantations could not hold
Her Jason; nor could Circe's witchcraft keep
Ulysses when he wished to flee from her.

    "A lady should take care to give no gift
180 Of any value to her friend, though he
May claim her love. A pillow she may give,
Or napkin, kerchief, hood, if not too dear,
A needlecase, a leash, or even a belt
With clasp not too expensive, or a knife
That's small but fair, or little ball of wool
Such as the cloistered nuns are wont to give.
But to associate with them is rash;
To love the worldly women's better far.
There is less chance of being blamed for that,
190 And they more freedom have to do their will.

Well they know how to feed with specious words
Their husbands and their other relatives;
And, though it well may be that neither costs
More than she's worth, the sisters cost the most.

    "The man who would be wise will doubt all gifts
A woman makes him; for, to tell the truth,
They are but nets set to entrap a male.
Against her nature every woman sins
Who shows the fault of liberality.
200 Leave largesse to the men; when dames are free
With gifts, it is great mishap and great vice.
It is the devil who has made them soft.
But naught care I, for women are but few
Who are accustomed to give much away.

    "Such gifts as I have mentioned will do well,
Unless they're given deceivingly, to please
The boobies better. And be sure you keep
All that is given you. Have well in mind
The bourne toward which is tending all your youth,
210 If you may live so long; that is old age,
Which never, day nor night, will intermit
To press upon us. When that time shall come,
Be no such one as men will call a fool;
Have then a well-lined purse, and be not mocked;
For acquisition without husbanding
Is hardly worth a grain of mustard seed.

    "Alas! I did not thus, and now I'm poor
By reason of my own neglectfulness.
Great gifts from those who gave themselves to me
220 I gave in turn to those I better loved.
Men gave to me; I gave to men; and now
There's nothing I've retained. Munificence
Has brought me indigence. I never thought
Of my old age, in which I've such distress.
I let time go as lightly as it came;
I feared not poverty and took no care
To moderate my rash expenditures.

    "Had I been wise, I might, upon my soul,
Have been a wealthy woman; for I knew,
230 When I was young and bettter dressed, great men

From whom I could have any price secured;
But whatsoever presents I received
From them, by God and Saint Thibaud I swear,
I gave unto a wretch who shamed me much,
But it was he who then pleased me the most.
I called the rest my friends; but him I loved.
Know well, for me a pea he did not care,
And even told me so. A bad one he!
I've never seen a worse. He loved me not,
240 The wretch, and to despise me never ceased.
He used to say I was a common whore!
Poor judgment have all women; I was one,
Decidedly. I never loved a man
Who loved me in return. But do you know
If he had thrown my shoulder out of joint
Or broke my head, I would have thanked the wretch!
He ne'er beat me so much that I refused
To do his will; he well could make his peace,
No matter how he had mistreated me.
250 Against me he had never done so much—
Beaten and dragged me, scratched and blackened my face,
And called me shameful names—that he'd not ask
My pardon ere he went, and beg a truce.
He would entice me to the game of Love,
And then we'd quiet be and in accord.
He had me on his leash, the traitorous wretch,
For he was a fierce lover, I'll admit.
I could not live without him; and I wished,
So much he solaced and delighted me,
260 Always to follow him. If he had fled,
To London, England, I had gone with him.
He shamed me, and I him; for he would lead,
Upon my gifts to him, a riotous life.
He would not put my savings in the bank,
But spent them all in taverns and on dice.
He never learned another trade than this,
And this he never mastered to his gain.
All men were then my tenants; what they paid
He freely spent, and always in debauch,
270 His body e'er inflamed with lechery.

He was so tender mouthed that he could bear
No bridle. He would occupy himself
With nothing good; it pleased him not to live
Except in pleasure and in laziness.
But toward the end, when gifts less often came,
He spent a sorry life in poverty;
He had to beg his bread, for by that time
I had not cash to buy two hackle combs,
Nor had I wedded spouse to succor me.
280 Then came I here, as I've already told,
My temples scratched with all the underbrush.
    "May my estate example be to you,
My fair, sweet son; keep it in memory.
After my tutelage, may you be wise
To act so that you'll be the better off!
For when your Rose is withered, and white hair
Besieges your creased brow, you'll feel the lack of gifts."

65. Fair Welcome thanks the Duenna and agrees to receive the Lover
[14547–14718]

WHILE the Duenna preached, Fair Welcome spoke
No word, but gladly heard all that she said.
Much less he feared her than he had before;
For now he'd come to see that easily
The castle might be seized, had it not been
For Jealousy and her gatekeepers three,
In whom she had such faith, and who remained,
Running forever all about the fort,
Madly attempting to defend the place.
10 Their energetic cares successful were;
'Twas not yet taken, as he thought 'twould be.
    Not one of them lamented Evil Tongue,
Who now was dead. He'd not been loved by them;
For always he had slandered and betrayed

Them all to Jealousy. They hated him
So much that none who with him ever lived
Would toward his ransom give a garlic stem;
Unless 'twere Jealousy herself, who loved
To hear his jangling. She would lend her ear,
20 Whene'er the liar started up his band,
Though marvelously sad she'd been before.
Naught that he could recall would he conceal
From her if trouble were to come of it;
And, worst of all, he often told as truth
More than he really knew. He'd ever add
Embellishments to all the things he heard.
He'd make a bigger story of each tale
That was not good or fair; from those that were
He would omit at least the better parts.
30 Thus, like a man who'd wasted all his life
In envy and detraction, he would please
The vicious appetite of Jealousy.
None hired masses chanted for his soul,
For all were glad when of his death they knew.
It seemed to them that they had nothing lost;
For, when they counsel took, they were agreed
That they could guard the place, as ne'er before,
From being taken by five thousand men.

THE GUARDIANS

Said they, "We certainly would be most weak
40 If we, without that wretch, could not defend
All that we have. That false and treacherous knave,
May he be burned and utterly destroyed
In stinking fire of Hell! He was no good!"
Three guardians of the gate thus had their way;
But they were weakened, whatsoe'er they thought.
    When the Duenna ceased to tell her tale,
Fair Welcome spoke, and though he late commenced
He said but little, and as one well taught:
"My lady, when you teach to me your art   FAIR WELCOME
50 So debonairly, I must thank you well;
But whate'er you have said to me of love—
That sweet, but often bitter, malady—
Is on a subject that's unknown to me.

Except by hearsay I have nothing learned
Of it, nor anything desired to know.
And as to what you've said to me of wealth
And how I might amass it plenteously,
I answer that I have sufficient now.
On courtesy alone my mind's intent.
60 I put no trust in magic, devilish art,
Whether its power is fabulous or real.

 "As to the youth whose praises you have sung,
In whom all merit, grace, and good unite—
May he retain them. I am nothing bent
To get them from him; rather I resign
Them all to him. But, on the other hand,
Though certainly I feel for him no hate,
I love him not too well. Although I took
His chaplet, and I therefore call him friend,
70 'Tis but as everybody commonly
Says to another, 'Friend, you're welcome here,'
Or, 'Friend, may God you bless!' I neither love
Nor but most honorably honor him.
But since a present he has given me,
And I've accepted it, I should be pleased,
And it would fitting be, that he should come
To visit me, if 'twould be opportune,
And if he wants to see me. He'll not find
Me slow most willingly to welcome him.
80 But he must choose a time when Jealousy,
Who hates and vilifies him without bounds,
Is out of town; and, even then, I fear
Lest unexpectedly she might return.
For often when her things have all been packed
As for a trip, and when she's taken leave
Of those remaining, and they think she's gone,
She turns about when halfway to her goal,
And her return upsets and shocks us all.
If she should chance to come when he was here,
90 So cruel and so hard is she with me,
That though I might be guiltless of all blame
She might, in wrath, dismember me alive."
 Then the Duenna this assurance gave:

"Leave all of that to me. To find him here   THE DUENNA
Would be impossible, though she returned.
By God and by Saint Rémy, I've in view
So many hiding places that she'd find
An ant's egg in a mow more easily,
Than him when he is safely stowed away,
100 So well how to conceal him I shall know."

"Then I am willing that he come," said he,   FAIR WELCOME
"If properly he will conduct himself,
Refraining from all outrage."

"By God's flesh,   THE DUENNA
You wisely speak, like prudent, thoughtful youth
Who's worthy, and who knows how much he's worth."

Their conversation ceased; they left the room;
Fair Welcome sought his chamber, while the crone
Busied herself about her household tasks.
But when time, place, and season all were right
110 And she perceived Fair Welcome was alone
And unemployed, so one might talk to him,
She hastened down the stairs and left the tower
And, without stopping, trotted to my home,
Where she arrived quite tired and out of breath
To let me know how the affair progressed.

THE DUENNA
"Come I in time," she wheezed, "to get the gloves,
If I can give you tidings fresh and new?"

"The gloves!" I answered. "Lady, I will give   THE LOVER
A fur-trimmed hat, a mantle, and a robe,
120 And any kind of shoes you wish to name,
If you have anything of worth to tell."

Then the Duenna said that I should go
Straight to the tower, where one awaited me;
Nor did she leave until she had explained
How I might enter there. Said she, "You'll walk   THE DUENNA
Straight to the postern gate, and I'll be there
To open it for you and so best keep
The matter secret. It's a covered way
Which was first opened but ten weeks ago."
130 "By Saint Rémy I swear, lady," said I,   THE LOVER
"That though the stuff cost ten or twenty pounds

A yard (for I remembered well my Friend
Had warned me to make promises enough
Though they were such as I could not fulfill)
You'll have a lovely dress of blue or green,
Provided that I find that gate unlocked for me."

66. The Lover gains entry into the Castle of Jealousy
[14719–14807]

THE woman left, and, for my part, I went
Straight to the postern gate she'd told me of,
Beseeching God to guide me to my goal.
I reached the gateway silently, and found
That she'd unlocked and left it half ajar.
I entered in and closed the door behind;
And then I felt secure, especially
Because I knew that Evil Tongue was dead.
No one's demise e'er pleased me half so much!
10 Beyond I saw his doorway battered down,
And entering there found Love within the gate
With all his host who came to bear me aid.
Great help they gave me when they broke that door!
May they be blessed by God and Saint Benoît!
There were False Seeming, traitorous son of Fraud,
Pretended priest, Hypocrisy, his dame,
Who against virtue feels such bitterness,
Also Forced Abstinence, who is with child,
And ready to give birth to antichrist,
20 Whose father is False Seeming, as I've read.
'Twas they destroyed the gate, beyond a doubt,
And so I prayed for them, whate'er might hap.
Seignors who traitors wish to learn to be
Should hire False Seeming as their pedagogue
And take unto themselves Forced Abstinence;
For both of these, of feigned simplicity,

Are masters of duplicity itself.
    When I perceived the door was smashed and seized,
And found the weaponed host already there
30 Ready to make assault before my eyes,
No one need ask if I was joyful then.
As I profoundly pondered how to find
Sweet Sight again, God bless him! there he was,
For Love had summoned him to comfort me.
Too long I'd lost him! When I saw him there,
I almost fainted for excess of joy;
And he, when he perceived me, was most glad
Of my return, and me Fair Welcome showed,
Who, leaping from his seat, came to me straight,
40 Like the well-taught and courteous youth he was
By training of his mother. My salute
Most promptly he returned, and gave me grace
Because I'd sent the wreath to him. Said I,   THE LOVER
"Sir, do not take the trouble; 'tis not you
Should thank me, but 'tis I have you to thank
One hundred thousand times because you've done
Such honor to me in accepting it.
Know well that, if it please you, I have not
A single thing but that belongs to you—
50 With which you may do whatsoe'er you wish,
Though it should make a man to laugh or cry.
All that I wish is but to be your slave,
To honor and to serve you all my life.
If you in anything give me commands,
Or let me know what's wanted without speech,
Or if in other ways I find it out,
Body and goods and, truly, even soul
I'll cast into the balance, nor will have
The least remorse of conscience. Now I pray,
60 In order that you may be sure of me,
That you'll put me to trial, and, if I fail,
Never again may I feel sensual joy."

                                                   FAIR WELCOME
    "I thank you, sir," said he, "and I would add
That if I've anything that might you please
You're welcome to it. Take it without leave;

My goods, my honor, and myself are yours."

"One hundred thousand times I give you thanks,"
Said I, "for all the grace you've shown to me;
But though you offer to me all you have,
70 I must reply that I have no desire
Or expectation of another thing
Than that which you've already tendered me
And which has given my heart a greater joy
Than all the gold of Alexandria could give."

67. Danger again prevents the Lover from attaining the Rose
[14808–14942]

THEN I advanced that I might stretch my hand
To reach the Rose I so much wished to have,
With which I hoped to accomplish my desire;
For surely, thought I, all these gentle words
That were so sweet, and our acquaintanceship
That seemed so pleasing, his deportment fair
Which he so artlessly seemed to affect,
Had given me good reason to have hope.
But it turned out quite otherwise for me.
10 More oft remains to do than fools suppose.
Too cruel defense I found 'gainst my essay,
For, soon as I approached the Rose, the path
Was blocked by Danger (may some evil wolf
The villain strangle!), who had hid himself
Behind us in a corner, and had spied
And word for word recorded all our speech.
My tentatives were halted by his shout:
"Flee, varlet, flee! You trouble me too much!   DANGER
The devils must have brought you back again!
20 The cursed fiends would share this ritual
And ere they left partake of everything.

No holy person e'er comes nigh this place.
God help me, but I'll nearly break your head!"
    Fear arose, and thither Shame then sped
At hearing Danger yell, "Flee, varlet, flee."
Nor did he stop at that; 'twas he that brought
The devils there and chased the saints away.
My God, how that miscreant cleared the place!
All three with one accord converged on me
30 And pushed my hands away with scolding rage.

THE GUARDIANS

"You'll never have," said they, "or more or less
Than you have had, for well you understand
How to put evil sense into the gift
Fair Welcome offered when you talked to him.
Gladly he offered you his benefits,
Provided you would use them honestly.
You have no care for the proprieties,
But take his simple offer in a sense
In which no man should take it, for it goes
40 Without declaring, and is understood,
That when an honest man his service gives
'Tis to be taken only in good guise
And as the promiser intended it.
Now tell us, Sir Deceiver, why you failed,
When well you understood the words he spoke,
To take them in the right and proper way.
Misunderstanding him so villainously
Must come from sheer stupidity, or you
Are pleased to play the part of foolish wit.
50 He never offered you the Rose for that
Would be a most disgraceful thing to do;
Nor should you ask it, or without request
Attempt to have it. How did you intend
That he should take the offer that you made
Of all you had? Did you by that design
To cozen him and so to steal the Rose?
You wished to serve him thus that you might trick
And fool him better, being all the while
His enemy in secret. Ne'er in book
60 Were written acts that more might grieve and harm.

Now you must quit this place, and we'll not care
Although your heart should burst with suffering.
The demons must have forced you to return,
For well you still recall that other time
When you were chased away. Now get you gone;
Seek to supply your wants some other place.
She was not wise who entry gave such fool!
She did not know your thoughts—your purposed guile.
She ne'er had sought you out had she conceived
70 Such great disloyalty. Grossly misled
Fair Welcome was himself, defenseless one,
When privately he entertained you here.
He sought to serve you, but you do him harm.
My faith! Such gratitude a man receives
Who's barked at for his pains when to the land
He helps a drowning dog. Go seek your prey
Some other place! These precincts leave at once!
Go back downstairs politely, with good grace,
Or you will have no chance to count the steps;
80 For such a one may suddenly arrive
As, if he should but get you in his grasp,
Happening to come upon you face to face,
Would make you reckon badly your descent.
Presumptuous fool, void of all loyalty,
What has Fair Welcome ever done to you?
For what misdeed or fault have you so soon
Begun to hate him that you would betray
Him just as you have offered him your all?
Was it because he let you visit here?
90 Was it because he fooled us for your sake?
Was it because he offered you his dogs
And birds? I know he foolishly behaved,
And for his acts of now and once before,
If Heaven and Saint Faith will be our guards,
He will in such a prison cell be placed
That no man will have strength to enter there;
To such rings he'll be riveted that ne'er
On any day you'll see him walk abroad,
Now he's deceived and circumvented us.
100 By him we're all befooled. Woe worth the day

When you so freely came to see this youth!"
　　They seized him then and pummeled him so much
That as he fled they drove him to the tower
With imprecations vile, and shut him in,
Though not with irons or chains, with threefold locks
Fastened with threefold keys. No further care
They took at once, for they were in such haste;
But worse they promised him at the first chance they had.

68. The Lover begs to be imprisoned with Fair Welcome, but his request is denied
[14943–15067]

THEIR task detained them but a little time,
And then all three returned and fell on me,
Who outside lingered, grieving, overcome,
Doleful, and in tears. Now they assailed
Me once again with comminations dire.
God grant they may someday repent their crimes!
My heart at their attack almost stopped still,
For though I offered willingly to yield
They seemed determined not to let me live.
10　I undertook to make my peace with them,
And gladly would have shared Fair Welcome's cell.
　　"Danger," said I, "most charming gentleman,　　THE LOVER
Of nature frank, of body valorous,
More pious than all others that I know,
And you, fair Shame and lovely Fear, two maids
Frank, noble, wise, well taught in word and deed,
Of Reason's lineage born, permit that I
Become your slave by such a covenant
That I Fair Welcome's prison house may share
20　Without a hope of ultimate release.
Most loyally I promise you to give
Such service as may please you to devise
If you will put me in your castle tower.

If I were traitor, thief, or ravisher,
Accused of murder or some other crime
For which I might deserve imprisonment,
My faith! I would not need to beg, by God,
For I'd be jailed, without my own request,
Provided I arrested were by law.
30 If I to be dismembered were condemned
None would allow me to escape that fate,
Provided they could catch me. Now I ask
For God's sake let me share imprisonment
With him forever, and if I be found,
Whether by proof or not, to be so vile
As not to serve your ends without defect,
Out of your jail for good I will depart.
No man is faultless; but, if I default,
Then make me pack my clothes and sally forth
40 Out of your precincts. If I you offend,
Then let me feel the rod of your revenge.
Be you my judges; I'll have none but you.
In high or low on you I rest my fate—
On just you three—unless Fair Welcome join
With you to make a fourth; that I accept.
Let him recall the facts, and if you three
Cannot agree to tolerate my stay
Then let him bring you to accord, and hold
To his decision. Fear not I'll escape,
50 Though I be beaten or e'en put to death."
　　Then Danger cried, "By God, a fine request!　　DANGER
To put you both together in one cell—
You with your philandering, and he
So debonair! One might as well pen up
Sir Reynard with the chickens and expect
True love. Whatever service you might do for us,
Well know we that you have but one design:
To shame us and to bring us to disgrace.
We care not for your service. You must be
60 Devoid of sense to ask that he be judge.
Judge! By the gracious King of Heaven above!
How can a person, taken and condemned
Already, be a judge and make decrees?

Fair Welcome has been caught and brought to trial,
And yet you think him of such dignity
That he might arbitrator be himself!
The flood shall come again ere he escape
From out our tower. When we return to him,
He'll be destroyed as he so well deserves
70 For one thing that he did, if for no more,
When he debased himself by offering you
All that he had. The roses all are lost
Through him. Each dotard thinks to pluck a rose
When he is well received. There is but one
Alternative: to keep him in a cage
Where no one can do harm and where no man
Alive can rescue him, more than the wind,
Unless it were some churl who force would use.
If he did that, such sin he would commit
80 That he would hanged or banished be for it."

   "But certainly," said I, "most grievous wrong   THE LOVER
A man would do who someone else destroyed
Without a reason, or imprisoned him.
Most evilly you act when you arrest,
Without occasion, such a worthy man
As is Fair Welcome, so benevolent
That for the world he makes a festival,
And just because he granted me good cheer
And favored my acquaintanceship with him.
90 It were more reasonable, I submit,
That he were out of prison. So I pray
That he may issue forth—be of the charge
Considered quit. Too much you've punished him
Already. See to it that he is freed."

                           THE GUARDIANS
   "My faith," cried they, "this fool is mocking us.
We must appear to him such men as live
On semblances, when thus he would betray
Us by his speech to set at large his friend.
He asks what cannot be; never again
100 Will that one show his face at door or even grill."

Love's barons are called to assist the Lover. *Morgan 132, f. 111v.*

69. Love's barons are summoned to save the Lover from a beating
[15068–15134]

THEN all the three assailed me once again,
And each one tried to kick me out-of-doors;
Nor could this trial have given me more grief
If they had tried to crucify me there.
I tried to cry for mercy, but my voice
Was weak; my piteous shout could scarcely reach
My friends, whose duty 'twas to succor me,
And call them to the assault. It was perceived
By sentinels they'd set to guard the host,
10 Who, when they heard the noise, set up a shout:
"Up, barons, up! Let each appear in arms   THE SENTINELS
Quickly to aid this faithful lover here,
Who's surely lost unless God lends His love.
The guardians have bound and beaten him—
Belabored him with rods. He will be killed
Or crucified. Just now we heard him cry
For mercy in a voice so faint, though clear,
That scarcely could we hear him; but 'twould seem
To one who heard that stifled scream or yell
20 Some clutch upon his throat had made him hoarse
Or that by strangling they were killing him.
Already have they so shut off his breath
That he dare not, or cannot, cry aloud.
We don't know what he's going to do; but they
Are adversaries far too strong for him.
He can but die unless he's helped at once.
Fair Welcome, who had comforted him so much,
Fled at full speed. Now he needs other help
That he Fair Welcome's comfort may regain.
30 From now on there is need for armored knights."
    The three had surely killed me, had the host

Delayed their coming. But the barons jumped
To arms as soon as they heard, saw, and knew
That I had lost my solace and my joy.
As for myself, so tangled in the snares,
In which so many folk by Love are caught,
Was I, that without stirring from the spot
I watched the tournament that fiercely broke.
    Soon as the guardians knew how great a host
40 They had against them, they themselves allied
With oaths and pledges swearing to give aid
Each to the other to their utmost power
And never to submit to any truce
Or separate peace so long as each should live.
I grieved at this alliance as I watched
Their faces and their manner resolute.
    Those of the host, when they saw, in their turn,
The alliance made, assembled and joined hands.
They would not separate, but rather swore
50 To fight till in the place they should lie dead
Or till they should be overcome and seized
Or till they should have won the victory.
All were wrought up to quell the guardians' pride.
    Now to the battle we shall come ere long,
And you shall hear how stoutly each of them could fight.

70. The Poet apologizes for his book
[15135–15302]

NOW, loyal lovers, may the God of Love
Grant that your sweethearts you may all enjoy!
If you can understand what I shall say,
You'll hear the baying dogs pursue the hare
You seek yourself; the ferret you will see,
Which, without fail, shall make the rabbit jump
Into the snare. If what I say you note,
You'll know sufficiently the Art of Love;

And if you chance to find obscurity
10 I'll throw a light upon the troublous point
When I elucidate the dream, and gloss
Upon the text. Then you will know enough,
If anyone objections interpose,
Wisely to answer him in Love's behalf.
By what I then will write you'll understand
What I've already written and shall write.
But ere you listen further to my tale
I'll now defend myself a little while
Against the evil-minded folk; nor strive
20 To swindle you, but to protect myself.
     Sir lovers, I beseech, by Love's sweet game,
That, if you here find words that seem unwise
Or bawdy, whereof scandalmongering tongues
Might make occasion to say slanderous things
Of us because of what we have to tell,
You'll courteously gainsay their criticism.
And when you shall have stopped their calumny,
Denied their charges, and reproved their speech,
If still there shall remain some words of mine
30 For which I rightfully should pardon beg,
I pray that you will make excuse for them
And make response to critics, as for me,
That they are necessary to the tale,
Which leads me to the words by its own traits.
This is the reason why I use such words.
According to the good authority
Of Sallust, this procedure is correct
And proper, as he tells us in these lines:
"Although the glory cannot be the same   SALLUST
40 Of him who did the deeds and him who wrote
Descriptions of the deeds within a book
As best he could to chronicle the truth,
Yet is the latter of no light renown,
For 'tis no easy thing to write things well.
If he who writes would neither maim the truth
Nor puzzle you, then he must make his tale
Have likeness to the facts; the neighbor words
Should be at least the cousins of the deeds."

Thus must I speak if the right path I'd tread.
50   So, worthy women, whether maids or wives,
Heart free or bound in love, I pray you all,
If you have found some words included here
That seem malicious or satirical
Against the ways of womankind, that you
Will not blame me therefor, nor scorn my book,
Which is but written for instruction's sake.
For certainly I have not said one thing,
Nor would I say, in drunkenness or ire
Or hate or envy, 'gainst a living dame;
60   Since no man but the vilest of the vile
Would have the heart a woman to despise.
Men write such things that you and I may have
Acquaintance with ourselves and know the truth
When we find you and me described in books.

And furthermore, most honorable dames,
If you think I say things that are not true,
Say not I lie, but search authorities
Who've written in their books what I have said
And shall. In no respect speak I untruth
70   Unless wise men who wrote the ancient books
Were lying, too. They all agree with me
When manners feminine they chronicle;
Nor were they drunken fools when thus they wrote.
Twas by experience they knew the ways
Of women, and they found them proven thus
In many an age; so you should pardon me.
I but repeat their words; though for my game,
Which costs you little, I additions make
As all the poets have been wont to do
80   To order matters which they're pleased to treat.
For, as their writings prove, their only aim
Is to delight and profit those who read.

And if some folk against me make complaint
As troubled and upset because they feel
That them I criticized when I composed
The chapter which contains False Seeming's words
And so conspire to shame or punish me
Because those words have given them some grief,

I here declare 'twas never my intent
90 To speak against a single living man
Who follows Holy Church, nor one who leads
A life devoted to religious works,
Whatever robe he wears. I bend my bow,
And, sinner that I am, at random speed
My arrow, finding lodgment where it will,
To wound those faithless folk, cleric or lay,
Whom Jesus Christ condemned as hypocrites,
Many of whom, to seem the more sincere,
Forswear the use of flesh at any time
100 As food, and this their penitence they call,
Abstaining thus as we in Lent abstain;
Yet they devour their neighbors with the teeth
Of foul detraction, with a bad intent.
They are the only butt at which I shoot;
Would that my darts in them might find their mark!
My volley's aimed at them, but if it chance
That someone else before the target sits
And wilfully receives an arrow wound,
Misled by pride, when he might dodge the shaft,
110 And then complains because I've injured him,
It would not be my fault though he should die;
For I can hit no one who well knows how
To look to his estate and ward the blow.
And those who feel the damage of my steel
Will soon recover from the wound if they
Cease to be hypocrites. And howsoe'er
Men feign nobility and therefore make
Complaint of me, I make this my defense,
That never, to my knowledge, have I said,
120 However much they may deny my claim,
One word for which I cannot give good proof,
To those to whom it may distasteful be,
By reasoning or by good evidence.
If Holy Church can find a single word
Which she may foolish deem, I ready stand
To make amends, if they will satisfy
Whenever she may deign to fix a fitting time.

71. The battle begins, and Danger overcomes
Dame Franchise
[15303-15381]

FIRST, Franchise in humility advanced
Toward Danger, who was fierce and valorous,
And contumelious and savage seemed.
Within his fist he grasped a mighty club
And grimly brandished it and whirled it round
With blows so perilous that never a shield,
Were it not magic, could the blows withstand.
If one who made a stand opposing him
Were once but fairly smitten with that mace,
10 He might as well for vanquished yield himself;
For Danger could quite overcome and crush
A man who knew not well the art of arms.
From our Refusal's Wood he got his club,
The ugly churl, whom I repudiate!
Vilification formed the embroidery
Upon his shield, which was made up of Strife.
    Franchise, for her part, was so strongly armed
That she could not be easily o'ercome.
Because she knew so well herself to guard,
20 She rushed at Danger first, to force the gate.
In hand she held a stout lance, polished fair,
Brought from the Forest of Cajolery.
No better timber grows in Fontainebleau.
Seductive Imploration steeled the shaft.
With great devotion she had formed her shield
Of Supplication such as monks ne'er made,
And its embroidery was palm-joined hands
And promises and covenants and vows
And pledges colored most entrancingly.
30 You would have said it was Largesse had lent
A shield that she herself had carved and dyed,

Franchise is rejected by Danger, Shame, and Fear. *Morgan 324, f. 102v.*

So much it seemed to be her handiwork.
Protecting now her body with this shield,
She raised her lance and threw it at the churl.
Then he no coward proved, but rather seemed
Renoart of the Pole come back to life.
His shield was pierced, but it so sturdy proved
That his coat armor felt no injury;
And with it he contrived to fend the blow
40 So well that he no body-wound received.
The lance head broke and lessened thus its force.
The furious, savage churl was well supplied
With arms. He seized and broke her lance
In little pieces with his mighty mace;
And then he aimed a fierce and powerful stroke,
Meanwhile exclaiming, "Dirty, lecherous whore,   DANGER
What now prevents that I should strike you down?
How comes it you're so hardy as to dare
Assail a nobleman?" Then with sure blow
50 He struck the shield of that sweet, worthy maid
So courteous, and made her back recoil
More than a fathom and in agony
Fall to her knees, while he insulted her
And rained more blows, the least of which had killed
If she had had a shield of common wood.
Said he, "In former times I trusted you,   DANGER
Foul harlot! Worn-out wench! No good e'er came
Of it; your flattery betrayed me quite.
To ease that libertine, at your request,
60 I granted him his wish to kiss the Rose.
The Devil must have made me say that word!
Good-natured fool he found me! By God's flesh,
'Twas evil day when he assailed our tower;
And so it is but fitting now that you should die!"

72. Pity rescues Franchise and is attacked by Shame, but aided by Delight
[15382–15486]

THE fair one cried for mercy in God's name,
Beseeching him that he would not destroy
Her life as she lay helpless at his feet.
The villain shook his owl-like head in rage
And swore by all the saints that she must die
Without a respite. Pity saw it all
With great dismay, then to the villain ran
In haste to rescue her companion.
Pity, who gives her aid to each good cause,
10 Carried, in place of sword, a misericorde
Dripping continually with sob-wept tears.
Unless my author lies, this sword could strike
Through adamant, so sharp was it of point,
If well the blow were aimed. Her shield was made
Of Solace, but its whole embroidery
Consisted of complaints and sighs and groans.
Pity, though weeping ceaselessly, attacked
The villain, thrusting at him everywhere.
Like leopard at the first he made defense,
20 But, when she had well soaked him with her tears,
The dirty, filthy wretch began to melt.
It seemed to him that he was stupefied
And swimming in a flood, for ne'er before
Had he been so o'ercome with words or deeds.
His hardness failed him; weak and limp he swayed
And tottered; and he gladly would have fled.
    "O Danger, Danger, villain proved," cried Shame,   SHAME
"We'll all be captured if you're recreant now.
Fair Welcome will be freed and will at once
30 Betray the Rose which we have kept shut up.

I tell you truly, and you know, yourself,
That, if Fair Welcome should expose the Rose
To that voluptuary, she would be
Soon wan and pallid, withered and inert.
Besides, I can predict, if once the gate
Were opened, such a wind therein might blow
As would endamage all and cause us loss.
It might too much the rose seed agitate
Or shower alien sperm upon the bloom.
40 God grant that no such seed on her may fall
As would with cumbrous burden trammel her!
Too great calamity 'twould be for us;
For, ere she could get rid of it, the Rose
Might, without recourse, perish utterly.
Or, if such fate she should escape, the wind
Might deal such blows as would inmix some seed
That might o'erwhelm the flower with its load,
In its descent the leaves dissevering
Until the fissure in the foliage
50 Disclosed the undeveloped bud beneath.
May God ne'er let such accident occur!
For then 'twould commonly be said that rakes
Had had her at their will. Then we should know
The hate of Jealousy, who would learn all,
And of that knowledge such affliction feel
That she'd deliver all of us to death.
The devils must have made you act so drunk!"

DANGER

"Help! Help!" cried Danger. Thereupon Shame rushed
At Pity rapidly and threatened her
60 So that she greatly feared the menacing.

SHAME

Said Shame, "You've lived too long; I'll break your shield.
You'll bite the dust today for making war."
She bore a mighty sword, well made and fair,
Whose blade, well tempered, she had fearfully
Forged of stuff called Dread of Discovery.
Her shield, named Fear of Evil Name, was strong
As wood could make it, and its border showed
A fringe of tongues. Shame struck so hard a blow

That Pity back recoiled, about to yield.
70 But at that moment to her came Delight,
An eligible, comely bachelor,
Mighty in arms, and combated with Shame.
He had a sword called Joyous Life, a shield
Such as I've never owned—its name was Ease,
And it was decked with Happiness and Bliss.
He struck at Shame, but she so skillfully
Warded the blow that she received no wound.
Then Shame invoked her might against Delight
And struck him such an agonizing blow
80 That splintered was the shield held o'er his head
And he himself was stretched upon the earth.
She would have cleft his head down to his teeth;
But God a champion sent, and Hide-Well was his name.

73. Hide-Well overcomes Shame, but Fear defeats Hardihood
[15487-15555]

A VERY skillful warrior Hide-Well was,
A sly and crafty land-possessing lord.
His silent sword, like tongue split half in two,
He brandished quietly; a fathom off
One could not hear its stroke; no clash or clang
Was by vibration of its best blows made.
His target was Obscure Retreat. No bird
E'er laid her eggs in better hidden nest.
Blind alleys and screened paths bordered its edge.
10 He raised his sword and struck Shame such a stroke
As stunned her quite, and almost broke her brow.
"That miserable wretch, Dame Jealousy,   HIDE-WELL
Long as she lives shall ne'er know what is done,"
Said he. "I will assurance give of that,
And raise my hand to swear a hundred oaths.
Is not that guarantee enough for you?
Since Evil Tongue is killed, and you are seized,

You'll not escape to cause us further woe."
　　Shame scarce could make reply to what he said;
20 But Fear, who usually a coward is,
　　Leaped up, now filled with ire, as she saw Shame,
　　Her cousin, so subdued, and grasped her sword,
　　Which was of terrible efficiency.
　　Fear of Ostentation it was called,
　　For it was made of that; and when 'twas drawn
　　From out its sheath, brighter than beryl shone.
　　Fear had a shield that Doubt of Peril hight,
　　With Labor and with Difficulty decked.
　　Hide-Well she tried to cleave from top to toe
30 With it, and so revenge her cousin's fate.
　　She struck his shield so strongly that the stroke
　　He could not stand, but tottered as though dazed.
　　He called for Hardihood, who leaped to aid;
　　For, had Fear given another blow like that,
　　Ill work she'd done, and Hide-Well had been dead.
　　He scarcely could have stood another round.
　　　　Hardihood was valiant, bold, and true
　　In word and deed. His good, well-polished sword
　　Was made of Fury's steel. His famous shield
40 Was called Death-Scorner, and its broidery
　　Was Rash Abandonment to Jeopardy.
　　He rushed at Fear and aimed an evil blow.
　　The stroke she fended, making it fall short;
　　For all the art of fencing she knew well.
　　Then, ere he could recover from the thrust,
　　She struck him to the ground; for never a shield
　　Could offer guarantee against her might.
　　He found himself laid low, and then he begged,
　　With hands conjoined, that she would spare his life
50 For love of God. But harshly she refused the plea.

74. After a general battle, a truce is declared
[15556–15658]

THEN cried Security, "What can this be?   SECURITY
Though you should do the worst that you know how,
Here you shall die, O Fear, I swear to God.
Your custom is to shake as with an ague,
A hundred times more timorous than a hare;
But now you have put off your cowardice.
The Devil himself, it must be, makes you brave
Thus to face Hardihood, who loves the lists
And, if he but recall it, knows so much
10 Of tourneying that he no rival has;
While ne'er in all your life you've fought before.
You knew not how to make one fencing thrust
At other times. In all your other bouts
You've either fled or else you've come to terms—
You who this time so well defend yourself.
With Cacus you escaped from Hercules
When you saw him come running, club in hand.
Quite disconcerted then, you lent winged heels,
Such as he'd never had before, to him
20 When Cacus stole from Hercules his cows
And, dragging them all backward by the tails
That none might track them thither, in his cave,
That distant was, concealed them cleverly.
Then was your valor tried. Beyond a doubt
You showed you were worth nothing in a fight;
Nor have you frequented the battlefield
Since then. You've naught, or little, learned of war.
Now it behooves you to give up your arms
Or flee and not defend yourself. You'll pay
30 Most dearly for opposing such as he."
    A hardened sword of Flight from Every Care
Security possessed and shield of Peace

Bordered with Concord, surely excellent.
She struck at Fear, thinking to kill her quite;
But Fear took care to cover with her shield
Her body, meeting luckily the blow,
Which grieved her not at all, but, glancing off,
Fell harmless. Then she dealt Security
A blow that stunned her and almost caused her death;
40 So mighty 'twas, it robbed her of her shield
And sword. What did Security do then?
To give example to the rest, she seized
Her enemy by both the ears; and Fear
To her did likewise. Others intervened
And, grabbing one another similarly,
Struggled in pairs. Never was battle seen
So joined before! The fight was reinforced
On every hand; the struggle was so great
That ne'er before in any tournament
50 Was there such give-and-take of deadly blows.
Both sides called reinforcements. Here and there
Pell-mell they ran. I never saw strokes given
So thick as then they fell, like hail or snow.
I never saw folk mingle so in fight.
Not one of them but battered was or bruised.
　　But now, to tell the truth, the besieging host
Was getting the worst of it. The God of Love,
Distrusting lest his men should all be killed,
Sent Franchise and Sweet Sight to tell his dame
60 That she should come—that no necessity
Should hold her back. Meanwhile he made a truce
To last ten days or twelve, or more or less;
The length was not precisely limited.
Indeed, they might have made it last for aye
Had they desired, but it could broken be
By violation upon either side.
Had not Love seen that it was best for him,
He to the armistice had ne'er agreed;
And if the guardians had not supposed
70 That Love was desperate and could not break
The truce, they had not freely granted it.
Their anger had flared up had he displayed

Of his intentions but a single sign.
Had Venus' intervention been surmised,
There ne'er had been this truce, which to Love's cause
So advantageous proved; since there was naught
For him to do but flee or respite gain,
As oft occurs when armies fail to rout
Their foes and need to gather force for fresh attack.

75. Venus agrees to come to Love's aid
[15659–15778]

WISE messengers departed from the host
And journeyed till they came to Venus' home,
Where with great honor they were well received.
Within a wooded plain is Cythera,
A mount so high that ne'er an arbalest,
However strong and competent to shoot,
Could send a shaft or arrow to its height.
Venus, who inspires all womankind,
Her principal pavilion perches there.
10 I'd bore you if I should describe it all,
And so I'll let it go; I would be brief.
   Dame Venus had descended to the plain
To hunt. Her dearest friend attended her—
Adonis, prepossessing, fair, and young—
Coming to manhood, hardly more than boy,
He had a happy heart and loved the chase.
'Twas just past noon, and, wearied with the sport,
Beneath a poplar on the grass they sat
Beside a shaded pool. Their tired dogs,
20 Panting from exercise, the water lapped.
Their bows and arrows and their quivers stood
Against the tree behind them. They enjoyed
The birds they heard above them in the boughs.
After their hunting, Venus on her knees
Held him embraced, and, as she kissed his lips,

Gave him instructions how to course the woods
According to the manner she employed.

　"Dearest, when you go forth with ready pack　　VENUS
To hunt wild boars that flee from your pursuit,
30 Pursue them boldly till they turn at bay;
But against one that fiercely shows his tusks
Defend your body lest you shall be gored.
Facing the brave, be slow and hesitant;
For against those that have a hardy heart
No hardihood will give security.
The brave against the brave make deadly fight.
Reindeer and other deer, roebucks and hinds,
Rabbits and hares and goats and lesser game
You may pursue at will. Enjoy yourself
40 In hunting such. But bears and wolves and boars
And lions I forbid; pursue none such
Against my interdiction. They defend
Themselves too well and kill or maim the dogs.
They make the best hunters lose the day,
Or serious wounds sustain, or even die.
Most sorely grieved, I'd have no joy in you
If you did otherwise than as I bid."

　Thus Venus counseled and sincerely prayed
That he would heed her words or hunt no more.
50 Adonis little prized his sweetheart's words
And to their truth or falseness gave no thought;
But, to have peace, accepted what she said,
Although he valued not her counseling.
Her efforts were in vain. He had in mind
That she might give him what advice she pleased,
But, once away, she'd not see what he did.
He'd not believe her, so he later died
When Venus was not there to give him aid;
Then hers it was to weep and grieve for him.
60 　A boar he hunted that he thought to catch
And throttle; but he neither caught that boar
Nor cut him up. The boar had his revenge
Like proud and fiery beast; he couched his head
Against Adonis, and he slashed his teeth
Into his groin. Then with a twist of his snout

He stretched Adonis dead upon the earth.
   Fair sirs, whatever hap, keep well in mind
This sad example. You who disbelieve
Your sweethearts' words should know that you are fools.
70 Trust them completely, for what they may say
Is true as chronicle. If they should swear,
"We are entirely yours," believe them just
As you believe, "Our Father who's in Heaven."
Never prove recreant to such a creed.
If Reason counter comes, believe her not
Though she should bring to you a crucifix;
Have no more trust in her than I have had.
Had Venus by Adonis been believed,
He had enjoyed a longer lease of life.
80   After Venus' speech the lovers toyed
Each with the other, as delighted them,
And took their pleasure. Then to Cythera
They both returned; and there the messengers,
Ere Venus had had time to change her clothes,
Recited, point by point, the narrative
Of all that had occurred. "My faith," said she,   VENUS
" 'Twill be an evil hour when Jealousy
A castle or even a cottage can maintain
Against my son's desires. My bow and brand
90 I'd not consider worth a wooden clog
If I did not the guardians set on fire,
With all their garrison, unless they yield the keys."

                     ·

76. The truce is broken, and the Castle of Jealousy holds out
against the God of Love
[15779–15890]

VENUS her meinie summoned, then gave word
Her chariot to prepare; for in the mud
She would not go afoot. Her car was bright,
Rolling on four gold wheels begemmed with pearls.

Venus sets out in her chariot to attack Chastity. *Morgan 132, f. 117v.*

In place of collared horses, six fair doves
She chose from out her dovecots for the shafts.
　All things are ready, so she mounts her car
And starts to wage her war with Chastity.
The birds do not cavort, but beat their wings
10 And then are on their way; the air divides
Before them as they cleave it in their flight.
Betimes they come upon the battlefield.
No sooner there than from her chariot
Venus descends, and to her in great haste
Her famous son, with great rejoicing, comes.
Already, by his own command, the truce
Is broken, ere the enemy show signs
Of violating it; for Cupid keeps
No faith or vow or even covenant.
20 　Then forcefully they gave their heed to war—
These to attack, the others to defend.
The besiegers aimed their mighty mangonels.
Most moving Prayers, like heavy rocks, were hurled
To break the walls. The guardians fortified
The towers with hurdles of Refusal made,
With flexible birch switches interlaced,
Which they with great brutality had culled
From Danger's hedge. Love's army shot at them
Barbed arrows feathered with great Promises
30 That soon they'd have whatever they deserved
In gifts and services; for never a yard
Ungraced with Promises could enter there,
Or any shaft unfortified with steel
Made of Assurances of plighted troth.
The guardians were not slow in self-defense
But screened themselves with targets hard and strong,
Neither too light nor heavy, rightly made
From that same wood that Danger had supplied
From out his hedge. To shoot at them was vain.
40 　As thus the combat went, the God of Love
Approached his mother, telling of the case
That he was in and asking for her aid.
Said she, "May evil death o'erpower me soon　　**VENUS**
If Chastity I suffer to uphold

Dominion over any living dame,
No matter how much Jealousy may strive.
Too oft she's made us suffer painfully.
Fair son, swear all your men that they'll advance
Only employing your accustomed paths."

THE GOD OF LOVE

50   "Right willingly, my dame," he answered her.
"There shall be no exception made; no man
Can truthfully assert that he is mine
Unless he's now in love or once has been.
Great dolor 'tis that any man alive,
If he is able, should renounce the joys
Of Love. May he arrive at some bad end!
I hate them so that if I could confound
Their ways of life I'd do so willingly.
Of such men I complain and always shall;
60 Nor my displeasure will I strive to screen.
I'd injure them whene'er I got a chance
That I might be revenged, and that their pride
Might be laid low, or that they all should be
Condemned. Cursed be the day when they were born
Of Adam's line, who dare to cross my will!
Within their bodies may their foul hearts burst
When they attempt love's joys to abrogate!
'Twould seem no worse if one should beat me well
Or, with pickaxes, even break my head.
70 I am not mortal. If I were, I'd die,
Such grief and anger I endure from this;
For if my game should fail I would have lost
All that I have of worth except my clothes,
My body, and my weapons, and my crown.
At least, if Cupid's joy should lose its power
So that all men would fain abandon it,
They'd feel chagrin and curb their hearts in grief.
Where could man seek to find a better life
Than that of being in his sweetheart's arms?"
80   Straightway the host all ratified the oath,
And in the place of relics swore upon
Their quivers, arrows, bows, and darts, and brands.
They said, "No better relics can we ask   THE BARONS

And none more pleasing have. If on such things
We swore false oaths, we'd ne'er be credited."
And what they swore was truth; for they believed
In these as much as in the Trinity,
And would not swear an oath on any other thing.

77. The Poet tells how Nature strives to contravene
the work of Death
[15891–16004]

SOON as the barons shouted loud their oath
So that it could be heard both far and wide,
Dame Nature, who takes cognizance of all
That haps beneath the sky's blue covering.
Entered her workshop, busying herself
With forging individual entities
To save the species' continuity
Against the assaults of Death, who ne'er attains
The mastery, no matter how he speeds,
10 So many reinforcements she creates;
For Nature's reproduction follows Death
So closely that whene'er with club he kills
Some individuals who are his due—
For they are so decrepit that they have
No fear of death, since they are in decline
(They waste away in time and then decay
To furnish nourishment for other things)—
Then when Death thinks the race to extirpate
He never can get hold of all at once.
20 When one he seizes here, another there
Escapes him; and, when he the father kills,
A wife or son or daughter still remains,
Who, when they see the father lying dead,
Themselves in face of Death betake to flight,
Though later they must die, howe'er they flee;
For medicine and vows are nothing worth.

Nephews and nieces straightway fare afar,
Fast as their feet will carry them. They run
To seek distraction from the thought of Death:
30 Some to a dance, and others to a cell;
Some to a school, and others to their shops;
Some to the arts that they perchance have learned;
Others to joys in goblet, board, or bed;
Some mount their steeds with gilded stirrups decked,
Hoping to flee more rapidly from Death;
And others put their trust in wooden ships,
With due regard for starry influence,
For oars, and sails, and tackle for the boats;
And some humiliate themselves by vow
40 And take a mantle of hypocrisy
With which in flight they hope to hide their thoughts,
Though by their actions they're identified.
Thus all who live attempt to flee from Death—
From black-faced Death, who follows in pursuit.
They run a cruel race ere they are caught;
They flee, and Death gives chase—ten, twenty years,
Thirty, forty, fifty, sixty-five,
Yes, seventy, eighty, ninety, or fivescore—
And always crushing those whom he can seize.
50 Though it may seem that he has passed some by,
He ne'er forgets them but to them returns
Until, in spite of the physicians' skill,
He has them in his power. Doctors themselves
We never see escaping from Death's grasp.
Hippocrates and Galen, though both skilled,
Rhazes, Avicenna, Constantine,
All had to leave their skins; those less expert
Could salvage nothing more from Death than they.
So Death, who never can be satisfied,
60 Swallows each individual gluttonously.
His chase continues over land and sea
Till in the end he has engulfed them all.
But never can he get them all at once,
So fails he in his purpose to destroy
The species, which knows well how to escape:
If but a sole survivor can remain,

The common mold will live. This we may see
Well illustrated in the phoenix' case;
The species lasts, though there's but one on earth.
70   Always a single phoenix is alive,
Who, ere his death, has lived five hundred years;
Then at the last he builds a funeral pyre
Covered with spices, and thereon he leaps
And burns himself to death. But that the race
Of phoenixes may not become extinct,
However much the fire may burn him up,
Another phoenix from the ashes springs,
Or it may be the same one thus revived
By Nature, who this species values so
80 That she would lose her being if the bird
Could not be re-created when destroyed.
When Death devours the phoenix, ne'ertheless
Another phoenix still remains alive,
And would remain though thousands were destroyed.
   This is but one example of the way
That Nature works new creatures to create
So that when all of them shall come to death
They will leave others still alive. 'Tis thus
That all things living 'neath the circling moon
90 Have come to birth; and if but one remained
The species would by it be resupplied
And so Death never would succeed to gain his end.

78. The Poet tells how Art strives with Nature
[16005–16248]

DAME NATURE is so pitiful and good
That when she sees Corruption league himself
With envious Death, and both together come
To ruin the productions of her shop,
She forges and she hammers tirelessly,
Ever renewing individuals

By generation new. No better plan
Can she conceive than to imprint the stamp
Of such a letter as shall guarantee
10 That they are genuine; as men are wont
To stamp the various values on their coins,
Of which by Art we some examples have,
Though Art can never fashion forms so true.
With most attentive care, upon his knees,
Of Nature Art implores, demands, and prays,
Like wretched mendicant, of sorry skill
And strength, who struggles to pursue her ways,
That she will teach him how she manages
To reproduce all creatures properly
20 In her designs, by her creative power.
He watches how she works, and, most intent
To do as well, like ape he copies her.
But Art's so naked and devoid of skill
That he can never bring a thing to life
Or make it seem that it is natural.
Howe'er he tries, with greatest care and pains,
To make things as they are, with figures such
As Nature gives them—howsoe'er he carves
And forges, and then colors them or paints
30 Knights armed for battle on their coursers fair,
Bearing their shields emblazoned blue or green
Or yellow or with variegated hues,
If more variety he wishes them to have—
Fair birds in forests fresh—fish in the flood—
All savage beasts that feed in woodland dells—
And all the flowers and herbs that in the spring
Maidens and youths go happily to cull
When first come forth the flower and the leaf—
Domestic animals and captive birds—
40 Balls, dances, farandoles with comely dames
Holding the hands of gallant bachelors,
Well dressed, well figured, and depicted well
On metal, wood, or wax, or other stuff,
In pictures or on walls—Art never makes,
For all the traits that he can reproduce,
His figures live and move and feel and speak.

Though Art so much of alchemy should learn
That he all metals could with colors tint,
Though he should work himself to death, he ne'er
50 One species could transmute to other kind;
The best that he can do is to reduce
Each to its constitution primitive.
He'll ne'er attain to Nature's subtlety
Though he should strive to do so all his life.
If he would labor till he knows the way
To transmute metals to their first estate,
'Twere needful he should have much sapience
To reach the right degree of tempering,
When he would his elixir make, from which
60 The final composition should result.
Who best knows how to reach successful end
Must comprehend essential differences,
Which to define he's often at a loss,
Between the substances that he manipulates.
    However, 'tis well known that alchemy
Is veritably an art, and one will find
Great marvels in it if he practices
With wisdom; for, however it may be
Concerning species, individuals
70 Subjected to intelligent control
Are mutable into as many forms
As their complexions will delimitate,
By transformations various, and change
So that they will of different species seem
Once they have lost their aspect primitive.
Does not one see how those in glasswork skilled
Of ferns make ashes first and then clear glass
By easy depuration? And we know
That fern is glass no more than glass is fern.
80 When lightning flashes and the thunder rolls,
Men sometimes see a stone fall from the clouds,
Which certainly are not of stone themselves.
The sage may know the reason why these things
Have changed to matter so dissimilar.
In one case Nature—in the other, Art—
Has utterly transformed materials,

In form and substance, into different stuff.
   Those who know how to consummate the work
Can do likewise with metals, from the ore
90 Extracting all the dross and rendering it
Pure bullion, using the affinity
Of substances that like complexions have;
Which shows that they a common nature own,
However Nature may have sundered them.
For, as the books assert, all ores are born
In various ways within terrestrial mines,
Of mercury and sulphur. One who knew
How skillfully the spirits to prepare
That they might enter into substances
100 And not depart when they had entered in
Until they found the substance purified
Might work his will with metals if he had
In calorific sulphur to depinct
Ore white or red. Those who have mastery
Of the alchemist's art can bring to birth
From finest silver finest gold, and give
It weight and color from an ore less dear;
And of fine gold they fashion precious stones
Most clear and enviable. Some other ores
110 They sunder from their species and transform
Into fine silver, using chemicals
That penetrating are, and clear and fine.
But sophisters can ne'er accomplish this;
Though they may work as long as they may live,
They never can attain to Nature's skill.
   Ingenious Nature, who is so intent
Upon her much-loved works, worried and grieved,
Now made complaint and most profoundly wept
So that no heart that felt a bit of love
120 Or pity could perceive her suffering
And not join with her in those bitter tears.
Such dolor seized her heart because she'd done
A deed of which she now repented so
That she would willingly have left her work
And given it no further thought at all,
Provided only she could from her lord

Obtain permission, which she'd gladly seek,
Her heart was so tormented and oppressed.
　　Nature would I gladly describe to you,
130 But insufficient would my wit appear.
My wit! What say I? It is far too weak.
That without saying goes, quite naturally.
No human wit could that description make
Most certainly, in writing or in speech.
Though Aristotle, Plato, Ptolemy,
Algus, or Euclid, who've so great renown
As writers good, should dare attempt the task,
Their ingenuity would be in vain;
For they could hardly comprehend the theme.
140 　　Pygmalion could not carve Nature's mold;
Parrhasius would work to no good end;
Indeed, Apelles, whom I call the best
Of all the painters, howe'er long he lived,
Would not be able to portray her charms;
Myron and Polycletus could attain
To no such skill as such a task would take.
　　Zeuxis, the painter, strove in vain to draw
The form of Nature when employed to make
An image for a temple. He secured
150 As models five young girls, the fairest five
That could be found by searching all the land.
As Cicero reminds us in his book
On rhetoric, a most authentic work,
These maidens were directed to appear
Before him all unclothed, and one by one,
That he might see if he could find defect
Of limb or body in a single case.
He found no fault, but even with such aids,
And though he had great skill in portraiture
160 And coloring, he failed to imitate
Nature's perfectionment of pulchritude.
　　As Zeuxis failed, so have all masters failed
Whom Nature's brought to birth. However well
Her beauty they perceived, they'd waste their time
At such a task, and never teach their hands
To reproduce all Nature's loveliness.

'Tis God alone can claim such workmanship.
Had I been able, I had willingly
At least attempted to perform the task;
170 Had I the wit and skill, I'd penned for you
Such a description; but I have, myself,
Wasted my time, though all my lore I used,
Like foolish and presumptuous wight I was,
A hundred times more than you can conceive.
By sheer presumption I did undertake
Too much when I my resolution turned
To the achievement of such lofty work.
It rather seems as if my heart would burst,
So noble and so worthy have I found
180 Nature's great beauty, which I prize so much
That I would comprehend it with my mind.
And yet, whatever labor I employ,
However much I set my thought on it,
I do not dare to say a single word;
So I keep silent and renounce the thought.
The more I think of it, the more it seems
Far greater beauty than I can conceive;
For God, whose beauty is quite measureless,
When He this loveliness to Nature gave
190 Within her fixed a fountain, full and free,
From which all beauty flows. But none can tell
Either its source or limits. 'Twere not right
That I should give account of Nature's form
Or of her face, which is more fresh and fair
Than fleur-de-lis new sprung in month of May.
The rose upon the branch is not more red;
And no more white is snow upon a limb.
Why should I try to find a simile
When I cannot compare to anything
200 A beauty and a worth that men cannot conceive?

79. Nature goes to Genius for confession
[16249–16346]

WHEN Nature heard the barons swear their oath,
A great alleviation of the grief
That weighed her down she felt within her heart;
And yet to be deceived she feared, and said:
"Alas! What have I done! I do repent   NATURE
Of nothing that has happened soon or late
Except one deed committed long ago
When this fair world was young. In that I erred
Most miserably, and for that one act
10 I call myself a fool. When I regard
My foolishness, it seems to me but right
That I should make repentance for my sin.
Unhappy wretch! Most miserable dunce!
One hundred times unfortunate mischance!
Where can good faith be found? How well have I
Employed my pains! I certainly must be
Devoid of wit, who, to deserve their grace,
Have always taken care to serve my friends;
And yet my efforts turn out finally
20 To aid my enemies. By kindness I'm misled."
    Then Nature went to parley with the priest
Who in her chapel celebrated mass—
The same liturgics that he had performed
Since first he had been cleric in the church.
Boldly, in place of other rites, the priest
Before the goddess Nature, in accord
With her, recalled in open audience
The figures representative of all
Things mortal, that he'd written in his book
30 As Nature had delivered them to him.
    "Genius," said she, "my gentle priest, who are   NATURE
The god and master of this place, and who,

According to their qualities, direct
All creatures in the works to them assigned,
And well perform your task, as to each one
Is needful, of one foolishness I did,
Of which I've never given full account,
Although repentance I've expressed for it,
I now would make confession unto you."

40   "My lady, queen of all the world," he said,   GENIUS
"Before whom all things earthly bow the knee,
If there is anything that gives you grief,
Of which you would repent, or which to speak
Would please you, whatsoe'er the matter is,
Of joy or dolor, well you may confess
To me at leisure and as you desire;
For I'm entirely at your command.
I'll gladly give you what advice I can
And keep the matter secret, if it's such
50 A thing as is not proper to be told;
And, if you absolution need, I'd not
Withhold it from you. But first dry your tears."

      "Good Genius, that I weep is certainly   NATURE
No wonder."

                "Ne'ertheless, I counsel you   GENIUS
To cease your crying and consider well
That which you have to say, if you would make
A good confession. Well may I believe
You're moved by some great outrage, for I know
No noble heart would be by trivial thing
60 So daunted. What fool dares to trouble you?
But it is true that easily inflamed
With ire is woman. Vergil testifies,
And well he knew the female character,
That never any woman was so stanch
As not to be capricious and unfixed—
An easily offended animal.
Solomon says, 'There is no head above   SOLOMON
The cruel serpent's, and there is no wrath
Above an angry woman's, and no thing
70 Of such maliciousness.' So much of vice   GENIUS
There is in woman that her traits perverse

Cannot be told in meter or in rhyme.
So Titus Livius, who knew the modes
And manners of the female sex, declares
That prayers are less effective to reform
Their customs than are lies and blandishments,
So pliable and foolish are their hearts;
And Scripture also says that all the vice
Of women has its origin in avarice."

80. Genius pictures the life of a man with an avaricious wife
[16347–16706]

"A MAN who trusts his secrets to his wife   GENIUS
Makes her his mistress. None of women born,
Unless he's drunk or crazy, will reveal
To women anything that should be hid,
Unless he wants to hear it coming back
To him from others. Better 'twere to flee
From out the land than tell his wife to keep
A secret, though she meek and loyal be.
Nor will he any secret act perform
10 In presence of a woman, for she'll tell
About it soon or late, though it involve
For him a mortal peril. Though none ask
Her secret, she will tell it just the same
Without an invitation; naught will keep
Her silent. She will think she might as well
Be dead as that the secret should remain
Unspoken, though great peril or reproach
Should come of it. And if it's such a thing,
The man who's told it ne'er will dare to raise
20 His hand to punish her with slaps or blows
A single time—much less three times or four.
No sooner will he touch her than she'll throw
It in his face, then tell it to the world.
The man who trusts a woman loses her.

"Do you know what the miserable man
Who places confidence in woman does?
He puts a halter round his neck; he binds
His hands behind him. For, if only once
He ever dares to make complaint to her
30 Or scold or punish her for what she's done,
He puts his life in peril. If the crime
That he's revealed to her is capital—
Punishable with hanging by the neck—
The judge may seize him then with her consent,
Or clansmen may avenge their friend on him,
To such an evil pass he will have come.
And yet the fool must go to bed with her
And lie all night beside her on their couch
Where he dares not to sleep, e'en if he could,
40 Because he's done, or mayhap planned to do
Some murder or some other crime for which
He fears to die if it should be revealed.
Then, when he turns and twists and groans and sighs,
His wife, who well perceives he's ill at ease,
Draws him to her with kiss, caress, and hug,
And lays her hand upon his breast and says:

THE WIFE

" 'What's wrong? What makes you shiver so and sigh
And wallow? We're alone in secret here,
Just you and I—we two—of all the world
50 The persons who should love each other most
With true and unembittered, loyal hearts.
I locked the chamber door with my own hand,
As I remember well; and I am glad
To say our walls are forty inches thick;
The rafters are so high that we should be
Secure beneath them; no one can espy
Our secrets, for the room is unexposed
And from the windows we are far away,
Which no man living could unlock and ope
60 More than the wind, unless he shattered them.
In brief, there's not a crevice in the room
Where any eavesdropper could prick his ear.
No one can hear your voice excepting me;

Therefore it is I tenderly implore,
By all our love, that you confide in me
Enough to tell me what is ailing you.'
    " 'My dear,' he says, 'as I am in God's sight,   THE HUSBAND
I would not tell it you for anything;
It's not a thing that should be talked about.'
70   " 'Alas! My dear, sweet husband,' she replies,   THE WIFE
'Are you suspicious, then, of even me
Who am your loyal spouse? When we were wed,
Lord Jesus Christ, whom we have never found
Ungenerous in grace, made of us two
One body; now if we are but one flesh
By right of common law there should not be
Within one body but a single heart
Upon the left. Our hearts are therefore one.
I have yours and you have mine. There's naught
80 That yours should know that is not known to mine.
Therefore I pray that you, in recompense
And as my due desert, confide in me;
For never shall I have a happy soul
Till I know all. And if you will not speak
I'll know that you impugn my honesty;
I'll know what love you bear me when you say
That I'm your sweet companion, sister, friend!
Who do you think it is for whom you pare
Such chestnuts? Certainly, if you don't tell
90 'Twill surely seem that you're betraying me,
Who, since the day when we were first betrothed,
Have so confided in you that I've told
You everything that's come into my head.
For you I've left my mother and my sire,
My uncles, nephews, sisters, brothers, friends,
And all my family, as you well know.
Most certainly I've made an ill exchange
If now so hostile I find you to me
While I adore you best of living things
100 Although you value me less than a leek,
When you conceive that I so ill could act
Toward you as any secret to reveal.
I never would, by Christ, the King of Heaven!

Who should protect you more than I myself?
At least consider me, and if you find
Good reason to misdoubt my loyalty,
You have my body in your power. What gage
Could be a better guarantee than that?
Would you have better hostage? Then I'm worse
110 Than other women; for I see my friends
Their households' mistresses. Their husbands tell
Them all their secrets; for they confidence
Have in their wives, with whom they counsel take,
When sleepless they together lie in bed,
And privately each one confession makes
Unto the other, so that naught remains
That should be told. This they, to tell the truth,
More often do than go to see the priest.
I have their words for it, for many a time
120 Complete avowal they have made to me
Of all they've seen or heard or even thought,
So do they purge and so relieve themselves.
But they are not like me, nor I like them—
Not garrulous or quarrelsome or light;
I'm chaste of body, howsoever vile
My soul may seem to God on judgment day.
You never hear that with adultery
I have been charged, unless mischievously
Some fool tells untrue tales of me to you.
130 You've proved me well; and have you found me false?
Fair sir, be careful how you keep your faith
With me! You must have evilly forsworn
Yourself when first you pledged to me your vows
And on my finger placed your wedding ring.
I don't know how you dared to do it then.
Who made you marry me whom now you fear
To trust? Now let me know what deed you hide;
I pray you, keep your faith at least this once.
I truly promise, pledge my faith, and swear
140 By holy Peter, what you tell to me
I'll keep as close as if 'twere in the tomb.
Now certainly I'd be most indiscreet.
If from my mouth a word should issue forth

By which you might be injured or disgraced.
'Twould shame my lineage, and most of all
Myself; and never in my life have I
Disgraced my family. 'Tis true, they say,
"Who cuts his nose off just to spite his face
Is but a fool." Now, by your faith in God,
150 Tell me, what is it disconcerts your heart;
Or, if you don't, you will have caused my death.'
    "She pulls the clothes from off his head and breast   GENIUS
And kisses him repeatedly and weeps
Upon him many tears, with ardor feigned.
    "The wretched man then all his shame recounts
And tells his deed and thereby hangs himself;
Though when the words are spoken he repents.
But, once a word has taken wing, it ne'er
Can be recalled. Forthwith he prays his wife
160 (And he's more ill at ease than he had been
When she knew naught) that she will hold her tongue,
And she repeats her promise to keep still
Whatever hap. What does the fool expect?
He couldn't keep his secret; does he think
That he can make his wife more secretive?
Does he know what the end of this will be?
He sees that she has now the upper hand,
And knows that ne'er again he'll dare complain
Or scold her for whatever thing she does.
170 Now that she has the wherewithal, she'll keep
Him cowed and mute. Her promise she may hold
Until some quarrel rise between the two;
She may restrain herself to that extent,
But scarcely to such point that she'll not have
His heart in balance, therefore causing grief.
    "Whoever feels affection for mankind
Should preach to them this sermon, which is good
For all occasions, to the end that they,
Thus warned, so great a peril may escape.
180 It may displeasing be to nagging wives,
But verity will not in corners hide.
    "Fair sirs, beware of women, if you love
Your bodies and your souls; at least don't be

So bungling in your conduct as to tell
Them secrets you should keep locked in your breasts.
Beware! Beware! Beware! Beware! Beware!
Good fellows, flee, I charge and counsel you,
Without deceit or guile, from such a beast!
Note Vergil's words, and plant them in your hearts
190 So that they never can be rooted out:
   'O children, who pluck strawberries and flowers   VERGIL
So clean and fresh, flee from the serpent cold
That's lying in the grass.' She'll surely sting   GENIUS
And poison and envenom everyone
Who comes too close; and so, young folk who go
Seeking the flowers and berries of this world,
Beware the evil serpent, the cold snake
Who so maliciously is lurking here,
Who hides her venom, keeping it concealed,
200 Secreting it beneath the tender grass
Until such time as she can pour it forth
To injure and deceive. Consider well
How to escape and never to be caught,
If you would be safeguarded from sure death.
The beast's so venomous in head and tail
And body that if you approach her close
You'll find yourselves empoisoned, for she stings
And kills most traitorously; and when once stung
A man can find no soothing antidote.
210 No treacle can cure that venom's burns:
No herb or root is of the least avail.
The only remedy is found in flight.
   "It is not my intention, ne'ertheless,
To say that you should not hold women dear
Or lie with them—you should not flee so far.
Rather it's my command that you them prize
And reasonably advance their every cause,
Provide them clothes and shoes, both of the best,
And ever strive to serve and honor them
220 In order to maintain the human race,
That Death may ne'er succeed to root it out;
But never should you trust in them so much
That you'll reveal to them what should be hid.

If they've ability for such-like cares,
Let them maintain the household and the home,
And come and go; or if it chance that they
Know how efficiently to buy and sell,
To such affairs they rightly may attend;
Or if they're mistresses of any craft
230 Let them pursue it if they feel the urge;
And let them know such things as all may know—
Such things as have no need to be concealed.
But if you e'er entrust too much to them,
Or give them too much power, you'll late repent
When finally their malice you shall feel.
We're warned by Scripture that if sovereignty
A woman have, she will oppose her spouse
In whatsoever thing he says or does;
Therefore beware that your house does not fall
240 Into such evil way, for e'en at best
Man loses much. A wise man guards his own.
    "You men who have your sweethearts, show yourselves
Good fellows; each provide sufficiently
With common duties. But if you are wise
And prudent, when you hold them in your arms
And hug and kiss them, you will silent keep.
Be still! Be still! Be still! Be still! Be still!
Think well, and hold your tongue; no good can come
From making them your coparticipants
250 In secrets. They are all too proud and vain.
Too venomous and biting are their tongues.
In such a situation many a fool,
Held tight within his sweetheart's arms, and kissed
And fondled, in the midst of amorous game
That pleases them so much, can naught conceal.
Then are his secrets all revealed, and then
The husband bares his heart. From such an act
Much grief and trouble come. All but the wise,
Who think before they speak, reveal their thoughts.
260   "Delilah, the malicious wedded wife
Of Samson, who was valorous and strong,
A crafty warrior, by her flattery,
Which was so venomous, the while she held

Him sleeping in her lap complaisantly,
With shears cut off his hair, with which he lost
His strength. He was too great a fool to know
That he should keep his secret, so he told
His wife that with his locks he'd lose his power,
Revealing all his inmost privity.
270   "No more examples need I cite for you;
You well may make the one suffice for all.
But, since I love you, I'll to you commend
A proverb written down by Solomon:
'To free yourself from peril and reproach,   SOLOMON
Guard and keep locked the portals of your lips
Against the wife who sleeps upon your breast.'
All who hold mankind dear should preach this lore, GENIUS
That they may guard themselves from womankind
And never give them any confidence.
280   'Tis not for you that I this sermon preach,
Dame Nature, for you're always stanch and true.
Scripture affirms that God so boundlessly
Has dowered you that you are now omniscient."

81.   Nature begins her confession
[16707–17038]

HIS comforting to Nature Genius gave,
Exhorting her, so far as in her lay,
To banish all her grief; for, as he said,
In dole and sorrow one no conquests makes—
Unprofitable wounds are won by woe.
When he had had his will in speech, he sat
Upon a settle near the altar placed,
Remitting longer prayer. Upon her knees
Before the parson Nature humbly knelt.
10   To tell the truth, she could not yet forget
Her dolefulness; nor did he strive anew
To free her from it, for he clearly saw

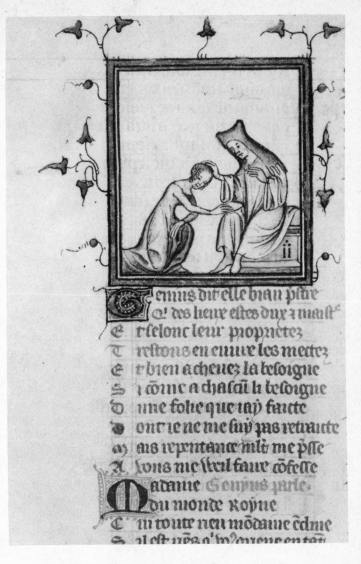

enius dit elle bian pstre
Q. des lieur estes duy z maist
Et selonc leur propnetez
Trestons en euure les mectez
Et bien acheuez la besoigne
Si come a chascū li besoigne
Une folie que ray faicte
Dont ie ne me suy pas retraicte
Mais repentance mlt me psse
Alons me sueil faire cōfesse
Madame Genius parle.
Du monde Royne
En toute riē mōdaine cōme
Sil est nꝰꝰ qꝰ ꝑꝛ enreur en tēꝯ

Nature confesses to Genius. *Morgan 132, f. 121v.*

His pains were wasted—all his efforts lost.
Instead, he listened silent to the dame,
Who most devoutly, hindered by her tears,
Recited this confession, which I quote
As she pronounced it to him, word for word:
      "When God, who in all beauties so abounds,   NATURE
First made so beautiful this lovely earth,
20   Whose foreseen form of fairness in His mind
He had before He gave it outward shape,
Thence taking His design and whatsoe'er
To its fulfillment was expedient
(For, had He elsewhere sought, He had not found,
In heaven or beneath, a single thing
That could have aided His accomplishment,
Since naught outside Himself existence had,
And He, who could not fail in anything,
From nothing could make all things come to birth)
30   No other thought urged Him to this employ—
Unenvious, benign, and generous—
Save His good will, the wellspring of all life.
      "In the beginning Chaos He ordained,
Which had but mass, and in whose every part
Confused disorder—indistinction—reigned.
He separated then the elements,
Which never since have been anatomized,
And numbered all of them and knew their sum,
And limits set to every firmament
40   In reasonable measure, and decreed
That each, in order to include the more
And move the better, should be round in shape,
According to the purposes of all.
Each one He stationed in its proper place
As He perceived that all should be arranged:
The lighter rose aloft; the heavy sank
Down to the center—medials between.
In time and space He rightly each ordained.
      "When He, according to his fixed design,
50   Had thus His other creatures all disposed,
With His own grace God honored me so much—
Held me so dear—that He established me

As chamberlain of all, to serve Him thus
Permitting me, as e'er He will permit
While it shall be His will. No other right
Claim I to such a bounty, but I thank
Him for His love of such unworthy maid
And for His prizing me so much that He,
Great lord of such a vast and fair estate,
60 Appointed me His constable—indeed,
His steward and His vicar-general—
A dignity which little I deserved
Except through His benign benevolence.

   "God honors me so much that in my ward
He leaves the lovely golden chain that binds
The elements, which bow before my face.
To me He has entrusted everything
Within those rings of gold, and all their forms
It is my duty to perpetuate.
70 His will it is that all should me obey
And to my rules conform—forget no laws,
But keep and guard them everlastingly.
In truth, this commonly is done with care
By all His creatures, saving one alone.

   "It is not of the sky that I complain.
Forever, without fault, it turns and turns
And with it in its shining circle bears
The twinkling stars, whose virtuosity
Is of more worth than any precious stone.
80 As it pursues its course from east to west,
And never stops or turns the other way,
O'ercoming all the orbits that impede
And would arrest its movement if they could,
It furnishes delight to all the world.
No retardation can a man perceive
That will prevent the starry firmament,
After a space of thrice twelve thousand years,
From circling back precisely to that point
At which it was when first it was create,
90 Having accomplishèd its entire course—
Its pathway's length around the zodiac,
That mighty circle which it wheels upon.

So perfectly the sky revolves above
That in its track no error can be found.
'Aplanos,' for this reason, it is called
By those who've found it not to deviate;
For this Greek signifies, in modern tongue,
A thing that's errorless. Man has not seen
The other heavens I might name to you,
100 But their existence is by reason proved
By those who demonstrate by evidence.

 "Nor of the seven planets do I make
Complaint, for each throughout its course shines bright,
Spotless, and clear. 'Tis true, the moon may seem
Less purely white—obscure in certain parts—
But 'tis the double nature of that orb
To show some troubled features on its face—
In one part shining, in another dark—
At once possessing and devoid of light.
110 Transparencies upon the lunar globe
Cannot reflect the shining of the sun,
But in these portions are its rays absorbed;
Thus is the brilliance of such parts destroyed.
But all the thicker portions of the moon,
Which offer more resistance to the rays
And conquer them, throw off a shining glow.
To make this easier to understand,
I may, instead of further glossing, give
A brief example to explain my text.
120 Transparent glass through which the light can shine
When nothing thick on either side is placed
To throw it back cannot reflect the face
Because the rays of light that meet the eye
Strike nothing that will make them back rebound;
But coat the glass with lead or something else
As dense as that, which intercepts the rays,
And straightway in the glass your face appears—
For if they are opaque or can be backed,
All polished surfaces reflect the light—
130 So the transparent surface of the moon,
Which may be likened to a crystal sphere,
Does not retard the rays, which enter it

And can, therefore, no bright reflection make;
But denser parts, which no rays penetrate,
Strongly reflect them back and make that orb
Seem brighter in those portions than it is
In other parts which seem the more obscure.
     "The figure of a creature marvelous
Is formed by darker patches on the moon.
140 It is a dragon that inclines its head
A little toward the west, and toward the east
Couches its tail; upon its back it bears
A towering tree, whose branches eastward stretch,
But upside down. These topsy-turvy limbs
Support a man, who, hanging by his arms,
Kicks toward the west with both his legs and feet.
Thus are the semblances interpreted.
     "Good works perform the planets: each of them
So labors that all seven never stop.
150 Through all degrees of their twelve hours they wheel,
Resting in each but the appointed time,
And, as is meet to do their duty well,
Their motion is contrariwise to that
Of all the heavens; so each day they win
To new positions which their portions are
Of the tremendous circles they complete.
Then without pause they recommence their round,
Opposing contrary motions to the stars
To guard the elements, which could not live
160 Beneath a sky that circled unrestrained.
     "The glorious sun, the fountainhead of light,   *heliocentric universe*
Which gives the day its being, like a king
Sits in the center crowned with flaming beams.
Most reasonable 'tis that in the midst
He have his home, since God, so fair and wise
And strong, has willed that there he have his place,
For if he nearer came the earth would burn—
If farther strayed, the frost would doom to death.
From thence the sun dispenses common light
170 To moon and planets—makes them shine so fair
That Night as candles lights them every eve
That she before her husband, Acheron,

Setting her table, may less dreadful seem,
Because of which his heart knows bitterness,
For rather would he be without a light
In union with his inky-featured spouse,
As first they lay together long ago
When Night conceived, through their fond interplay,
The Furies three, fierce ministers of Hell,
180 Felonious whores. But ne'ertheless Night thinks,
When she within her closet scans her glass,
Or in her cellar or her cave, that she
Would be too colorless and hideous
If shining down through the tenebrous air
No joyful light she had from flaming stars
Which in their spheres revolve as God Himself
Established them. Sweet harmonies they make,
Which are the source of all the melodies
And divers tunes that we in concord set
190 In all our sorts of song. There is no thing
That would not chant in unison with them.
   "The planets by their influence control
The accidents and substances of all
The things existing 'neath the moon on earth;
And by their communal divergencies
They sometimes darken the clear element
And then in turn the darkness clarify.
Cold and hot and moist and dry through them,
As in a coffer, in each body meet
200 To hold the parts together closely joined,
Howe'er contrary their propensities.
Among four enemies they bring accord,
When to complexion reasonable reduced
By suitable attempering, to form
In worthiest shape the things that I create;
Or, if it happens that they are not good,
It is the fault of their material.
   "But one who will examine well may know
That heat the sap of life will ceaselessly,
210 How good so ever the accord may be,
Suck and devour and waste from day to day
Till death, which is their due, shall come to all

By my most just decree, if it, indeed,
Come not in other ways, hastened by chance,
Ere spent is all the sap; for no one can,
By any medicine that he may take
Or any ointment that he may apply,
Lengthen the body's life, though easily
Each one may much abridge and shorten it;
220 For some by noose or drowning end their days
Before the sap has failed, or undertake
Some perilous exploit in which they burn
Or are interred alive ere they can flee,
Or meet destruction by some foolish act,
Or undeservedly by enemies
With false and cruel hearts are doomed to die
By stroke of sword or draft of poison cup,
Or by an unwise regimen of life—
By too much sleep or waking, work or rest;
230 Eating or drinking; joyfulness or grief;
Getting too fat or losing too much flesh
(For sin in any one of these may lie);
By too long fasts; by joining in delights
Too much; by suffering too much misease;
By too much change of state, as oft appears
When one with sudden heat o'erwhelms himself,
Or sudden cold, which he repents too late;
By changing clothes too often, which brings death
To some whose bodies can't accommodate
240 Themselves to sudden shifts, while others fall
In sickness from a change that Nature hates—
So that they make me vainly force myself
To lead them toward a natural decease.
But, howsoever much men may misdo
When they procure such deaths in my despite,
I ne'ertheless am much disturbed when they
Halt on life's road like wretches recreant,
Vanquished by ill-starred death, who easily
Had held their way unto the very end
250 Had they been willing to restrain themselves
From folly and excess which clipped their lives
Ere they attained the good I had in store for them."

82. Nature discusses destiny and free will
[17039–17874]

"EMPEDOCLES, who read so many books   NATURE
And loved philosophy so much, did wrong
When, melancholy, he, not fearing death,
Within the depths of Etna sought his end,
And there, feet bound, was burned alive, to show
That men are weak of heart who dread to die;
Therefore he willingly embraced his fate.
No honey sweet he gained thereby, but chose
A sulphurous and boiling sepulcher.
10   "His case but little aids my argument;
But Origen his own testes cut off
With his own hand, that he might better serve
The nuns, and no suspicion rouse that he
Made opportunity to lie with them.
     "Some say, a certain fate at certain hour
By destiny had been decreed to each
When he was first conceived—that they were born
Beneath such constellations that they must,
By sheer necessity and with no chance
20 Or power to avoid, accept their fate,
However grievous it might be to them.
But I know well the truth: however much
The heavens labor, and on men bestow
Their natural morals and their tendencies
To do such things as lead them to such ends,
Obeying the material force their hearts
Would fain elude, yet may they easily
By doctrine and by wholesome nouriture
Or medicines, if they are pure and fine—
30 By cultivating high companionship
Furnished with virtue and with common sense—
Or by superior mentality—

Succeed in leading lives quite otherwise,
If sensibly their natures they restrain.
Though men and women naturally spurn
The good, and turn to evil, Reason can
Turn them about again, if they believe
In her alone. Then things go differently;
For other outcome ever can be gained
40 Than that decreed by the celestial orbs,
Which doubtless have great force unless the aid
Of Reason be against them brought. But they
Are lacking power o'er her. Each wise man knows
That Reason is not subject to the stars;
For 'neath their power she was not brought to birth.

"The problem's not for lay folk to resolve
And show how man's free will can coexist
With foresight and foreknowledge heavenly
And with predestination. He who'd try
50 Would find the proposition much too hard
To explicate, although he might succeed
To meet objections urged against his case.
But it is true, howe'er it seems, that these
Together may accord; or else 'twere true
That by necessity all things occur.
Those who do well would never merit praise,
And those who sin would never blame deserve;
For who would do good works could never will
To do aught else, nor could he who would sin
60 Help sinning. Since it was predestinate,
Willing or not, he'd do it just the same.

"A man may well assert in argument
That God may never be at all deceived
In facts that He has pondered in advance,
Which doubtlessly must happen as He planned;
For He knows when and how they will take place
And to what end they tend. If it could be
That in advance God knew not, then He were
Not of unbounded might, unbounded good,
70 Unbounded knowledge, and full sovereignty—
The fair, the sweet, the premier of all!
He would not be aware of what we do,

But would believe as humans think of us
Who must depend on dubious surmise
Without the certainty that knowledge gives.
'Twere deviltry such error to ascribe
To God! No reasonable man would hear
Such charge preferred. Then we are led perforce
To say that when the will of man directs
80 Him how or when to act or speak or think
Or will or instigate, then 'tis a thing
Predestinate, which cannot be escaped.
Then it should follow that no one has free will.

   "But if stern destiny decrees all things
That happen, as this argument appears
To prove, and men do well or ill because
They can't do otherwise, then what reward
Or punishment do they deserve from God?
Though he had taken vows, a man could act
90 No otherwise. Then God could not be just
In scourging evil or rewarding good;
For on what basis could He judge a case?
He who considers well will see that then
No virtues and no vices could exist,
And, without them, no prayer or sacrifice
In chalices would any virtue have.
God would be most unfair when He mounts high
Upon the throne of justice, if He took
Of vice or virtue no account, but set
100 The murderers and usurers and thieves
All free, and judged to be of equal weight
The acts of hypocrites and honest men.
Then shamed were those who strive to love their God
If in the end they failed to get His love;
And fail they must, for it would come to this:
That no good works might gain them grace divine.

   "However, God is not unjust, but fair,
And goodness throughout all His being shines,
Else in perfection would appear defect.
110 Then He must mete his gain or loss to each
According to his merit; all good works
Are recompensed, and destiny ignored,

At least so far as lay folk understand,
Who all things good or bad or false or true
Impute to it as needful happenings.
So free will does exist, however much
It is ill-treated by such sort of folk.

   "Should some oppose, and deprecate free will,
Defending destiny, as many men
120 Have been inclined to do, and say of things
Improbable but possible, when once
They have occurred, 'Had one foreseen this fact
And said, "Such thing shall come to pass, nor can
A man avoid it," would he not have told
The truth? Then this would be necessity;
For it ensued, beyond the slightest doubt.
So interchangeability exists
Between necessity and certitude;
And when necessity compels a thing
130 It must, perforce, occur.' By what reply
Can one escape from this predicament?
A man's foretelling may be true, and yet
It may not illustrate necessity;
For, notwithstanding his foreseeing it,
Not necessary—only possible—
Was its occurrence. If one thinks it out,
A relative necessity he finds,
Not clear necessity, as he had thought;
Not worth a wimple is that argument!
140 If it is true that something must occur,
Its happening is then necessity;
But although simple truth may correspond
To what I clear necessity have named,
Possible verity may not at all.
Such arguments cannot disprove free will.

   "Besides, consider that 'twould please no man
To take account of any thing on earth
Or work to satisfy his needs; for why
Should he do this if all were foreordained
150 And fixed by force of destiny? He'd win
By counsel or by handiwork no more
Or less; because of it he'd never be

The worse or better off. And vain it were
To choose between things born and things to come—
Between things done and unattempted things—
Between words said and thinking unexpressed.
No one would learn a trade, for each would know
The art as well without his mastering it
As if he worked and studied all his life.
160 But this conclusion's not to be allowed.

    " 'Tis clear, then, that a person should deny
That human works come from necessity.
Rather, men freely good and bad perform
Entirely as they will. To tell the truth,
There is no force outside themselves that makes
Them will to choose that which they are not free
To take or leave, if Reason they employ.

    "Too great a task 'twould be for me to try
To answer all the arguments men bring
170 Against free will. But those who take the pains
To reason subtly tell us that divine
Foreknowledge places no necessity
Upon the acts of men. For well they say
That just because God knows what men will do
It does not follow that they're forced to act
So that they will attain to such an end;
But, since it happens that such tendency
They have toward such an end, therefore God knows.
However, too unskillfully such folk
180 Unsnarl the knot of all this argument;
For he who follows out their reasoning,
If their grounds are correct, must clearly see
That future facts to God His prescience give
And His foreknowledge make necessity.
Great folly 'tis to think God's wit so small
That on exterior facts He must depend.
Those who this sort of reasoning accept
Are striving evilly against their God
When they are willing to belittle Him
190 And His foreknowledge by such vain discourse.
Reason would teach that God can nothing learn
From man, for surely not all-wise were He

Could He be proved to suffer such default.
Then worthless is this answer, which impairs
God's foresight, and His providence conceals
Beneath the shadowing of ignorance;
For it is certain God can scarcely learn
From human works, and doubtless if He could
'Twould prove His lack of power, which were a sin
200 To mention and a shame even to think.
    "Others think otherwise and answer thus,
According to their judgment: they agree
That when a thing's by free will done, as choice
Allows, then to what end it tends God knows,
And what will come of it; they also add
That He knows in what manner 'twill turn out.
Thus they would prove there's no necessity,
But rather possibility, because
He only knows to what end they will come
210 If they do thus and so or do it not.
He knows that of two roads each must take one,
Shunning the second, or the other choosing,
Yet not so absolutely but that things
Might not end otherwise, conceivably,
If by free will a man should choose to act.
    "How dare they say this? How dare so despise?
Such foresight only to allow to Him
As does but dubiously a thing perceive
And knows the truth but ineffectually!
220 They'd let Him know the effect of every deed
But never know 'twould not be otherwise;
And, if another end ensued than that
He had foreseen, as I have pointed out,
His prescience were deceived as if it judged
No better than opinion fallible.
    "Others have gone about it differently,
And many accept their logic when they say
Of what occurs by possibility
That all comes by necessity on earth
230 As far as God's concerned, not otherwise;
For absolutely—ever without fail—
Howe'er free will may act—He knows all things

Before they happen, and what ends they'll have.
Doubtless they speak the truth; for all agree
Upon the fact that He has needful wit—
Forever free from any ignorance—
To know how everything will come about.
There's no constraint on either man or God;
His knowledge of all possibilities,
240 And of the sum and substance of all things,
Out from His goodness, might, and wisdom come,
Before which attributes naught can be hid.
A man would lie who said necessity
Compelled him; for, I dare assert, 'tis not
God's prescience that compels a thing to be,
Nor yet the fact that something will occur
That gives Him prescience. His omnipotence,
His goodness, His omniscience give him that;
He cannot be deceived in any thing,
250 Or blind to it, for He knows all the truth.
    "He who would ambulate the shortest road
In trying to make clear this reasoning,
Which is quite difficult to understand,
Some simple illustration should employ
For laymen who may be illiterate;
For such folk something obvious require
Without much glossing or much subtlety.
    "Suppose a man by free will undertakes
Some task, or, fearing that someone will see
260 And shame him for it, fails to carry through
The work in full accordance with his need,
And no one knows of it before the task
Is done—or left, if he forsake the work;
A man who afterward learns of the thing
Would place thereon neither necessity
Nor, to be sure, constraint. If he had known
Even before, if he took no offense
But merely was informed of what was done,
His information by no means deters
270 The other one from doing what he will
Or having done what most convenient seems;
Or, on the other hand, from stopping work

If it is his free will to leave the task.
Thus he can do or from his deed abstain.
    "So God more nobly and more surely knows
The future facts and to what end they tend,
Howe'er the affair may be in the free will
Of the performer, who the power holds
Of free election, and inclines this way
280 Or that, led by his folly or good sense.
However they are compassed and performed,
God knows the things accomplished; and He knows
The reason why some people leave their work
For shame or other cause rightly or not,
According as they're influenced by free will.
I'm very certain that there many are
Who turn from crime to which they are inclined,
And some—though few they be—abandon sin
And, for the love of God, lead virtuous lives,
290 Learning refinement, grace, and courtesy.
Others, tempted to evil, though they think
They will no hindrance find, nevertheless
Curb their desires, fearing remorse or shame.
All this as though displayed before His eyes
God clearly sees, and all conditions knows
Of all intentions and of every deed.
Naught can be kept from Him or hid awhile;
For howsoever distant it may be
It's seen by God as if before Him placed.
300 Though it occurred ten, twenty, thirty—yes,
Five hundred or a thousand—years ago,
In town or country, honestly or not,
It is to Him as if it were today;
In plainest show it always has appeared
Within the everlasting mirror clear
Which none but He knows how to polish bright
Without detracting somewhat from free will.
This mirror is Himself, whence all things spring.
In this fair, shining glass, which e'er remains
310 Within His presence, He sees every act
That will occur as though it present were:
He sees where souls that serve Him loyally

Will go; and of the ones who have no care
For loyalty and truth He sees the fate.
According to the works that they perform,
Salvation or damnation He assigns,
Within His mind, to each. Prescience divine
This is—what we predestination call—
That knows all things and nothing needs to guess,
320 That knows how to extend its grace to us
When our intention to do good appears,
Yet free will's power by no means circumvents;
For right or wrong each man does by free will.

   "This is man's present vision. He who'd frame
The definition of eternity
Would call it having whole and perfect life
Unending and uninterruptable.

   "But this world's ordinance, which God has fixed
By His wise providence, He must maintain,
330 Through universal causes, to the end.
These necessarily must be such ones
As shall persist throughout all time to come.
Ever the stars their transmutation make
And by their revolutions force exert,
By necessary influence, on things
Enclosed within terrestrial elements,
As they receive the light that on them falls;
And all things that have power to give new life
Bring forth their likenesses, or hybrid forms,
340 By mingling of complexions natural
According as they have affinities.
He who must die will die; but he will live
Long as he can. By natural desire
The hearts of some would lie in lazy ease—
This one in virtue, that in wickedness.

   "But yet perhaps not always is man's fate
Pursued according to the stars' design,
If something interferes with the events
Which always would the guiding stars obey
350 Were they not turned aside by chance or will.
All men are ever tempted to do that
Toward which their hearts incline, but do not reach

Inevitably the end toward which they're drawn.
So I concede that destiny may be
A disposition subpredestinate
Applied to variable human hearts
As they are found most easily inclined.
    "Perhaps predestinate a man might seem,
Up from the moment of his birth, to be
360 Valiant and bold in all of his concerns
And wise and generous and debonair—
Renowned for attributes of gentlemen—
With friends and wealth enough—or might appear
Foredoomed to adverse fortune all his days.
Let him beware what kind of life he leads;
For all may be, by good or ill, reversed.
If he knows that he's close or miserly,
Let him bethink himself that no such man
Is truly rich, and with sufficiency
370 Let him content himself, and reason take
As a defense against his natural bent.
With generous heart let him bestow and spend
Money and food and clothes. But let him not
Acquire the name of foolish prodigal.
He should beware of avarice, which leads
A man to hoard his goods, and makes him live
In such a torment that he's not content
With anything; for it constricts and blinds
And lets him do no good, and makes him lose
380 All virtue, if he gives its promptings heed.
So may a man, if he be not a fool,
Guard against other vices which would turn
His heart from virtuous life—make him go wrong.
But free will has such potency for one
Who knows himself aright, that he his path
May always guarantee, howe'er the stars
Would have him go, if he can but perceive
Within his heart that vice would master him;
For he who could foreknow what deeds the stars
390 Would have him do might easily forfend.
Suppose the heavens should desiccate the air
So that all men were like to burn to death;

If they knew in advance, they'd build new homes
In marshlands or upon the riverbanks,
Or caverns excavate within the earth
Where they could hide themselves, nor fear the heat.
Or if they could foresee that some great flood
Would come in later times, the ones who knew
Some refuge could in season leave the plains
400 And seek the mountains, or could build great ships
In which to save themselves amidst the flood.
    "That is what formerly Deucalion
And Pyrrha did, escaping in a skiff,
On which embarked they braved the waters' wrath.
When finally they safely reached a port
And saw the world stagnant in marshy plains—
And then the valleys when the waters sank—
And realized that now no lord was there
Or lady in the world, but just themselves,
410 Deucalion and his wife to worship went
In Themis' temple. She the goddess was
Who passed her judgment on all destinies.
Upon their knees they fell and counsel craved
From Themis, begging her to teach them how
They might renew the human lineage.
She listened to their plea, which proper was,
And told them they should cast their mother's bones
Behind them when they left the temple gates.
Pyrrha so bitter found this strange response
420 That to accept the counsel she refused,
And justified herself with this remark:
'No one should ever scatter or unearth   PYRRHA
His mother's bones.' But soon Deucalion
This explanation gave: 'Another sense   DEUCALION
I place upon the words; our mother's bones
Are stones, for our great mother is the earth,
And they are certainly the bones that we
Must throw behind us to restore our race.'
It was no sooner said than done. Straightway   NATURE
430 The stones Deucalion threw leapt up as men,
And women sprang from those that Pyrrha cast.
In soul and body they were all complete

As Themis promised, whispering in their ears.
Now since the race no other parents knew
Than stones, in them there always will appear
A certain hardness. Thus they wisely worked
Who in a skiff their lives saved from that flood
As anyone foreknowing might have done.

   "Suppose a famine came, and all the crops
440 So badly failed that men were like to starve
Because of lack of grain. Foreknowing ones,
Two years, or three, or four before the time,
Might store up grain enough to overcome
The hunger of all people high and low
When finally there came a time of dearth,
As Joseph did in Egypt, with good sense
And foresight saving such a store of grain
That all might their salvation find therein
And, free from hunger and misease, survive.

450   "Or could men but foresee when killing cold
In winter would unreasonably appear,
They might take care to lay in store of clothes
And pile up firewood in great wagonloads
To feed their chimney fires; and they might strew
Their homes with clean, white straw from out the barn,
And close the doors and windows, and so be
Within their habitations safe and sound.
Kept warm by heated stoves, they might engage
All nude in bawdy dances if they wished;
460 And when they heard the windy tempests rage,
Seizing and binding every stream with ice,
And hailstones fall, killing the pastured beasts,
Though menaced, they might laugh at all the threats
Of storm and cold, and, caroling within,
From peril quite protected and set free,
So fortified, might mock the elements.

   "But, unless God performed a miracle
By vision or by oracle, no man,
I am quite sure, unless astrology
470 Taught him to know the functions of the stars
And their diverse positions in the sky
And on what climes their greatest influence falls,

Could know future events by wit or wealth.
   "If bodies are so strong as to escape
The stars' unwholesome influence, and thus
Negate their labors and protect themselves
Against them, still more powerful must be
The soul than any body, for its force
Stirs and informs with life the lifeless form
480 Which without it would be inanimate.
More easily and better, by the use
Of good intelligence, free will avoids
Whatever thing might bring the soul to grief;
Only what it allows may cause it woe.
'Twere well to learn by heart this fact: that man
Is for his own misease responsible;
Occasions only are exterior trials.
If man knows his estate and has regard
For his nativity, he may scorn fate.
490 What is this sermon worth? It says that man,
Whatever be for him predestinate,
Is over every destiny supreme.
   "I might more fully destiny discuss—
Fortune and chance I might discriminate—
And willingly I would expound it all,
Refuting more as more might be opposed,
And many illustrations I might give;
But ere I finished it would prove too long.
Consult some clerk who reads and understands.
500   "I should be silent now, and certainly
I'd talk no more but that I must explain
More fully, lest my enemy should say,
When he hears me thus make complaint of him,
To overcome his great disloyalty
In blaming his creator, that my wish
Is wrongly to defame him. I have heard
Him say that he has no free will to choose,
For God by His prevision holds him so
In full subjection that his every thought
510 And deed is governed but by destiny—
That, if he wills to lead a virtuous life,
'Tis but God's doing; if to sin he turns,

It is because he is compelled by God
More firmly far than if he by the hand
Led him and made him do whate'er he does:
All sin, almsgiving, blasphemy, fair speech,
Marriage or reconcilement, right or wrong.
 " 'Thus must it be,' says one; 'God brought to birth
This woman for this man, nor may he have
520 Another spouse by bribe or trickery;
He destined was for her.' Then, if the match
Is badly made, though one of them should be
Insane, and someone protest makes, and blames
Those who arranged and gave it their consent,
The senseless one replies: 'To God we owe
This marriage; 'twas His will that things go thus;
Doubtless 'twas He who brought this all about.'
He swears that things could not be otherwise.
 "No, no; this explanation is a lie!
530 The true God would not serve folk such a sauce;
He can do nothing false, and would not make
Them give consent to such unholy banns.
'Twas from themselves the crazy thought arose
To countenance such evil and perform
Such wicked works, from which they should abstain;
And easily they could abstain from them
If they but knew themselves. Let them address
Their prayers to God. If they give Him their love,
He'll love them in return. The only way
540 Wisely to love is fully to know oneself.
 "Dumb beasts, of reason void and destitute,
Are naturally ignorant of self;
But, if they were endowed with speech and sense
To understand each other and themselves,
It would go hard with man. Maned coursers fair
Would never let themselves be curbed with bit
Or mounted by the knights—no ox would place
His horned head beneath the plowshare yoke—
No ass or mule or camel would transport
550 A burden for the masters they'd despise
As hardly worth a cake—no elephant,
Who with his trunk can blow and trumpet loud

And feed himself at morning and at night
As well as can a man with his two hands,
Would bear a castle high upon his back—
No cat or dog would serve, for well enough
They could support themselves without mankind—
Bears, wolves, and lions, leopards and wild boars
Would strangle all mankind; and even rats
560 Would choke men in their trundle beds at night—
No bird would risk his skin at any call,
But pick men's eyes out as they lay asleep.
And if man answered with a careful scheme
To overthrow them all with armament—
With helms and hauberks, bows and arbalests,
And hardy swords—so animals might plan.
Are there no apes and monkeys who could make
Themselves good coats of mail of skin or steel,
And even doublets? Since they use their hands,
570 They'd hesitate at nothing, and so armed
They would not be inferior to man.
They might, indeed, the art of writing learn!
Their efforts would not be so much in vain
That all together they could not succeed
To learn the military art, and forge
Artillery that men might grievous find.
Even the fleas and earwigs might annoy
Most seriously if they could penetrate
Within man's ears as he lay fast asleep.
580 Bugs and nits and flesh worms oft attack
So boldly that a man must leave his work
To beat them down and drive the pests away;
He twists and dodges, jumps and skips about,
Struggles and scratches, till at last he strips
His clothes and shoes off, he is so pursued.
Even the flies that light upon man's food
And at the table oft assail his face
Great danger sometimes bring, and never care
Whether their victim be a king or page.
590 Ants and little vermin could become
A great annoyance if they knew their power.
From their own nature comes their ignorance.

But reasonable creatures—mortal men
And heavenly angels—all owe praise to God.
If they like fools refuse to know themselves,
The fault comes from their wickedness and vice,
Which dull their senses and intoxicate;
Whereas they easily might use free will
And follow reason. If a man does not,
600 There's nothing he can give as his excuse.
    "It is because of this I've said so much
And brought to bear so many arguments:
That I would all their quarreling suppress
And for a refutation leave no further grounds."

83. Nature explains the influence of the heavens
[17875–18152]

"NOW, to pursue my first intent, which I   NATURE
Would fain fulfill, that was to state the grief
Which troubles me in body and in soul,
This matter I'll discuss no more, but turn
Back to the heavens that well their duty do
To creatures who receive their influence
According to their divers substances.
    "They make the contrary winds inflame the air
And shriek and howl and burst on many a place
10 In thunder and in vivid lightning flash;
The trumpets, kettledrums, and tambourines
Of the celestial orchestra they sound
So loudly that the vapors which they raise
Disrupt the very clouds, whose bellies burst
With heat engendered by the thunderbolts
Which horribly in tournaments engage
And shake the very earth and raise the dust,
Bell towers and turrets overwhelming quite—
And many an ancient tree so lash and beat
20 That it is torn, uprooted, from the ground,

Its roots, no matter how they were attached,
Availing naught to keep the trunk upright
Or save the branches wholly or in part.
   "Some say the demons bring all this about
With hooks and cables, or with teeth and nails;
But such an explanation is not worth
Two turnips; those accepting it are wrong,
For nothing but the tempest and the wind
Are needed to explain the havoc wrought;
30 These are the things that cause the injury—
Blow down the grain and shrivel up the vines,
Knock flowers and fruit from trees and shake them so
That naught stays on the branches till it's ripe.
   "The heavens make the air at divers times
Weep heavy tears; the clouds such sorrow feel
That they divest themselves of all their clothes.
They do not care a straw for those black cloaks
That they have worn, but tear them piecemeal off,
So much they've given themselves up to their grief.
40 As if one murdered them, they shed their tears
So thick and fast, and so profoundly weep,
That they cause streams to overflow their banks
And flood the fields—the neighboring forests sack
With their outrageous, inundating waves.
Destruction of the grain makes hard times come;
Then the poor men who cultivate the fields
Give themselves up to anguish, all hope lost.
But, when the rivers break their banks, the fish
Which, as is reasonable and right, pursue
50 The streams, like lords and masters wandering,
Go feeding 'mongst the vineyards or o'er fields
And meadows; toward the ash trees, oaks, and pines
They dash, and disinherit savage beasts
From their estates and manors, swimming free.
Bacchus and Ceres, Pan and Cybele
Are much enraged when they see troops of fish
Invading, on the fin, their happy homes.
With heavy hearts satyrs and fairies lose
Their charming groves to inundating floods.
60 The nymphs lament their fountains; when they find

Them full and overflowing, covered quite
With river water, they resent their loss.
Wood sprites and dryads are so sick with grief
That they all think they're ruined when they see
Their woods cut off, and of the river-gods
Complain that they new villainy have wrought
Upon them, undeserving innocents,
Who naught have done to merit such abuse.
The fish are guests in many a neighboring town,
70 Low lying by the river, where they find
The miserable guest rooms poor and vile;
But there is not a cellar or a barn,
Or any place so costly or so dear,
That they therein do not install themselves;
The temples and the churches they invade,
And rob of services the deities;
From dim-lit chambers they chase household gods
And for their images have scant respect.
     "But when good weather comes and drives away
80 The bad, the heavens, which are displeased and bored
In time of rain and tempest, clear the air
Of all its wrath and make it laugh with joy;
Then, when the clouds perceive that they are fed
With such rejoicing air, they smile again,
After their mourning trim and deck themselves,
To be more fair and pleasing, in bright robes
Of many colors, and their fleeces dry
Beneath the sun's most pleasant, cheerful rays,
And take advantage of the weather bright
90 And clear to comb them in the open air;
And then they spin their wool, and when it's spun
Draw out great needlefuls of snowy thread
As if they were about to lace their sleeves.
And then, when they take heart again to go
On a long pilgrimage, they hitch up steeds
And mount and ride like mad o'er hill and vale;
For Æolus, as he is called, the god
Of winds, when he has safely harnessed them
(For there's no other charioteer who knows
100 The way to manage horses such as they),

Puts on their feet such wings as birds ne'er had.
   "Straightway the air then dons the mantle blue
Which she in India is wont to wear,
And dressed in it prepares to look her best,
As for a festival, while she awaits,
In fine array, the absent clouds' return.
They, meanwhile, to give solace to the earth,
And that they may be ready for a hunt,
Are wont to bear, ready at hand, a bow
110 Or two or even three if they prefer,
The which celestial arcs are rainbows called,
Regarding which nobody can explain,
Unless he teaches optics in some school,
How they are varicolored by the sun,
How many and what sorts of hues they show,
Wherefore so many and such different kinds,
Or why they are displayed in such a form.
Such teacher should take care to read the book
Of Aristotle, who has more observed
120 Of nature than has any other man
Since times of Tubal Cain. An optics book
Was written by Alhazen, of the line
Of Huchaïn, which none but fools neglect.
He who would well this rainbow understand
Should study this, and he should be, besides,
A good observer and a careful judge
And learned in nature and geometry,
Knowledge of which is most prerequisite
For one who would the book on optics con.
130 Therein he'll find explained the mirror's powers
And why a glass can make the smallest things—
Grains of powdered sand, or letters small—
Seem great, and to the observer bring them close:
Enable him to choose among them all
And count them, or to read the smallest script
From so far off that one who has not seen
Would not believe the tale of him who knows
The causes and observes their great effects.
This need not be accepted on belief,
140 For knowledge of it such a one can gain.

   "If Mars and Venus, ere they went to bed
And as they there together lay were trapped,
Had looked in such a glass, so held that they
Could in it see the bed, they had escaped
The subtle, tenuous net that Vulcan made
And set for them, of which they nothing knew,
But in which they were captured and enmeshed.
For though that net had been of workmanship
Finer than spiderweb, it had been seen
150 And Vulcan had been foiled, for never they
Would then have gone to bed, if they perceived
Each thread more thick and longer, seemingly,
Than some great beam. Then Vulcan, wicked wretch,
Raging with anger and with jealous ire,
Never had proven their adultery,
Nor would the gods have known of the affair
If Mars and Venus had such glasses used,
For they immediately had fled the room
When they perceived the network spread for them,
160 And they had run to find some other place
To lie, where their amour had been concealed,
Or else they had contrived some other scheme
All mishap to avoid, and shame and grief.
Now, by your faith, have I not told the truth
In all these matters you've heard me confess?"
   "Yes, certainly," replied the priest. "That glass,   GENIUS
To tell the truth, had useful been to them;
For elsewhere they could easily conjoin
When once they knew their peril; or with sword,
170 Were it well made, strong Mars, the god of war,
Could certainly have cut the net apart
And so had vengeance on the jealous spouse,
And on that selfsame bed made Venus feel
That she was safe, without the care to find
Another place, unless one near at hand
Within the very room, upon the floor.
Then, if by some unfortunate mischance,
Which had been hard, indeed, Vulcan had come
Upon them while Mars held her in his arms,
180 Venus is smart enough (all women are

Most clever in intrigue), soon as she heard
Her husband at the door, to cover up
Her nakedness in time, and find defense
Against what accusation he might bring,
Offering some plausible excuse
Why Mars had come to visit in their home,
And swearing to whate'er he made her say,
Provided that she robbed him of his proof
And made him necessarily believe
190 That none of his malicious thoughts were true.
Nay, though his very eyes had seen her sin,
She might convince him that his sight was bad.
She knows how to employ a double tongue,
Twisting this way and that to find excuse;
For there's no creature can more hardily
Than women commit perjury and lie.
So Mars must have retired discomfited."

"Most certainly, sir priest, you've spoken well, NATURE
Like one who's worthy, courteous, and wise.
200 Too much of subtlety and craftiness
The hearts of women harbor. He's a fool
Or ignoramus who doubts not their guile,
And never shall he be excused by me.
More boldly will they lie and falsely swear
Than any man, and even when they find
Themselves convicted of an obvious fault;
Indeed, especially when they are caught.
So I may honestly and well declare
That he who learns a woman's heart should be
210 Unboastful, for he'll ne'er know it so well
That it may not delude him in some way."

Here Nature and Genius seem to reach accord;
But ne'ertheless wise Solomon has said,
And I go by the truth in Scripture writ:

SOLOMON

"The man who one good woman finds is surely blest."

84. Nature expounds the properties of mirrors and glasses
[18153–18298]

"STILL other properties these glasses have,"   NATURE
Nature resumed, "and they are powerful;
For large things near at hand appear far off
As seen through them. Even the highest mount
Between Sardinia and France would seem so small
And so remote that he who looked for it
At longest leisure scarce could make it out.
    "Some other glasses truly show the size
Of things seen through them, if the man who looks
10 Is one who can manipulate them well.
    "Then there are glasses which will burn things up
When focused on them, if one knows but how
To bring together in a point the rays
Of sunlight shining brightly on the glass.
    "Some mirrors of material diverse
In various reflections things display—
Some upright, some reversed, and some stretched out—
And he who gains the mirror's mastery
Can make it one to many multiply:
20 For instance, in one visage show four eyes,
If he the right glass ready have to hand—
Or make phantasmic forms appears to one
Who looks therein—or even make appear
Outside, in air or water, living shapes.
A man may see them play before the eye
And mirror if the latter is composed
Of divers angles which depend upon
Whether the medium is a composite
Or simple—of one nature or diverse.
30 Sometimes the form's reversed or multiplied
By the responsive glass, so that it comes
In various phases to the observer's eyes,

According as the rays are variously
Absorbed by the material, and thus
The sight of the observer is deceived.
   "Aristotle knew these matters well,
Loving all science, and he cites this case:
A man fell ill with such a malady
As dimmed his eyesight—made the atmosphere
40 Seem dark and troubled. But where'er he went
He saw his face before him in the air.
Glasses, if unimpaired by obstacles,
Make many miracles appear. Their lack
Causes mistakes at divers distances;
For things far sundered may together seem
Or quite conjoined, or one thing may seem two,
By some diversity of view, or three
Seem six, or four seem eight, or less or more,
According as a man may please himself.
50 One who knows how to separate or bring
Closer together the focus of his eyes
May make a group of objects seem but one.
Glasses may make a very tiny man
Whom people call a dwarf appear to be
Big as ten giants, so that those who look
May shake with fear, although the little man
Could pass beneath the branches in a wood
And never break or even bend a bough.
Similarly a giant may appear
60 A dwarf to eyes abnormally deranged,
Which see a great diversity in things.
How many times when men have been deceived
By mirrors or the effect of distances
Which have made things appear as they are not,
They straightway to their neighbors run, and boast,
Not telling truth, but lies, that they have seen
The demons, so their eyes have been betrayed!
An eye diseased makes one thing seem like two—
Two candles where there's but a single one,
70 Or double moon in heaven. There is no man
Who sees so well that he may never be
Deceived in vision; wherefore many things

Have been adjudged quite other than they are.
　"It is not now my purpose to explain
The figures of these mirrors, or to say
How they reflect the rays that on them fall.
You'll find that written elsewhere in a book.
Nor do I wish their angles to describe;
Nor tell why images of things observed
80 In glasses are reversed before the eyes
Of anyone who gazes on them there,
Nor how they cause deception, nor the grounds
For their appearances. Nor do I wish,
Dear priest, to tell where all such images
Their being have—without or in the glass.
Moreover, I'll forbear to analyze
The other visions just as marvelous—
Pleasing and dolorous—that come to man
Quite unexpectedly, to know if they
90 Objective are or only in the mind.
I'll none of this unfold, for it is now
No part of my intent; so silently
I'll pass it by, with other things I named
But never did expound. 'Twould surely be
Too big a subject, and a grievous one
To talk about, and hard to understand,
Especially for laymen, unless I
Confined myself to generalities.
Lay folk could not believe the facts are true,
100 Especially of glasses which produce
Such different effects, unless they saw
The instruments themselves, and had a clerk
Willing to show them and to demonstrate
That they might have this knowledge marvelous.
Indeed, the vulgar could not give belief
To demonstrations one might make for them,
So grand and wonderful the visions are.
Nor the deceptions could they realize
That from such visions come, and much amaze
110 Many a man while sleeping or awake.
Therefore I'll pass them by. I would not tire
Myself to speak or you to hear of them;

For all prolixity 'twere well I should avoid."

85. Nature discourses on dreams and frenzies
[18299–18606]

"WOMEN are likely to be troublesome   NATURE
And boresome in their talk; but I perceive
The truth so clearly that your leave I ask
To give you now some more particulars.
    "Many a man is so deceived by dreams
That, jumping from his bed, he dons his clothes
And shoes, and gathers all his other gear,
As if his common sense were still asleep
While all his other senses were awake.
10 He takes his staff and scrip or bill and bow
Or sickle and goes, traveling afar—
He knows not where; may even mount a steed
And ride o'er hill and dale through dust and mire,
Arriving at some unfamiliar place;
And, when his common sense at last awakes,
He marvels and is very much amazed.
When to his rightful state he has returned
And mingled with his neighbors, he declares—
And not at all as something fabulous—
20 That demons bore him off, removing him
From his own home; whereas it was himself.
    "Sometimes a frenzy seizes on a man
In illness; and, if he has lain alone
And is not guarded well, he may get up
And run away; nor does his wandering cease
Until he finds himself in some wild place—
A meadow, vineyard, or a wood—and there
He falls. When friends come, possibly quite late,
Because he had no nurse, or stupid ones,
30 From cold and illness he is found quite dead.
    "One often sees even a healthy man

Who lives unwisely or whose native bent
Inclines him oft to meditate too much
Or to be melancholy or to fear
Unreasonably, who pictures to himself
Apparitions numerous and strange—
Quite other than the ones we talked about
When we, too briefly, of the mirrors spoke.
These phantoms seem to him as good as real.
40   "Some will with great devotion meditate,
And too much meditation makes appear
Before them things of which they have but thought;
But they believe they see them openly.
    "This is but lying and deceit. Thus he
Who dreams believes that he before him sees
Substances spiritual, as Scipio
Once dreamed that he saw Hell and Paradise
And sky and air and sea and earth beneath
And all the things that are contained therein.
50 He sees the stars appear, and birds in flight,
The fish that swim the sea, and animals
Disporting in the woods and circling there
Gently and graciously. All sorts of men
He sees—some taking chamber joy, and some
The chase pursuing o'er the countryside
Through forests, vineyards, fallows, and tilled fields,
Over the mountains, by the riverbanks.
One dreams of pleas and judgments, or of wars
And tournaments, or caroling and dance,
60 And hears the citoles and the violins,
Smells spicy odors, tastes delicious food,
Feels his fair sweetheart (though she isn't there)
As if she really were within his arms.
Then perhaps Jealousy appears to him,
Her pestle on her shoulder, having learned
From Evil Tongue that they together are;
For he invents his tales before the facts,
Wherefore all lovers are by day alarmed.
When ardently they give their passion rein,
70 Those who lay claim to being lovers true
Have much to bear that's hard and dolorous.

(I know the symptoms by experience.)
In bed at night after they long have thought
Of her whom all day they've implored, she comes
Into their dreams, where rivals may appear,
Opposing them and causing dreariment.
If mortal hate possess their souls, they dream—
Associating contrary ideas
Or similar—of contests, quarrels, fights,
80 And all that appertains to war with those
Who caused their anger and are enemies.
If they've been put in prison for some crime,
They dream of pardons if they hope to gain
Deliverance; or, if they feel despair,
They dream of gallows tree and hangman's rope
Or other things as disagreeable
Which are by no means there, but in their minds.
But they think all are actualities,
And put on mourning or a festive mien
90 According to the dreams within their brains
Which, by the phantoms that the mind accepts,
All the five senses master with deceit.
    "Because of this some foolishly suppose
That sorceresses, wandering by night,
Are led by Dame Abundance; and they say
That one in three of all the children born
In all the earth displays her attributes,
And that three nights a week they issue forth,
As destiny directs, and force their way
100 Into each house, in spite of lock and bar
(For they can enter by a chink or crack
Or cat hole, since their souls have power to leave
Their bodies); and through dwellings and through yards
They wander with those fays that people call
Good Ladies. If for this belief one ask
The reason, folk reply that all the things
They see have never come to them in bed;
So it must be their souls that labor so
And thus go coursing over all the earth.
110 They would have us believe that while their souls
Are on these trips their bodies must not be

Turned over, or the souls no entry find
On their return. But monstrous foolishness
Is this, and quite impossible to trust.
The human body dies soon as the soul
Inhabits it no longer. Therefore they
Who thrice a week this sort of journey make
Thrice die and thrice revive each seven days.
Disciples of that convent may well claim
120 Great frequency of resurrection days!
    "I dare assert without an argument,
For well 'tis proved, no mortal man need die
More than one death; nor will he be revived
Until the day of judgment, unless God
Shall manifest some special miracle,
As in the case of holy Lazarus
We read about and do not contradict.
    "Now, on the other hand, when some men say
That if the soul the body once deserts
130 It never can get back if it should find
The body has been turned when it was gone,
Who would attempt such fable to maintain?
It must be that the liberated soul
Is freer, subtler, wiser than it was
When to its earthly body 'twas confined,
From which it e'er must its complexion take,
Which hinders it. Therefore the soul should gain
The entry, though the body had been turned,
More easily than exit theretofore.
140   "As to the statement that one third of all
The human race with Dame Abundance speed,
If this is true, as foolish old wives try
To prove by citing visions they have had,
Then, doubtless, all the world must speed with her;
For there's nobody who does not have dreams
Of truth or falsehood, not three times a week,
Perhaps, but five times every fifteen days,
Or more or less, perchance, as fancy wills.
    "I will not say that dreams are true or false,
150 Or whether men should all reject or none,
Or why, when one may be most horrible,

Another's most agreeable and fair,
According as the apparitions come
In various complexions of the mind
Resulting from a difference of age
Or habit; nor shall I attempt to say
If God sends revelations by such dreams,
Or if the evil spirits by them try
To tempt men to their peril. None of this
160 Will I discuss, but to my theme return.
  "I say, then, that the clouds, when they are worn
Or tired of casting arrows through the sky,
Which are more often wet than dry, for they
Are always watered with the rain and dew,
If heat has given them nothing dry to throw,
Consider that they have had sport enough
And all together they unbend their bows.
The fashion of the bows these archers bend
Is strange enough, for when they are unstrung
170 And sheathed, their colors straightway disappear;
We never see them use those bows again,
But if they wish to shoot another day
They make new bows, which nothing but the sun
Can color, for they'll take no other gloss.
  "The heavens' influence more wonders works,
Such powers they have on sea and land and air;
They make appear the comets, never fixed
In heaven but in the upper air aflame,
And once they have been formed their life is short.
180 Many a fable is of comets told:
Astrologers who such predictions make
Foretell the death of princes by their means.
But comets do not guard or cast their rays
Or throw their influence more strongly o'er
Great emperors than over common folk,
Or over commoners than over kings;
And we are certain that they hold their sway
O'er all earth's regions as they climates find
And men and beasts disposed to yield themselves
190 To the great influence stars and planets have.
Celestial powers have great significance,

And, as they find things subject to their force,
They often change the temper of affairs.
  "I do not say that any king should be
Considered richer than a common man
Who wends his way afoot. Sufficiency
Is wealth, and avarice is poverty.
Be he a king or man not worth two peas,
The more he covets things the poorer he.
200 Kings are like pictures, if we may believe
The Scriptures. He who wrote the *Almagest*
This illustration gives: he who would view
A picture best should never stand too near;
However pleasing it may be afar,
It loses something when too closely scanned.
And this of powerful friends is also true:
Lacking experience of acquaintanceship
A man would think their help and friendship sweet;
But one who's proved them well such bitterness
210 Will know that disappointment he will have,
So much to be discounted is their grace.
Horace describes their love and favor thus.
  "Princes unworthy are that stars should give
More warning of their deaths than of the ends
Of other men. Their bodies are not worth
An apple more than those of laborers
Or clerks or squires; for I make all alike,
As when they're born they one and all appear.
Equally naked they are brought to birth—
220 Highborn or low, and powerful or weak.
I place them all upon an equal plane
As far as human status is concerned.
Fortune may do the rest, but ne'er displays
Dependability; for she bestows
Her favors as she pleases, and on whom
She chooses, without care; and when she will
She takes away, or will take, all that she has given."

86. Nature discusses gentility
[18607–18946]

"IF ANYONE should dare to contradict   NATURE
What I have said, and vaunt his gentle birth
And name of gentleman, declaring he
Is better by nobility of race
Than those who cultivate the fields, and live
By their own labor, I should answer thus:
That no man's gentle who is not intent
On virtue, and that none ungentle are
Except by foolish outrage or by vice.
10   "Nobility comes from an upright heart;
Gentility of birth is nothing worth
If he who has it lacks goodheartedness.
In him the prowess should be shown of those
Who were his forebears, and their name achieved
By the good works to which they set themselves.
When from the world they went, they with them took
Their virtues, leaving only to their heirs—
Who nothing more could claim—their property.
These have their fathers' wealth, but nothing more—
20 No nobleness or worth—unless they do,
By reason of their virtue or good sense,
That which discloses true nobility.
  "A greater chance have learned men to be
Gentle and courteous and wise, than kings
And princes who may be illiterate.
This is the reason: clerks may find in books
By reason demonstrated—proved by lore—
The good they must pursue, the ill to flee.
Whate'er the world has known in word or deed
30 Has been recorded. In the ancient lives
Clerks see the wickedness of all the bad
And all the goodnesses of gentlemen

Who were compendiums of courtesy.
Briefly, they find recorded in their books
Whatever they should follow or eschew.
Disciple or master, therefore, every clerk
Is truly—or should be—a gentleman.
His evil heart's to blame if he is not;
For his advantages are greater far
40 Than those of men who hunt the forest deer.
No one is valued less than learned clerk
Whose soul lacks fineness and nobility
And who forsakes known virtues to pursue
That which he clearly sees is naught but vice.
Before the King of Heaven, worse punishment
That man should have, when he succumbs to sin,
Than any layman, simple and unwise,
Scorned by the clerks as underbred and vile,
Who may have never learned to read a book
50 In which the nobler virtues were set forth.
Although a prince may well know how to read,
He has so much to busy him that he
May have no time to study much or learn.
In their pursuit of true nobility
The clerks have some advantages more great
And fairer than those had by lords of land.
   "To make a conquest of gentility,
Than which pursuit naught is more honorable,
One should learn well this rule: he who would have
60 True nobleness must guard himself from pride
And, whether he choose the study or the field,
Be void of villainy and idleness.
Let him in heart be humble, courteous,
And gentle, in all places, toward all men
Except the enemies whom he has failed
To reconcile. All damsels and all dames
He ought to honor, but small confidence
Repose in them, for no one is too good,
However she may seem. Such gentleman
70 Should have the name of true gentility,
Honor, and praise—without reproof or blame.
No others can deserve so great renown.

"Knights strong in arms and courteous in speech
And, like Sir Gawain, doughty in their deeds,
Whom no one would inscribe among the weak,
Or like the good count Robert of Artois,
Who from the cradle practiced all his life
Nobility, largesse, and chivalry,
Nor e'er was pleased to take ignoble ease,
80 But rather was a man before his time—
Such knights, valiant and true and generous
And courteous and trustworthy in arms,
Should everywhere be welcomed, praised, and loved.

"Much should one honor, too, the learnèd clerks
Who labor with intelligence, and strive
To practice virtues set forth in their books.
Of such there many were in ancient days;
The names of ten or more I could recite—
Indeed, so many that the list would tire.
90 In former days the valiant gentlemen,
As they are called in literature—the kings,
Dukes, emperors, and counts, of whom I'll say
No more—honored the great philosophers.
Villas and gardens, honorable estates,
And many other most delightful gifts
They gave even to poets. Vergil was made
The Lord of Naples, a more lovely town
Than Lavardin or even Paris is.
Fair gardens in Calabria were given
100 To Ennius by friends in ancient times.
But why should I for more examples seek?
Well could I prove my point by many such,
Who, though lowborn, yet had much nobler souls
Than many a son of count or even king,
And so were rightly known as gentlemen;
But of all these I'll give you no account.
The times have come to such a pass that now
Good men who give their lives to learning's quest,
Becoming doctors of philosophy,
110 And journeying to many a foreign land,
Get into debt and suffer poverty,
And almost naked beg their barefoot way

In search of knowledge; yet they are not loved.
Less than an apple princes prize them now,
And yet they are far worthier gentlemen
(God grant I get no fever saying this!)
Than those who spend their time in hunting hares,
Or those whose sole ambition seems to be
The dung heaps of their fathers to maintain.
120   "Is he a gentleman who name and praise
Would have because he has inherited
Nobility from others, yet has not
Their merit and their prowess? I say, no!
Rather he should be deemed a villain wretch,
And less esteemed than son of vagabond.
I'll never flatter such a one as he
Though he were born the son of Alexander,
Who dared so much in arms and made such wars
That he became the lord of all the lands.
130 When those surrendered who had fought with him,
And others yielded without trial of arms,
With pride he was so swollen that he said
He found the world too small—no longer wished
To stay where he could scarcely turn around,
But longed to seek another, larger world
Where he might institute another war.
To gain more fame he smote the gates of Hell,
Whereat the devils trembled with alarm;
For they believed he was the destined one
140 Who, by the power of the wooden cross
Erected for the souls who die in sin,
Should break the gates of Hell, subdue their pride,
And from the pit deliver all His friends.
    "Let us suppose, though it could never be,
That I no gentleman to birth had brought
And that of common folk I had no care,
What would gentility then have been worth?
A man who strives to comprehend the truth
Must certainly agree that there's no good
150 In it unless a man would emulate
The prowess of his noble ancestors.
In this attempt should live each gentleman

Who would show semblance of gentility,
Unless he'd steal nobility, and have
The credit for it without real desert;
For I make bold to assert this axiom:
Gentility confers no other good
Upon a man but the necessity
Of his performing deeds befitting it.
160 Know well that no man merits having praise
By virtue of the good in someone else;
Nor does he merit blame for others' sins.
Honor to him to whom the honor's due!
But he who does no good—in whom are found
Depravity, ill-humor, villainy,
Lying, blustering, and boastfulness,
Vanity, deceit, and insolence,
Uncharitableness, and lack of alms,
Stinginess, and negligence (alas,
170 Too many of this sort a man may find!)—
Though born of parents whose good deeds shine clear,
Does not, of right, deserve to have the name
His ancestry confers; but he should be
Considered viler than those lower born.
    "No person of intelligence denies
That there exists a mighty difference,
As touching unrestrained philanthropy,
Between a man of sense and nobleness
Who gains his reputation by his worth
180 And one who spends his life in toil to gain
Great property and wealth and ornaments.
For he who has a great desire to work
To gain such money, jewelry, and land,
Though he a hundred thousand marks in gold,
Or even more, amass, may leave it all
To whomsoever of his friends he will.
But he who works to gain such other things
As I have mentioned, which are merited,
Cannot be led by friendship to do that;
190 For he cannot bequeath them anything.
Can he bequeath them knowledge? Not at all;
Nor his renown, nor his gentility.

But he may teach them how to gain all these
If they will take example from his life.
They are no better than mere idle oafs
Who boast nobility that others own.
They do not tell the truth, but rather lie,
And steal the name of gentleman, when they
To their good parents no resemblance show.
200   "Whereas as equals I bring men to birth,
If they wish any other nobleness
Than what I give them, which is fine enough—
Their native frankness, that I grant to all,
With reason, which is given them by God,
Who, in His wisdom and His goodness, makes
Them like Himself and like the angel host,
Excepting for the difference that's made
By their mortality—they must acquire,
If they are worthy, new gentility;
210 And, if they can't achieve it by themselves,
They'll ne'er be gentlemen by other means.
I make exception of no count or king.
A carter, cobbler, swineherd might be shamed
To have a son who proved a reprobate:
But greater shame it is for any prince
To be offensive, vicious, or a fool.
Had he the offspring of some coward been,
Who by the fire, all dusty, sat at home,
It had been more to valiant Gawain's praise
220 Than if he had a coward been himself
And noble Renoart had had as sire.
    "But it's no fable that a prince's death
Is than a peasant's much more notable,
And when his body lying dead is found
More widespread is the rumor of the event.
Therefore the simple folk suppose that when
They see a comet it is for a prince;
But if all men were equal on the earth
In peace or war, and there was neither king
230 Nor prince to reign in province or in realm,
Still would celestial bodies, when they come
In proper influence to do such work,

At proper times bring comets into birth,
If but the air sufficiency supply
Of right material to nourish them.
The simple folk consider them to be
Like flying dragons scattering twinkling stars
Which, as they fall, descend from out the skies.
But reason holds that nothing from the heavens
240 Can fall, for there exists in heavenly things
Nothing corruptible; but all is firm
And strong and stable. Naught that touches them
Can break them or leave imprint on their forms;
Nor yet can aught their substances invade,
However sharp or subtle it may be,
Unless it were a spiritual thing
Like light, the rays of which may well pass through
And do no harm or damage to the heavens.
By various influences they produce
250 Hot summers, freezing winters; and they make
Fall snow or hail in large or tiny flakes;
And, by their oppositions, other weather,
According as they separate or join.
When in the sky he sees eclipses come,
Many a man is very much dismayed
Or thinks himself in a precarious state
From loss of influence which seems to fail
When some familiar planet disappears;
But, if he knew why they were lost to sight,
260 No longer would he be measurably disturbed."

87. Nature absolves the heavens, elements, plants,
birds, animals, and insects
[18947-19020]

"IN windy war the ocean waves are raised   NATURE
And foam-lipped breakers kiss the very clouds;
Then peace comes o'er the sea, which roars no more,

And stills its bounding billows, but for tides
Which ebb and flow, by influence of the moon
Compelled to motion; naught can hinder them.
If more profoundly one investigate
The miracles that heavenly bodies cause
Upon the earth, he'll find in them so much
10 That's marvelous that never he'll succeed
To put it all in writing in a book.
So I acquit the heavens of revolt
Against me, for by their beneficence
They do so much of good that I perceive
That duly all their duty they fulfill.

  "Nor do I of the elements complain;
For my commandments fully they obey,
Blending and resolving, each in turn.
All is corruptible beneath the moon;
20 Naught is so nourished that it cannot rot.
By their own composition and the intent
Of nature all must follow this fixed law
Which never fails: all whence it comes returns.
So general this rule, it cannot fail
To function in respect to elements.

  "Nor do I of the vegetable world
Complain. The plants are never slow to heed
My will, but are attentive to my laws.
Long as they live they spread their roots and leaves—
30 Expand in trunk and branches, flower and fruit.
Each year each one produces what it can,
As herb or bush or tree, until it dies.

  "Nor do I of the fish and fowl complain.
They are most fair to see, and well they know
And follow all my rules. Good scholars they!
All tug the traces fastened to my yoke.
They breed according to their several wonts,
And thus do honor to their lineage.
Great comfort 'tis to see how each of them
40 Strives to prevent his race from dying out.

  "Nor do I of the animals complain,
Who bow their heads continually to earth
And never warfare wage against my rule.

All do my service as their fathers did.
Each male goes with his female, and they mate
Fairly and pleasingly, and in their joy
Their young engender, coupling just as oft
As may seem good to them. No bargaining
Delays their union when they're in accord.
50 With courtesy that is most debonair
It pleases each to do the other's will;
And all for what they do feel amply paid
By blessings that upon them I bestow.
So do my fairest insects: flies and ants
And butterflies. Even the worms that breed
In rottenness cease not to keep my laws.
Adders and snakes are studious to do my work."

88. Nature denounces mankind
[19021–19334]

"MANKIND alone, to whom I've freely given   NATURE
All blessings that I know how to bestow—
Mankind alone, whom I have so devised
And made that he toward Heaven turns his face—
Mankind alone, whom I have brought to birth
Bearing the very likeness of his God—
Mankind alone, for whom I toil and moil,
Who is the very culmination of my work,
Who has no more, except what I have given,
10 As to his body, in his trunk and limbs,
Than what a ball of pomander would buy,
And, as to soul, but just one single thing:
For, as I may assert who am his dame,
He has from me in body and in soul
Three energies—existence, feeling, life—
Of great advantage to the wretch if he
Were wise and good, for he's provided well
With all the good things God has placed on earth—

Companion he to creatures everywhere
20 And sharer of the blessings they enjoy—
Being he owns in common with the stones;
Life he enjoys in common with the herbs;
Feeling he has in common with the beasts;
Thinking in common with the angel host
He has, excelling all the others thus
(What more need I enumerate of him?)
He has whatever humans can conceive;
He is a microcosm in himself—
Yet worse than any wolf cub uses me.

30   "Man's understanding I well recognize
As something not provided him by me;
My jurisdiction does not stretch to that.
I'm neither wise nor powerful enough
To make a creature so intelligent.
Whate'er I make is mortal; I create
Nothing that lasts throughout eternity.
Plato gives testimony when he speaks
Of my domain and of the deathless gods.
They're kept by their Creator, and maintained
40 Eternally, and by His will alone;
For they would die if not sustained by Him.
'Perishable are Nature's works,' he says;   PLATO
'Her power is but obscure and weak, compared
To that of God, who in His presence sees,
In one eternal moment, present, past,
And future—triple temporality.'
God is the king and emperor who tells   NATURE
The other gods that He their father is,
According to the words that Plato wrote,
50 Which in modern tongue this signify:
'O gods, I am your maker and your sire;   GOD
Creator and the God of gods am I;
You are my creatures and my handiwork;
By Nature you are mortal, but I make
My works to be immortal by my will;
For nothing made by Nature can but fail,
In season due, however carefully
She fashion it; but whatsoever God

Joins and rules with good intelligence
60 Is wise and good and strong without a flaw;
He never willed nor wills that it dissolve
Or to corruption come. So I conclude
That, though you had by your Creator's will
Beginning of your being, and by that
Engendered were and formed, and still are kept
And will be kept, yet not completely you
Are freed from dissolution and from death;
For I should see you dying, one and all,
If I did not sustain you. You would die
70 By nature if I did not will your life.
My will has jurisdiction o'er the threads
Of life for you, which bind your being fast;
Thence comes your hope of immortality.'
       "This is the substance of what Plato wrote,   NATURE
Who better far might dare to write of God,
Since he more prized and feared Him, than might all
The rest of worldly old philosophers.
But certainly he could not say enough;
For he could never fully understand
80 The mystery that could not be explained
Till comprehended in the virgin womb.
Yet doubtless she whose womb was swollen thus
Knew more of it than even Plato could;
For just as soon as she perceived she bore
That comfortable weight, she knew that it
Must be that marvelous, eternal sphere
Whose center would be fixed in every place
But whose circumference would nowhere be;
She knew it was the mystic triangle
90 Whose angles superpose in unity
So that the three are one and one is three.
Triangular the circle is, or else
The triangle is round, that found a home
Within the Virgin. Plato did not know
So much as that; no trinal unity
In that most simple trinity he saw
(Nor deity hid in a human skin).
It was the God who Maker calls Himself

Who planned and formed the intelligence of man
100 And gave it to him. How was God repaid?
Most badly, for man thought he could deceive
His God, though really he deceived himself.
Because of this my Lord came to His death,
Having, without my aid, assumed man's flesh,
To rescue that poor wretch from punishment.
I know not how, without me, He became
A mortal man, except that His command's
Omnipotent; and much I was amazed
When He was of the Virgin Mary born,
110 And then, incarnate, hanged upon the cross
For wretched man; since it could never be
By Nature that a virgin could give birth.
And yet by Jews and Paynims, formerly,
This incarnation had been prophesied
To ease men's hearts and give them greater faith
That what was prophesied would come to pass.
In Vergil's books, *Bucolics* called, we read
The Sibyl's saying, by the Holy Ghost
Inspired, 'New lineage has now been sent   SIBYL
120 From Heaven above to us on earth below,
Upon the proper road to set the feet
Of such men as have gone astray, and end
The iron age and bring the age of gold.'
And even Albumazer testifies   NATURE
That he knew well that in the virgin sign
A worthy maiden should be born, who'd be
A virgin and a mother both at once
And give her father suck, and lie beside
Her husband, who'd not know her carnally.
130 He who will seek in Albumazer's book,
Where 'twill be found ready to meet his eye,
May read this statement. Therefore Christian folk
Every September hold a holiday
Commemorating that nativity.
     "Jesus, our Lord, knows how I've worked for man,
As what I've said would indicate. I've had
That labor for the wretch; he is the end
And consummation of my work. And yet

The traitorous renegade is satisfied
140 With nothing I can do, and he alone
Thinks he's ill paid. Against my rules he works.
What further can I say? What is the use?
I've honored him more than I can recount,
Yet countless and immeasurable shames
He heaps upon me, thus repaying me!
Fair chaplain, gentle priest, is it then right
That I should reverence and love a wretch
Whom I have found in such a way of life?
Therefore, so help me God the Crucified,
150 I much regret that e'er I made mankind.
But, by the death He suffered on the Cross
Whom Judas kissed, Longinus pierced with lance,
Man's fall I will recount before that God
Who when he first was in God's image made
Gave him to me, since that he thwarts me so.
As I'm a woman, I canot keep still
But will tell all, for women naught conceal.
I'll shame him as he ne'er was shamed before.
Evil the day when he deserted me!
160 His vices I'll recite, and tell the truth.
   "Man is a boastful thief and murderer—
A tricky felon, covetous and mean—
A glutton, evil-mouthed and desperate—
A hateful, spiteful, lying miscreant—
An envious forger and a perjured fool—
A changeful, silly, vain idolater—
Disgusting traitor and false hypocrite—
A lazy sodomite. In brief, the wretch
So simple is he makes himself a slave
170 To all the vices—gives them harborage,
And of them forges chains more strong than steel.
Does he not purchase death who to such sins
Devotes himself? And since all things must go
Back to their source, when man shall stand before
His Maker, whom he should forever serve
And honor with his best ability,
And keep himself from sin, how can he dare
To look his Lord and Master in the face?

And with what eye will He who is the Judge
180 Regard mankind, disloyal proved to be
Toward Him, and found to be in such default,
Poor wretch, whose heart is so infirm and weak
That with his talent he can do no good?
Saving their honors, both the small and great
Do but the very worst that they know how,
As if together they had sworn an oath;
But honor is not saved to anyone
By such a vow, which should instead result
In death or suffering or worldly shame.
190 What can the caitiff think when he reviews
His crimes as he shall stand before the Judge
Whose sentence none can circumvent or dodge,
Who sums and weighs all things in equity
And does no wrong? What fate can he expect
Except a halter knotted at his throat
To drag him to be miserably hanged
Upon a gibbet tree in deepest Hell,
Where first he will be bound in iron chains
Welded to an adamantine ring
200 Before the prince of all the lower world?
There in a caldron he will scalded be,
Or roasted front and back on glowing coals
Or on a grill, or pinned like Ixion
Upon an ever-turning, sharp-edged wheel
With heavy spikes, propelled by demon paws;
Or else with thirst and hunger put to death,
Pinioned in a swamp like Tantalus,
Who stood in water reaching to his chin,
But, howsoever much he suffered thirst,
210 Could ne'er succeed to reach it with his lips
Because it lowered as toward it he bent,
And who with hunger sorely was oppressed
Yet could not be appeased, but died insane,
Since he could never reach the apple hung
Before his nose because it always rose
Whene'er he tried to seize it with his teeth;
Or ceaselessly employed like Sisyphus,
Compelled to roll forever up a hill

A millstone which as oft rolled down again
220 And must be sought anew and upward rolled;
Or made to fill a barrel bottomless
And so unfillable, as, for their sins,
The Danaïdes were compelled to do.
You know, fair Genius, how the vulture tore
At Tityus' liver, nor could be driven off;
And there are many other punishments
Cruel and vile and great, to which mankind
Will be subjected, and I'll be revenged
By all their tribulation and great pain,
230 Their awful torture, and their suffering.
If He who judges every word and deed
Were merciful alone, then laudable
And right would be the loans of usurers;
But He is ever just and to be feared
By those who enter on the sinful path.
    "I leave to God the sins with which mankind
Is fouled; He'll punish as it pleases Him,
Or let the wretches exculpate themselves.
As for the ones of whom Love makes complaint,
240 Which I indeed have heard, these I myself,
As best I can, denounce, and should denounce,
Since they refuse the tribute they should pay,
Which all, so long as they enjoy my tools
Have owed, and owe, and evermore will owe to me."

89. Nature sends Genius to encourage the God of Love
[19335-19438]

"ELOQUENT Genius, now I bid you seek   NATURE
The host of barons of the God of Love,
Who, I am certain, is so fond of me,
So frank and debonair is he of heart,
That much he strives to serve me, and is drawn,
More than a steel to magnet, to my work.

My greetings give to him and my good friend
Dame Venus, and to all the barony
Except False Seeming, who associates
10 With hypocrites most dangerous and vain
And felons whom the Scriptures designate
As pseudo-prophets. Of Forced Abstinence
I've much suspicion that she's also proud
And like False Seeming, howsoever much
Humility and charity she wear.
So if False Seeming and Forced Abstinence,
His lady love, are still associates
Of proven traitors, greet them not from me.
Such folk are to be feared. Love would do well
20 To drive them from his army, if he would,
Unless their aid is indispensable
And lacking it he can accomplish naught.
But if they give their aid to true love's cause
And lessen lovers' pains, I pardon them.
       "Go, friend, to Cupid; carry my complaints
And griefs; though not that he can justice gain
For me, but that some comfort he may find
In hearing news that should most welcome be
To him, and grievous to our enemies,
30 Leaving him free from care if not from pain
Which I see burdens him. Tell him that I
Send you to excommunicate all those
Who us withstand, and freely to absolve
The valiant hearts who labor to observe
Rightly the rules found written in my book,
And strongly strive to multiply the race,
And give themselves to love. I call them friends
And will delight their souls, if they will guard
Themselves from vices that I've named before,
40 Which would destroy all good. Indulgence give,
Not for ten years, which were not worth a cent,
But plenary, for all they may have done
At any time, as soon as they confess.
When you have reached the host, who'll welcome you,
And as you best know how, my greeting given,
Within their hearing publish this decree

And absolution, which I'll dictate now."
   He wrote as she directed, and 'twas sealed.
She bade him haste, and asked to be absolved
50 If she had failed to think of anything.
Soon as Dame Nature thus had made her shrift,
As law and custom bade, the valiant priest
Gave absolution, and some penance slight,
As her slight fault deserved, assigned to her.
Back to her forge he said that she should go
And work as she had worked before she felt
Conviction of her fault, and serve until
The King who all can do and all undo
And all redress should other counsel give.
60   "Fair sir," said she, "I'll do it willingly."   NATURE
   "And I," said he, "shall go without delay,   GENIUS
Faster than running, to give succor due
To all true lovers, soon as I put off
This silken rochet, chasuble, and alb."
   He hung them on a hook, and dressed himself
In clothing secular that left his limbs
More free, as if he would attend a dance;
And taking to his wings he swiftly flew away.

90. Genius goes to reveal Nature's will to Cupid's hosts
[19439–19504]

THEN Nature to her workshop turned again,
Wielding her sledges, as her custom is,
And forging as before. No more delayed
Genius, but swifter than the rushing wind
Pursued his wingèd way and reached Love's host.
False Seeming was not there. He had decamped
In greatest haste, nor stopped to say good-by,
Ill liking pause, soon as they seized the hag
Who oped for me the gate into the close
10 And with Fair Welcome so advanced my cause

That I might talk with him. But, to be sure,
Forced Abstinence was found by Genius there.
She tried her best False Seeming to ensue
As soon as she saw Nature's priest appear,
And scarce could be restrained. Little she liked
To let us see her converse hold with him,
And four gold besants gladly would have paid
That of her plight False Seeming might not know.
    Genius, without delay, in that same hour
20 The host saluted as was seemliest
And told, omitting nothing, why he came.
I need not say how much they all rejoiced
To hear the news he brought. I will abridge
My tale, lest I too much should tire your ears;
For often he who preaches at great length
His hearers loses by prolixity.
    In chasuble was Genius soon arrayed
By Cupid, who a ring and cross supplied
And miter clearer than a crystal glass.
30 But for no richer tiring would they wait,
So eager were they all to hear him read.
O'erwhelmed with laughter, Venus scarce kept still;
Inspired by jollity and gaiety,
She placed within his fist a taper bright,
Which certainly was not of virgin wax,
To make more forceful his anathema,
When he revealed the theme of his discourse.
    Genius no more delayed, but mounted high
Upon a scaffold, where he best could read
40 The scripture that Dame Nature's will revealed.
The barons, wishing for no better seats,
Stretched on the ground, while he displayed to them
His charter. Then with motions of his hand
He signed to all the circle to be still.
His words were pleasing, and with wink and nod
They silenced one another, listening well
As he his exhortation forcefully began.

91. Genius begins his exhortation to fecundity
[19505–19906]

"BY VIRTUE of the high authority   GENIUS
Of Nature, who the custody of earth
As vicar or as constable maintains
For God, this sempiternal emperor
Who sits as in a tower, the sovereign
Of all this noble city called the world,
Of which Dame Nature is His deputy
Who there administers all benefits
According to the influence of the stars
10 By which all earthly happenings are ordained
In full accordance with the imperial rights
Of which she is the sole executor,
Who since the world was first an entity
Has brought all things to birth, and given term
Unto their growth and unto their increase,
Nor ever anything has made in vain
Beneath the sky, which turns unceasingly
About the earth, above the world as high
As it is low beneath, nor night nor day
20 Ceases its motion for a space of rest,
May all be cursed and excommunicate
As men disloyal, renegade, condemned
Without respite, be they or high or low,
Who in contempt hold Nature's processes
By which life is sustained! But he who strives
With all his might to further Nature's ends,
Takes pains to love, without one villain thought,
And labors loyally, may he be crowned,
When he goes there, with flowers in Paradise!
30 Provided he has full confession made,
I'll take upon myself all of his sins
And bear them with what strength I may possess,

Nor ever the least pardon for them ask.

   "Woe worth the day when Nature freely gave,
According to her custom and her rule,
Unto false folk a tablet and a style,
Hammer or anvil, coulter pointed well
To use as plow on fertile, fallow ground—
Not stony, but with tender grass o'ergrown—
40 Which they should plow and therein deeply delve
With labor that she meant they should enjoy;
But they refuse to serve or honor her
By working as they should, and rather seek
Her blessings to destroy, when they desert
Her tablets, plowshares, and rich, fallow land,
Which she has made so precious and so dear
To aid perpetuation of the race
That Death may ne'er succeed to conquer all!

   "Shame on the thriftless ones of whom I speak,
50 Who never deign to set themselves to work
To write their names upon the tablets fair
Or stamp their likenesses, which might endure!
So bitter their contempt, so scornful they,
That soon the anvils will grow green with moss
And perish for the want of hammer blows;
For rust will soon destroy them if the ring
Of sledges beating on them is not heard,
And fallow land that is not deeply plowed
Soon becomes barren through its own disuse.
60 Buried alive that man should be who dares
Neglect the instruments that God has made
With His own hand, and to my lady lent
That she with them may reproductions form
To give a mortal race eternal life.

   "It truly seems that evilly they act,
Since if for sixty years all living men
Should follow their example, there would be
No children born again forevermore.
Were this God's will, mankind were at an end
70 And all the earth deserted, certainly,
Or peopled but with animals—dumb beasts—
Unless God pleased a new race to create,

Or bring those back to live on earth again
Who were deceased. Or if all women held
To their virginity for sixty years
The same result would follow. God must then,
If He so willed, create mankind anew.
    "If it be said that God removes desire
From some, by His good grace, but not from all,
80 Then, since because of His omnipotence
His judgment cannot err, we may be sure
That every man should do as others do
That all may have of grace an equal share.
Then my conclusion is as 'twas before,
That to perdition this would bring the race.
From such dilemma one cannot escape
Unless belief can be sustained by faith;
For God in the beginning equally
Loved all mankind, and reasonable souls
90 Gave men as well as women. I believe
That 'tis His will that all—not just a few—
Pursue the road that best will lead to Him.
If 'tis His will that some lead virgin lives,
The better to follow Him, then why not all?
What reason should deter a man from that?
So it would seem that He were not displeased
If generation of mankind should cease.
Let those respond who will; I know no more
About the business. Bring on the divines,
100 Who may discuss, but never will conclude.
    "But those who with their stylets scorn to write
Upon the precious tablets delicate
By means of which all mortals come to life,
Which Nature never lent us for disuse
But rather that we all should scriveners
Become, since each of us his livelihood
Gains in this way—yes, every he and she—
And those who two strong hammers have been lent
But will not as they should use them to forge
110 Upon the proper anvil properly—
And those who are so blinded by their sins
Or by the pride by which they are deranged

That they despise the furrow, fair and straight
Amidst the blooming and luxuriant field,
And to the proper roadway never keep
But go like wretches to the desert wastes
Where they misuse their plows and lose their seed
And prove their evil rules no other way
Than by exceptions most anomalous
120 When they desire to follow and observe
The example set by Orpheus, who scorned
To write on tablets, plow a furrow, forge—
May all such men be hanged up by the neck!
When they contrive such rules, they prove themselves
Opposed to Nature. May those who so despise
So fair a mistress that they read her rules
All upside down, and will not ever hold
Them right side up that they may understand
Their proper sense, but when they come to read
130 Pervert the Scripture, be condemned to Hell,
With total excommunication cursed!
And, since to their bad rule they have adhered,
Before they die may they all lose the signs
That they are males: the pilgrim scrip and stones!
May they those pendants lose with which their purse
Is heavy now! The hammers hung within
Be torn away! And may they be deprived
Of that convenient stylus they refused
To write withal upon the tablets fair!
140 And, since they have refused to plow aright
With them, may all the framework be removed
From out their coulters and their unused plows
So that they never can be raised again!
May all who follow them lead lives of shame!
And, that their foul and horrid wickedness
May dolorous and painful punishment
Receive, may they be scourged in every place
That all who meet them may perceive their sin!
    "For God's sake, lords, you who are still alive,
150 To follow such examples e'er refuse;
Be active in your functions natural—
More active than the squirrel, and more deft

And lively than the birds or than the breeze.
Provided only you work manfully,
I pardon all your sins; lose not that boon!
Exert yourselves gaily to leap and dance,
And rest not, lest your members grow lukewarm.
All your utensils in the task employ;
He who works well by work will warm himself.
160 Plow, barons, plow—your lineage repair;
For if you do not there'll be nothing left
To build upon. Bend well your sturdy backs
Like sails that belly to take in the wind.
Though, if you please, your bodies be quite bare,
You'll never feel too cold, nor yet too warm.
The plow hales lift with your two naked hands,
And with your arms strongly assist the beam
And strive to thrust the coulter firmly home
And keep it in its proper place, to sink
170 More deeply in the furrow. Urge your steeds
More sharply forward; never let them rest;
Whip them along with the severest blows
That you can deal, when you most deep would pierce.
Or, if you work with horny-headed beasts
Yoked to your plow, urge them with goads. Thus you
Will amplify the benefits you reap.
You'll plow the best if oft you spur their speed.
　　"And when you've worked till you exhausted are,
You needs must take a suitable repose;
180 For in no task can one continue long
Without a rest. Nor need you recommence
Too soon, in order to advance the work,
Lest all your interest in the labor lag.
　　"Cadmus, obedient to Pallas' will,
More than an acre plowed, and sowed therein
The dragon's teeth, from whence sprang up a crop
Of armored knights, who such a fight began
That on the spot they all were killed but five
Who later, as his good companions, helped
190 Him build its walls when he had founded Thebes.
With him they set the stones in mortarwork,
And afterward they peopled all the town.

Good sowing Cadmus made, who so advanced
  His people. If you do as well as he,
Your lineage may well endure as long.
    "Two great advantages do you possess
To save your line, and if you lose the third
'Twill be because you are no more than fools.
A single disadvantage you must own:
200 On one side you're assailed; guard that wall well.
Most impotent would be three champions,
And well deserve their beating, if a fourth
They could not overcome. I speak of three
Who sisters are, of whom two are your aides.
The third alone will grieve you. She it is
Who cuts the thread of life. The two who help
Are Clotho, who the distaff always bears,
And Lachesis, who spins the living thread;
But Atropos dissevers it the while,
210 However much her sisters strive to spin.
'Tis Atropos who seeks to baffle you.
She's never far away, and all your line
Will sepulcher. On you she has her eyes!
There never was a fiercer animal;
No greater enemy you'll ever have.
    "Have pity on yourselves, my noble lords!
Remember your old mothers and good sires.
'Tis by their deeds you're of their lineage;
See that their line's not forfeited by you—
220 Regard their prowess; see what they have done!
Themselves they well defended from the charge
Of slothfulness, for they to you gave life.
Had it not been for their good horsemanship,
You would not be here now. Great love for you
They had, and for the others who should come
Your lineage to maintain forevermore.
    "Yourself should have a thought of friendliness.
Be not dismayed! The style you have; now write.
Don't muffle up your arms—blow, forge, and beat!
230 Aid Lachesis and Clotho, so that they,
  If Atropos, who is so villainous,
Cuts off six threads, may spin a dozen more.

Bend all your powers to multiply the race;
So best the schemes of Atropos defy.
Felonious and cross-grained traitor wretch,
She ever seeks the living to destroy.
This woman foul, striving against all life,
Has heart so hardy that she feeds the dead
To Cerberus, the hellhound, who desires
240 So much their bodies he with longing burns
And well-nigh dies of hunger-nourished rage
Unless the harlot hastens to his aid;
For otherwise he'd have no sustenance
But she to feed him well will never cease;
And when this triple-headed dog's athirst,
He hangs upon her breasts, which are not twins
But triplets to accommodate three mouths.
His groins he pillows in her tender lap,
Muzzles her dugs and sucks and draws her milk.
250 He never has been weaned, nor e'er will be;
No other drink will satisfy his thirst,
Nor will another food his hunger end
Except the corpses of the human race.
Into his triple throat she mountains casts
Of men and women, which alone he eats,
And ever she attempts to fill his maw
But finds it empty, spite of all her pains.
The three avengers of all felonies—
Felons themselves, and harlots every one—
260 Alecto and Tisiphone by name;
Megaera is the third—I know them all—
Hover about in great anxiety
Around his food; and each would eat you whole
If Cerberus would give her any chance.
    "These three await your entry into Hell.
They bind and beat and scourge and strangle you;
They scratch and wound and scorch and give you pain;
They choke and burn and grill and scald and boil
In presence of three provosts sitting there
270 In full consistory to judge those men
Who have committed crimes while still alive.
These provosts by their torturing extort

Confessions of the sins that men commit
From birth to death while living on the earth.
Before these judges all the people quake.
I'd be a coward not to name them here:
Three brothers—Rhadamanthus, Æacus,
And Minos—all the sons of Jupiter.
These three, on earth, according to the tale,
280 Such wise men were, and justice so maintained,
That they became, when dead, judges in Hell;
For Pluto waited long until their souls
Had left their bodies; then as fit reward
He gave them the office they so well deserved.

"For God's sake, seignors, fight against the sins
That our fair mistress, Nature, named to me
When she heard me say mass. She told me all.
I could not stay when more than twenty-six
I heard—more noxious sins than you'd believe.
290 If from the ordure of these crimes you're free,
The precincts of the harlots I have named,
Who have such ill renown, you'll never view;
Nor need you fear the condemnation just
Of those three provosts. I'd recount to you
These sins but that they too outrageous are.
But if it please you to consider them,
That from such vices you may guard yourselves,
Then read the rollicking *Romance of the Rose*,
Which briefly will present them all to you.

300   "Strive, then, to lead the good life, one and all;
Let each embrace his sweetheart, and let her
In turn embrace her lover. Let them kiss,
Solace, and comfort one another so.
You never will be blamed for loyal love;
And, when you've played enough, as I advise,
Make your confession well, and promise give
All evil to forsake, to follow good,
And pray to God in Heaven, whom Nature owns
As her great master, that He will, in the end,
310 Come to your aid when Atropos shall seek
To bury you in Hell. He is the cure
Of body and of soul—the mirror He

Of Lady Nature. She had nothing known
Were it not for that mirror true and fair.
He rules and governs her; no other law
Has she than His. Whate'er she knows she learned
From Him when she at first was made His chamberlain."

92. Genius describes the life of the blest in Paradise
[19907–20036]

"NOW, lords, it is my will and her command,   GENIUS
Since you don't always have your book with you,
And 'tis, besides, most wearisome to write,
That each of you attend this sermon well
And learn it all by heart—yes, word for word,
As I have spoken it—so when you come
To any place—to castle, village, town,
Or burg—in summer or in winter time,
You may recite it to those not here now.
10 'Tis well to know by heart the lore that comes
From a good school—and better to repeat,
For one may thus attain to high esteem.
My counselings are wise—one hundred times
Than sapphires, rubies, other precious stones
More valuable. My lady has great need
Of preachers those who disobey her rules
To chasten so that they may thenceforth keep
Her laws and spread her precepts through the earth.
    "If you thus preach, you never will be stopped,
20 According to my judgment and the facts,
From entering the paradisiacal fields
Wherein the offspring of a virgin lamb,
Arrayed in whitest wool, conducts with Him
His sheep, who revel o'er the pastures green.
He's followed by no mighty company
But fitting few, along the narrow paths
Bordered with blooming flowers and fresh herbs

So little trodden that they're not bent down.
Beasts debonair and free—the lambkins white—
30 Nibble about the new-spring herbage green
And feed upon the grass along the way.
Know well, their pasture is so marvelous
That all the pretty flowers growing there,
So virginal and tender in the spring,
Retain their youth, ever as new and bright
As flaming stars upon the verdant mead,
From dewy morn through noonday heat till eve,
Nor ever age, but keep their native charm
With colors lively, fresh, and fine, till night,
40 And can be gathered just as well at dusk
As in the morning, let him pluck who will.
    "Nor are these flowers either immature
Or overblown, but in the herbage glow
In full perfection of their perfect age.
They're never scorched by too-bright-shining sun
Or drowned by dewdrops bathing them at dawn,
But e'er their roots the sweetest sap provide
To keep them in their perfect loveliness.
    "And should you say that lambkins cannot graze
50 Forever on the selfsame grass and flowers
Without destroying them, then be assured
That ever, as they eat, the herbage springs
Anew; and furthermore (deem it no lie!)
The flowers and grass are indestructible,
However much the flocks may them devour.
Their pasture nothing costs, and so their fleece
Is never sold to stranger folk for wool,
Their skin is never stripped for coverings,
Their flesh is never flayed to make a feast.
60 No malady will e'er o'ertake them there;
No foul corruption will upon them seize.
I doubt not the Good Shepherd who attends
Them in their pasture never clipped a lock
Nor e'er despoiled them of a feather's worth
That He might clothe Himself in their white wool,
But wears a fleecy robe, it seems to me,
Because it pleases Him to look like them.

"Did I not fear to weary you, I'd tell
How they enjoy an everlasting day;
70 For never yet has twilight fallen there.
There's neither dawning morn nor darkling night;
The evening and the morning are the same.
Each hour is like a minute, yet the day
Never declines to night, nor is there strife
Between the light and darkness. Measureless
Is time in that abode. Delightful day
Endures forever, and clear weather smiles
In one eternal present, without past
Or future; for one tense is there as three.
80 No portion of the present has had end,
And there is naught to come; for there exists
No preterite or future tense. The one
Can never be; the other has not been.
All time has but a stable permanence.
The sun, resplendent, ever is in sight;
The day stands still as if the hour were noon;
The season stays as if 'twere always spring,
So fair and pure that none e'er saw its like—
Not even in the time of Saturn's reign,
90 Which was the Golden Age, till Jupiter,
His son, committed such an outrage vile—
Tormented so his aged sire—when he
Bereft his regal father of his testicles."

93. Genius gives an account of Jupiter's reign
[20037–20278]

"IF ONE takes true account, he must agree   GENIUS
Castration is an act which will inflict
The greatest shame and loss upon a man.
Besides the great discomfort and disgrace,
He loses his sweetheart's love, however close
As lovers they had been allied before.

If he is married, worse go his affairs,
For, howsoever debonair she's been,
Now will his wife all her affection lose.
10 Castration should be named a mortal sin;
For one who gelds a man not only steals
His manhood, the affection of his friend,
Who'll never love him more—nor will his wife—
But also takes away his chivalry—
The bravery that valiant men should have—
And makes him cowardly, perverse, and base;
Or alters him with manners feminine.
Eunuchs display no trace of hardihood
Unless it be in some malicious vice;
20 Like women, they are strong in deviltry,
And in some other ways resemble them.
Although the gelder is no murderer,
Thief, or committer of a mortal crime,
Against Dame Nature he has sinned, at least,
When means of propagation he destroys.
No matter how a man may search his mind,
He cannot find excuse for such a wrong.
At least I can't; for when I ponder well
And canvass all the facts, I can't refrain
30 From lashing with my tongue the criminal
Who gelds a fellow man, such is his sin
Against the precepts which Dame Nature gives.
　　"But, howsoever great this crime may be,
Jove cared little, if he could have the reins
Of power in his hands. When he became
The ruler and the lord of all the world,
To teach the people how they ought to live
His laws and his commandments he ordained,
And his establishments, and had the banns
40 Promptly and frankly cried in audience,
The substance of which notice I'll repeat:
　　"'Jupiter, who rules the world, commands　　**JUPITER**
And hereby as a law establishes
The custom that each man shall be at ease
And do such things as please his appetite,
If he is able, solacing his heart.'

No other rule he made, but did concede   GENIUS
That all in common, each one for himself,
Should do what most delightful seemed to each.
50 Said he, 'Delight's the best thing that can be—   JUPITER
The sovereign good in life, which all should seek.'
In order that all folk might keep this rule,   GENIUS
He furnished them example by his deeds,
Indulging every sense, prizing delights,
And thus became the jolly Jupiter.

    "Within another book the *Georgics* called,
We're told by him who the *Bucolics* wrote
That from Greek works he learned what Jove achieved.
Before his time, inhabitants of earth
60 Followed no plow to cultivate the fields,
And spaded up no ground. The simple folk,
Peaceful and good, had set about their lands
No boundaries, but commonly enjoyed
The benefits which came to them unsought.
But Jove gave orders to divide the land,
Of which no man before had claimed his share,
And measured it by acres. Then to snakes
He gave their venom, and he taught the wolves
To hunt their prey, such malice he aroused.
70 The honey-bearing oak trees he cut down,
And stopped the sources of wine-flowing streams.
He all the fires extinguished, scheming thus
To annoy the folk and make them learn with flint
To kindle flame, so subtly did he work
His wiles upon them. New and various arts
He then contrived: counted and named the stars,
Taught men to catch the savage beasts in nets
And birds with snares and bird lime, made the dog
Obey man's will as he'd not done before.
80 He overmastered all the birds of prey
Which had tormented man maliciously.
Assaults and battles then he brought about
Between the hawks and partridges and quails,
Ordaining tournaments high in the clouds
Betwixt the falcons and the kites and cranes.
He made them all to man's enticement yield,

Provided they were fed each night and morn,
That man might thus their favor e'er retain
And they return unquestioning to his hand.
90 The gallant by this practice came to be
In servitude unto these felon birds
Who formerly were thought his enemies,
As ravishers of other, peaceful fowl.
These flew so high he could not capture them,
Nor did he wish to live without their flesh;
So great a connoisseur he had become
That he considered them his daintiest food.
He put the ferrets in the rabbit holes
To storm their trenches and to drive them out.
100 The fishes of the rivers and the seas
He scaled and boiled or roasted, making sauce
With divers herbs and many spices mixed
To stimulate his dainty appetite.
Thus arts arose, for mastered are all things
With labor goaded by necessity,
Which is a care to all of humankind.
Hardship arouses ingenuity
To find a means to lessen suffering.
So Ovid says, who, when he was alive,
110 Knew good and evil, eminence and shame,
As he himself recounts. But Jupiter,
When he held all the earth, for nothing cared
Except to change his empire's first estate
From good to bad and then from bad to worse.
A weak administrator he became.
He shortened springtime, quartering the year
Into four seasons, as we have them now—
The winter, spring, and summer, and the fall—
Thus making of the former constant spring
120 Four seasons quite diverse; for he would have
Things as they were no longer. When he gained
His throne, he banished quite the Golden Age;
And soon the Silver Age that then ensued
Degenerated to the Age of Brass,
For humankind continued to decline,
So much they were ensnared in wickedness,

Till now, their state is so degenerate,
The Iron Age succeeds. The infernal gods
Are greatly pleased, for, ever foul and dark,
130 They envy men their life upon the earth.
These demons in their stables have secured—
And never will release—the black-fleeced sheep,
Ill-fortuned, wretched, sad, and sick to death,
Who would not keep the straight and narrow path—
Appointed for them by the Snowy Lamb—
In which they had been set at liberty,
And their black fleeces whitened, but the broad
And ample avenue they chose to take,
Filled with innumerable company,
140 Which led them to the lodgings they now have.
        "No sheep that walks therein can bear a fleece
Of any worth, of which a man might make
Befitting clothes—but rough and horrid hair
Which would be harsh and prickly to the skin
If it were worn, as would a mantle made
Of hedgehogs' skin beset with spiny quills.
But any man would gladly comb the wool
That could be gathered from the snowy sheep—
So fleecy, soft, and smooth, and plentiful—
150 And garments make fit to be worn at feasts
By kings or emperors, or angels e'en.
If, indeed, angels woolen clothes assume;
For you should know that he who could obtain
Such raiment would be clothed most royally
And therefore such adornment dear would hold,
For, truly, such-like animals are rare.
        "The Shepherd, who is not a fool, keeps guard
Over the flock enclosed within a park,
Allowing no black sheep to enter there,
160 However much they beg, for He prefers
To choose the white, who well their Shepherd know
Because they've come to make their home with Him;
And well He knows them when He welcomes them.
        "Most gentle, rare, and beautiful of all
This worthy flock is that white, joyful Lamb
That leads the sheep out to their pasturage

With most painstaking care; for well He knows
If one should miss her way and be perceived
Alone by that fierce Wolf that haunts the road
170 And tracks no other prey, the moment she
Ceases to trail the footsteps of the Lamb
Who leads them all, the enemy will seize
And drag her off, which no one can prevent,
And eat her up alive, in spite of all.

    "Seignors, this Lamb awaits you there. But now
We'll cease to talk to Him, except to pray
To God the Father that He'll lend an ear
Unto His mother's plea that He will lead
His flock so that the Wolf may not annoy
180 The sheep, and that they may not fail, through sin,
To enter and enjoy the paradise
Which so delightful is and beautiful,
With tender grass, and blossoms odorous
Of violets and roses—and of all good things!"

94. Genius contrasts the Shepherd's Park with the garden of Sir Mirth
[20279–20682]

"NOW whosoe'er would make comparison   GENIUS
Between that garden square, whose little gate
Was closed with bars, wherein the Lover saw
Sir Mirth and all his meinie caroling,
And Fairfield Park I've just described to you
Would err as greatly if he thought them like
As one who should consider fable truth.
Whoe'er might come into this paradise,
Or even glance therein, would dare assert
10 That garden to be nothing as compared
To this enclosure, which is not square built
But subtly round, so that no ivory sphere
Or beryl ever had more perfect shape.

What would you have me tell you? Let us talk
Of all the things the Lover saw at first
Within the garden and without. In brief
I'll summarize, omitting the details.
   "He saw the ugly images portrayed
Outside—but if a man should scan this wall
20 He'd find the infernal demons pictured here,
Most foul and fearful, and each outrage vile
That's suffered by the inhabitants of Hell,
And Cerberus, who keeps them under guard.
Here would he see depicted the whole earth
With all its worldly wealth of ancient things.
Here would he see the ocean faithfully
Portrayed with all its store of things marine—
The fishes that inhabit the salt seas
Or live in rivers fresh, muddy, or clear,
30 And all things great and small the lakes contain—
The sky, with all that make the air resound—
The birds and butterflies and even gnats—
The fire that girdles all the furniture
And tenements of other elements.
Here would he see the constellations bright
All fastened in their spheres. Here would he see,
Excluded from the garden, all these things
Pictured as plainly as in fact they appear.
   "Let us once more the garden enter now
40 And name the things within. The Lover saw
Delight conduct a dance upon the grass,
And all her fellows decked with odorous flowers
A-caroling with her. He says he saw
Grass, trees, and beasts and birds, fountains and brooks
Rippling and splashing over gravel beds—
Especially the stream beneath the pine
Of which he boasts that such another tree
Has ne'er been seen since old King Pepin's time,
Nor any fountain with such beauty filled.
50   "For love of God, lords, be upon your guard
If you are looking for the naked truth.
These things are fables—vain imaginings—
No stable facts, but fictions that will fade.

Dances will reach their end and dancers fail.
So all he saw within the garden walls
Inevitably must crumble and decay;
For Atropos, the nurse of Cerberus,
Whose practices mankind cannot prevent
Or her attack avoid when 'tis her will
60 To use her strength, as she does ceaselessly,
And nothing spares, lies in wait for all
Except the gods, whom she cannot destroy,
For things divine never descend to death.
   "But now let's talk of all the lovely things
The Shepherd's Park includes. I must be brief;
For I this sermon shortly must conclude.
Though I'd proceed aright, I do not know
How properly to speak; for there's no heart
That can conceive—no human tongue describe—
70 The mighty worth and beauty of the things
Contained therein, nor the delightful games,
The everlasting joys, sincere and great,
That are experienced by those within.
All things delightful, permanent, and true
Have those who in this park take their delight;
And right it is, for they all good imbibe
From that same spring of wealth and happiness
That is so precious, fair, and clear, and pure,
And waters all the place, a flowing brook
80 From which the sheep who enter Fairfield Park,
Forsaking the black flock thus to deserve
Admission to these precincts, gladly drink.
Soon as they're watered, no more thirst they have,
But live together as they will, nor feel
The blight of illness or the sting of death.
In lucky hour they pass within these gates;
In lucky hour they see the Lamb of God,
Whom they may follow in the narrow path,
While the Good Shepherd guards, whose only wish
90 Is to purvey them harborage with Him.
None who once drink from that pure stream can die;
For this is not the fountain 'neath the tree
The Lover saw enclosed in marble verge.

He should be ridiculed who praised that spring—
The bitter, poisonous Fountain Perilous
That killed the fair Narcissus, who therein
Admired himself until he pined away.
The Lover himself was not ashamed, indeed,
To recognize and testimony give
100 About that fountain's character, nor hide
Its cruelty, when he applied the name
Of Mirror Perilous to it, and said
That when he looked therein he felt a throb
Of painful grief, and heaved a heavy sigh.
You see what sweetness in the spring he found!
Fine fountain this, that makes well people ill!
What good turn was he doing for himself
When he therein on his reflection gazed?
  "The water flows, he says, in welling waves
110 From two deep, hollow sources. Well I know
That in itself the spring has no supply
Of water, but whatever qualities
It has all come to it from somewhere else.
Then he says further that it never fails,
And that its surface shines like silver fine.
Behold what trumpery he's telling you!
The water is so troubled and so dark
That one who bends his head above, to see
Himself reflected there, sees naught at all,
120 And might grow crazy with bewilderment
Because he could not recognize himself.
A double crystal in the depths, he says,
Reflects the sun when it is shining bright
And shows one half the park to him who peers
Within; whereas the other moiety
Can from the other side be clearly seen,
So magical and fair the crystals are.
But, truly, they seem cloudy and most dull,
Or why do they not at a single view
130 Show all the garden when the sun is bright?
And since they don't, my faith! it seems to me
That some obscurity must them becloud
So that they cannot all reveal to him

Who gazes in them when they borrow light
From sources not themselves. And if the sun
Shed not its rays upon the crystals there,
They have no power to show forth anything.
Now prick your ears and hear the marvelous tale
That I shall tell about the beauteous fount
140 Which I have mentioned formerly to you.
    "This fountain fair, which so much virtue has
To cure, with its sweet waters, ailing sheep,
Flows from a Triple Well, unfailing, clear.
These sources are so close together set
That all together gather in one stream
So that when one sees all he can perceive
But one, or three in one—a Trinity.
However many times one tries to count,
He'll never make the number up to four;
150 For it's their common, mystic property
Forever to be three, forever one.
The like of such a fountain ne'er was seen,
For 'tis itself the source from which it flows;
Whereas all other springs have their supply
Through veins from alien sources far away.
'Tis its own conduit; extraneous veins
It never needs. More sure than native rock,
The living stream depends upon itself.
It needs no marble curb, no sheltering tree;
160 Its waters issue from so high a source
That they can never fail. No tree could grow
So high that 'twould surmount this fountain jet.
    "But on the slope, as though 'twere coursing down
The hill, a little olive tree is seen,
Beneath which all the waters gently flow;
And when the tiny olive feels the stream
Moisten its roots with liquid fresh and sweet,
It sucks up such life-giving nourishment
That it grows strong and puts forth leaves and fruit;
170 Then it becomes so broad and towering
That not the pine the Lover has described
E'er stretched so high from earth into the sky
Or spread its branches in so fair a screen.

This olive standing there extends its boughs
Above the fountain and o'ershadows it.
There come the lambkins to enjoy its shade
And suck the moisture that the spray spreads round
Upon the flowers and the tender grass.
Written in tiny letters on a scroll
180 Upon the olive an inscription hangs,
Which those who, coming there to lie beneath
The branches and enjoy their shade, may read:
'Here flows, beneath this leafy olive tree
Which bear's salvation's fruit, the Fount of Life.'
What treasure had the pine compared to this?
  "Though foolish folk would hardly credit me
And many will as fable hold my tale,
I tell you that within this fountain shines,
More marvelous than any precious stone,
190 A round carbuncle, in three facets cut;
So high it hangs that it lights all the park,
And one may see it plainly far away.
No wind or rain or fog can dim its beams,
So bright it is and of such nobleness.
Such is the virtue of this wondrous stone
That every facet's worth the other two,
However bright each by itself appears;
Nor can all one surpass, however fair
Each seems alone. None can distinction make,
200 By taking thought, among the facets three;
Nor can one in his mind the three unite
So that among them no distinction lies.
No sun illumines it, and yet it has
So fine a color, and it shines so clear,
That the resplendent sun which falls upon
The double crystal in that other spring
Would seem obscure and dull compared to it.
What need I tell you more? No other sun
But this carbuncle ever needs to shine.
210 It is this garden's sun—its glow more bright
Than any other that e'er shone on earth.
It sends the night to exile—makes the day
Endure forever, never having end,

As no beginning it has ever had,
Spontaneously holding to one point
And never by a minute or degree
Or any other fraction of an hour
Advancing toward another house or sign
Along the zodiac. It has a force
220 So marvelous that whatsoever man
Beholds it hanging there and then perceives
His face reflected in the spring below
Always, from whatsoever side he looks,
Sees all the things contained within the park
And recognizes each for what it is,
And ever knows its worth. He who has seen
Himself reflected there at once becomes
So wise a master that he nevermore
Can be deceived by aught that may occur.
230   "Another marvel I'll recount to you:
The rays of this carbuncle never harm
Or daze the eyes of those who on it gaze,
Or make them dizzy; it invigorates
Their eyesight and delights and strengthens it
By its clear beauty and its temperate heat,
Which with a pleasing odor fills the park,
So marvelous a sweetness it exhales.
  "I will detain you but for one word more
That you may know that whosoever sees
240 The form and substance of this beauteous place
Might well assert that Adam was not formed
To occupy a fairer paradise.
  "What think you of this park that I've described
And of the Lover's garden? Tell me, lords.
On accident and substance give your votes
And reasonable verdict. By your faith
Declare which seems to you more beautiful.
Consider the two fountains, and decide
Which furnishes the more health-giving stream
250 And water the more pure and virtuous.
Judging the nature of the conduits,
Say which is more praiseworthy. Judge the pine
And olive which o'ershade the living streams;

And judge the precious stones the fountains hold.
I'll stand by your decision if you give,
According to the evidence I've read,
A verdict just. I say without deceit
From first to last that I have added naught.
Should you speak falsely or withhold the truth,
260 And thus do wrong (I'll not dissimulate!)
I'd call in others as my jurymen.
That sooner an agreement you may reach
I'll briefly summarize what I have said
About the fountains' virtues and true worth:
The one intoxicates a living man
And brings him to his death; whereas, in truth,
The dead are by the other spring revived.

    "Seignors, if you would wisely act, and do
That which you should, you'd from this fountain drink.
270 That you more easily may keep in mind
My teaching (for the lesson in few words
Contained is that which is remembered best)
Again I will repeat what you should do:
Honor Dame Nature; serve her by good works;
If others' goods you hold, restore them straight,
Or, if you can't restore what you have spent,
Or lost in play, remember willingly
Your creditors when you have means again;
Keep clear of murder; let your hands and lips
280 Alike be clean; be pitying and leal.
Then you shall walk in that Elysian field
And follow in the footsteps of the Lamb
In everlasting life, and freely drink
The water of that spring which is so fair,
Health-giving, clear, and sweet, that none may die
Who drink thereof, but happily they'll walk,
Singing their everlasting songs and chants
And canzonets, upon the verdant grass.
Or dancing 'neath the olive midst the flowers.
290   "What's this I pipe to you? High time it is
I put my flute away. The sweetest tune
Ofttimes annoys. I might keep you too long.
So here I'll end my sermon. Now let's see

What you will do when you have mounted high
To preach a pulpit sermon o'er the breach!"
    Thus Genius preached, renewing hope and strength
Among the barons. Then amidst the throng
He threw the waxen torch, whose smoking flame
Sets fire to all the world. No woman lives
300 Who can resist it. Venus spreads the fire
Until aloft it's borne upon the wind
And every female body, heart, and mind
Is as intoxicated with its smell.
News of the charter then did Cupid spread
Until all valiant men were quite agreed thereto.

95. Love's barons prepare for the final assault on the
Castle of Jealousy
[20683–20784]

WHEN Genius ended, all the lords rejoiced.
Never a better sermon, so they said,
Had been pronounced to them; nor since their birth
Had they a fuller pardon e'er received;
Nor ever such a just anathema
Against all men who might that pardon scorn
Had they e'er heard. They all at once adhered
Unto that creed and cried, "Fiat! Amen!"   THE BARONS
    Things being so appointed, they would brook
10 No more delay. Each one who had paid heed
To that sweet sermon loved its text so well
That word for word he locked it in his heart.
Gladly they'd heard it, for its pardon seemed
Most salutary and compassionate.
Then Genius vanished, so that no one knew
What had become of him. A shout arose
From twenty of the host, "To arms! To arms!   THE BARONS
No more delay! Greatly our enemy
Will fear us if we heed our lord's decree!"

20 Then, jumping to their feet, they ready stood
To carry on the war until each tower
Should captured be or leveled to the ground.
    Venus, all ready for the fray, demands
First of the guards that they give up the fort.
What do they answer? Shame and Fear respond:

SHAME AND FEAR

"Certainly, Venus, you we need not fear;
You'll never set one foot within our walls";
And Shame adds, "Though I stood alone on guard,   SHAME
Truly I would not feel the least dismay."

VENUS

30   Then, answering Shame, the goddess cries, "Vile trull,
Out of my way! Who are you to resist?
Unless the castle is surrendered straight
To me, you never will survive the storm
That I shall raise; for never can you hope
To make defense. Resistance is in vain
Against my army. By the flesh of God!
You'll give it up or I'll burn you alive
Like miserable caitiff that you are!
The whole enclosure I will set on fire;
40 Turrets and towers I will raze to earth.
I'll burn your fences, walls, and columns down.
I'll scorch your fosses, fill your ditches full.
No matter how you rear up straight and tall
Your barbicans, that stand so proudly there,
I'll bend them double, and you'll not prevent
Me when I stretch them low upon the ground.
Fair Welcome I'll permit to pluck at will
Blossoms and buds, as purchases or gifts,
When I have opened wide the garden gate.
50 However furious you may be, you'll see
That all men in procession shall go there,
Without exception, midst the trees and flowers,
And everybody roses pluck and buds.
To outwit Jealousy, I will enlarge
The passages, that all the world may go
To plunder mead and prairie of their blooms.
Cleric and layman then shall gather there,

Without delay or hindrance, buds and flowers.
None will be able to restrain themselves,
60 Be they religious men or secular,
From paying there appropriate penance.
But not alike will they perform their vows—
Some openly, some secretly will come—
Though those who hide love's mysteries will be
Held nobler; others will be oft defamed—
Called ribalds and puerile profligates—
While they may never be so much at fault
As those avoiding all reproach and blame.
    "It's true that some abandoned men desert
70 The roses for the weeds. May God confound
(The holy Pope at Rome assisting him)
Both them and their affairs! Satan it is
Who to such crimes incites, and he will give
Them nettle hats in Hell. For, by command
Of Nature, Genius sentences them all,
Both for their sins and for their nastiness,
To punishment with all our enemies.
    "Shame, if I don't outwit you, hold my bow
And arrow of but little worth, for ne'er
80 I'll boast again if now I don't succeed.
You and your mother Reason both I hate,
So harsh you are to lovers. Whosoe'er
Believes the one or other scarce can hope
To love." No more said Venus, thinking 'twould suffice.

96. Venus begins the attack on the Tower of Shame
[20785–20816]

THEN did Dame Venus tuck her skirts up high
And like an angry woman seize her bow
And cock the shaft, well fitted at the notch,
Drawing the bowstring backward to her ear
(The arrow was not more than fathom long!)

And like a skillful archeress take aim,
Pointing it at a loophole in the tower
That Nature had with cunning workmanship
Seated between two columns, visible
10 In front, indeed, but not on either side.
　　These columns were of finest ivory,
Supporting piously a sort of shrine—
A maiden form of silver, not too short
Nor yet too tall; not fat, nor yet too thin;
But perfect in proportions generally—
In shoulders, arms, and hands. All other parts
Were fairly sculptured. There was seen within
A sanctuary covered with a shroud
Nobler and more precious and more fair
20 Than could be found from here to Istanbul.
A pomander perfume the place exhaled.
If one should reasonably strive to think
Of fit comparison, he'd find as like
As lion to a mouse that sculpturing
Compared with that one old Pygmalion once made.

97. The Poet tells the story of Pygmalion, and of Cinyras and Myrrha
[20817–21214]

PYGMALION a sculptor was, who wrought
In wax, wood, metal, stone, and ivory,
And all materials known to the craft,
To prove his genius; and no other man
Has shown such cunning or such honor gained.
Wishing for his own pleasure to create,
He made an ivory image of a maid,
Devoting so much care to each detail
That it became as graceful and as fair
10 As the most beautiful of womankind.
Not Helen or Lavinia had such

A fine complexion or such pleasing form
Or e'en one tenth such fairness, though they were
Both famed for beauty. When Pygmalion gazed
Entranced upon his work, he little knew
How fast the God of Love was binding him
Until he'd nothing left to do but grieve,
Without a means to satisfy desire.

PYGMALION

　　"Alas!" he cried, "I dream; what have I done?
20 Full many an image have I carved or forged
Of which no man can estimate the worth,
But never have I fallen in love with them.
Now does love sickness seize me, and I feel
All of my senses failing 'neath its power.
Whence comes this thought? How was such love conceived?
I love a statue motionless and mute,
Deaf to my pleas, unfit to grant me grace!
How can such passion wound me? Love so strange
No one e'er knew till now. I am amazed.
30 In such astounding case what shall I do?
I am the maddest man in all the world.
My faith! If I had loved a queen, I might
At least for favor hope; 'twere not absurd.
But this preposterous love's unnatural.
So evilly I find myself inclined,
Basest of Nature's children I must be
My better genius to dishonor so.
She lowered herself when she formed me so vile.
If I am moved so foolishly to love,
40 I surely can't blame anybody else.
Not since I've been Pygmalion and could walk
On my two feet have I of such love heard.
　　"But possibly my love is not too fond;
For there's been many another senseless love
Unless the Scriptures lie. In leafy wood,
Stooping to quench his thirst at fountain pure,
Narcissus fell in love with his own face;
Nor ever could recover, but expired,
According to the well-known history.
50 At least I am less foolish than was he,

Pygmalion kneels before his sculpture. *Morgan 245, f. 150v.*

For I the object of my love can touch,
Fondle, and clasp, and kiss; and thereby gain
Solace in my misease, which he ne'er had
From his own face reflected in the fount.
Besides, in many a land dames have been loved
By those who served them most devotedly
But never gained a kiss to ease their pain.
Am I not favored more by Love than these?
Ah, no! For they had, doubtless, constant hope
60 Of kisses or of other sweeter bliss;
But I'm denied e'en hope for such a joy
As those expect who wait on Love's delights.
For when I would enjoy a kiss or hug
I find my sweetheart rigid as a stake
And so congealing that I freeze my lips.
Ah! Pardon, sweetest love, my too rude words!
I pray that reparation you'll accept.
If notwithstanding my insanity
You'd smile, 'twould pay for all my suffering;
70 For loving looks delight true lovers best."
      Then, weeping, on his knees Pygmalion falls,
Offering his vows as if they'd make amends.
But she cares not for his apology;
She neither feels nor sees him or his gift.
He loses labor loving such a maid.
Yet he would not take back his offered heart,
By Cupid quite bereft of mind and sense,
Though not insensible to all his pain.
He scarcely knows if she be live or dead.
80 His gentle fingers touch her, and he thinks
That it is flesh he touches; but, alas,
The suppleness he feels is in his hands!
Then in his strife he finds no peace or truce.
In no condition can he long remain—
Now loves, now hates; now happy is, now sad;
Now laughs, now cries; now rages, now is calm.
      Then he attires and reattires his love,
Getting from costumers full many a dress
Of linen white, and softest scarlet wool,

90 Of linsey-woolsey, and of costliest stuff,
   Of green and blue and brown—the freshest dyes
   And colors fine and pure—and all well trimmed
   With squirrel, ermine, fox, and other fur.
   Again, these robes discarded, he assays
   How best become the figure, gowns of silk,
   Sendal and satin, tabby cloth, moiré,
   Of blue and scarlet, yellow, green, and tan.
   Samite, diapered stuff, and camelot,
   As if she were an angel, she can wear,
100 Preserving still her modest countenance.
    Another time he clothes her in a guimpe,
    A kerchief falling o'er it from her head.
    But never will he veil her lovely face;
    For he likes not the style of Saracens,
    Who hide their ladies' faces from man's sight
    With folds of cloth, when they go on the street,
    So are their hearts fulfilled with jealousy.
    Another time Pygmalion's fond desire
    Leads him to quite disrobe his ivory saint
110 And grace her limbs only with ornaments—
    Yellow, vermilion, azure, green in hue—
    With fine and dainty laces, silk and gold,
    And tiny pearls. Above her coiffure high
    A precious brooch he pins, holding in place
    A coronet of finest gold, beset
    With many precious stones in fair designs
    Composed of semicircles and of squares,
    Not to record the other jewelry
    That plentifully decks her other parts,
120 As pendent earrings of the finest gold
    Set in her little ears, and golden clasps
    To hold a coif about her dainty neck.
    Between her breasts he hangs a jewel rare;
    Then with her cincture does he take great pains,
    Designing such a belt as ne'er before
    Adorned a maiden's waist, to which he hangs
    A dainty purse well stocked with golden coin;
    And, chosen, from the seashore, five small stones

Such as maids for a game of marbles use
130 When they find them round and fair, he adds.
He gives her little balls and singing birds
And all the novelties that please young girls.
Then next, with tender care, her two small feet
He clothes in stockings finely made, and shoes
Raising her from the street two fingers' breadth.
No boots he gives her; no Parisian she!
Too rude such footwear for so tender a maid!
With golden needle drawing golden thread
He sews her sleeves till they fit perfectly.
140 Then he brings new-blown flowers, which pretty girls
Delight to weave in wreaths in early spring,
And of the blossoms chaplets makes more fine,
By artist skill, than ever man has seen.
On her ring finger he a golden band
Places, and says, like loving, loyal spouse,
"With this ring I thee wed, and thus become   PYGMALION
All thine, as you all mine. Let Hymen hear
And Juno heed my vows, and present be
At this our marriage. If they're witnesses
150 (And they of wedlock are the very gods),
Sufficient are our rites; no priest, or clerk,
Or mitered prelate do I wish, or cross."
   Then with uplifted voice he sweetly sings,
Expressing all his happy-heartedness,
In place of masses, pretty chansonettes
Of lovers' secrets; and the instruments,
Of which he many owned, he makes resound
Till one had thought the gods were back on earth.
More skillful are his hands upon the strings
160 Than Theban Amphion's fingers ever were;
Zithers and harps, lutes and guitars he played.
He had constructed clever chiming clocks,
The artful wheels of which ran ceaselessly—
Organs which could be carried in one hand,
Which he himself not only blows and plays
But sings to their accompaniment sweet
Full-voiced motets in tenor or treble strains.

Then each in turn he sounds, and plays with care
Cymbals and pipes and fifes and tambourines,
170 Timbrels and chalms and flutes and psalteries,
Bagpipes and trumpets, Cornish pipes and viols.
    See how he capers, dances, clogs, and trips,
Cuts pigeonwings the whole length of the hall,
Seizes her by the hand, and begs a dance!
But now the weight falls on his heart again;
For in response to neither speech nor prayer
Will she take part with him in dance or song.
    Next he again embraces her and lays her form
Upon a couch, striving with kiss and hug
180 To rouse some warmth as she lies in his arms.
But the result is not what it should be
When lovers kiss; rather, to him it seems
That most distasteful is his kiss to her.
By frantic fancy almost overcome,
Half crazy and half dead with foolish love,
Pygmalion his senseless image woos,
Thinking her lovelier naked than when dressed,
Then dressing her and thinking her more fair.
    It happened that there came a festival
190 Much celebrated in that countryside
Because of marvels that had oft occurred.
The eve before, a swarm of people came
To Venus' temple there. Pygmalion
Among the rest observed the festive rites
That he might gain some counsel in his love,
Complaining to the goddess mournfully
Of the sad passion that tormented him.
    "Fair gods," he cried, "if it's within your power, PYGMALION
And if it pleases you, hear my request;
200 And you especially, this temple's dame,
Saint Venus, satisfy my soul with grace.
Although in worshiping of Chastity
I may have angered you, and pain deserved,
Without delay I now repentance make
And beg your pardon. Pity have for me;
In friendship and gentility pray deign,
Provided that I Chastity desert,

To make that fair one, now of ivory
(She who has robbed me of my loving heart),
210 Taking a woman's body, soul, and life,
Become my loyal love. If you perform
My wishes promptly, and then ever find
That I am chaste, I gladly will be hanged,
Or cut in pieces with some headsman's ax,
Or, bound with cords or irons, given up
Alive to Hell's gatekeeper, Cerberus,
To grind with triple jaws and swallow down."
  When she his prayer had heard, Venus rejoiced
That he'd left Chastity and come to her
220 To serve like one who truly did repent
And long to prove his naked penitence
Within the arms of her whom most he loved,
If she indeed would furnish her with life.
So Venus to the image sent a soul,
And she became so beautiful a maid
That never in the land more fair was seen.
  No longer did Pygmalion sojourn
In Venus' temple, but with greatest haste,
As soon as he had tendered his request,
230 Back home to see and touch his image went.
Running with little leaps, he reached the house,
Burning the more, the nearer he approached;
For, though he knew not of the miracle,
In Venus he had greatest confidence.
To learn the truth he stripped the statue bare,
And when he saw his love was living flesh,
And marveled at the comely yellow curls
Flooding her shoulders with their graceful waves,
And when he felt her bones and saw her veins
240 Filled full of flowing blood, and beating pulse,
He knew not if 'twere trickery or truth.
He stumbled back; he knew not what to do;
He kept his distance, fearing sorcery.
"What's this?" he cried. "Am I now being tried?   PYGMALION
Am I awake? Ah, no! It is a dream;
But ne'er saw I a vision so complete.
A dream? My faith! 'Tis not! I'm not asleep!

Or if I'm not, whence comes this marvel then?
Has phantom shape or demon her possessed?"
250   Then did the maid, so pleasing and so fair,
Enshrouded in her golden curls, respond:
"It is no demon and no phantom shape,   MAID
Dear lover, but your sweetheart, ready now
To be your partner in accouplement
If you'll accept the offer of her love."
    Soon as he hears the miracle is real—
Soon as he sees the marvel is a fact—
He closer comes as if for further proof,
And freely offers to be wholly hers.
260 In loving words they're mutually allied;
Each gives the other thanks for love received;
In mutual embrace they both find joy;
Like turtledoves they mutually exchange
Their kisses, winning mutual delight.
Then to the gods they offer up their thanks,
Especially to Venus, who has shown
More courtesy and aid than all the rest.
    Now is Pygmalion quite at his ease;
Nothing displeases him, for there is naught
270 Which he may long for that she will refuse.
Whatever he proposes she provides,
As the conclusion to the premises
In syllogism offering herself.
Or, if 'tis she commands, he promptly acts;
In nothing would he disappoint his bride
Or have her lack for her most fond desire.
Now may he lie in pleasure with his love;
She ne'er demurs and never makes complaint.
    Love's play continued till the wife conceived
280 The infant Paphus, from whom that famed isle
Of Paphos took its name. Paphus begot
A son who later was King Cinyras,
Who was, with one exception, a fine man
And would good fortune ever have deserved
Had he by Myrrha never been deceived.
She was his daughter, beautiful and blonde,
Whom an old woman (may the gods confound

Her since her conscience would permit such sin)
Brought to her father in his bed one night,
290 The queen being absent at a festival.
Impetuous Cinyras clipped the maid
Quite ignorant that she was his own child.
When the duenna brought things to this pass,
She played a trick against Nature herself.
The fair Adonis from this match was born,
His mother having been to tree transformed,
Else by her father had she murdered been
When finally he learned of her deceit.
He would have killed his daughter on the spot
300 If he had known; but she escaped that end,
For when he ordered that a light be brought
The one who never more would be a maid
Escaped her father's ire by rapid flight.
    But from my story I too long depart,
And I should force myself to keep to it.
However, you shall find what all this means
Before my tale shall finally have reached its end.

98. Venus sets on fire and overthrows the Tower of Shame
[21215–21345]

I'LL not detain you longer; I'll return
To my narration, for I've other fields
To plow. As I have said, he who'd compare
The image I've described and that one made
In ancient times by great Pygmalion
Would find no similarity at all.
Just as the lion is by far more great
In body, and more valorous and strong
Than is the mouse, by so much this excels
10 In beauty that one which has been so praised.
    Dame Venus took good aim, as I have said,
At this fair shape between the pillars placed

Right in the middle of the ivory tower.
I never saw a place I'd gaze upon
More gladly. On my knees I'd worship it.
The sanctuary I would ne'er desert,
Nor leave the loophole—not for any bow
Or arrow any marksman might let fly—
Nor yield the right freely to enter there.
20 At least I'd struggle with my utmost power,
How e'er I might succeed, to stay therein,
If I could find one who would offer me
Admission, or, if nothing better happed,
At least would not resent my being there.
I've made a vow to God that I will go
To make a visit to this holy shrine
And touch the relics that I have described.
So soon as I find opportunity,
If time and place conform to my desire,
30 Please God, I'll seek them with my staff and scrip.
May nothing mock my plans or so disturb
That I may not enjoy my darling Rose!
  No more delaying, Venus then let fly
Her feathered arrow full of flaming fire
That should discomfit all her enemies
That still within the castle might remain.
So subtly Venus worked that none of them—
No man or woman—had the power of choice,
However they had held to it before.
40 Soon as the bolt was shot, the place caught fire
And all went crazy, thinking they were lost.

DEFENDERS

They cried, "Betrayed; betrayed! We all are dead.
Alas! alas! Let's flee and get away!"
Each wicked warden cast away his keys.
Danger, the horrid wretch, when first he felt
The heat, ran swift as stag upon the heath.
None waited for another. Skirts tucked up,
Each gave his whole attention to his flight.
Fear rushed away. Shame galloped in retreat.
50 They left the castle towers all aflame.
There was not one who could or would delay

To make an argument, as Reason taught.
  Then came Dame Courtesy, so fair and proud
And worthy, when her son's discomfiture
She saw; and with her also Pity came
And Lady Franchise. All together leaped
Into the enclosure. They pursued their way
Until they reached the place Fair Welcome kept.
Then Courtesy, not slow to speak fair words,

COURTESY

60 Thus first addressed him, "Much I've grieved, fair son;
Great sorrow has enthralled my heart since you
So long have been in prison thus confined.
May evil fires and fiendish flames consume
The one who first condemned you to such ward!
Now, God be thanked, you're free; for out there lies,
Together with his drunken Norman knights,
Foul-spoken Evil Tongue, dead in a ditch,
Unable to o'erhear me any more.
Jealousy's no longer to be feared;
70 To lead the good life one no longer dreads
Because of her, nor need one fear to take
His secret solace with a loving friend,
Especially since she has no more power
To see or hear whatever may occur.
There's no one now can carry tales to her,
So she is able to surprise no more.
Likewise our other discomfited foes
Are fled or quite destroyed, presumptuous fools!
The castle is quite free of all the rout.
80 Now, for the love of God, most fair, sweet son,
Don't let yourself get burned by staying here.
Franchise, Pity, and I in friendship beg
That you permit to make the due amend
This loyal Lover who so long has borne
For you such insults, nor a single fault
Has e'er committed that should anger you,
So frank and free from guile he's always been.
Receive him, then, and that which he presents;
For what he offers is his very soul.
90 In God's name, fair, sweet son, refuse it not;

Take it upon the faith you owe to me
And for the sake of Love, who succors him
And all his power has placed at his command.
Fair son, 'Love conquers all;' and with his key
Are all things kept protected. Vergil says,
In confirmation, these most courteous words,
Which you in his *Bucolics* may peruse:
'Love conquers all, and we must cede to him.'   VERGIL
Firmly and well he speaks the very truth.
100 No better saying can be found than he
Has stated for us in this single verse.
Fair son, assist that Lover; as a gift
Present his Rose to him; and then may God
Be gracious in his gifts to both of you!"
    Fair Welcome then replied, "Most willingly FAIR WELCOME
I offer her to him; and since we two
Are now alone, he may the blossom pluck
At leisure. I perceive that guilelessly
He loves and should have had his guerdon long ago."

99. The Lover makes his way into the Ivory Tower
[21346–21694]

A HUNDRED thousand thanks I offered him
And promptly, like a pilgrim most devout,
Precipitate, but fervent and sincere,
After that sweet permission, made my way
Like loyal lover toward the loophole fair,
The end of all my pilgrimage to achieve.
    With greatest effort I conveyed with me
My scrip and pilgrim staff so stiff and stout
That it no ferrule needed to assure
10 That it would hold the path and never slip.
The scrip was of a supple leather made
Most skillfully, without a single seam;
Nor was it empty. As it seemed to me,

Since none had opened it, Nature had placed
Most diligently, with the greatest care,
The hammers therewithin together laid.
When she had subtly manufactured it,
Excelling Daedalus in craftsmanship,
She lent the scrip to me. I think 'twas done
20 Because she thought that I might have to shoe
My palfreys when I felt their footsteps slip.
So should I do, if I but felt the need,
Most certainly; for, thanks be unto God!
I well know how to do such smithy work.
Truly I tell you that I better love
My scrip and hammers than my lute and harp.
When such equipment Nature furnished me,
Much was I honored; and I learned its use
Till I became a craftsman wise and good.
30   It was she, too, who furnished me my staff—
Another gift—and ere I went to school,
To polish it would have me set to work;
But for a ferrule she cared not a straw,
Nor valued less the staff for want of it.
Since I received it, I have always kept
The staff with me. I've never lost it yet;
Nor shall I lose it if I can prevent
Its loss; and not for fifty million pounds
Would I e'er part with it. Dame Nature made,
40 When she presented it, a lovely gift;
And therefore I must ever guard it well.
When I upon it gaze, I'm always glad
And thank her for the present. When I feel
Its sturdiness, I'm overjoyed and gay.
Much comfort has it given me many a time,
And well it's served me in full many a place,
Where I have put it. Know you how it serves?
When I am journeying and chance upon
A hidden place obscure, I thrust my staff
50 Into the ditches bottomless to sight,
Or test with it the depths of dubious fords.
Now I can boast that I've so well assayed
Such depths that I have often saved myself

From perishing therein. By springs and streams
I make my way in perfect confidence.
If e'er I find the bed too deep—the banks
Too steep—I much prefer to coast the flood
And make my way two leagues along the shore.
I suffer less fatigue than I should feel
60 In risking water that is perilous,
As I know well by sore experience;
Though in such waters I have ne'er been drowned.
Soon as I test the depths that I would ford
And find no bottom with my staff or oar,
I go around, and, keeping near the banks,
Find my way out, at least eventually.
To find an exit I could ne'er be sure
Had I not the equipment Nature gave.
      Now let us leave these dangerous, slippery trails
70 To those who willingly would travel them,
And hold our way, not by the wagon roads
But by delightful footpaths, pretty lanes
Which lead the happy man to fond delights.
There's more productive gain in trodden roads
Than in new-broken paths; and there men find
Fair properties that livings will provide.
It is by Juvenal himself affirmed
That one who'd quickly come to great estate
Can find no shorter road—no better way—
80 Than to invest in some old, moneyed dame;
For if she finds his service to her taste
She soon will raise him to a high degree.
Ovid repeats a maxim proved and true
That whoso will a wealthy widow take
Soonest attains the greatest recompense.
Great riches are acquired most rapidly
By sending goods to market by such roads.
      But he who'd steal an older woman's love,
Or even purchase it most lawfully
90 When Cupid catches him within his net,
Should take good care that naught he says or does
Resembles subterfuge or trickery;
For tough old pallid dames, who've left their youth,

Having of yore been flattered, duped, and tricked,
When they're deceived again, more readily
Perceive the subtlety of flatterers
Than do the tender maids who doubt no ruse
When they give ear to their deceivers' talk
And think all guileful lies the gospel truth,
100 Since they have not been scorched. But wrinkled dames,
Malicious and hard baked, are in the art
Of fraud so well instructed that they know
The science well by old experience.
When they are thus approached by flatterers
Who hope to capture them with fairy tales,
And play upon their ears, and labor long
To gain their grace by humbleness and sighs
And begging mercy with hands joined in prayer,
With bowed heads kneeling, weeping lavish tears,
110 And torturing themselves that they may gain
Better belief, making feigned promises
Of heart and body, services and wealth,
Calling to witness all the holy saints
That are, have been, or ever more shall be,
And thus with windy words attempt deceit
As does the fowler hidden in the woods,
Who with his whistled notes decoys the birds
To come within the nets where they'll be caught,
And is abroached by all the foolish fowl
120 Who don't know how to meet his sophistries
But are deceived as by a metaphor,
As are the silly quail who hear the sound
The fowler makes to win them to his trap
And hover round, and then beneath the net,
Which he has stretched upon the springtime grass
So thick and fresh, they flutter and are lost,
Unless some older quail refuse the snare
Because she has been singed and almost caught,
Having seen other netting likewise spread,
130 From which she has escaped by miracle—
So older women who have once been lured,
And by their suitors tricked by flatteries,
Hearing the words that they have heard before

And seeing the attitudes that they have seen,
The more they've been deceived, the more they're sly
To recognize, far off, the trick again.
   If suitors seriously make their vows
To gain their just deserts from Cupid's game,
Like those in fact entangled in the net,
140 Whose torture is so pleasant, and whose toil
Is so delightful that there's nothing else
Half so agreeable to them as hope
Which grieves them more than it encourages,
Then do they fear to swallow hook with bait,
And listen close and try to figure out
Whether it's truth or fable they are told.
They weigh each word, so much they fear deceit
Because they have experienced it before
And of it have a lively memory.
150 All try to please her, thinks each aged dame.
   You, if you wish, may turn your hearts to these,
The sooner to enrich yourselves; or you
Who study your delight, and pleasure find
In them, may jog along such well-worn roads
As will provide most solace and most joy.
You others who prefer the younger girls
(That you may never be by me deceived,
Whate'er my masters may command—and good
Are all behests that they have given me)
160 Again I tell you for the very truth—
Believe it he who will—that one does well
To try them all that he may better know
How to regale himself with what is best.
'Tis thus that gourmands do who of all food
Are connoisseurs, and many viands taste—
Roasted, and boiled, and fried, in gelatin,
In batter, or in souse—when they inspect
Their kitchens, and know well what should be praised
Or blamed, and what should be or sweet or sour;
170 For many a time they've tasted all the foods.
Know well, and have no doubt of it, that he
Who never tastes the bad can hardly know
How good things ought to taste; who knows not shame

Will scarcely recognize what honor means;
Who learns not first what real discomfort is
Will scarcely know what things are comfortable;
And he who's never suffered any pain
Will scarcely realize when he's at ease.
No one should offer solace to a man
180 Who has not learned its worth through suffering.
'Tis thus with all such opposites: the one
Explains the other. He who would define
A thing must have in mind its opposite
Or else no definition can he frame;
For he who knows not both cannot conceive
The difference between them. This unknown,
No proper definition can there be.
    The sacred relics of the ivory tower
I hoped to touch with all my equipage
190 If I so close approach might win for it
And get it through the little opening.
So after all my wanderings and toil—
Like pilgrim agile still and vigorous—
I knelt at last, and without more delay,
Between the two fair pillars I've described,
With staff unshod; for very fain was I,
With heart devout and full of piety,
To worship in that sanctuary sweet,
Which to be highly honored well deserved
200 Though now it lay flat fallen on the ground.
None of the structure had escaped the fire
Which toppled down all that was not destroyed.
A little then I pushed aside the shroud
That curtained the fair relics, and approached
The image that I knew was close within.
Devotedly I kissed the sacred place.
Safely to sheathe my staff within the shrine,
I thrust it through the loophole, while the scrip
Dangled behind it. Carefully I tried
210 To thrust it in; it bounded back again.
Once more I thrust it in without avail;
Always it back recoiled. Try as I might,
Nothing could force the staff to enter there.

Then I perceived a little barricade,
Which though I well could feel I could not see,
Quite near the border of the opening,
Which from the inside fortified the shrine,
Having been placed there when it first was made,
And still remaining fast and quite secure.
220 More vigorously then I made assault;
But often as I thrust, so oft I failed.
    If you had seen me there thus tourneying,
You would have been much taken with the sight
And would have thought of Hercules the Great
And, to dismember Cacus, how he strove.
Three times he assailed the gate, and thrice he failed;
Three times he struck, and thrice, exhausted, fell;
Three times he sat, hard-breathing, in the glen,
Such labor and such pain he had endured.
230 So I, when I had struggled there so long
That I perspired in very agony
Because the palisade would not give way,
Was just as tired, I think, as Hercules,
Or even more. However, at the last,
My battery availed to this extent
That I perceived a narrow passageway
By which I thought to gain admission there,
Though I must quite destroy the palisade.
Pushing within this little, narrow path
240 By which I entrance sought, as I have said,
I broke down the obstruction with my staff.
Then through the passageway that I had made,
Though 'twas too narrow and too small for me,
I got inside—or, rather, half inside.
Sorely I grieved no farther to get in,
But could not do what was beyond my power,
Though not for anything would I relax
My efforts till the staff was quite inside.
At last I got it in, but still the scrip
250 Remained outside, its hammers knocking there
For entrance; and so narrow was the path
That therein I was placed in great distress.
The passage would have been by far too small

For me to traverse it, and well I knew
By this that none had ever passed that way.
I was the first of men to tread that road;
The place was not accustomed to receive
The tributes pilgrims well might bring to it.
I know not whether it has offered since
260 Of its advantages to more than me;
But I assure you, even if it had,
I love it so that I would not believe
The truth, for no one readily mistrusts
That which he loves, no matter how defamed.
I'd be the last to credit evil tales.
However, at the least, I know that then
It never had been pierced or battered down.
I myself entered there because I ne'er
Without such entrance could have plucked the bud.
270 Imagine how I acted when I found
That quite at my disposal was my Rose!
Listen while I describe the deed itself,
So if you, too, should have a chance to go,
When spring's sweet season shall have come again,
To pluck a full-blown flower or tight-closed bud,
You then so wisely may conduct yourself
That you may never fail to gain your end.
Unless a better method you have learned,
Employ that one you hear me now explain.
280 If you can make the passage more at ease,
Or better, or with greater subtlety,
And not too much exert or tire yourself,
Use your own system when you've heard my plan.
At least this much advantage you will have,
That I will teach you, without asking pay,
My method. Listen to me, therefore, willingly.

100. The Lover wins his Rose
[21695–21780]

TORMENTED by my labors, I approached
So near the rose tree that I could at will
Lay hands upon her limbs to pluck the bud.
Fair Welcome begged me, for the love of God,
That no outrageous act I should perform,
And to his frequent prayers I gave assent
And made a covenant with him that I
Would nothing do beyond what he might wish.
    I seized the rose tree by her tender limbs
10 That are more lithe than any willow bough,
And pulled her close to me with my two hands.
Most gently, that I might avoid the thorns,
I set myself to loosen that sweet bud
That scarcely without shaking could be plucked.
I did this all by sheer necessity.
Trembling and soft vibration shook her limbs;
But they were quite uninjured, for I strove
To make no wound, though I could not avoid
Breaking a trifling fissure in the skin,
20 Since otherwise I could have found no way
To gain the favor I so much desired.
    This much more I'll tell you: at the end,
When I dislodged the bud, a little seed
I spilled just in the center, as I spread
The petals to admire their loveliness,
Searching the calyx to its inmost depths,
As it seemed good to me. It there remained
And scarcely could unmingle from the bud.
The consequence of all this play of mine
30 Was that the bud expanded and enlarged.
But I'd not misbehaved more than I've told;
Rather, I'd done so well in my attempt

That never did the sweet bud turn from me
Or think it any harm, but e'er complied
And let me do whatever she supposed
I ought to do most to delight myself.
　　Of course she did remind me of my pledge
And say I was outrageous in demands,
And that I'd done what I should not have done;
40 But ne'ertheless she never did forbid
That I should seize and strip and quite deflower
Both trunk and limbs of every leaf and bloom.
　　When I perceived that I had such success
That my affair no longer was in doubt
And that I nobly had achieved my end,
I felt most thankful and recognizant,
As any honest debtor ought to feel,
Toward all the friends who had so aided me.
I felt myself beholden much to them,
50 Since by their aid I had become so rich
That, to affirm the truth, not Wealth herself
Was half so wealthy. First unto the God
Of Love and Venus, who had helped me most,
And then to all the barons in his train,
Then to Fair Welcome and that other Friend
Who proved himself to be a friend indeed,
Whom I pray God that He will ne'er restrain
From aiding loyal lovers, I gave thanks
With savory kisses, ten or twenty times.
60 But Reason I forgot, whose hortatives
Had made me waste so many pangs in vain,
As well as Wealth, that ancient villainess
Who had no thought of pity when she warned
Me from the footpath where she kept her ward.
Thank God she did not guard that passageway
By which I made my entrance secretly,
Little by little, notwithstanding all
The efforts of my mortal enemies
Who held me back so much, especially
70 The guardian Jealousy, with her sad wreath
Of care, who keeps true lovers from the Rose.
Much good their guardianship is doing now!

Ere I remove from that delightful place
Where 'tis my hope I ever can remain,
With greatest happiness I'll pluck the blooms
From off the rosebush, fair in flower and leaf.
    This, then, is how I won my vermeil Rose.
Then morning came, and from my dream at last I woke.

SELECTIVE LIST OF PROPER NAMES AND PLACE NAMES

SELECTIVE LIST OF PROPER NAMES AND PLACE NAMES

(Reference is to Robbins' chapter number. Classical and biblical topics are omitted)

A

Abélard, Peter (1079–1142), French philosopher, lover of Héloïse, §42

Abstinence, Forced (*Astenance Constrainte* in the original), personified abstraction of debased celibacy, §§50ff.

Abundance, Dame, legendary witch, §85

Algus, Arab mathematician, §§59, 78

Alhazen, eleventh-century Arab scientist, of the line of Huchaïn, author of book on optics, §83

Amand, Saint, of Bordeaux, §63

Amiens, city in France, §48

Anjou, see Charles of

Argenteuil, village in Seine-et-Oise, France, where Héloïse was abbess, §42

Arnold, Saint, patron of cuckolds, §44

Arras, capital of Pas-de-Calais, France, famous for wool manufacture, §4

Arthur of Britain, legendary king, §§4, 58

Artois, Robert II, Count of, brother of King Louis IX, §86

Aureole, book ascribed to Theophrastus (preserved in Jerome's *Adversus Jovinianum*), §41

Avicenna, Arab philosopher (died 1037), §78

B

Béguin, Beghard, member of religious community of laymen not bound by vows, §55

Béguine, member of religious community of laywomen not bound by vows, §§55, 56

Belin, Don, the ram celebrated in the Reynard tales, §52

Black Monks, members of Benedictine order, §55

Boethius, author of *Consolation of Philosophy* (written 524), §§25, 42

Boreas (in the French original, *Bise*), personification of north wind, §29

Breton, inhabitant of Brittany, §51

C

Calabria, area in southern Italy, §86

Canons Regular, Augustinian (Black) canons, §55

Carmelites (in French, *Barrés*), White friars, §56

Charlemagne, King of Franks, Holy Roman Emperor, §§6, 36, 37

Charles the Great, see Charlemagne

Charles of Anjou, Count of Provence (died 1285), won Sicily from Manfred, condemned Conradin to death, imprisoned Henry, brother of the King of Castile, §32

Conradin, nephew of Manfred, decapitated (in 1268) by order of Charles of Anjou, §32

Constantine (Afer), eleventh-century Carthaginian physician, §78

Cordeliers, Franciscan friars, §56

Cornish pipes and pipers, §§19, 97

D

Danger (old French *Dangier* from Latin *dominarium*), personified abstraction of feminine restraint (corresponding to the *Pudor* of Ovid), §§13ff.

Denis, Saint, traditional apostle to France and first Bishop of Paris, §§41, 44

Istanbul (Constantinople), capital of Turkey, §96

J

Jacobins, Dominican friars, §56
Jean Chopinel de Meun, §50
Julian, Saint, patron of hospitality, §42

K

Kay, insolent seneschal of King Arthur, §9

L

Lavardin, town in Loire-et-Cher, France, §86
Leonard, Saint, patron of prisoners, §42
Lifard, Saint, patron of church of Meun (Meung), §60
Loire, river in France, §50
London, capital of England, §64
Lorraine, province of France, §3
Lorris, see William de Lorris

M

Macrobius, late Roman grammarian, commentator on the *Dream of Scipio*, §1
Maine, French province, conquered by Charlemagne, §37
Manfred, King of Naples and Sicily, conquered (in 1266) by Charles of Anjou and killed, §32
Marseilles, city in Provence, conquered by Charles of Anjou, §32
Meaux, village in the department of Seine-et-Marne, France, §§18, 45
Mendicants, begging friars, §38
Meun (Meung), village in the department of Loiret, France, birthplace of Jean Chopinel, §50
Milan, city in Italy, §55